Bedlam in the Bog

(Book IV of The Osten Chronicles)

Author: Daniel Thorman

ISBN: 978-1-963913-26-2

Imprint: Native Publishers, The

The Osten Chronicles

Dedicated to:

Sister Shirley Le Blanc

May her gentle rhythms echo ever down the halls of time, spreading joy among all whom they touch.

The Prophecy of the Verdant Child

(as given by Sybell Dunham, oracle of Conclave)

The enemy doth spread his seed,
the northern lands to ravage.
The verdant child, in time of need,
must go confront the savage.

Let all beware the verdant child,
by whose power the land doth drown.
A kingdom shall be reconciled,
and none shall wear its thorny crown.

CHAPTER ONE

The Sapling

"Have patience, the grass will be milk soon enough."

~ Chinese Proverb ~

I touched the cluster of delicate petals bunched within their leafy crown and expelled the briefest whisper of magic from my fingertip. The bud burst open to form a flat, spongy brown cake ringed by a halo of yellow petals perfectly positioned within the hedge. I stepped back to survey my handiwork. I was most pleased to find it a fitting match for the others. The long stems of the sunflowers grew straight up through the topiary I'd been grooming for House Owl. Their blossoms were centered in the eye sockets of the sculpted birds, which no longer bore any resemblance whatsoever to chickens. I grinned with satisfaction.

Although I was now a full journeyman, and thus no longer a resident of House Blue Jay, I thought it best to honor my previous commitment to complete the hedgerow of the aspirant dwellings. With this final flourish, I'd more than made good on my promise, and Lorraine could stop badgering me about it. Since Franklin's departure, the young lady from Freemark took her new duties as head of house quite seriously.

I longed to join Roy and Sholeena at Mistress Julia's grand estate. Sholeena had found her homunculus almost at once and was free to join Roy there a mere week after her choosing. Sadly, I was still sequestered by night in the academy's basement, making little progress toward surmounting that hurdle. My sessions with Mistress Dunham were frustrating. Whatever did she mean by 'listen for its voice.' Vines didn't have voices. Thus far, I'd only managed to produce a lumpy brownish husk as a permanent fixture in the center of my inner garden. It stood there as though staked in place and uttered nary a sound.

My daily lessons with Mistress Julia weren't any more interesting. Upon learning that I have a secondary affinity for working earth, she had immediately assigned me an enormous stack of reading on the topic of geomancy. Conclave's library had little to offer on the topic of my primary magic, verdumancy, and most of this was only theoretical. But there were stacks and stacks of information about clay, earth, sand, stone, and the many uses to which they could be put. Hundreds of geomancers had passed through Conclave over the years and all had something tedious to say about it. A dry, flat tone seemed to be a prerequisite to writing a treatise on geomancy.

Reading some of the references sparked a sense of déjà vu. I struggled to recall what it had been like casting some of these spells as Grandma Abbey. She had, after all, been a geomancer. Since purging her possessing spirit from my dreams and my psyche, I still had access to some of her memories. Thankfully, these were now detached from any animating force and felt more like something I'd read somewhere. Sometimes, I just knew in my bones what it was like to perform a particular earth shaping. But try as I might, I couldn't connect to this at a conscious level. What stood out from her jumbled memories were only the emotional highlights of her misspent life. These proved pretty useless as study aids.

Suddenly, the owl sculpture I was viewing took to shaking, and a voice emerged from its depths.

"Now that ye've finished with me," it said in a piping falsetto, "I've a mind to stretch me wings and fly. Could ye please sever me tethering roots that I might enjoy the sky?"

I blinked, startled from my reverie.

"I think not," I recited with amusement, "oh prankster sprite. All know that owls fly only at night."

And out from the shrubbery stepped a familiar fellow, parting the branches with his walking stick. He stood only as high as my waist, but he carried himself with a strut that belied his modest size. Terwilliger wore a mischievous grin, but I sensed that all was not right with the Brownie. He turned to review my sculpture with a critical eye, at last saying:

"Tis a fine effort I trow. I doubt e'en Fengári could find fault with these leafy-feathered fellows."

"Thanks," I grunted. "What's on your mind?"

He wrung his hat in his hands. It seemed to run contrary to fairy etiquette to ever come straight to the point, so I waited patiently for him to overcome his reticence to do so.

"Ah, well," he finally put forth. "Far be it from me to cast aspersions on the Mistress and her nurturin' way, but as deep as her roots may run, she's clearly out of her depth today. I wondered whether ye'd time to stop by and call on her in the glade. I'll wager she'd find it a welcome relief if a friendly visit were paid."

He blinked up at me expectantly. This was as close as Terwilliger had ever come to asking for a favor. Among the fey, to do so was to invite an exchange of a boon I could name later. The fair folk were most jealous custodians of their boons and could be quite cruel in exacting inordinate retribution upon him who failed to uphold such a bargain. I had tried explaining friendship to the Brownie, but in his world this translated roughly to 'stupidity.'

Still, I was now curious about what had Hazel's roots in a twist.

"Alright," I replied carefully. "I'm finished here, as you can see, and I'd fancy such a visit myself. If someone would stow my tools back in the shed, I could set off at once."

"I'd be happy to be of such service, me lad. Tis but a trifle. I'll see them all polished and sharpened to boot."

The twinkle had returned to Terwilliger's eye as he found an immediate way to repay the favor with no loss of dignity. It was a jolly good thing I had traded in my sheers and most of my other small tools for versions made of bronze. As envoy to the woodland fey, it would be unseemly to carry too many items made of iron, the touch of which was anathema to them. I hefted my bob and made for the glade.

***

As I waded through the thicket, well off the beaten path, I could sense the unquiet that stirred the artificial woodland. It had been only a few months since the semi-wilderness tract and its surrounds had been given over to the fair folk's management, and already the lush growth had taken on an untamed feel. It was as though the woodland itself had awakened, shaken itself, and decided to be ornery. More than that, today the very trees seemed to quiver with upset as the greenery all about cowered and thrashed in an undertone of anxiety. It could mean only one thing.

Long before I entered the small glen at the center of the glade, I could hear the commotion. The sprites were sounding off in alarm, and snippets of soothing words could be heard between the loud fretting wails of Holly. I wondered what had set her off this time. Thrusting aside the last of the leafy boughs and stepping into the clearing, I beheld a disturbing scene.

The stone bench had been overturned, and flailing vines thrashed about, twitching in the throes of the temper tantrum of the glade's newest denizen. Pixies darted willy-nilly, trying to soothe the birds, bees and other creatures in their purview. Unsurprisingly, Bogalump was nowhere in sight, doubtless having retreated within the safety and relative peace of his 'embassy.' It was a wattle and daub affair that somewhat resembled a small hill.

The tiny terror of the trees stood with her fists balled and wailing to beat the band. Hazel stood nearby, looking tentative and uncertain. When I'd first met Hazel in this very glade, I'd thought the tree sprite to be rather moody and impetuous. But now I saw her as the epitome of calm and maturity when contrasted to the fretful hysteria of her firstborn. Holly was but a sapling. I'd planted her myself barely a few months gone.

When Holly had first emerged, I thought her the living embodiment of sweetness and light. But this stage had lasted barely a month. Young dryads, it seemed, grew at an astonishing pace. Her tree was already twice my own modest height, and her green, springy trunk was darkening and roughening. Patches of scabby grey bark had become evident as her outer casing gave the task of drinking the sunlight over to her emerging and ever-multiplying leaves. Hazel told me the itching discomfort this caused was quite irritating in the first year of growth, so allowances had to be made. I guessed it to be akin to when human babies were teething.

No human babe, however, had as profound an impact on her surroundings. The chaos went on unabated, despite Hazel's best efforts to mitigate it. I wished, not for the first time, the solution could be as simple as giving her a teething ring or rubbing her gums with a touch of corn spirits. Holly's aspect roughly resembled that of a gawky, pre-adolescent girl. Though one could clearly see in her slender form the beginnings of the elegant traits that characterized her kindred, she had yet to fill out and fully adopt the graceful gliding movements of her folk. She stomped around in her fury, waving her fists at the offending sky, an angry scowl marring her exquisitely chiseled features.

"There there, dearest," Hazel soothed, "He's not hurting the birch. He was only seeking a meal and relieving her of pests. Woodpeckers aren't malevolent. Consider them our guests. Calm yourself, my daughter, and be not so distressed."

Reluctantly, I approached.

"Heed your mother, Holly," I chimed in sternly over the wailing din.

A look of relief crossed Hazel's face as her emerald eyes caught mine. But Holly was having none of it.

"He beat on the birch and broke her bark," she sobbed, "and all *she'll* do is stand there and *rhyme* about it."

I glared at the waif until she stilled.

"Your mother is wise in the ways of the woods and has lived here longer than you. You should calm down, as she suggested, and apologize to her for disrupting the peace of the glade. *Don't make me use your true name.*"

Her lips bunched up in a stubborn set, but she quieted and stilled, nonetheless. No dryad wanted her true name bandied about, and she knew I was one of the few beings who could do it.

"Yes, godfather," she sullenly spat.

Turning to her mother, she rolled her eyes and begrudgingly announced: "Sorry I made a mess."

Her stance was still defiant, but it would have to do. I fervently hoped Hazel would accept this small victory rather than prolonging the dispute.

"Well met, Lucas," Hazel belatedly greeted. "Be welcome to the glade. You've caught us at an unseemly moment; I'm afraid."

"Fear not, Mistress," said I, addressing her with her proper title in response to the formal greeting. "I hope you won't mind a friendly visit. I can come back later if you're too busy."

"No. No," she hastily assured me, a look of panic crossing her features. "I was just teaching Holly here how to commune with the forest when she became troubled by a marauding bird."

"Wood-*pecker.*"

Holly said it like a curse. Before she could get all worked up again I quickly cut in with: "Well, perhaps I could take over for a bit. I'd fancy a visit with my goddaughter, and as you know, I've yet to find anyone else who can teach me the ins and outs of talking with plants."

Hazel offered me a smile that was at once acceptance and relief.

"Certainly," she said. "I could use a little rest to get my sap flowing aright."

And with that, the hamadryad glided gracefully toward her tree, melding into its trunk in that eerie way to which I still hadn't quite grown accustomed.

Holly blinked up at me, silent but assessing.

The top of the young tree sprite's head came nearly up to my shoulder by now. It was a considerable increase from the spriteling who only a fortnight ago had stood no taller than my waist. She had her mother's emerald eyes, but these contained a distant, distracted look when she was calm, as was fast becoming the case.

I sat down in the grass and crossed my legs before me. Holly stifled a grin. It always amused the dryads when we humans bent in the middle and 'pretzeled' ourselves. Dryads had no such need to recline.

"So how far is your reach now?" I asked.

"Mom says our real roots run as deep as our tree is tall," she replied. "Our energy roots can stretch out to about five times that all around, and we can sense out to about twice that far."

Quickly doing the math, I realized Holly should now be able to affect things about fifty feet out and sense things perhaps a hundred feet away. I'd seen Hazel reach farther than this rule would warrant, based on her own height, but perhaps there were tricks and mitigating factors a more experienced dryad could command.

Two satyrs were already righting the stone bench, and from the hole in the embassy's front, I spied Bogalump cautiously peering out.

"Can you shake that bush over there?" I asked, indicating a shrub just to his right.

"Of course," she replied with an impish grin.

Holly's head lowered and her eyes became half-lidded. I felt a rush of green energy pass beneath us. I still couldn't quite fathom how the fey worked their magic. Most of it remained invisible to my mage sight. And while I could feel its presence via the fey mark that graced the back of my hand, this perception conferred only the vaguest sense of direction. The nuance of what she did escaped me.

Suddenly, the shrub that was her target gave a mighty shudder and writhed in a manner an ordinary bush could not. Ambassador Bogalump was just emerging into the glen when the lavender erupted as though possessed. The great toad nearly swallowed his pipe as he scuttled back within, disappearing from our sight.

"Why are you laughing?" asked the dryad girl after observing me carefully for a time.

"I don't think I've ever seen Bogalump retreat in such an undignified manner. You've really got the old sot spooked."

It amused me to see the Grudge who had put me through so much heartache get a bit of comeuppance at the hands (or roots) of the juvenile wood nymph.

"Should I startle him some more?"

What passed for humor among the fey could sometimes be strange to my human sensibilities. Some pranks that they found hilarious seemed just downright mean-spirited. Similarly, the fair folk often failed to fathom human notions of comedy. Fairies were quite literal-minded. This sometimes led to strained relations between the two races.

"Maybe later," I hedged.

I went on to explain that some things were funny only once. Some others were funny three times, especially when it was a little different the third time around. Only a rare few jokes were reliably funny every time they were played, and even these needed some time in-between before they were funny once more. A jester with whom I'd traveled had explained all this to me, and I'd found it to be true enough. Holly attended me with a most serious expression. We whiled away our afternoon on this and other trivial topics as a relieved Hazel concentrated on the carefree conversion of sunlight to sustenance.

***

I was glad that mess at the grove was sorted out. Who knew baby dryads could be so temperamental? One would think as a tree spirit, she would develop a steadier personality to match the passivity of her native form. Alas, the mercurial whimsy of the fey seemed to overshadow even the most gentle-natured of such good folk. It was surprising that more conflicts hadn't yet arisen between the humans of Conclave and the new owners of the sacred glade. The treaty had been touch-and-go for a while there, but our offer to form an alliance had finally been accepted. I suppose we should count our blessings. At least the interaction shed some light on our adversaries, the unseelie fey, with whom I suppose we were now technically at war.

"You're not concentrating."

Her words snatched me from my reverie. My eyes moved once more to rest upon the old woman seated across from me on the mat. Her eyebrows were drawn up and a sober frown graced her lips. Not for the first time I marveled at her patience. When seated thus and focusing within, I knew my mind tended to wander. I seemed to lack the concentration needed to make any headway on the task at hand. Whereas Roy had dispatched the assignment in just over a week, and Sholeena had spent barely three days in sequestration, it seemed that my stay in the tower of meditation was to be never-ending.

I knew better than to answer her aloud. Instead, I drew another deep breath and let my mind settle. I could envision my inner garden perfectly well, having trained to do so for nearly two years now. But rather than reaching for my magic, I reclined in its midst, feeling my magic's pulse and bathing in its lush ambiance. I sat (metaphorically) facing the brownish lump that had been my only success to date. It had congealed here in the center of my inner field amid a confluence of vines that had arisen at my beckoning, slithering forth and knotting together. It had since lain unmoving and gradually dried out and faded in hue while I poked at it and cajoled it to do something more interesting.

Mistress Dunham had urged patience. 'Just listen,' she had advised. 'You will know when you are ready.' I was beginning to think the stupid desiccated husk was laughing at me. I could scarcely wait until my hour was up today. I was getting a bit thirsty (thirsssty) just staring at the thing. Wait. What?

I was getting a bit thirsty...

I paused. Then I heard it again, this time more distinctly. It was a low rasping thought that was no proper sound at all, but rather an echo of my own inner voice.

(Thirrrssstyy), it drawled.

I considered invoking 'tenera pluviam' my spell of gentle rain. Though my water magic lacked strength, I thought I might be able to draw down a feeble trickle or some such. As I gathered my will, I hesitated. The incantation died on my lips. It felt wrong somehow.

I could feel Mistress Dunham observing me most intently, silently urging me to some action, but I put her from my mind and focused instead on the feeling. This was my own puzzle to solve. A notion gnawed at my awareness. It invaded my thoughts like a pup greets its master, all eager and tail-waggingly expectant. Suddenly I knew what was needed, and it wasn't water. This inner thirst could be quenched only by my gift, a draught of pure, unadulterated magic. I smiled. This answer felt right. Finally, something was about to happen. I scooped energies from the surrounding haze and slathered them liberally upon the brown lump lying before me.

It began to twitch.

Now awash in my verdant energies, it wriggled and pulsed. I felt it tug at my magical strength like a fish caught on a line. And while my swirling energies diminished, funneling into the pulsing cocoon, the draw became an unpleasant scraping that set my teeth on edge. It reminded me of the time Master Chadwick had siphoned my magic to use in his grand working on Westarbor's gate.

This wasn't right; was it? Its incessant demand for more suddenly met my firm denial as I withdrew my gift. And the husk soon lay turgid, torpid and still. Had I killed it? I think not. For in the aftermath of its infusion, I noted the husk had lost its lifeless quality. Though unmoving, it seemed to shine and effervesce with the silent promise of something more to come. As to what this might be, I had nary a clue, but evidently it wasn't happening anytime soon. Reluctantly, I withdrew, increased my breathing, and ended the meditation.

I was surprised to find Mistress Dunham absent and all the sand piled at the bottom of the hourglass. My joints were stiff and I felt a bit lightheaded and fatigued. I heard a clattering off to my left as I eased myself up from the mat and looked about. I soon spied the old woman approaching with a tray. The sharp, tannic aroma drifting from the steaming mugs thereon soon overpowered the light fragrance of burning sandalwood that wafted about the circular room. Subdued light from the morning sun filtered through its frilly curtains to bathe the open space in a warm glow.

Tea would be most welcome indeed. I prepared to resettle myself on the plush divan. As she rested the tray on a low table before it and took her seat, Mistress Dunham was the first to break the silence.

"An interesting choice, journeyman. Usually I advise establishing a deeper dialog before empowering one's homunculus, but each gift brings its own special requirements."

Is that what I had done? What in the blue blazes *was* my homunculus? Over time, I'd seen my cousin empower one of his magic specs until it metamorphosed into something entirely different. He called her 'the queen bee of his inner hive' and could communicate with her quite readily. In actuality, she was merely a manifestation of Roy's unconscious mind and governed his magic while he slept or focused on other tasks. That was the goal, after all, and he had achieved it quite handily. Sholeena too had discovered a little fish in her inner pond. It told her secrets which I suspected were her own unconscious observations and could even do tricks. Evidently, *my* homunculus was to be a brownish lump of twisted imagination that lay completely still and sometimes ate my magic. Lucky me.

"It seemed the right thing to do," I replied uncertainly, taking a sip of my tea.

"Well, I won't second-guess you. I'm here only to guide and assess. But it seems to me that 'thirsty' isn't much of a vocabulary. Nor is it much of a basis on which to turn over a portion of your power."

I mulled over the admonishment. It was, perhaps, well-deserved. I was supposed to be connecting to my unconscious mind, understanding it, and setting boundaries. One's unconscious thoughts and desires, when unrestrained by reason and social mores, were capable of terrible and selfish acts one would never consider were one aware. If someone's worst impulses and daydreams became reality what destruction might be wrought? Doubly so for a mage. Mayhap I'd let my impatience get the better of me (or the worst, as the case may be).

"I think it needed the energy to evolve to the next stage," I justified. "I'll start holding it to account as we discussed once it can communicate better."

"So it's still genderless?" she prompted. "I thought you may have gotten a sense of that during your joining."

"As far as I can tell, it could be anything."

"Well, get some rest," she advised. "It seems a boy with your wit and imagination would have a livelier unconscious mind. Perhaps that's the problem. With all your daydreaming, you don't leave a lot for your sleeping mind to mull over. Mayhap it's grown lazy."

Shrugging, I thanked the old woman, drained the last of my tea, and made ready to depart.

***

I approached the entrance to Mistress Julia's private estate. It was still early enough to at least get a decent meal before being consigned to my stuffy cell for the night. My new home-to-be stood a fair distance from the academy and was somewhat isolated. It rested within one of the few wooded lots at the conclave. All around me, nature played its soothing summer melody. The low hum of buzzing insects, birdsong and all the rest created a susurrus of gentle murmuring one would usually only note by its absence. The sun warmed my skin, and the breeze kissed my cheek as I made my way along.

When I'd first arrived at Mistress Julia's private retreat, I'd been astonished by the grounds at its frontage. A meandering stone walkway led through a spacious courtyard, at the center of which rested a deep pond surrounded by lush greenery. Mistress Julia tended the unusual plants herself, and I could find no fault with her gardening skills. The verdure seemed to thrive under her care. Nor was I invited to help with such. In fact, other than managing our own needs, we journeymen had been assigned no tasks apart from our studies as yet (this, despite the fact that our mistress kept only a few servants). I'd come to understand that self-sufficiency was a cultural trait of the Elves (the *nuvapua watheesh*, I hastily amended). Approaching the estate, I sighted one of these servants lugging a heavy wooden trunk out onto the front stoop.

"Hello, Jase," I greeted. "What's in the trunk?"

He looked my way and flashed me a friendly smile. The boy had entered my lady's service but six short months ago himself. Mistress Julia had initially sought him out to assist with some repairs on the estate. The quiet young man had grown up in lakeside, the third son of a fisherman. Although not formally apprenticed to any profession, Jase had a reputation as a right good Jack of all trades. On seeing the kindly way he automatically helped Griselda tote and carry, my master had offered him a permanent position, and the young man had accepted.

"Journeyman," he returned as he straightened. "The mistress is stowing some of her belongings into storage at the academy. The porters'll be by for 'em sometime today."

That was odd. Despite the recent addition of three new journeymen, the estate was spacious enough. There seemed to be room aplenty in its spartan halls. My new master's tastes ran toward the plain in a motif one might name 'austere elegance.' I left Jason to his labors and entered the house.

In the entryway, I remembered to pull off my boots after stamping the dirt off as best I could on the front mat.

On entering my lady's service, Royland, Sholeena and I had each been given a set of house shoes and told in no uncertain terms that muddy boots were to be shucked before entering the house proper. Although a bat wouldn't envy her eyesight, it seemed Madam Mattingly had a sixth sense allowing her to instantly perceive when this rule was flouted. It was at times like these that I most missed the services of Terwilliger. I'd grown accustomed to freshly polished boots each morning. But the brownie had opted to remain the house sprite of House Blue Jay and its new clutch of aspirants.

So I ambled down the hall toward Royland's room, wishing the stiff soles of my new shoes were more thoroughly broken in. I arrived to find it empty. Upon overhearing voices from Sholeena's room, I continued on, pausing at its open doorway.

"I think you're right, Filbert," she was saying. "Mistress Julia is planning a trip."

The girl stood quite alone, sorting through a basket of laundry and folding various items into neat stacks at the foot of her bed. I cleared my throat to announce my presence. She turned my way and shot me a sheepish grin.

"Hello Lucas," she said demurely. "Have they finally let you out of the cellar?"

"Not yet," I replied. "I've just come for dinner. I'm also looking for Royland. He promised to help me with something today."

"I think he's in the library," she said, balling up a set of stockings and tossing them onto the pile.

I shouldn't be surprised. My cousin loved to read, and Julia's eclectic collection of books was just the sort of thing to draw my cousin's eye. I, too, could scarcely wait to be a full-time resident here with constant access to it. This, despite the fact that nine-tenths of her collection was in Elven. As I prepared to leave and seek out my cousin, I paused.

"Your diction has gotten a lot better, Sholeena. One might almost mistake you for a native speaker of Ostinian,"

"Thanksh," she drawled, her Paluda grin broadening a notch. The slight orange tinge of her cheeks emphasized the intentional nature of her jape. "Mistress Julia gave me a poem to practice with. You wanna hear it?"

"Sure," I returned gamely, leaning on the door jamb to await this rare treat.

With most people, Sholeena was painfully shy. That she'd offered to recite a poem spoke volumes about her trust in me. Laying aside her laundry, she faced me fully and began.

"She SELLS SEA-shells on the SEA-shore.

The shells she SELLS are SEA-shells, I'm sure.

For if she SELLS SEA-shells on the SEA-shore

Then I'm sure she SELLS - - SEA-shore SHELLS!"

I almost laughed for joy at the pride evident in her eye over hitting all her S's, but I stifled it so as not to give offense. I applauded instead. Truth be told, I never minded Sholeena's soft slurring of her sibilants. I had found it quite endearing and would, in fact, quite miss it. We were all hitting our stride and learning new things. One day I knew I would look back with longing on these more innocent days of my youth, ignoring all the tedium and daily aggravations which presently took center stage. So it was with a sense of wistful ennui that I left Sholeena to return to her folding and departed.

***

Julia's library was a cozy little nook near the back of the main house. Like the rest of the estate, it was kept tidy and understated. On a floor of fitted planks devoid of rugs stood several well waxed tables. These were of simple design but finely wrought from exquisite hardwoods. They gleamed in the afternoon light that filtered in through the bay window. Ringed about the area, wall-mounted shelves jutted out, each laden with its precious burdens.

The only nods to decor were some delicate ferns that grew from glazed clay pots in the window bay and just to either side of the entryway. These urns depicted peaceful woodland scenes that put one in awe of the artistry of their maker. My gift automatically stretched out to the plants and informed me they were quite content.

The only sound to disturb the stillness of the room was the slight scrape of parchment from a large grimoire which lay open upon the central table where my cousin stood leafing carefully through its pages. Though I knew Roy sensed my presence, he remained focused on the colorful pages fanned out before him. Royland had recently shown a willingness to engage in the social niceties, but I knew his first instinct remained cold indifference toward the world around himself until it suited him to depart from his silence. I had grown comfortable with this, and so I bided, content to soak in what I could through observation alone without pestering the man.

Laying at Roy's elbow was the knitted scarf he'd been gifted by his grandma. Mistress Gretta was still deeply withdrawn and remained uncommunicative, but she seemed a bit more capable each time we'd visited her. Recovering from her long imprisonment by the dark druids was a slow process, but Mistress Dunham assured us Gretta was making steady progress. Roy had cherished the scarf and wore it often in the early spring, just after he'd been gifted it during the old woman's singular moment of clarity. But as the summer progressed, it had been reluctantly set aside and packed in mothballs along with his other out-of-season garments.

What was he doing with the ugly thing? His eyes flitted between it and the pages he was perusing, as if seeking something. The book didn't have much in the way of text, seeming to be more a picture book of some sort. No. That wasn't it. Stepping closer, I made out the distinctive lines and symbols of a map, like the baron had in his map room at Westarbor Keep. So it was an atlas furrowing my cousin's brow, one depicting forests and waterways and fraught with Elven runes and symbols.

Finally, my cousin's frantic page-turning ceased. He steepled his fingers before his lips while his eyes lay locked upon the tome.

"Hello cousin," he greeted me at last.

Naturally, I had some questions, but I resisted the impulse to pose them. I'd only just gotten back into Royland's good graces, and I was loath to annoy him by asking the obvious. Instead, I thought to try a different tack.

"Hey Roy," I returned. "You promised to help me learn an enchantment today. I came to see whether you had some time."

Royland frowned. His eyes slid toward mine in a sly attempt to assess my mind, but I avoided his gaze, concentrating instead on a speck on the ceiling and taking a slow, serene breath.

"I'm busy right now," he grumbled. "You should take it up with our master. Enchantment is no proper pursuit for a journeyman who's yet to master his homunculus. Why do you insist on this?"

"I have my reasons," I assured him earnestly. "And we all know that even aspirants dabble in enchantment a bit on the sly. *You* did."

"That was under a master's direct oversight. Master Reinhardt was with me every step of the way. And besides, I'd already learned the enchantment when Master Chadwick fortified the keep's gates. Perhaps you should have paid better attention at the time."

"That would've been a bit difficult while his grand working was leeching all the magic from me."

"Concentration is the hallmark of a good mage. It's a shame you're gifted with so little of it. Anyway, it's like I said. I'm busy now. I've just made a discovery. Perhaps tomorrow."

I could tell my cousin was just itching for me to ask. Again, I denied him this, refusing to be diverted.

"Okay," I said. "I'll hold you to that."

As I turned to take my leave, Roy's compulsive nature finally forced him to broach the topic himself.

"I said 'perhaps'," he snapped. "And don't you want to know what I've discovered?"

Hesitating in mid stride, I turned back to meet his gaze.

"Tell me, then," I commanded.

With relief evident on his face, Roy lifted the scarf.

"The patterns on this aren't random," he exclaimed. "They mark the steps of a journey, Gretta's last journey south."

He said it with a conviction that left no room for doubt. Perhaps his certainty arose from when he had touched the old woman's mind. Or maybe he'd confirmed his suspicions in the tedious and obsessive way that Roy tackled all manner of trivia he 'researched.' I believed in my cousin, but I remained silent to let him speak on.

Beckoning me closer, he held the unseasonal garment up against the page to which the atlas lay open. There did indeed seem to be a rough correlation between Grandma Gretta's scarf and the map in question.

"See this blue circle?" he continued. "That represents Lake Placid. And this meandering brown line swerves exactly like the high south road toward Lorédon. I've confirmed several other landmarks in this remarkably detailed rendering. Enough to affirm it's no mere coincidence."

"What do the red dots represent?" I asked, intrigued.

"That's uncertain as yet. I believe Gretta or her homunculus was trying to tell us something important."

"Whatever could it mean?" I wondered aloud.

"I don't know," said my cousin absently, "but I certainly intend to find out."

***

Dinner at the House of the Twilight Sun (*jaweehay chosha julia*) was simmering in its kitchen. And from its spicy aroma, it'd be well worth my earlier hike up from the academy. Griselda was fussing over the place settings, of which there were four. Zelda would sup at the small table in the kitchen with Jase after the rest of us had been served. We were only just moving toward our seats when there came a clapping sound at the front door. This was accompanied by a melodious male voice spouting a greeting in Elven.

"Jisusha jaweehay quash quin quem!" announced the visitor.

Mistress Julia arched an eyebrow and turned to Zelda saying: 'Set another place for dinner, dear.' Then, rather than having a servant do so, she strode out toward the entry hall to greet the visitor herself. Uncertain whether we should seat ourselves, we journeymen milled about, waiting to see what would come next. Surprisingly, it was Sholeena who soon took charge.

"Well?" she chided. "You heard the master. Whoever he is, he'll be shtaying for dinner. That means introductions. Make a receiving line and get ready to greet the man!"

I glanced at Roy, who adopted an amused expression as he quietly complied. It was thus they found us, standing in a line eldest to youngest, looking like butter wouldn't melt in our mouths. Our hasty facade of cultured indifference should stand up to casual scrutiny.

On first sighting the visitor, my expectations were confirmed. He was an Elf. Though tall and fairly slender, he was a bit thicker about his middle than most Elves I'd seen. Moreover, he carried himself with an informal bearing. It was graceful enough but bore hints of a slothful ease that matched the sloppy grin he sported. Mistress Julia walked beside him. The two were carrying on a low conversation in Elven, which abruptly ceased upon their entry into the dining room.

"Journeymen," my master announced, "It is my honor to introduce my life-mate, Hazhi Dia Quobias. Hazhi, these are my new journeymen: Royland Wagge and Lucas Harper of Meadowfork, and Sholeena Blorlafargalish of the Paludaria."

"I am honored by the gift of your names," he said, his grin broadening.

"*Sowee batla shey jhey*," I returned, taking extra care with my pronunciation.

So this was Mistress Julia's husband. He seemed less stuffy than how I'd imagined the spouse of the prim matron. As Griselda finished setting a fifth place at the dining table, Mistress Julia indicated we should all be seated. Never one to stand on ceremony, Royland eschewed his usual place near our master and slouched around to assume a spot at the table's foot.

Mistress Julia claimed her accustomed seat at the table's head and Hazhi sat to the right of her. It seemed strange somehow. I was used to seeing lords seated at the table's head with their wives just to the left of them. Then I recalled that the Elves favored a matriarchal tradition. Women were the 'lords' of the household, and their men were treated more like their honored guests. We all held hands in the Elven fashion, and Mistress Julia invoked the blessing.

"*Quordusha tivia vam soja pop sodazh*," she intoned (something about enjoying the family meal to honor our foremothers).

As we began passing the various dishes and helping ourselves to whatever we fancied. Mistress Julia herself served our smiling guest.

"So these are the *biddle-tessen puqua* you mentioned in your letter," he remarked in a laconic drawl. "Whatever possessed you to take on such a responsibility, pookie? And at this of all times?"

My chest spasmed, and I nearly dropped the bowl of sugar beets I was passing. I knew my master's full name was Puquabeth Chosha Julia, but I was having serious difficulty imagining her as a 'pookie.' If my master noted my lapse, she gave no hint of it.

"Dark times are upon us, beloved," she replied. "The headmaster urged us all to make selections that Osten may muster its full magical might sooner rather than later. I agreed in principle and felt it meet to set an example. It is time to look beyond our differences and serve the greater good."

So saying, she heaped his plate with an extra portion of asparagus, which he eyed skeptically.

"What's a biddle-tessen?" I inquired.

Mistress Julia pursed her lips and glared stonily at Hazhi.

"It's a term used by the more ill-mannered of my folk to describe those *not of* the first people," she admitted. "It loosely translates to 'half-ear' or 'round-ear,'" she explained in clipped tones.

I like to think I was raised right. For most of my life, I'd been fairly sheltered in my small and provincial hamlet, surrounded by customs and rules of behavior well understood by all. However, since traveling abroad, I'd encountered many other cultures and had discovered there were just as many forms of politeness as there were people. The fairies had their own ways. The southerners had theirs. Even the goblins presumably had some code or other that governed what passed for civility among them. But one rule always seemed to hold true. It was inevitably deemed the height of good manners to make a guest feel comfortable and welcome.

And so I laughed.

What could better ease the tension in a new acquaintance than a bit of shared laughter? Hazhi smiled and nodded, speared an asparagus and commenced chewing it with gusto. And even Mistress Julia's stern expression dissolved into a reluctant grin as she began partaking of her own selections.

***

After the meal, Mistress Julia gathered us into the sitting parlor for an announcement. She bade us all be seated but remained herself aloof, pacing before the steady flames in our hearth until we had settled. A single lock of her dark chestnut hair strayed from its coiffure onto her unlined brow.

"My husband has brought us some joyous news," she began, her tone uncertain. "I am to be recalled to fair Lorédon to attend the birth of our first grandchild. My replacement is even now setting her affairs in order and should arrive within a fortnight."

There was silence for several breaths as our thoughts ran wild with unfettered speculation. Then Roy dragged his regard up from the floorboards and posed the obvious questions in a dispassionate manner any barrister might envy.

"Who is this replacement?" he put forth. "Will she become our new master, or must we again await selection?"

Julia met his questioning gaze with a thoughtful glance before delivering her reply.

"You all have vowed to obey me as your master. I, in turn, have sworn an oath no less binding to nurture your gifts and guide them to fulfillment of your masteries. Such oaths are not taken lightly, nor can they be readily set aside when inconvenient. I therefore propose to bring you with me on my journey south that your studies may continue without interruption."

"What about my sequestration?" I asked.

"I've spoken with Mistress Dunham, Lucas. She assures me you're well on your way. If you haven't got a handle on it in the next several weeks, I feel certain I can assist you in completing that bit of training."

Clasping her hands before her and addressing all, she continued.

"I understand that this mayn't be easy for you so soon after your selection. On the plus side, introduction to a different culture is an eventual requirement for *all* masters. I can attest that it yields many benefits. If, however, you don't feel up to this challenge, simply let me know it and a more suitable arrangement can be made. Think on it. I'll expect your answers by tomorrow night."

Roy said nothing, and Sholeena was looking green around the gills, a certain sign the Paluda girl was anxious. Thus far, I'd been fretting over my own situation. But how much worse for Sholeena, who'd already had to learn one foreign language and culture to be so soon thrust headlong into another? I placed my hand on her shoulder, and she quickly covered it with her own.

In the silence of my cell, I considered my options.

The Elves I'd met to date had seemed a decent enough folk. Some were whimsical and some more serious. Best not to lump them all together. Language would be a difficulty. I'd never in all my life been at a loss for words. I dreaded being unable to know what was said around me or stuttering through the simplest of requests. What would Royland choose? Since leaving Meadowfork, he'd been the one constant in my life. Despite some recent quarreling, he's always been the yin to my yang.

Ultimately, it came down to a matter of courage. Mistress Julia had been truly brave to take charge of three unruly biddle-tessens and offer to share her wisdom with us. Add to that, as our master, she could have simply commanded we accompany her. Put in those terms, how could I let my master down? As a certain dairy maid had once reminded me, 'oaths were sworn for a reason.' It would be both cowardly and ungrateful to bail on her at this point. I appreciated the time to mull it over, but my decision was made at that moment. I was certain Roy would arrive at the same conclusion. As for Sholeena, I supposed we'd find out tomorrow.

At least I had several weeks to say my goodbyes. I thought of all the friendships I had forged here at Conclave. I'd been here scarcely five short months, and already it felt like a second home. Strangely, this gave me hope. Surely, in Lorédon, I would make *new* friends and find *new* things to pique my interest. I'd miss Lorraine, Lloyd, Hazel and all the rest. I'd have to have a long talk with the tree sprite. She could commiserate with me. She'd be able to relate, if anyone would, to what it felt like to be uprooted.

CHAPTER TWO

The Stonemason

"The highest tribute to the dead is not grief
but gratitude."
~ Thornton Wilder ~

'This is it,' I thought with excitement as I stepped down the gangplank. We were now officially on our way. Our barge had made the crossing in less than an hour, thanks in no small part to the favorable winds summoned by my master. It now lay moored to the dock awaiting the new Elven master and her entourage. Originally, I had supposed we might welcome Mistress Talia at the estate, but the plan was now to meet her carriage here at Gentle Repose on the lake's southern shore.

Once all our baggage was unloaded and settled, we were free to explore the grounds. I struck out at once. Sholeena wanted to tag along, but I claimed a need for some private time to reflect. In truth, my bladder was full near to bursting. Unlike the sailors and stevedores who had crewed our barge, I was squeamish about relieving myself over the railing while we were under sail. I was paying the price now as I stiff-walked toward a copse of trees a short distance off.

For a cemetery, Gentle Repose had a pleasant feel. Well-trimmed ivy grew up the sides of the crypts visible from the lake's shore. Within these stone edifices were interred the remains of past masters who had once dwelt at the conclave. I wondered which of these structures might have been the site of the grizzly offense so recently perpetrated by the necromancer. In the Prowd family crypt, he and his undead minions had lain in wait to assault poor Luther's funeral procession.

Only one man had escaped the ambush to bear witness to the depraved and wanton slaughter. Master Sheppard was even now leading a squad of his seneschals in pursuit of the abomination once known as 'Adam.' After committing the vile deed, the creature had fled east, leaving the dead strewn about in his wake. Worse still, he had stolen the former headmaster's arms and head. He clearly intended to use these to replace the monstrous ones he'd inherited from Franklin's innocent experiment. I shuddered as I relieved myself against the bole of the tree.

On emerging from the thicket, I approached the cluster of crypts. I ambled among them, recognizing the names and heraldic symbols of such notables as Southerland, Willoughby, and all the rest. Angels adorned some of these, as though to bear their occupants off to their final rewards.

And there it was, 'PROWD.' Unlike some of the more recent structures, this one stood among those at the forefront, its pitted and weathered brown stone a mute testament to its historic nature. From my reading on the topic, I knew Greyson Prowd was one of the seven wizards who had established the conclave hundreds of years in the past. Many of Luther's ancestors had served the conclave in a Prowd tradition, dating back to its very founding. It was sad to see the last of his long line pass in such a horrific manner. I removed my hat, inclined my head, and offered a short prayer that Luther's soul might find rest.

I wondered what other sights I might explore in this venerable necropolis. Beyond the crypts lay a meandering trail that wound back into a field of burial sites which sported various markers and headstones. It was here where the ordinary citizens of Conclave had, for generations, been laid to rest.

These more modern habitats of the dead were interspersed amid an old-growth cypress forest heavily bearded by moss. The shade cast down by these made the lighting subdued. The pyramidical tops of the blue-green trees pointed heavenward as though beseeching a blessing. And their shed needles abounded to form a thick, soft mat that threw up a pleasant citrus fragrance when trod upon.

I soon arrived at the first of the markers and gravely regarded its chiseled message.

Here lie the bones of

WILLIAM BAKER

Fell off the spire

And met his maker

MCLXIII

I'd heard of this, but was still a bit put off by the irreverence. Long ago, the stonecutter at conclave had shown his morbid sense of humor in his penchant for inscribing the manner of death into the headstones' epitaphs (this, or some horrible jape about the deceased loved one's personality or proclivities). The man's apprentices had upheld the tradition, and the inhabitants of Conclave even liked to suggest their own prior to their passing.

I scanned a few others and found them to be much the same. I suppose it was a little livelier than a dull rendering of names and dates. This seemed a cruel prank to play on grieving loved ones, but I'm told the locals actually found it very cathartic. 'To each his own,' I allowed.

The notion got stuck in my head. I found it nigh impossible to dislodge, it having taken firm root in my overactive imagination. There, as I meandered through the cypress grove, I couldn't help but consider how the awful stonecutter might have described my own dearly departed. My mother first came to mind.

ISABELL HARPER NÉE WAGGE

Escaped from the witch

and married the miller

bearing a son

was this lady's killer

MCCIX

As I gnashed my teeth with guilt at my betrayal of her memory, an odd laughter rang out from within the depths of my mind. Wait. I knew that voice. It was my own, but... not. The rasping echo of mirth continued, and a shiver ran down my spine as realization dawned that my unconscious mind was speaking to me at long last. Despite Mistress Dunham's assurance that all was proceeding normally, the husk that lay in my inner field had made no further forays into speech since first declaring it was 'thirsty.' Mistress Julia had said it was of little consequence. We would see to my homunculus once we arrived in Lorédon.

I sat down and cautiously peered within, worried at what I might find. There, nestled amidst my vines, lay the husk. It no longer shone with the infusion of my gift, but lay lifeless and still with a deep, jagged split running lengthwise down its middle. Crouched over it was a gaunt, green figure with knobby knees and elbows. Its head put me in mind of a wrinkled canvas sac beneath which odd bulges shifted about. Its lips were parted in a grinning leer that somehow failed to convey any sense of good cheer. Almost skeletal, it peered up at me from two hollow, empty eye sockets, looking otherwise like a praying mantis ready to strike.

"*You should have saved him,*" it accused.

"Saved who?" I asked, mystified.

A swirling vision erupted as if from nowhere, and in it, I witnessed Kyle Digby laying dead on the field just as I had last seen him. He sank below the ground and another cenotaph arose in his place.

KYLE DIGBY

Defending the kingdom

to his final breath

By giant spiders

he was bitten to death

MCCXXIII

"I... I couldn't have *saved* him," I protested. "I did my best!"

"*Not good enough*," the thing insisted.

I think I saw where all this angst was coming from. If this bizarre haunt arose from my own unconscious mind, then it was trying to come to grips with my own guilty feelings and lingering doubts. I didn't like thinking about death and had always sought ways to put it from my mind. I guess this had merely suppressed such issues and forced my subconscious to deal with them. Now here he was, throwing them back at me.

"I'm sorry," I said after some thought. "I should have worked through our feelings on these matters and not just ignored them. I was an ass."

The thing arose from its crouch and took a tentative step towards me.

"*Thirsssty?*" it keened plaintively.

"Not just yet," I forestalled. "We must talk again and at great length about how our powers are to be used before I entrust any more of them to you."

Standing erect, the creature resembled less a leafy bug than he did a slender man, one made all out of sticks and stems. His pale, wrinkly face sitting atop the parody of a man's body, put me in mind of a scarecrow. Although my inner garden had never, to my knowledge, been threatened by avian pests, this image solidified in my mind. And as it did, the creature stood a bit straighter and became garbed in loose-fitting, shabby clothing and a straw hat.

I resisted the urge to name the fellow. According to Mistress Dunham, to do so was to cement our relationship, which was only in its earliest stage. Naming one's homunculus was a special treat reserved for a time when rules of behavior had been completely codified and settled. For now, the clothes would have to suffice.

"You've given me a lot to think about," I said. "We'll talk again very soon. I promise to do some honest soul-searching and grieving over those troubling matters I've neglected from our past. Meanwhile, *you* should consider what else you want and how you would use more power and autonomy should I choose to grant you such."

With that, I ended the impromptu meditation to resume my place in the world without. As the dismal surroundings swam back into focus, I was startled to discover I wasn't alone.

***

Two men loomed above me where I sat among the graves.

"I think he's asleep," one was muttering to the other.

"Lucas?" prompted the taller of the two. "Are you all right?"

It was a familiar young fellow with a mop of dusty blond hair. I craned my neck upward and gave voice to my astonishment.

"Franklin? What are *you* doing here? I thought you were off chasing a murderous beast."

"Well, I was," he replied. "Still am, actually. It's just that the trail has gone cold. Master Sheppard sent me back to dig for clues."

As I made to stand, Franklin offered his hand and helped haul me up to my feet. Franklin was my former head of house and a dear friend who had helped me battle an unseelie wight. I recognized the other man with him. He was Arnold Clark, the soldier who had escaped the attack on Master Prowd's funeral barge. Both young men were now journeymen to the conclave's chief seneschal and part of the task force pursuing the monster responsible.

"I thought Master Sheppard was an expert tracker," I put forth as I brushed the pine needles from the seat of my breeches.

"He is," Franklin confirmed. "The problem is: Adam doesn't need to sleep. Moreover, on those bovine legs I gave him, he runs nearly as fast as a horse can gallop. As near as we can tell, he's been running for more than a week now, stopping only to recharge his necromantic energies. We lost track of him somewhere near the outskirts of Fairglen duchy."

"So why are you here, then?" I asked.

"We're looking for the Moore family burial plots," Arnold put forth. "Do you perchance know where they are?"

"No."

"Well, we'd best be about our search, then. The caretaker said they were farther down this path and on the left."

"I'll help you look," I offered. "I've some time. We're just waiting for a carriage to arrive."

With that, I fell into step with the two men, and we headed down the trail. Every so often, we would spread out to read the headstones when we came upon a cluster of them.

"What's in the Moore family burial plots?" I asked. "You mentioned clues."

"Not what - who," said Arnold. "As you may know, Franklin here can commune with the dead. He reminded our master that the necromancer had been possessing that Russel Moore fellow for a week or so as he worked his villainy at Conclave. We think there's a chance Franklin can enter that corpse and learn of the creature's plans. That way, we can try getting out ahead of this thing."

I was astonished and more than a little repulsed by this idea. Something of this must have shown on my face, for Franklin grimaced and looked away.

"Believe you me, Lucas," he groused, "it isn't my idea of a pleasant little frolic, but if it can help, I must buck up and do it."

I knew Franklin felt personally responsible for unleashing this terror upon the kingdom. True, he had provided a superior body, which now served the necromancer as a host. But Franklin's intentions had been pure. He hadn't meant for his creation to be stolen and so sorely misused.

We continued in silence for a time.

"So..." Arnold began conversationally. "Whatever were you doing napping in the middle of a graveyard, Lucas? Lookin' forward to your final rest, were ya?"

"I was taken with a sudden need to meditate," I carefully replied.

"Trouble with your homunculus?" Franklin asked with an uncanny burst of perception.

Had he been taking lessons from Roy? As Franklin was also a new journeyman, perhaps he'd encountered similar difficulties.

"Something like that," I equivocated. "What's *your* homunculus, anyway?"

Franklin got a distant look and wet his lips before answering.

"Don't ask," he replied.

We continued in silence for a time.

The way grew rougher. Our boots crunched on the cypress needles as we surveyed yet another cluster of tombstones arranged to the left of the path. This section seemed older. Ivy and other creepers had intruded, and the trees pressed closer about us.

"Over here," shouted Arnold. "I think this is one."

Franklin and I hustled over. Arn had pulled back some vines to reveal the writing on the marker.

Here lie the bones of

LESTER MOORE

Buried six feet down

No Les, No More

MCXXXV

"Yep," said Franklin. "This must be the right area. Look for a fresh one."

As we spread out among the shaded plots, an idea occurred to me. I reached for my magic. Not my vines, but rather my secondary, earth affinity. Submerging myself into my inner hill, I cast about. All around me, the earth lay packed and firm. I could feel its gritty texture. But straight ahead and just off to my right lay a crumbly disturbance. I strode over to it and shifted the ground cover aside.

"It's this one here," I announced.

I was soon joined by the others, and we regarded the writing on this more recent stone.

RUSSELL MOORE

A jolly fellow

with life all aglow,

Till a necromancer

Laid him low

MCCXXIV

"I feel... something," Franklin declared, crouching down and placing his palm flat on the bare earth. "It's very faint, though. I'm afraid I'll have to get a lot closer to gain any impressions."

"So we dig?" asked Arnold.

At Franklin's nod, the more senior journeyman began stripping off his shirt. I recalled Arnold was a therianthrope. I believe he meant to sprout digging claws and have at it right then and there.

"Maybe I can help," I quickly asserted. "Stand back and let me try something."

Back at Fowler Ranch, I had learned the spell: 'Earth Furrow.' We used it for farming. At the time, my pathetic efforts would barely scratch the surface. This had been prior to acquiring my earth affinity, however, and I'd yet to test my current limits. I'd once seen my app-master carve out an entire castle moat in one grand casting.

I focused on my inner hill until I felt a firm connection. I planted my feet and steadied my breathing as I'd been instructed.

"Terram aratro," I pronounced with what I imagined was a suitably dramatic rumble.

It wasn't like my verdumancy. Nor did it resemble the minor earth shapings I had attempted to date. Shifting sand back at the créche had been a simple matter that taxed me not a whit. But here I could sense the full weight of the earth I intended to move. I felt the strain deep in my gut and loins.

First, a rough gouge formed in the loose earth before the tombstone. The dirt within it rattled around and came spewing out to either side. A shower of debris issued forth. Some scattered far and wide, while the bulk of it formed loose mounds just to the left and right. This was how 'Earth Furrow' was *supposed* to be performed, I thought with glee.

Despite the cloud of fine grit thrown up from the gaping hole and obscuring normal vision, I could still sense what I was doing. Once my burrowing encountered what must be the casket, I released the spell and promptly sat down, exhausted.

When the dust cleared, my friends approached to stare down into the excavated gravesite.

"Well," said Arnold, "that's gonna make things a mite easier."

Looking within, I noted my inner hill was more like an inner mole-hill. Only a pittance of my earth power remained, and I felt the loss like a deep ache in my lower back. So much so, I wasn't even certain I could stand. Franklin looked over at me with a crooked smile I'd rarely seen grace those lips.

"You've grown," he remarked.

I thought such praise might be a tad premature. I'd definitely overexerted myself. I could feel my eyelids beginning to droop.

"Ah... I'll just leave you to it, then," I announced. "I need to check back in at the barge in case Mistress Julia needs something."

I put on a brave face and stood slowly to my feet, taking care not to swoon. I pulled upon my wakefulness spell, but it seemed to make little difference. Franklin flashed me a look of disappointment, but soon turned back excitedly to our dig site. Arn had already climbed down and was prying at the lid. Having no great desire to see what lay within, I turned and headed back the way we'd come.

"Stay safe," I entreated them. "And if you catch up to that Truman fellow, give the knife an extra twist for old Russell there."

"We will most assuredly do so," shouted Franklin to my retreating back.

As I strolled along the trail, I began to feel somewhat stronger. The lightheaded feeling passed, and my stride became more natural. Moreover, my magic was recovering far quicker than was usual. A smile tugged at the corners of my mouth, but it failed to fully form as the cold realization struck. I glanced back over my shoulder to confirm my fretful conjecture. The headstones just to my rear were now devoid of vines and creepers. Only defoliated and withered stalks protruded from the ground about them.

What was going on? I hadn't invoked 'ambulare interitus', my withering stride - not consciously.

Not... consciously.

A certain scarecrow came to mind. In depleting my magic, had I made a certain someone 'thirssty' enough to take independent action? It occurred to me that new journeymen were sequestered for a very good reason. Also, though empowering my homunculus had seemed like the right answer at the time, perhaps it wasn't such a genius move after all. In magic, dangerous shortcuts were to be avoided like flames in a mill. I realized with chagrin I would need to inform my master of this development at once. I quickened my pace and sought to clamp down on my involuntary magic as I scurried back to the boat.

***

On hearing of my adventure in the cemetery and subsequent troubles with my homunculus, my master became most distraught. She forbade me to make any further use of my magic until such time as we might properly resume daily meditations. I was to consider myself semi-sequestered for the duration of our journey.

Franklin and Arnold came wandering back a few hours later. Their horses awaited them here. Their leads were affixed to a shade tree in front of the caretaker's meager dwelling. Their saddles were slung over a fence railing nearby. Once the two men had washed off the reek of the grave with a quick dip in the lake and a change of clothing, they joined us for a bit. The two didn't stay overlong, just long enough to share a cold meal from our traveling stores and share news. Then they were off. We wished them good hunting ere they galloped east to rejoin their fellows.

By this time, Mistress Talia was noticeably overdue. My master fretted over what could be delaying her. As it was verging on nightfall, she gave permission to the crew of 'Greyson's Lament' to weigh anchor and return to the master's dock back at Conclave. Our party would camp here on the lake shore to await the elves should they arrive during the nighttime hours. We lit a small watch fire and spread our bedrolls nearby.

The refreshing lake breeze had stilled and begun to reverse. According to my master, an expert in such matters, hot air liked to rise. It was why smoke flued up from our fire rather than spreading out in a choking cloud all about. In the heat of the summer and so near to a sizable body of water like Lake Placid, the air tended to rise to be replaced by the cooler air from the lake. This resulted in a continuous inbound breeze we called a 'lake breeze.' After sunset, as the land began to cool, the reverse was true, causing the wind to go out to the lake as a 'land breeze,' or an 'offshore breeze,' as the sailors would have it. In any event, I supposed those of us living near a lake or the sea were fortunate. We enjoyed a much milder climate thereby. It was lucky for us that water was so slow to surrender its heat.

Hazhi sat near his wife, looking out upon the lake. The stars had come out and the offshore breeze brought us the soothing aroma of cypress. I wouldn't have imagined spending the night by a cemetery in which zombies had recently arisen to slaughter the living could be so serene. And yet it was. Add to that; I'd only just come from exhuming a months-dead corpse which had played host to a necromancer while a creepy scarecrow seized control of my magic...

"Tater?" said a voice just to my left, disturbing my silent litany of dread.

I blinked and turned to gaze up at the man. It was Sam Pfitzner, the caretaker. Sam was a stone cutter by trade. He managed the grounds of Gentle Repose. It was he who carried on the tradition of carving the irreverent epitaphs on the headstones hereabout. Earlier, Sam had buried a dozen potatoes beneath the edge of our fire to bake in the heat of its coals. He now stood clutching a basket of them and proffering one to me on the end of his knife.

"Thanks," I answered.

I rummaged through my bob to retrieve my mess kit. I plucked the tuber from off the knife and swiftly set it on my tin plate, careful not to burn my fingers in the process. As he shuffled back toward the fire, I hastened to join him and the others there. I broke the blackened rind down the middle to reveal the steaming, pale yellow goodness within. The others were by now digging in, but I thought it best to wait for mine to cool a bit more.

"So, Hazhi," I put forth. "Ever since we were introduced, I've been wondering about your name."

"Oh?" he prompted after swallowing a mouthful.

"Well, to the best of my meager translation skill, it means something like 'Happy Danger.' That can't be right, can it?"

"Close," he said and grunted.

From an elf, a grunt came out more like a little 'aha.'

"'Laughs in the face of adversity' would be closer to its intended meaning. My parents told me it was for the devil-may-care attitude I'd had as a child."

"Not just as a child, dear," Mistress Julia muttered.

Was that a jolly jab from my normally reserved master? I stifled a laugh at the thought of it.

Hazhi leered over at her, then turned back to me saying: 'Never be reluctant to laugh, journeyman. The creator above granted us this gladsome gift. She herself is possessed of a magnificent sense of humor.'

"What makes you say so?" inquired Roy.

The elf paused, as though seeking just the right words before answering my cousin.

"When we expel waste gasses from our bowels, we do so between the two largest flaps of flesh we own. This makes a merry little toot accompanied by a foul little stink. Now I ask you, isn't this her way of assuring we don't take ourselves too seriously?"

Sholeena snickered.

"He means farts!" she laughingly announced.

It was an odd reflection on the nature and intent of our maker, but I was soon to learn this was typical of my master's mate. For his life path, or *vallahimay*, he'd chosen to be a poet. This was a highly respected profession among the first people and had even won him the heart of my mistress back in the days before even my grandfather was alive. We had him recite one of his odes for us.

It had the melodic and fluid lilt that characterized all Elven speech. The effect of this oration on Julia was immediate and profound. Her eyes shone in the reflected light of our fire and a faint smile pierced her customary mask of disinterest. It didn't strike me as poetry *per se*. I could detect no rhymes or metered cadence. Perhaps as a 'biddle-tessen' I lacked the proper ears to judge it.

As I settled within my bedding, I thought long and hard of the deaths I had witnessed and began working through the guilt and loss they stirred in me. It was the first thing my unconscious self had asked of me, and I could put it off no longer. I reasoned that if I dealt with my suppressed emotions in a stalwart manner, it would lift their burdens from my soul. Hopefully, this would, in turn, make my homunculus more manageable.

Roy and Sholeena had undoubtedly gone through something similar. During his sequestration, hadn't Roy explicitly mentioned 'cutting ties with the ghosts of his past?' Only *I* had been too pigheaded to get on with the *true* challenge of confronting one's homunculus.

I considered the mother I had never known and all the soldiers who had died during the siege. I winced to recall the goblin scout who had died with my quarrel in his chest. I thought about my failure to save Kyle Digby and how I had crushed Grandma Abbey's last link to life. Though most, if not all, of these events had been necessary or their circumstances beyond my control, I let my thoughts dwell on each and allowed myself to grieve.

In the days to come, my hollow-eyed scarecrow would dredge up many more neglected shades from my sorry past to be banished by the bright light of awareness. My trek south was thus to become also a journey of self-discovery.

***

"...*Jiquosa jithosia tua*," sang the voice.

"I confess I was worried, Talia," my master replied. "And though my ears rejoice to hear the mother tongue again, let us instead converse in the human language. You need the practice. You'll be living among them for some time to come."

Bleary and befuddled, I came more fully awake. The low-toned conversation disturbing my slumber had been going on for some time, only gradually becoming separate from the dreams I'd been enjoying.

I cracked my eyes open a slit.

Five figures sat surrounding the remnants of our fire, the dim coals of which shed an orange glow. I could make out my master and Hazhi. The others were facing away from me, their shadowy silhouettes backlit by the lambent embers. The one to the left must be Mistress Talia. It was she who was speaking. Her diction was spot on, even having noble overtones, but her grammar struck me at once as odd.

"All right, Chosha. Let it be as you are asking. I am sorry for the lateness of my arrival. I was... detained... not avoidably.

"My, you *are* rusty. What was this 'matter' that detained you?" asked Julia, speaking slowly and enunciating clearly.

"Nothing very dangerous. It was another swarm of blade moths at a village east of *Boma-sud Hoodah*. It is all poor Shon can do to keep the southern reaches safe. And since your daughter is not helping, it fell on me. Fell to me? To repel them. Also, what is this 'rusty?'"

"Rust is the *ragha* that forms on iron tools that have not been used for a long time. It simply means you have not spoken Ostinian for a while and are out of practice. Humans use such idioms all the time. It's frustrating at first. Just smile and nod a lot until you... 'get the hang of it.'"

Rather than being an eavesdropper, I decided it was time to announce my return to a state of consciousness. I sat up, yawned noisily, and rubbed at my eyes to clear them. I marked that Sholeena and Roy were slumbering quietly nearby, still huddled beneath their blankets. Despite the gentle offshore breeze, blankets weren't really needed on a warm summer night such as this. But I always felt safer and less exposed when tucked under one. I peeled mine back and emerged to meet the newcomers.

I was introduced to Mistress Talia and her apprentice. Her husband, Tamil, was a tall fellow who built houses and other structures for his *valihimay*. He was here only to help get his wife settled in, but then would be heading back to their home in Lorédon.

The coach in which they'd arrived was to be ours for the return journey. It was an impressive sight and far larger than the carriage I'd been envisioning. The Elven wainwrights seemed to prefer gentle curving lines. Its massive main cabin was a roundish enclosure that put me in mind of a gigantic, hollowed-out pumpkin. It was replete with ornamental filigree throughout and boasted many other fine appointments. The matched team of four horses that had pulled it stood picketed nearby.

Because dawn wasn't far off, it was decided to let the others sleep on. After all, there was really nothing to be done until after 'Greyson's Lament' returned in the morning. The horses had been hauling long into the night and would require further rest before setting out once again. We sat by the fire, we six, while Mistress Julia imparted many final bits of advice to the conclave's new mage.

I couldn't keep my mind focused on the topics they discussed. My thoughts kept drifting to the dangers Mistress Talia had mentioned. I'd known the kingdom was under continuous assault along its southern border, but I hadn't considered just what that might mean for us. The war had always seemed a distant thing. Talia's simple statements had brought it home to me. Although Osten's primary attention remained on the battlefront at Eagle's Keep, Lorédon too, was suffering its own share of incursions by the horrific creatures raised by our enemy.

A swarm of 'blade moths' didn't sound like anything pleasant. Yet these had been dismissed as 'nothing very dangerous.' Did that mean the Elves and 'poor Shon' were facing more serious threats so often they'd become used to them? I pulled my blanket tighter about my shoulders and listened on.

***

The summer blessed us with clear skies and fragrant breezes as we plodded along the winding road south. The rattle of the reins and the soft clop of hoofbeats made a pleasant backdrop to my thoughts. I sat atop the driver's bench of the Elven carriage. Owing to our recent experience with the Tomcats' caravan, Roy and I were charged with driving the grand coach and caring for its animals at each stop along the way.

We took it in turns. One of us would drive while the other attended Mistress Julia's language lessons within the coach itself. I was thankful for the break. Elven was a difficult language. Its words could change their meanings drastically based on where they fell within a sentence. Moreover, every sodding inanimate *thing* was assigned a gender of which one needed to be mindful. I couldn't for the life of me determine by what logic a coil of rope was deemed female while fence railings were considered masculine. Rote memorization of these lingual peculiarities seemed the only possible path to success.

Elves were batty.

Since bypassing the duchy's capital of Deerfield, encounters with the duke's patrols had become far less frequent. So too had other traffic diminished. In fact, we'd only seen one other traveler all morning, some sort of fast horse messenger heading north. He hadn't even stopped to share news, passing us by with but a hasty nod and basic greeting. Farmsteads and other signs of habitation which had heretofore littered the surrounding countryside had grown sparse. And the 'road' was now naught but a simple dirt track which stretched ever onward.

The horses' ears pricked up, and I sensed a sudden eagerness in their gait. I emerged from my musings and grew more attentive.

Then, in the distance, I saw it.

Beyond the arid savanna through which we'd been wending our way was a line of lusher green growth. Surely such greenery was fostered by the very watercourse we'd been anticipating, the Washburn River. This would mark the southern boundary of Deerfield. By nightfall, we would be crossing into *puhi Lorédon nagemmahia*, the beautiful, forested land of Lorédon. I slowed the horses and prepared to step down and share the news. The door to the coach swung open as we rattled to a rest.

"Lucas?" came my master's voice from within. "Is aught amiss?"

"Quite the reverse, my lady," I answered cheerfully. "I sense we are nearing our destination and thought you might appreciate some forewarning to freshen up and prepare to greet your countrymen."

Just across the bridge that straddled the Washburn, I'd been told, was the Elven settlement of *Ngema Sorihap*. It was there where most commerce with the Elves was conducted. In it, one would find human traders, diplomats and the like mixing freely with their counterparts among the first people, the Elves. It was to be our stop for the night. As we went farther into Lorédon's interior, the human presence would taper off, eventually dwindling to only a rare few scholars and visitors. The southern reaches of the *nuvapua watheesh* welcomed only those having special permission.

"Thank you. That was most thoughtful. We shall stop here for our mid day meal and to prepare ourselves."

Roy and I unhitched the team and saw to the animals' grooming and hoof care while Sholeena began assembling lunch from our food stores. Hazhi scrambled up to the coachman's bench to confirm my sighting, and Mistress Julia started a fire. She had earlier used her aeromancy to corral and capture several Abodarian wind-thistle bushes she'd seen rolling by. As I understood it, these were the skeletal remains of the Salosa plant, a bright green shrub that sheep find rather tasty. When its bush matures and dies, what remains breaks off at the root and is blown away with the winds, scattering its seeds far and wide. Some people call them 'tumbleweeds.' Crushed up, they make dandy fire-starters. The weeds flared to life and were quickly consumed, leaving only a bed of smoking debris to which my master added a few sticks. Wandering over, I fished out something more substantial from my Bob.

It was true that aspirants sometimes dabbled in enchantment even before their selection as journeymen. Royland's pillowcase was one example of this. Henry Sutherland, then an aspirant from House Falcon, had gifted it to him to spare his housemates from Roy's godawful snoring. The pillowcase bore an enchantment that could be used to muffle all sound around it.

One day, a week or so prior to our departure, my Bob went missing. I searched all over the place to find where I'd left it. It turned out that Lloyd had taken Bob, and my other friends had conspired with him to throw me off the scent. Several days before we were to set off, there was a going away party for Sholeena, Roy, and me. Many of our friends had gathered and there were parting gifts all around. Even Terwilliger attended (though he remained unseen by most). It was there that Lloyd proudly announced a new aspect of his gift.

I had seen Lloyd place things into an unseen non-space he called his 'void' and cause them to reappear elsewhere on command. But none of us yet suspected just how advanced he'd become with this skill. To the wonderment of all, Lloyd reached into his breast pocket and produced a never-ending chain of colored handkerchiefs tied together at their corners. I laughed with all the others. Apparently, Lloyd had discovered how to enchant an aperture (his pocket in this instance) to hold open a tiny window into his void. Moreover, he then stood to one side and introduced me to my new and improved 'Bob.' Stitched onto its side was a new pocket held closed by a brass buckle. The boy gleefully explained that he wanted me to have a 'void pocket' of my own to remember him by. Once I'd recovered from my shock at his astonishing and wondrous gift, I clapped him on the back and assured him he would always be in my thoughts. I damn near shed a tear.

Bob could now hold what was in my traveling trunk many times over. But due to the experimental nature of the gift, I was reluctant to entrust anything valuable to 'void storage.' Firewood, however, was a different matter. I sauntered over to Mistress Julia where she crouched above her nascent flames and handed her a heavy log. She arched her eyebrows as her gaze shifted from the log to my satchel and back in bewilderment. It was good to know something could still surprise my old master. Though she looked to be in her twenties, I knew her to be centuries old and, thus, normally unflappable.

"Lucas," she said archly, "I thought we agreed to discontinue use of your magic until such time as you have full mastery over your unconscious will."

"I haven't forgotten, Mistress," said I in reply. "It's an enchanted object, a parting gift from my former roommate at Conclave."

"He did this as an *aspirant*?" she said, arranging the log onto the kindling with a slight frown. "I'm surprised he's not been selected as yet."

I was proud of my friend, and glad for him as well. I thought it likely Mistress Julia would put a bug in someone's ear about Lloyd's uncanny acumen and worthiness when next she took up the quill.

As the flames began licking up the log's outer bark, Sholeena arrived amid a clatter of cook pots and accoutrements.

"We still got some stew from lasht night's supper," she reported.

"We still *have* some stew," my master gently corrected.

"Yes, we still do."

"When will we carve into that pig we procured?" I asked with feigned indifference. "Now would seem to be an apt time. It'll spoil if we hold off much longer."

Vegetable stew was filling enough, and the subtle spices used by the Elves made it a meal that was truly delectable. But I'd been eyeing that pig for the better part of two days now. Hazhi bought it at the farmer's market where we'd last restocked.

It lay untouched, all succulent and stomach-growlingly delicious in the boot on the back of our coach.

"That's for another occasion," said my master as a hint of a smile graced her lips. "The stew will do for now."

"Hang the kettle, dear" she said to Sholeena.

The Seeress

"Do not go where the path may lead, go instead where there is no path and leave a trail."

~ Ralph Waldo Emerson ~

The horses trudged along, lugging our coach across the great stone bridge that spanned the Washburn.

We journeymen all sat within the conveyance. Our master had said it would be best if the border patrol first spied familiar faces. Therefore, it was she and Hazhi who now perched atop the driver's bench urging our strangely reluctant animals forward.

We had all donned finer clothing than our usual sturdy traveler's attire. But instead of the flowing robes she'd worn at Conclave, Mistress Julia wore a blouse replete with ruffled sleeves beneath a simple vest. An odd set of breeches that billowed out below the knee completed this strange ensemble. If you squinted a bit, they would resemble a long skirt. 'pantaloons' she named them (or *broeka* in Elven). Hazhi sported the same. And even Sholeena had been provided a pair.

The sound of rushing water hissed in our ears as the river swept through the rocky gorge below.

Royland had claimed the backward facing seat, but he'd promptly turned about to peer out the front-facing window. This afforded Sholeena and I a rather uncomfortable, intimate view of my cousin's skinny posterior.

"There's something they're not telling us," said Roy.

I had learned to trust Royland's insights about people. He had the remarkable talent to sense the emotions of another on touch or when meeting their gaze. It was more than that. He was, in fact, compelled to experience whatever they felt. Roy found most people's emotions disagreeable and would therefore often shy from such contact. Back in our home village, this had gained him a reputation as peculiar. And although Roy was now striving to overcome this perception, he still often enjoyed an unwilling inside track on what others intended.

"Something bad?" I asked.

Roy peered back at us. His brows were knit above his soft brown eyes and his mouth twisted to one side as he considered.

"It's more like a joke or a surprise of some sort they're brewing. It's tough to tell. Elves are hard to read. But the horses sense it too. See how skittish they are?"

Sholeena wriggled up beside Roy to peer without as well. Carefully, I leaned in to join them. The Appaloosas were indeed showing signs of distress. Their ears lay flat and their tails were swishing in agitation. We braced ourselves for whatever high jinks the two elves might intend for us.

We approached the southern end of the bridge, having safely traversed almost the entire span. Just as it seemed we had worried for naught and had slowly begun to relax, the dreadful ordeal began.

It started when a hairy hand nearly the size of a wagon wheel slithered up to grip the railing of the bridge to our right. Then all at once, a monstrous head hove into view. It had a mop of greasy green hair and an overlong, pointed nose. Two mismatched eyes the size of saucers were squinted nearly closed. It scowled at us and the horses shied and surely would have fled, had they not been trapped within their tack. They shivered there instead.

"*Quavo, sotto joh. Quaquova yinniway!*" shouted Hazhi from atop the carriage.

I hadn't a clue what his exclamation meant, my language skills having abandoned me entirely at such a moment.

"Fear not, my lady, I will protect you with my life?" murmured Roy, his face a study in skepticism.

I didn't doubt my cousin's hasty translation. Roy had made a far more meticulous study of Elven than had I of late. Rather, I was astonished at Hazhi's declaration itself. If it came to a battle with this gruesome giant from under the bridge, I'd lay odds on the wizard over the poet.

The coach rocked and quivered a bit as someone descended the ladder on its side. All the while, the fearsome monster slobbered and scowled.

Then Hazhi appeared in our vantage. From the wagon's front, he strode past the horses and well to the fore, lugging the fat pig. He bowed low before the monster, then backed cautiously away.

From its misshapen face, the creature emitted a great snort. Then his other hand reached over the railing, stretched across to the pig, and snatched it up. Its forearm was covered in mottled patches of dingy brown fur which stuck out in ragged, unkempt tufts. Though larger by far than the ogres I'd seen, the creature seemed rather gaunt. With beady eyes, it examined its prize with drool dripping down to its chin. It gnashed its teeth. And with a gurgling howl, the great head withdrew, sinking below the bridge once more and passing from our view.

Mistress Julia soon strode forth to join her hero and gave him a peck on his cheek. Hazhi turned and made her a courtly bow in reply. Hand in hand, the two Elves turned to face the window from which we peeped. With a shrug in our direction, Hazhi spared us a sheepish grin. He returned to the coach and climbed to his seat after giving the lead horse's neck a gentle pat.

Julia also made her way back. We awaited her within. The door swung wide and our master stepped up, her face impassive once again. Directly beside me, she took her seat.

"So, what did you make of the show?" she inquired.

Until up to this point, Sholeena's face had been well-nigh invisible, so effectively had her involuntary camouflage been wrought. It was almost as though an empty set of clothing sat beside my cousin. I feared for the girl's composure to have taken such a fright. But before answering our master, color returned to her cheeks, the orange-tinged complexion that in a Paluda denoted mirth or glee.

"That was... awesome!" she squeed. "I nearly peed myself."

Royland drew back from her with a look of distaste, either from her outburst of emotion or the threat of becoming so sullied.

"I take it," said he with a diffident air, "this 'show' was staged for our benefit?"

"Not entirely," returned our master with a sigh. "It is now traditional to welcome all new travelers to Lorédon thus. Glarp has stood guard over the bridge (or under it, to be more precise) for several hundred years."

I sensed my mistress was in a rare, wistful mood. So I prompted her to continue.

"I sense a story in this," I said. "Please share the tale, master. How did this Glarp come to work for the Elves, and why didn't you forewarn us?"

The coach lurched gently forward, and I heard the clatter recommence as the hooves rang upon the stone.

"He doesn't 'work *for* us,' Lucas. As but a young troll, he arrived and took ownership of the bridge of his own accord, demanding a toll from any who would cross. We welcomed this.

"It was during the *lway jagha poH*, the blood enemy times. Lorédon was an independent realm, and the humans to the north were aggressive and eager to expand their kingdom. They wanted the first people to bend a knee to their king Raymond, abandoning our ancient ways. Thus, a troll guarding the bridge connecting to the north was deemed a good thing by all."

After a pause, she continued.

"For many years, Glarp claimed the bridge. When enemies came, he stood barring their path and roaring out his challenge. Most fled. Some took up his challenge and were lost. None knew to pay the simple toll he required, for they believed him only a beast. They failed to discern from among his mighty roars the gutteral language he spoke. With the help of the fey, our scholars had worked it out over time. If more than one foeman came at Glarp, our archers would dissuade them from such."

She paused again, glancing downward as a frown took shape on her pouty lips

"And you chose not to give us fair warning because..."

"We neglected to do so to honor the tradition," she replied. "After Lorédon allied with greater Osten, we shared the secret with the first merchants and diplomats to arrive. Being decidedly amused by the ordeal, they, in turn, established it as a rite of passage. Henceforth, all newcomers would face the wrath of the troll unprepared. My people acquiesced to this new tradition. It helped Glarp to overcome his insecurity over his defeat."

"His defeat?" exclaimed Sholeena. "What could cow such a big, nasty troll?"

"None other than King Raymond himself," muttered my master into the ensuing expectant silence.

There was a bump as the wheels of our coach departed the span and encountered the cobbles of the street beyond. Our carriage lurched along. And I noted Royland was scrutinizing our master's face.

"Wait. Were you actually *there?*" he asked. "What happened? You simply must tell us."

Doing the math, I reckoned it was barely possible that Mistress Julia could have been alive and present for King Raymond's first foray into the land of the Elves. Now this was a story I, too, would like to hear. A first-hand account of the historic event would be far more interesting than talk of geomancy or Elven language lessons.

"I would," she returned, "but I fear we haven't time for a proper telling. I wish you were better schooled in the speech of my people. Hazhi's "Ode to the Great Unifier" shines brightly among the proudest of his achievements. It is filled with all the sorrow and joy that can only be suitably expressed in *watheeshan*. Renditions by your human bards never seem to do it justice. Doubtless, at the hostelry, you will hear the full tale. They love reciting it to those who've just passed their inaugural rite of passage."

And so, in the late afternoon light, we plodded along toward our first stop in the land of the Elves. My master smiled as she amiably described the lodgings where we'd be staying. She seemed almost like a different person. Along with her high starched collar and billowing robes, she had shed much of the stiff correctness that had heretofore characterized her manner. She was more at her ease in the land of her ancestors, even to the point of playing pranks (traditional or no) on her journeymen.

I'd have to add Elven humor to the long list of things it would take some time to learn.

***

As mages, we occupied a special suite of rooms reserved for our use at the hostelry. After settling our gear, Hazhi offered to buy us dinner. Our master claimed fatigue and asked us to bring her back a baguette if they had any fresh. So we shuffled off to the common room while the kitchen was still servicing guests. Glarp had eaten our pig. To make it up to us, Hazhi treated us to ham steaks all around.

"My wife tells me I should eat more vegetables. Now that Pookie's back, she'll be forever nagging me about it. *Good* for me, I suppose," he grunted while patting his stomach.

There was pleasant music from a string quartet as we dined in the comfort of the mixed crowd. Before we'd finished, a man stepped up before the musicians with a glass in hand. He raised it high and started striking it with a spoon to gain everyone's attention. The musicians quieted at once.

"Some of you may know me. For those who don't, I'm Rory Nicholson, proprietor of this here establishment."

"Hello Rory," the guests all murmured in unison.

"I'm told we have some virgins here tonight," he said while pointing at our table.

Everyone laughed.

Royland made a smirk of disbelief while Sholeena discolored from embarrassment. I didn't know *what* to make of it.

"Today, for their first time, they faced the troll and paid the toll. And for this, we thank them."

A light smattering of applause broke out as the other guests all turned toward the stage.

"So once again, it's time for the telling."

"Tell it Rory!" chanted the crowd.

One of the serving maids lowered the chandelier and blew out its candles while another brought Rory a three-legged stool.

"Thank you my dear," he said as he made a great show of dusting it off and resting his portly bulk upon it.

The crowd stilled and awaited his words in the subdued light of the single hearth fire.

"It started more than a hundred and forty-five years ago. The Kingdom of Fairglen had only just united with the realm of Freemark under the Osten Alliance. The Farax pirates had barely been brought to heel by his righteous majesty, King Raymond, liberating those in their sway. It was then that we first felt the venomous bite of those blokes from the Black Plagued Marshes to the south. The Elven lands were the hardest hit... "

The tale was epic. It told of how Raymond Osten the first had ridden in at the head of an army of his knights, intent on denying the dark druids the prize of Lorédon. Although the enemy was fast overcoming the first people's militia in the south, the Elves distrusted the human king and his offer of aid. Better to defend the homeland on all fronts, they thought, than to surrender their autonomy to an occupying force.

Thus, when the Washburn Troll sprang atop the bridge to roar out his challenge, the people of *Ngema Sorihap* strung their bows and prepared to sell their lives dearly.

King Raymond knew that no flag of truce would be honored by the town's monstrous defender.

He could have sent in his knights to remove the creature, but this would surely provoke a response from the defenders. And then only by blood would his troops advance into *puhi Lorédon nagemmahia*.

Instead, he dismounted, girded himself, and strode alone to the center of the span.

"Have at thee then, creature," shouted the king to the troll, gripping his broad blade in both hands.

The astonished citizens looked on in amazement as the gigantic troll lumbered forth to meet the lone armored man. None intervened. The *nuvapua watheesh* were a people of honor, and they would honor the tradition of the challenge.

Surely Glarp would make quick work of this foolish human and hurl him off the bridge. But they would soon discover the battle was not so one-sided as they might have wished. At first, the sheer *reach* of the troll gave the man pause. But when he found his rhythm, he began fending off the blows. Nor could Glarp seize the man in his eager grip. Each attempt to do so was met with a punishing counterstrike to his arms.

Both combatants were veterans of many battles, and each, in his way, was a canny fighter. It quickly became evident that King Raymond was actually holding back. For rather than slicing into Glarp's flesh, he was striking only with the flat of his blade.

The Elves were at once baffled and amazed by the arrogance of the man. None wished Glarp harm, but trolls were fantastically hardy creatures. During a prior challenge, a knight had even severed one of Glarp's arms. The man was thrown screaming from off the bridge for this offense. Not two weeks afterward, Glarp had returned with the severed member intact. Either he'd regrown it or re-attached it somehow. Subduing an adult troll with only non-lethal strikes would indeed be a feat of legend.

As the battle raged on, the people's hearts became divided.

Both combatants were tiring fast, but in a final frenzy of motion, the man penetrated the troll's defenses and brought him to his knees. Raising his sword high above his head, the bloodied man shouted a single word.

"Yield!" he commanded.

Then Glarp did something unprecedented. Splaying his great hands to either side, he bent supine and touched his forehead to the stones. He then arose and, with a gurgling howl, leaped from the bridge and was gone.

The grim defenders of *Ngema Sorihap* shuffled about restlessly, uncertain how to respond and awed by the display of martial prowess they had just witnessed. A voice rang out from their midst.

"Peace!" she shouted.

It was the Bright One herself! Flanked by a contingent of her sword dancers and under a flag of truce, she stepped out onto the bridge. She walked out to meet the exhausted ruler midway across its span.

"And that, my friends, is how King Raymond won a reluctant truce," Rory said in conclusion.

"Glarp wasn't seen again for months,: he added. "Eventually, he reclaimed the bridge, but he was never the same. To this day, he runs when a sword is drawn. We all try to build him up by making sure everyone pays the toll. We think he's in his final years. Poor old thing."

At this, the candles were relit, coins were tossed into the storyteller's upturned hat. Though I hadn't much to spare, I gave him a whole shilling. If I hadn't seen the troll in question, I might have believed the whole thing had been exaggerated all out of proportion.

"That was a great story," said Sholeena "Better even than 'the Miller's Tale.' Poor Glarp. I'm *glad* he ate our pig.".

"Me too, I guess. What do *you* think, Roy?"

But my cousin wasn't listening. He was staring in stony silence at the flames in the fireplace. He'd been doing that for some time now. Oh no, I thought. Roy was no mere cat to be distracted by a shiny object. I recalled that each time he focused so intently on something, that something turned out to be of dire import later on. The infuriating part was that my cousin never shared his thoughts on such matters at the time.

Well, *this* time I was having *none* of it. I stared into the flames myself, even invoking my mage sight. *This* time, I would suss out my cousin's dire surprise *before* it changed my life.

There was... something?

It was like a pale echo of an enchantment, but so faint that it might simply be my imagination.

"You two are weird," said Sholeena.

"I concur," said Hazhi. "Let's go back to our suite."

"Don't forget the baguette," said the Paluda girl as the two strode off.

We stared in silence for a time more.

"How does it feel?" asked Roy.

"The fire?"

"No. To be seen as weird."

***

The hour was late when we crept down the stairs. The common room was silent as a tomb. With our darksight, we confirmed we had the place all to ourselves. We spared no words as we moved as one to the fireplace and arranged ourselves on the hearth before it. Roy shifted his backside to alleviate the discomfort caused by a bulge in his pocket. The unsubtle scent of wood-smoke quickly overpowered the lingering aromas of cheap wine and merriment and the sour smell of beer gone stale.

I soon wished Roy would get on with it as he paused to consider the still warm grate heaped high with ash and embers. On conferring in our rooms, we had concluded there was indeed some sort of enchantment in the fireplace. But it wasn't from the fire. It permeated the very bricks of the enclosure. And it was *old*.

Mages from both Lorédon and greater Osten had stayed here since the unification. The spell could be anything from something to harden the bricks to an air spell to aid the flue. Royland, however, suspected something far more consequential.

"Hurry up, Roy," I whispered.

"Patience, cousin," he replied. "I only had a week's practice with this spell before you put my master in the loony bin."

That was a low blow. Although I had indeed removed the unseelie wight from Gunther Brubaker, it was scarcely my fault the possession had addled his wits. It also neatly glossed over the fact that Roy had himself participated.

Finally, he seemed ready. Royland pressed his hands together as if in prayer, sighting along his thumbs. As he incanted, little sparks of energy emanated in several rapid streams to collide with one another just above the grate.

"Calidus ignis ardentis!" he forcefully intoned.

The sparks blossomed into a searing ball of magical flame. It was the very spell taught to my cousin to ignite the furnaces back in the conclave's foundry before his first master had gone off the rails. I leaned back from a sudden burst of heat that nearly scorched my eyebrows.

No sooner had the crimson orb taken shape, emitting a constant, smokeless heat, than a roiling mist began drifting toward it from the surrounding bricks. This mist began orbiting the blaze and taking on a rainbow of swirling hues. The heat diminished as the orb was enveloped and on its surface, dim shapes began to form.

"Is it *supposed* to do that?" I asked in startlement.

"Quiet!" Roy hissed. "There are voices and... no, it is not."

We stared in fascination as the shapes sharpened and the words became more clear. It was a man's face staring out at us.

"Hello? Ahem. Hello there, future unnamed person. I'm told we need to make a record, so here it shall begin."

He looked a bit like Roy, but with a somewhat firmer jaw. He also sported a mustache, and rather than the brown of my cousin's eyes, his were a pale blue. His next words explained the similarity.

"I am Hans Brubaker. And with me is my goodwife, Gretta. Say hello Gretta."

A familiar face swam into view. Familiar, but... not. The young woman was in the bloom of youth, but I could see within the pleasing lines of her aspect the elderly woman she was to become. She wore a wry smile, and a smattering of freckles graced the bridge of her nose.

"Hello," she sang, then passed back out of the image to be replaced by Hans.

"Um. We've been given a mission of utmost import. It has to do with the foul creatures bubbling up from the swamp to the south. Hopefully, by the time you hear this, the matter will be resolved. Until then, I'm afraid we're not to speak of it. I'm sure you understand."

With an amiable smile, the man glanced to one side, then hovered nearer in our view.

"I have it on good authority our mission will be a smashing success," he said with confidential overtones. "A young woman has just joined the conclave who possesses the most miraculous gift of foresight! Sybell Dunham is her name. We witnessed her vows, not a fortnight ago. An eager young thing, but a bit flighty if you ask me."

Mistress Dunham? An eager young thing? If these images that haunted the hearth were from Royland's grandparents, that would mean the enchantment was from twenty-six years ago. Gretta appeared a bit younger than the mother of an eight-year-old son, but perhaps she had married young. But I guessed Sybell Dunham to be much older than fifty. Perhaps she had come later in life to her powers.

"Anyway, her predictions of future events to date have been completely accurate. The woman's a *bona fide* oracle! We consulted her privately before setting out on our mission. And she prophesies we shall return victorious - although there was a bit of blather about hardships and the like. How did she put it dear? I wrote it down. One moment. Gretta's fetching it."

The orb became empty for a moment, and there were some shuffling noises. Then Master Hans' face filled it once more.

"Ah. Here we are. The prophecy. I asked her, 'will we survive our upcoming mission? And will we succeed in negating the threat? Here is what she said."

Hans held a parchment up to the orb. The writing curved oddly around the spheres rondure. It was blurry at first and wobbled back and forth a bit, but was overall legible.

Though fraught with pain and misery
Returning will be won.
Your journey will provide the key
To see the foe undone

Leave records of the trails you tread
Lest all be lost to time
It shall be used as Theseus' thread
The riddle to unwind

"There, you see? Gretta and I are of one mind on this. Whatever perils we must face, we shall endure them, secure in the knowledge we'll be returning and our journey will lead to ending this foul threat to the kingdom. And just as instructed, we're leaving a record of these events all along our route. It's a dandy little spell I call fire speech (or 'ignis loquela' in the old tongue). I'm afraid you'll need a pyromancer to read them, but... oho! If you're hearing this, you know that already. I had to look up that reference to Theseus' thread in the library. Ball of string through the labyrinth. Quite clever that!"

The image went completely dark, but after a moment, it burst back to life.

"Oh, and one other thing. The faeries can tell you where the next one lies. We're meeting with a man named Van tonight. Some sort of woodsman. He claims he can take us to where the faeries keep court. I hope you haven't any trouble finding it. The fey can be a bit brusk to outsiders, but they have a stake in this matter as well. Till next time, then. Fare thee well on the roads you travel. Say goodnight, Gretta!"

"Goodn--"

And the sphere went black again. Roy kept it going for a few minutes longer, but no other sounds or images appeared.

I became concerned for my cousin.

Roy's face had darkened, and he stared bitterly at the hovering sphere which once again burst into a writhing red ball of flame. With a disgusted swipe of his hand, my cousin released the spell. He then hauled back and struck the mantel with the heel of his open hand.

"What's wrong, Roy?" I asked, leaping up to my feet.

Roy continued staring at the wall, his hands clenched into fists. Then he turned toward me and speared me with a baleful glare.

"They were deceived," he said darkly.

"Well yes," I said. "The prophecy was obviously in error. Mayhap it didn't apply to them at all. You know that Mistress Dunham --"

"It applied all too well," he shot back. "The devils or beings that send these supposed glimpses of impending events knew just how to lure them to their doom."

"I don't know what you're going on about, Roy. Your grandparents were --"

"Were what? Heroes? More like fools duped by the powers that be. Little pawns to be trifled with, then cast aside. Don't you see, Lucas? The prophecy came true exactly as spoken -- but not as written. 'Though fraught with pain and misery, returning will be won' *should've* read 'Though fraught with pain and misery, returning will be ONE.' And return she did. After a delightful imprisonment of twenty-five-years, she returned to us so 'fraught.'

He reached into his pocket, the one with the bulge, and withdrew from it the knitted scarf. He set it on a table and unrolled it.

"I think the thrice-accursed oracle knew very well the prophecy would be misinterpreted. Else wise, they mightn't have gone. Hans' death; all Gretta's suffering. It was all just for this. Just so we might find our way in the wake of their failure. Well, I guess we now know what the red spots are for!"

His shaky forefinger stabbed down onto the scarf.

"We've just activated the first of them. Only eleven more to go. I say we just get on with our lives and tell the prophecy to go *piss off*."

I'd never seen Roy so emotional. I approached him with my eyes downcast and considered my next words carefully. I abandoned my conciliatory tone. It was time for honest speech.

"I can't do that, Roy, and you know it. I take your point, and you've a right to be angry. But we must remember, this is all Orenob's doing. It was *he* who slew your grandfather and ruined the lives of so many others. You're not the only one to lose a grandmother to his inhuman cruelty."

"With or without you, Roy, I must pursue this now. I've told you of the prophecy of the verdant child. And whether we follow them or not, prophecies have a way of coming true. If it isn't me, then it'll be Susie. She's only nine years old for star's sake! Better it be me than her. At least *I* have a chance. The demon

must be confronted, and I think, in the end, this task must fall to
me."

Royland was silent for a time. He rolled up the scarf, stuffed
it back into his pocket and gazed about the empty inne. When he
spoke it was in a calmer voice. He clasped my shoulder.

"You're right," he said. "It was just so... hard... to see them
like that. I had thought this my puzzle to solve, but I can see it
affects you too."

"I'm with you, cousin," he continued. "However this plays out,
we'll face its ending together."

***

Dear Lady Megan,

I pray this letter finds you safe and in good health. It has
now been three months since I received your last letter back at
Conclave. Where to begin? I wrote previously about my master's
reassignment to Lorédon. The journey here was interesting and
not *too* eventful. We arrived at a village called *Araceae Fontes*.
Strangely, this is not an Elven name, but one borrowed from the
more recent 'old tongue' of our own people. It translates loosely
to 'Palm Springs.' We're staying in Mistress Sithia's manor near
the middle of town.

Perhaps 'manor' is a tad generous. It's more like a
farmhouse, but perhaps twice the size of a typical one in
Westarbor. Elven society is extremely egalitarian. Even their
mages live not so differently than the common citizens.
Sometimes it's difficult to tell who's in charge. Those who *are*
lack any special trappings or attire. Nor are such positions
hereditary! They are awarded somehow based on merit and the
accumulation of *valladevhiwi*. This means something like 'clever
leadership.' It's all very strange.

I'm getting better with Elven speech, but it's a tough grind.
The important thing is to try. The Elves appreciate it, even if they
sometimes wince at my diction. The stuffy ones frown and
ignore me a lot, but most are encouraging. I'm told that the
words that give me the most trouble are the same ones that their

very young children tend to mispronounce. Many adults find this endearing and smile at my efforts. This has also earned me the nickname: 'Ghuji' among the younger elves, *Ghuji quich* being their phrase for 'Baby Talk.' Roy has a much broader vocabulary than I. He can make out the Elven writing very readily. However, since he speaks so sparingly, I've surpassed him by far in enunciation. Sholeena has us both beat.

Anyway, we've lived as guests of Mistress Sithia and her husband, Reh, for two months since our arrival, the former being Mistress Julia's daughter who is with child. She is also one of the three mages who reside here in Lorédon. Like her mother, she can command the winds somewhat, but her gift also grants her the power to pull lightning down from the heavens. I haven't seen her do this yet, but for a small demonstration, she made Reh's hair stand on end and stick out in every direction at once. He looked so silly that Sholeena's whole head turned orange.

It's been months since I've had my hair cut. I'm letting it grow long again. The style among the Elven men is to wear their hair at least down to their shoulder blades, tying it into a loose ponytail if this becomes bothersome. Some of the younger males shave their hair short, nearly to the top of their crowns, leaving but a single fulsome stripe that runs from their forehead to the nape of their neck. They aptly call this a 'horse mane.' I doubt I could pull off that look, and I lack the brazen will to try. My ears draw enough attention as it is.

Under my master's tutelage, we've discovered many novel uses for our magic. Although distracted by familial duties and occasional calls for magical assistance, Mistress Julia makes time to help each of us 'nurture our gifts.' To earn communal work credits, I wander about the village fostering health in the green and growing things. The first people value plants and make full use of them in all manner of ways. Even the hedgerows that divide plots of land from one another often produce esculent berries. Growing everywhere are the ferns I saw in Mistress Julia's library back at Conclave. It turns out they're edible as well. The elves call them *rakkanach. You* might know them as fiddlehead ferns. There are a few traditional tilled fields with more standard crops. But I've got to hand it to the elves; every square inch of decorative greenery in the village also serves some other purpose.

I could go on for hours about the elves' strange ways and amazing innovations. Alas, I have only so much ink and wouldn't wish to neglect other matters of greater import. I miss your gentle smile and wish I could hold your lovely hand and tell you in person of the matters closer to my heart. (Ouch). I just felt a punch to the shoulder in response to my bald-faced flattery. Very well, I shall move on.

I am troubled by my lack of progress with a certain aspect of my magical training. We mages must master our unconscious wills. I think mine is broken. It manages my inner garden as I sleep and has done nothing untoward as yet. But it rarely speaks to me, and when it does, I fail to gain its full agreement on rules of behavior. I have refused to name the thing. Nor have I granted it access to more of my power. And I fear it's grown resentful. We are at an impasse. Pray for me, my lady, that I might find the patience and wisdom to overcome this difficulty.

On another matter, the elves have finally agreed on the site for the first griffin hostelry to grace Lorédon. It is to be in a village halfway between here and something they call the 'singing green mountain.' It lies about a two-day trek east of here. I'm rushing to write these letters for you, father, and my friends back in Conclave. Many here in Palm Springs are hoping our letters can be waiting there prior to the griffin's historic first arrival. So please forgive my sloppy penmanship.

Your humble servant and greatest admirer,
Journeyman Lucas "the Just" (Baby Talk) Harper
Envoy Plenipotentiary to the Fey
Winder of Wool and Savant of the Green

There. That ought to do. I hadn't wanted to write openly about Roy's discovery or our plan to follow the trail laid down by his grandparents. So I'd hidden the references to such in the guise of my simple missive. I used the Arenson family code the baron entrusted to me last winter. It comprised a set of rules to interpret minor ink spills arranged throughout the text. It had taken me hours to puzzle this one out. And though I knew Megan was already dreadfully concerned about my role in the verdant prophecy, I'd sworn to the girl there would be no secrets between us. And that was an oath I planned to uphold.

For the final flourish, I dribbled hot wax on the envelope to seal the missive. As it began to cool and solidify, I pressed firmly down on the brass stamper to impress my mark. It was a stylish 'LH' that had cost me half of my hard-earned village credits and was now chief among Bob's proud offerings.

Royland never *had* helped me to learn that enchantment, insisting I needed my master's permission. I guess that sometimes, 'perhaps' meant 'no.' He said he sensed I intended something reckless and wouldn't be a party to it. And just who had died and made him the thought sheriff, eh? Since our agreement to proceed with our clandestine pursuit of the messages, Royland had reverted to his old pissy self, wrapped up in his own concerns. He had pestered me for a while to 'find the faeries,' as if that were an easy task. 'You have that mark thing,' he pressed. 'It's not like I can summon them, Roy,' I replied. 'Quite the reverse.'

And so, without his help, I had taught myself an enchantment. Granted, it was a simple one and not the one I ultimately sought. But it was a small step in the right direction. Leaning in, I focused my will on the cooling waxen seal.

"Ave cantus et flores," I intoned.

It was somewhat like casting a spell, but required a bit more effort. I had to embed the enchantment in the wax and affix it there to await release. This wasn't nearly as difficult as a permanent enchantment, such as Roy's pillowcase or Lloyd's void pocket. No, this spell need only bide until the wax was broken to activate it. All the energy it required was that which I placed in it now.

That should be enough, I thought. "Sigillum!"

And with that, the enchantment was done. I wished I could see Lady Megan's face when she opened it. My lady would be treated to the twittering of birdsong while the fragrance of wildflowers burst forth. I don't know what Master Chadwick did to his seals to secure them from unauthorized tampering. The very presence of an enchantment may give some people pause. But apart from all that, my enchantment was just for jolly good fun.

***

The summer was drawing to its end, though one could hardly tell by the balmy breeze that swept through the quiet Elven village this night. Here in these southern lands, snowfall was surpassingly rare and only the rainfall (or lack thereof) marked the change of seasons. We were heading into the dry season, that which passed for autumn, winter, and most of spring here. And though Jack Frost sometimes stepped beyond Lorédon's northernmost border, his visits were but occasional and still many months away.

Thus, the linden groves stood tall and shed their leaves but sporadically, replacing them gradually throughout the long 'winter.' I sat gathering the coiled tops of the Fiddlehead ferns that grew all along the lane. For the health of the plants, these were best harvested by night. My basket was nearly full, I noted as I swiped at a pesky fly. Before long, I would have enough to exchange for a work credit at the communal barn.

Then I heard it. Off in the distance, twining within the natural sounds of the night, arose a gentle chorus so soft it could have been merely the wind whispering through the trees. Rather than dismiss it, I stood and listened. As the sweet melody arose, the back of my hand began to tingle and thrum to the mesmerizing euphony of its rhythm. My feet began to shuffle of their own accord as I was beckoned by the familiar summons to the seelie court.

I shook myself.

Roy! Royland must be a part of this, I thought. We hadn't glimpsed any sign of the faire folk since leaving Conclave. And I knew my cousin was desperately eager to consult them regarding the next step of his grandparents' journey. I abandoned my harvest and sped down the lane toward Sithia's home near the center of town. Turning a corner, I encountered

66

another nighttime harvester strolling innocently along. I encountered him rather hard.

I was too slow (or rather too fast) to avoid the collision.

It was Pachtel bo'Degh, a boy from my Elven language class. I say boy, for though he was far into his twenties, this wasn't so old for an elf. A male elf in his twenties was only just having his final growth spurt toward adulthood. And though Swoop had achieved much of this growth, he was still considered a child. Swoop was one of the grumpy ones who rarely spoke to me. He sported the long, frilly horse mane the elves called a *sarghajib*. His was white as snow, stark white being one of the hair colors natural to elves. It put me in mind of a skunk stripe.

He glared down at me from beneath this pallid coiffure, his startled expression shifting to ire. At his feet lay his crushed basket with its contents spilling out on the cobbles.

"I beg your forgiveness," I hastily put forth in Elven.

"You are not forgiven, *Ghuji Tlhagh*," he spat back.

In his voice I heard an animosity unwarranted by the offense. And *I* took some offense at his perversion of my Elven name. Rather than 'baby talk', *Ghuji Tlhagh* meant 'baby fat'. It was a racial slur referencing my stockier build.

"Why do your eyes not govern your steps!" he sneered. "Oh. That's right. *Biddle-tessen ghuji* see poorly at night."

At this, he scooped up a cherimoya and hurled it straight at my face. Reflexively, I dodged aside. It seemed Taylor Allen's 'acorn' lessons had taken root. It was true the elves had superior night vision, but with my spell of darksight, I was more than capable. The bruised fruits lying strewn at the boy's feet were custard apples. Snarling, he snatched up another of them.

"Let me make it right," I offered. "Just over there is a whole basket of fiddleheads I picked. I offer them to replace what you lost. I'm in a hurry, Swoop. Please let there be peace between us."

"Do you want to make things right, *Ghuji Tlhagh*? Then return to your own people and leave Lorédon to those who belong here!"

He flung the cherimoya at the ground near my feet to burst and splatter about. Then he turned on his heel and stalked off in a fit of pique.

Tweenagers are the worst.

I hurried along to apprise my cousin of the fey presence I'd detected.

***

"It was off this way, Roy."

We were following a trail north of town which ran roughly toward where I'd heard the music. All was silent now, and from the mark on my hand, I felt not the tiniest tickle. The normal night sounds were subdued, and a strange stillness pervaded the linden forest.

"Look over to the right, Lucas," said Roy, pointing. "Could that be them? There's a faint light off in the distance."

And indeed, there was. Moreover, I felt a tug at my will and there was a sort of tinkling music I could almost hear. My mind went numb, and I felt a little loopy and befuddled. But then the mark burned on the back of my hand, bringing me back to myself. Roy had stepped off the trail and was stalking off in pursuit of the eerie light. I scrambled after, finally pausing to summon my magic.

"Cogitationes liberare," I cried, sending forth my vines to pierce the spell enshrouding my cousin's will.

Roy stiffened. Then, with a shudder, he turned back to face me.

"Trust me, cousin," said I. "You don't want to follow that. It does, however, mean that we're close. Elsewise, why would they send a will-o-wisp to lead us astray? Let's return to the trail and try off to the left."

Roy only nodded.

Linden trees were pleasant to look upon. The elves valued them for many reasons, not the least of which was their hardiness and ability to grow in all seasons. Their leaves and flowers are quite edible, making garnishes, sauces, and teas. Moreover, they imparted a most pleasant honey-lemon scent to the breeze. However, after three hours stomping around among them, I found their fragrance cloying, and the sticky sap that now covered my clothing was more than a trifle annoying.

Wait.

Why were my thoughts running to rhyme? I'd asked my friend Hazel about this one time.

I stopped, gnashed my teeth, and tamped down on this urge to versify. I had asked the tree sprite why all the fey spoke Ostenian standard speech. Laughing, she explained it was simply the nature of faeries. Their true speech sounded something like the tinkling of bells, but each listener heard it as if it were in his own native tongue. A part of this magic was the tendency toward alliteration and rhyme, especially when one was in or near a sacred glade.

"Hold up, Roy," I said. I think we've arrived.

"Arrived where?" asked Royland, peering about, perplexed.

We stood in a stretch of forest no different from any other. Reaching out with my gift, however, revealed that many of the trees and much of the undergrowth were illusory.

"You're right, Lucas," Roy exclaimed. "I can perceive the difference now. Hold a moment. Let me try something."

By my mage sight, I beheld Roy's magic stream upward and cluster around some winged shapes to render them apparent. It was a bevy of Lorédonian moon moths hitherto concealed. And by the gentle light that shone down from their glowing abdomens, the falsehood lay revealed.

CHAPTER FOUR

The Trapper

"To sleep -- perchance to dream. Ay, there's the rub!
For in that sleep of death what dreams may come..."

~ William Shakespeare ~

Many of the nearby trees rippled and vanished as if they never were, leaving a bleak landscape in their wake. We stood within a broad oval field of low weeds, tufts of grass and clover. Above us, the moon moths fluttered, their pale light shining down. Between them, I could see the stars in the dome of the night sky winking as thin clouds rolled by. Protruding here and there throughout the ill-lit glade were a half-dozen stumps. Upon the grandest of these, a merry little gentleman stood observing us intently.

"I heard the summons, so I came," said I. "I brought my cousin. I hope that's alright."

"You're early, me lad, if the court ye be seeking, by a full week at least. The band was just tuning up."

The faerie looked annoyed when we strode forward anyway, intent on asking our questions. But then he smiled serenely.

"You two are certainly most welcome in the Glade Forlorn, or my name isn't Sean O'Hennesey," he said with a wink.

We stepped closer. He was half the size of Terwilliger, but dressed in a similar way. He was garbed all in green, including his brimmed topper, whose black bow bore a buckle of brass. His full orange beard ended in twin points, but he sported no mustache.

"Careful, cousin," muttered Roy. "I mis-doubt this welcome. Mark his clever use of boolean logic."

Roy stood scrutinizing the tiny man's face. I didn't need Royland's special talent to detect the attempt to mislead. I'd already caught the incongruity and noted several others as well. The greeting didn't rhyme as was customary, a sure sign a faerie was being insincere. And never had I known a faerie to be so forthcoming with his name. That the name was suspect, ipso facto, the welcome was as well. So be it. Game on.

"Do you normally greet visitors with a falsehood, Sean, or whatever your name may be? My cousin and I deserve better and would prefer the truth."

There. That ought to set the proper tone. But the man's smile only broadened.

"Talk may be cheap, but truth is dear. I'll utter no lies. And just to be clear: a leprechaun's word is worth all his gold in such matters, truth be told."

"So you're a leprechaun," Roy mused. "Shouldn't you be sitting at the rainbow's end somewhere?"

I glared over at my cousin, willing him to silence. The leprechaun frowned. Before he could respond, I made the official request.

"May we speak to the Mistress of the Glade?"

"This glade has no mistress; it pains me to say. 'Tis a long sad tale we've no time for today. Now mindin' the store it's only just me, And 'tis *I* who'll be asking the questions of *ye*."

It was then I noticed the others. From the forest's edge, I spotted pairs of glowing eyes. As they differed in shape and size, they couldn't all be moon moths; could they? Moreover, some pixies were now buzzing forth to join the moths above. Their curious eyes peered down at our discussion. Several of these pixies were toting white flowers toward an indistinct shape over to my left. I was getting the feeling we should tread cautiously in this glade. These were not the familiar fey whom I'd befriended.

"Ask then, oh leprechaun, who would have us call him Sean." I said agreeably.

"Ye mages be clever. I'll grant ye that. Ye've pierced the veil of our seeming. Very well, then. What purpose brought ye hence? And what, pray tell, are ye scheming?"

"Haven't you heard? We now are allied against the unseelie threat in the south. I assumed your people had passed the word..."

He stared at me expectantly. I rolled my eyes and completed the verse as best I could.

"... ear to ear and mouth to mouth."

Nodding, he grinned and continued.

"Ye have the right of it. This tale be well known. Such news travels swiftly; it must. Not a faerie or spriteling remains unaware of the treaty of Lucas the Just."

"What in the world?" I exclaimed in surprise, for a shocking scene found my awareness...

It was a prone figure stretched out in the grass. He lay at the edge of the linden wood, his head propped up on a mound of moss. His long white beard flowed over his chest and stretched down nearly to his waist. The pixies I'd seen flitted about him, decorating his beard and hair with the flowers they'd brought. Behind his head lay a marker of sorts. 'R.I.P.' it said.

On noting my distraction, Sean turned and followed my gaze. Then a gleeful grin crept up his face.

"Pay him no mind. 'Tis only old Van. He's not dead, in case you did wonder. The slumber lilies are being refreshed to keep the old oath-breaker under."

"Van?" said Roy, turning to me. "Isn't that the name of the man Hans and Gretta hired to be their guide?"

"The very same," said our host with sudden suspicion. "Ye be well-informed."

"Why are you keeping him... um... under?" I asked.

The tiny man stiffened, but then his grin returned

"I may as well share the tale. 'Tis an epic prank we play. An object lesson to ungrateful sots who seek advantage o'er the fey."

On the stump where he stood, the leprechaun sat, and alighting from the sky above, wide-eyed pixies gathered round. One stood upon Roy's shoulder, the brazen little thing. When he turned his head to glare at her, she shyly blushed and looked away. But the tinkling laughter of the others rang in both our ears. In truth, she was a beauteous, dainty creature, so small and delicate of wing.

"That sorry bloke struck a deal with me," Sean began in a huff. "I held up my end right and fair. But he sought me out later, all pissin' and moanin' and reekin' of false despair. And here we get to the meat of it. He showed up right here in the glade, shedding his crocodile tears one night and regretting the bargain he'd made. He'd brought two others with him. Mages like you, they were. Thinking to bolster his unrighteous wrath and bully our queen to concur.

"'My son isn't growing,' the man complained (and this blame he would heap upon me). 'It's all due to your accursed bean. I grow older but never does he. A boy needs his father, so take back your boon if you've any compassion,' he says. 'Failing that, then extend my life to be just as long as his.'

"Fair Tinatia turned unto me with a dignity suiting her station. She bade me stand forth and gently intoned, 'How do you answer this accusation?'"

"And so I answered."

"If you used you boon unwisely, and regret in your heart be kindled, Moan not at us for redress of the wrong. 'Tis only yourself ye've swindled. Weep bitter tears and curse your ill luck but blame not the fey for your lack. For a bargain struck is a bargain struck and there be no taking it back!"

At this, a rousing cheer went up from the pixies. Their high-pitched voices joined, and they swirled aloft to cavort in an aerial ring. The one riding on Roy's shoulder tweaked his ear as she went.

"How did the queen decide the matter?" I asked.

"She didn't need to," he replied laughingly. "I offered to make amends."

The pixies were in a frenzy now. All were laughing and slapping at their knees. They flitted about, intoxicated by the leprechaun's enthralling tale, swarming about us like bees.

"To make amends, I offered a game, being a magnanimous sort. We'd reconcile our differences with a wee bit of honest sport. 'If ye can best me at nine-pins,' says I. 'Then this further boon ye shall win. Ye'll live out the fulsome span ye crave,' I said with a devilish grin."

"So, once each year at the harvest moon we wake old Van for the game. Before the Seelie Court is called, we play a single frame. Betweentimes, he lays sleeping, snoring in his bed. I've gotten worried in recent years. The man's three points ahead."

"Well, that's enough merriment for one night; I trow. Be off with ye. Gather your things and go," said Sean, the leprechaun.

"Wait," said Roy. "We need some questions answered. It's why we came here."

Hadn't my cousin grasped the point of the story we'd just heard? Don't annoy the leprechaun or petition him for favors. I wish he'd let me do the talking. At least with the mark of the fey, my words seemed to distress them less. It was why I was the envoy. But there was no stopping Roy when it came to one of his knowledge quests. He was like a hound with a bone to chew, grinding away at it relentlessly.

"In the spirit of the treaty," sighed Sean. "Three questions I bestow, if you agree that after that ye'll turn upon yer heels and go. I've wasted enough of my time on ye. I've places to be and people to see."

"Why only three?" I foolishly asked, as Roy looked dumbfounded and smacked his palm to his forehead.

"Only three is the number I set, for I have willed it so. That's one then. Ask me another. Ye've only got two more to go."

"Wait. That shouldn't count," I objected. "I wasn't ready. Besides, 'because I said so' isn't much of an answer."

"'Tis my game, me buck-o. I set the rules. And mama leprechaun raised me to never suffer fools. 'Tis my glade into which ye've wandered and not my fault the first was squandered."

"Of course, you are quite correct," I said respectfully, recalling my earlier silent admonition to Roy not to annoy the leprechaun.

"What became of the mages who accompanied old Van? It's news of their fate that we seek."

"For that, little human, you must ask our queen. She should be by sometime next week."

Who was *he* to call *me* little? He was repugnant, this leprechaun, who called himself Sean. His riddlesome ways were most annoying. It made me better appreciate the other faeries I'd known. Though whimsical and sometimes mischievous, at least none of them reveled in an old man's misery.

"Have you a question, Roy?" I asked, turning to my cousin.

"No, he does not," answered Sean, "for ye've just posed the very last one."

The pixies were practically in tears by now, pointing at me and buzzing about my head.

So that was it. I'd asked my third question. And as unsatisfying as the answers had been, at least he had given me something. If the faerie band had been practicing their summons here, and the queen would be 'by next week,' then it stood to reason the Seelie Court would meet in this very glen. As much as it chafed, we would have to await the event and seek a new audience then.

"Let's get out of here, Roy. We don't want to overstay our welcome."

The tiny man turned away from us and vanished from the stump. The moon moths scattered into the surrounding trees, and the faux forest surroundings swam back into view. My fey mark dimmed and settled. Of the Glade Forlorn, we could spy no trace, and the night insects resumed their chorus.

As promised, we turned and headed for the trail.

"That could have gone better," said Roy.

It may have been my imagination, but I thought I heard a fresh tinkling of laughter from the surrounding trees.

***

Our nighttime excursion hadn't gone unnoticed. It was nearly dawn when we were caught creeping back to our beds. Mistress Julia had taken one look at our rumpled clothing before commanding us to await her in the sitting parlor. So here I sat, stewing in my own guilt. Royland sat morosely by my side, saying nothing, as usual.

Our master had been distracted of late, and I hated having added to her worries. Mistress Sithia's blessed event could happen any day now, as she was presently in her sixteenth month. It was no wonder that births among the Elves were so infrequent. If human women had to endure such prolonged and taxing ordeals, I expect they'd avoid pregnancy as if it were a raging case of leprosy.

"What were you thinking?" asked my master, having quietly entered.

And though I knew she was displeased; I sensed the question wasn't rhetorical. She expected an answer.

"Well, as you know, mistress, I serve betimes as Osten's envoy to the fey. Last night, I heard the summons to their gathering and felt it meet to seek it out. I invited Royland because he had some questions he wanted to ask them."

She nodded at this. And although she seemed to accept my rather sketchy explanation for our prior night's escapade, I could tell by her posture the matter was far from settled.

"Could you not have left word of your plans?"

I cast my gaze downward, chagrined.

"What's really going on with you two?"

My master didn't deserve a half-truth. She'd been kind to us. Moreover, the travails we faced were momentous and more than a bit alarming. We were *supposed* to seek our master's advice on such matters. Resolving to confide in her, I opened my mouth to speak, but my cousin was quicker.

"As the senior journeyman, I take full responsibility," he announced.

"That's all well and good," she returned softly, "but I'll ask again; responsibility for what, exactly?"

"We should have come to you at once," Roy answered. "A matter has arisen that is possibly of great import to the kingdom. We needed to confirm a few things first before sharing our concerns. We were reluctant to worry you, especially given the current circumstances. Also, it strikes upon some private personal issues for each of us."

Without further prompting, the entire sorry mess came spilling out. Roy spoke of his grandparents, Gretta's scarf, and everything we'd surmised about the prophecies. I wasn't certain whether Roy and I were truly of a similar mind, or if he'd just sensed I was about to cave and decided to preempt it. You could never tell with Royland. When he finally trailed off, my cousin turned his hands upward and shrugged, as though offering the entire burden to our master.

Julia had been thoughtful and silent all throughout my cousin's narrative. Nor did she chime in immediately upon its conclusion. Her face remained inscrutable as her eyes lay upon him, drinking it all in. Finally, she spoke.

"I must reflect upon this," she announced.

She was granting it a fair hearing, at least. I was glad my master wasn't prone to making hasty judgments.

"The masters of the conclave have made a long and careful study of the prophecies given us by Sybell. While I admit your interpretations do seem to have some merit, many have sought to act on such foreknowledge, only to discover deeper layers shrouded in further mystery."

"Your human poet Virgil once stated that 'fortune favors the bold,'" she continued, "But *my* people follow the teachings of the Bright One. Although sometimes one must move swiftly, 'a venerable life is one governed by patience.'

"For now, continue your studies and other daily activities. I understand that you enjoy a special relationship with the fey, Lucas. But I doubt either of you is fully aware of the dangers their capricious natures can pose. As to the journey of your grandparents, Royland, I... appreciate your desire to pursue the matter. I will take this into account as I consider."

And that was it. Our master turned about and exited as quietly as she'd come.

***

I was brushing my teeth when there came a knock upon my door. Yes. You heard right.

Brushing.

My teeth.

Though I'd sometimes had to pick them clean after eating corn or particularly stringy meat, I'd not encountered this strange 'brushing' ritual until I'd come to dwell among the Elves. Hazhi had supplied each of us journeymen with a small, stiff-bristled brush and a strange yellow paste and instructed us on proper care for our choppers. Bemused, we had complied.

I had often wondered why none of the Elven elders had lacked a fulsome set of teeth. They were hundreds of years old, after all. And yet their bright smiles always displayed an even array of such. This special care they took in cleaning and polishing was one reason. Another, I was to learn, was a racial benefit the elves enjoy. Much like we humans, Elven toddlers lose their milk teeth when they're about ten to fifteen years old. Unlike us, their wisdom teeth don't emerge until they're well into their eighties. And rather than only four back molars, they gain an entirely new set! It is at this age that an elf is considered an adult and permitted to choose his or her *vallihimay*.

"Bjubst a mimanet," I yammered, hastily spitting out a mouthful.

Dabbing at the corners of my mouth with a wet washcloth, I hustled over to greet the visitor. It was Sholeena standing at my door wearing a smirk of amusement.

"Are you bum-busy? Should I comble back belater?" she laughingly gurgled.

"Not at all," I replied. "Crumble in and find a sheet. I was just brushing my teeth."

Entering, the girl patted over to a wooden chair and perched daintily on its lip. Finding my own seat on the foot of my bed, I smiled. Sholeena really did have a delightful sense of the absurd.

"What's on your mind, Sho?" I asked.

"Well," she began. "I know you and Royland have been shneaking around lately. Filbert says you have an important secret, and that Mistress Julia is in on it too. I was just wondering what it might be and if I could maybe help?"

She stared at me with those unblinking, wide-set, Paluda eyes.

"That Filbert is one smart fish," I began. "And I'm honored that you want to help us, but I just don't see how at the moment."

I went on to explain the basics of our quest and how we were uncertain when or even if we might continue it. Mistress

Julia had granted us permission to attend the Seelie Court. But we were to avoid making any commitments and were to report back to her immediately with our findings.

"It's dreadful what happened to Royland's grandparents," she said. "Are you sure you want to follow them? My people say: 'Chasing the wrong fish can lead you to dangerous waters.'"

Surely the wise course of action would be to do as the Paluda girl suggested. Stay here in the shallows and grow in strength. But there was something... urging me onward. I couldn't explain it. I felt in my gut the time for action was growing short. I think Roy felt it too. Normally a patient sort, he seemed driven to pursue this mystery. It was more than just wanting to avenge the wrongs which had befallen our families.

What did Orenob know that we didn't? Why was he so intent on drawing the verdant child to his side? Was this the 'time of need' of which Sybell had foretold? And what had she meant by 'a kingdom will be reconciled'? That could mean anything. I only knew that it must be me, and the thought of delay filled me with an unnamed dread.

"That's sound advice," I finally replied. "But my people also have a proverb: 'He who hesitates is lost.' And believe me, Sholeena, I'm starting to feel very lost in all this."

***

It was three days later when the call came.

I leapt from my bed and headed straight down the hall to rouse Roy. I was already mostly dressed, having taken to sleeping in my daytime attire in anticipation of the summons.

In the entryway, we paused to pull on our boots.

"Are you certain?" asked my cousin. "I don't hear anything."

There could be no doubt. The fey mark pricked on the back of my hand and the haunting tune swam in my head, urging me forth into the night.

"Only the fey-touched can hear the summons, Roy," I muttered, easing open the door and crossing its threshold.

This time, the way to advance was clear. The full moon shone down from a cloudless sky and an owl glided silently above. In the moonlight, the mark of the fey shed a faint radiance of its own. It somewhat resembled an oak leaf. I thrilled to recall the dryad's kiss that had placed it there only this past spring. Though visible only by moonlight, all faeries could perceive its presence and would mark its bearer as having won the favor of the wood sprites. We passed from the village and made our way into the linden wood. Though no trail marked the path through the darkness of the forest, the summons unerringly guided my footfalls, with Roy an eager step behind.

We first saw the flickering lights in the distance as we approached the Glade Forlorn.

"I hear something *now*," said Roy.

It was faint at first but grew in volume the nearer to it we trod. It was the tinkling sound of faerie laughter, rising to a crescendo, then petering off. It came in waves as various woofs, yips, and rumbles joined the chaotic cacophony of mirth.

Stepping from the forest into the open glade, a strange vista spread out before us. The clearing was abuzz with activity. Large red-capped mushrooms grew in clusters all about, and on these all manner of faeries reclined. Some, too, sat on the stumps we'd seen on our prior visit. I saw pixies and gnomes, and many creatures familiar to me. But some others were rare beings I'd not beheld before. All seemed to be intently watching an open strip down the middle.

At one end of it, stood Sean. High above him, the leprechaun held a duckpin ball nearly twice the size of his tiny head. He was scowling and squinting at the far end of the pitch, and his tongue protruded from the corner of his mouth. We watched in fascination as after a running start, he heaved the ball to roll across the green. At the other end, it encountered a rigid formation of wooden cylinders which stood in a diamond pattern. The ball carved a path of devastation through the ranks of wooden keglings I would soon come to know as 'pins.' They spun as they scattered, knocking into one another until all save but one lay flat on the lawn. The final pin wobbled but refused to fall.

Again, a mighty cheer went up with many a hoot and gibber. The fairies danced in excitement, but Sean scowled at the stubborn pin. With a tug on his beard, he stretched a fist forth. From it erupted a burst of fairy light trailing a sparkling green tail. It sped down the pitch to lay the last pin out as well.

"Well, that's hardly fair," came a masculine voice from just to his rear.

And there stood the old man, the one they called Van, having just arisen from the stump on which he sat. His stringy white beard dangled nearly to his waist and an offended look graced his sallow face.

"I was just havin' a go at ye, Rip," declared the leprechaun.

"That's only eight for you then," said Van.

"Aye, eight it is," confirmed Sean.

"Well, it's my turn then, you rascal. You'll see how a man bowls the pitch. When I knock them all down, you'll owe me a boon. That'll teach you my son to bewitch!"

"Hold yer horses, laddie. It's still anyone's game, don't ye know. I'm not in yer debt, as ye ain't won as yet. There still be four more frames to go."

"Get on with it, then, for I must make amends; I truly regret my sins. The sooner we start, the sooner it ends. Have your gnomes reset the pins!"

"Excuse me," I said, having sidled up to the pair. "Am I to understand that you're Van, the man who came here, accompanied by the wizard named Hans and his wife?"

The man looked down at me with steely eyes. Though outwardly he appeared quite frail and elderly, I could sense from him an inner strength belonging to a much younger man. He made me nervous.

"The name's Winkle. Van Winkle. And just who are you to be asking?"

"Oh. I'm Lucas Harper. And my cousin and I would very much like to know what happened to the two mages you guided here. Wait. *Winkle*, did you say? I once met a *William* Winkle. Any relation?"

"You know my son? William? How is he? *Where* is he?"

"Um. I believe he's a tailor now in the village of Belsby many leagues to the north. But that's neither here nor there. (Well. It's there, I suppose). Regardless, what happened to the two wizards you were escorting?"

"Them? Ain't seen 'em in a while. We parted ways about a week ago."

A week?

Was it possible that old Van wasn't aware that decades had since passed?

"Be that as it may," said Sean, sliding smoothly between us. "Ye be holdin' up the game. Stand back and let old Van make his feeble toss. The pins be awaitin' his tragic loss."

More fairy laughter rang about as the old man glowered down at his tiny tormentor. He took up the duckpin ball and lined up his shot. With three agile strides, Van raced forward and released the ball with a snap. The ball sped down the pitch and slammed into the leading pin.

"Hah! Turkey!" shouted Van with wicked glee. "I was already ahead by three in the score. Nine pins down. That puts me up by four!"

As the old man sauntered back, he suddenly looked more his age. And I saw pixies hovering above him waving white flowers by their stems. With his eyes glazing over, he stumbled toward the stump and sat.

"I want to go home," he murmured to no one in particular. "I feel it's getting late."

The leprechaun leapt up beside him, holding a tall wooden tankard topped with foam.

"Steady there, Rip," said the leprechaun in a soft voice. "The night is young as yet. Next one's the beer frame. Ye wouldna wanna miss that..."

"I should've stopped after I won that first game," muttered the old trapper with his eyes drooping shut.

"Aye, but ye didn't," replied Sean. "Now it's double or nothing; best two out of three. This one the decider be."

As the old man toppled over to one side, his fall was arrested by several sets of hairy hands. A small gang of hairy brown men bore old Van back toward the bed of moss where we'd seen him lying a few days before. As the gnomes cleared the pins from off the pitch, I spied a frolic of pixies hovering around Rip. They were adorning his hair and beard with a fresh bevy of slumber lilies.

"Should we help him?" whispered Roy.

"For now, it's best we bide," I replied. "This has been going on since before you and I were born. Let's wait and see what the queen has to say."

***

Once the round had concluded and the pitch had been cleared, the faeries filled the space and congregated all about. Roy and I wandered among them like two lost sheep. They accepted me readily enough but treated Roy as if he were invisible. It was more like he was beneath their notice, which was strange seeing as how large he was as compared to their generally diminutive statures.

Among the babble of fairy speech, I heard my name now and again, and some eyes flitted my way when they thought I wasn't looking. We found a gnome dispensing drinks. I cautioned Roy to take only small sips. The fey were fond of alcoholic drinks at their gatherings. And though sweet and unpretentious, the stuff was surprisingly potent.

As we sipped from our tiny cups, we were approached by a maiden in a flowing blue cloak. Her translucent skin was unnerving. Right straight through her, I could see. Only her cloak was substantial, opaque, and possessed of solidity. Her face was angelic and rather than hair, a watery mane billowed back, seeming ever to flow o'er her head to trail behind. I had seen her like only once before and but briefly when first I'd entered the Seelie Court at Conclave.

"I see from your mark that you speak for the trees, a much-needed talent in this sad place. I've never before seen a human at court, yet now, here be two of your race."

"Yes. Well, we're allies now. I'm Lucas and this is Roy. We hail from up north but are staying nearby, studying with the elves. And who might you be?"

She crossed her arms beneath her bosoms and smiled shyly.

"I am but a tributary. I haven't earned a name as yet. My mainstem is *Nom Quetbitig* who, in turn, feeds the Washburn at their confluence. I'm hopeful one day if I work very hard and erode the gully through which I run, I'll become a proper brook."

I sensed by her speech she was well on her way. She certainly babbled like a brook. I sought about for a polite response but was interrupted when a smaller flying fairy rounded the girl and slid between us.

"Make way. Make way," she crooned. "Kindly step aside, sweetie. Don't you know this is Lucas the Just, the one who suggested the treaty?"

She was shaped rather like a pear, and I didn't see how her tiny wings could keep her bulk aloft. Yet there she hovered, three feet off the ground. She was about the size of a teapot. On her head rested a conical hat with a long, flapping veil. In her hand, she gripped a stick of wood topped with a five-pointed star. This fizzled and popped and left a sparkling trail when it moved. She was draped in a plumb-colored, gauzy gown with pointed shoes to match.

"You are *that* Lucas, are you not? I won't waste my time on one lesser. If you be he, please confirm it for me. (I expected a snappier dresser.)

"Umm..."

"You have the right of it, madam," said Roy with a spreading grin. "My cousin is indeed known as Lucas the Just."

Sparing Royland but a brief glance, she hovered nearer to me.

"Then I'm very pleased to make your acquaintance. They call me Brunhilda the Buxom, for my obvious feminine charms."

"An honor, I'm sure," I replied.

"I heard you had planted a wee one and given her her name," she went on to say. "That makes you one of our proud kind, a distinction you should claim. We are the fairy godmothers, a group with style and flair. Come join us for the gathering. That's our circle over there."

And with this, she began tugging at the shoulder of my doublet to move me in the desired direction. I thought her rather pushy (though in truth she was pulling at the moment). Grudgingly, I followed the dame; for such, I supposed, was the price of fame. Looking back, I saw Roy already chatting amiably with the water nymph. I shouldn't be surprised. Roy always got the pretty ones.

I was soon introduced to a group of fairies very similar to Brunhilda. They questioned me about the acorn I had planted and spoke of their own duties, sharing many a fond remembrance. All were of a similar kind save for me, standing awkwardly among them. They'd given me names to call them by, but I'd be hard pressed to recall any. Instead, I thought of each by the color she sported, for each one was garbed in a different solid pastel.

"So this 'Hazel' entrusted you with the child's true name?" inquired Miss Yellow, as she hovered there. "You should be flattered by this; I trow. Such names by their owners are secrets well-cherished (and not for just any to know)."

I wondered when the court proper would commence. The small talk of the vapid fairies was beginning to wear my patience thin. As exciting as it was just to be here, I yearned for something more substantive to occur.

The blue one was cheerfully chatting to the others about a glass slipper. As 'my' circle of fairy godmothers nattered on about such unlikely apparel, I spotted an elf standing alone nearby. Apart from Rip. she was the only other non-fairy I'd seen this eve. When the moon crested the treetops, gracing the glade with its pale luminance, I spied a fey mark glimmering upon her brow. It was like my own, and by the light it shone, I reckoned that she must be, another proxy, just like me.

Nor was that the only thing strange about the woman. She was old, noticeably so. I'd never before seen an elf who looked her age. She must be elderly indeed. Despite this, there was a lively quality about her. From beneath her silver-gray hair and shining fey mark, her eyes shifted briefly to align with mine. With a simple nod, she acknowledged me as her peer, then returned her regard to the sky. She inclined her face upward as if greeting the moon and smiled serenely.

All about me, the faeries quieted. They were staring upward with expectant looks. It started low, then blossomed into a rousing refrain as hundreds of tinkling faerie voices were raised in unison.

When the queen comes

Fairest of us all

Heed HER words withaaaaal.

So then come ye hither

Dally NOT nor dither

Fair folk harken to the caaaaall.

And from beyond the forest's edge, a greenish light was seen. It rose above the treetops as the sun rises to greet the day. And from this verdant dawn emerged a shining emerald light, racing like a comet into our midst. It arced down to alight gently upon the tallest stump in the glade. As its brightness diminished, it resolved itself into a tall, slender woman bedecked in finery as green as a linden leaf. She had dragonfly wings like a pixie and a tall pointed hat on her head. She even had a pair of green boots to match, just like Terwilliger had said.

It was the fairy queen. It could be none other. Tinatia the Fair was here. And from the faeries hitherto assembled, there arose a raucous cheer. The queen smiled graciously as she looked out upon her gathered subjects, silently accepting their accolade. Then a hush descended once again when she raised her hand to speak.

"To the glade you are summoned, as the full harvest moon drifts up from the east to shine. 'Tis time for my people to gather in peace to deliberate matters of gravest import. The rules we enact here today shall bind us and all our fates entwine. And thus, it is with a sober heart I call to order this Seelie Court."

The ovation that followed was deafening.

I sought about for my cousin. I had to peel him away from his conversation and remind him of why we'd come. When we headed for the stump, we found, to our dismay, that a long line of petitioners had already formed. Worse still, when we queued up at the end, we were shouldered aside repeatedly by other hopefuls.

"Proxies to the rear," grunted a pig-like creature, who stepped directly in front of us.

I thought of asserting myself, but all the true fairies seemed to agree this was the rule. Even within their ranks, there looked to be some kind of unofficial hierarchy beyond my ken. I went up the line to where the fairy godmothers had a more prominent position, thinking to claim a place among them. But I was rebuffed.

"Sorry dearie," Miss Turquoise declared. "That title is but honorary here. I'm afraid you must wait for your proper turn. Proxies to the rear."

I returned only to find that a group of winged mice had also queued up in front of Roy. One was chattering away at my cousin about the teeth he and his brethren had collected from sleeping children. They were going to propose a clever new accounting system he'd devised for such.

It was going to be a long night.

"Did you learn anything from the nyad?" I asked of Roy.

"Brook? She told me where her gully lay and suggested I should come and wade in her one day."

Unbelievable.

"You're disgusting, Roy," I reproved him.

"What?" he said, all innocence. "You're not the only one who can have fairy friends."

"Well, if you go there, you should bring Sholeena along as chaperon. I should think as a water mage, she'd be delighted to meet such a sprite. Some of the faire folk are known to bewitch a man and compel him by their charms. And you, my friend, have a poor track record resisting such allure."

Just behind us stood the Elven woman I'd seen earlier. As she was the only other proxy in sight, I thought we might as well commiserate. Although my Elven speech lacked polish, I decided to give it a go.

"Honored elder," I began, "I am Lucas of Meadowfork, proxy for the dryad of Conclave. And this is my cousin, Royland."

She looked at me, intrigued, but said nothing in reply.

"I see you also bear the mark. Mine was received only earlier in this same year in the... er... springtime. As you are the more senior proxy, would you like to go before us?"

I stepped back and indicated she should precede us in the line. It wasn't much of an advance, but it seemed only proper. She looked bemused by the gesture, but when she spoke, it was in flawless Ostenian.

"I am content to bide. I have no need for an audience. Your politeness does you credit, young man. Pray, tell me what matter brought you hither? What conundrum would you lay before a queen?"

"Well," said I, "I suppose it won't be a secret ere long. My cousin and I seek information about his grandparents, who came this way twenty-five years ago. Hans and Gretta Brubaker were their names. They instructed us to seek from the fey a location where their next message could be found. They were on a mission, you see..."

She listened as I sketched out the basics, nodding sagely. From the reflected light of the moon, her mark still glimmered on her forehead like a third eye. When I'd finished, she uttered but a single syllable. It fell gently from her lips but landed with the full force of a word that expected to be obeyed.

"Bide," she commanded.

Then the old woman brushed past me and, with a measured stride, advanced to the head of the line. Nor did any fairy seek to impede her. She walked straight up to Queen Tinatia, making but a cursory obeisance. Then the queen stepped daintily down from her tree stump and leaned in as the old matron whispered something in her ear. The fairy queen looked flustered for a moment, nodded at the elf, then ascended back to her erstwhile perch.

As my fellow proxy made her way back to us, the queen carried on as though no interruption had occurred. I wondered at the sway the ancient elf had upon the fey. Roy was white as a sheet and wide-eyed with wonder as well.

"Who are you?" he asked as she approached.

"Come," she said as she stalked past us and into the forest beyond.

We followed at once, of course.

***

We followed the old woman into the darkened wood. I had to invoke my night vision to keep pace with her. No trail could I discern, but the Elven lady led us on with a sure and vigorous stride. Many questions begged me for release, but I sensed the time for this was not yet at hand. At one point, she stepped directly through a dense bit of underbrush that proved to be illusory and continued on. Again, I followed, and Roy came stumbling after.

We arrived at a small cottage. It wavered into existence on our close approach. Without pause, our mysterious guide stepped up to the door, turned its handle, and entered. Within rested only a few rough-hewn pieces of wooden furniture. Some crates and barrels lined the far wall. From a hook near the door hung an old oil lantern bathing the room in a soft, yellow light.

"Come in and find a seat," said our hostess. "It should be safe enough to talk in here. Its usual occupant is at the convocation, but she's quite a stickler for her privacy. Not many can even find the place. Another guest should be arriving shortly."

Once the lady had seated herself, Roy and I did likewise. She stared at Royland for a moment.

"As to who I am, I believe your people know me as Lady Brighton, Duchess of Lorédon."

"Your Grace?" yelped Royland, leaping from his seat and promptly falling to one knee before her.

I shifted, uncertain of the proper way to show deference to such a high noble. If what she said was true, it would certainly explain the faire folks' strange behavior toward her. Had the elves any royalty, she would be chief among them. *Wova zeja bosch tazbeth*, they called her, 'our bright and shining queen.' Still, the woman had bid me be seated. Shouldn't her command take precedence over my human notions of propriety?

"Arise, Royland, son of Robert," she said. "We've no time to stand on such ceremony. Be seated in comfort and let us speak of the urgent matters afflicting our fair land. For tonight, think of me only as she who speaks for the dryads who once proudly governed this wood.

I gulped. The stumps. It dawned on me now why the glade was forlorn.

"What happened to them?" I asked in a hoarse whisper.

"Can you not guess?" she replied. "More than a hundred years ago, the last of them succumbed to a scourge sent by the unseelie king, the one they call Orenob. Yes. I dare speak his name, for in this place I know we are well-guarded from the prying ears of his minions. A strange blue beetle gnaws its way ever northward, and in its wake, the hardwoods perish. Thus far, the linden have proven resistant, but the birch, hickory, oak, ash and yew and many others were purged from the land. Before she died, the mistress of this glade produced an acorn and implored me to bear it far to the north where her daughter might flourish. Hence, my status among the fey."

Absent the moon's touch, her shining mark was not in evidence, but I felt a kinship with this remarkable elf. Was it possible that Hazel and Holly were descended from that very acorn? What would that make the two of us? Second-god-cousins or some such?

"Not to be insensitive," said Roy, "but what has any of this to do with my grandparents?"

"They are as threads in the same tapestry, young man. The unseelie fey have some grand scheme to overturn the natural order and transform the land in ways more to their liking. We suspect the death of the hardwood forests is but one step along the twisted journey they would have us take. It is our belief that Orenob possesses a powerful artifact from ancient times known as 'the Heart of the Swamp.' Your council of mages tasked your grandam and her husband with locating and either retrieving or destroying it."

This caught my cousin's full attention.

"In what world was that deemed a good idea?" he groused.

"This one, I'm afraid. The fey thought it foolhardy for two so young to seek out the faerie king's lair. It is unwise to try to beard a lion in his den, is it not?. But the two insisted they were guided by a prophecy. They were very persuasive. They petitioned the queen for her aid in locating the monster.

"Now, Tinatia is no friend of Orenob (though technically they were married once). She believed anything to nettle him a worthy investment of her time. Therefore, she provided the two with what they sought and sent them on their way."

"What was it she gave them?" I asked.

"I believe it was a full lock of hair from Orenob's beard she'd acquired in her younger days. As mages, you may know that a strand of one's hair can be used in a potent spell to locate a person."

'Quaerite mihi amans,' I muttered softly to myself.

Roy looked over sharply.

"So where were they headed next?" I asked.

"We don't know," the lady lamented, "but there is one who does."

As if on cue, there came a knock on the cabin's door.

"Enter," said the duchess.

Sitting in this humble shack on a rickety wooden chair, the woman was nonetheless transformed. By her posture, tone and bearing, one would swear he was looking at a queen seated upon her throne. And though enchantments aplenty surrounded the hut, this aura of command must be natural, for it made no impression on my mage sight.

The door opened to reveal the old man. The one they called Rip, Van Winkle. He was flanked on either side by two satyrs from the glade. The one on the right stepped forward.

"We've brought him as our queen commanded," he bleated. "Sean was unhappy, but he soon bowed to her majesty's will."

"Then tell your queen," said the lady, "I am in her debt."

My breath caught in my throat. Among the fey, such words had meaning. I may have mentioned earlier that the faire folk were most literal-minded creatures.

"Your debt is acknowledged," returned the satyr with a wicked grin. "The queen will be most pleased. I imagine attendance at next year's activities will soar."

The two satyrs shuffled off, leaving Van at the threshold squinting suspiciously at the three of us.

"What's going on?" asked the old coot. "I've got a game to finish."

"Come in and have a seat, goodman."

Reluctantly, he did so. Stretching out his long legs, he

reclined on a stool with his back resting against the wall. His clothes had seen better days, and the man smelled awful.

"Do you recall the two wizards you came here with?"

"Of course I remember 'em. I was telling these two youngsters just a few minutes ago how I hadn't seen 'em in a week or so."

"Very good," the duchess continued. "Can you recall where you left them?"

"I ain't daft, woman. I guided 'em to where they was going, collected my fee, then circled back for my audience with the queen."

Now we were getting somewhere. Lady Brighton seemed to take no offense at the man's belligerent manner. And she was circling ever closer to the truth.

"Can you show us where you took them? Perhaps point it out on a map?"

"Well, I never had much use for maps, them swirling colored charts and such. But I'm a good pathfinder bona fide. Once I've finished my game, for two shillings, I could take you there."

The lady sighed.

"It shall have to do."

"Goodman Winkle," she continued. "know that your game is done. You've won. Lucas and Royland here would like to engage your services. Go and get cleaned up. You can meet them back at the glade on the morrow. You can collect your boon after taking them where they need to go. Now be off."

Rip looked like he might argue, but then thought better of it. He took his leave, promising to do as the lady commanded. After he'd gone, Roy turned to face her, puzzled.

"Are you suggesting we set out at once? Why?"

At this, the lady got a distant look, and a wrinkle creased her brow.

"You are probably unaware of precisely how bad things have become. Despite our best efforts, the land is failing. The king puts a glib spin on the war's progress so the common folk won't panic, but the elves know, and the fey do as well. Each season we suffer a new depredation, and that which sustains the land receives another crippling blow. Our sages and *puachoqua* tell me that the next might be the fatal one. We are desperate.

"The fey, too, have a prophecy. Long have they puzzled over its meaning, but it dangles one thin thread of hope o'er these grim goings on. Regarding the situation with Orenob, the fey consulted the eldest of the oreads in the northernmost reaches of the Echo Hills, and this is what he said:

The Verdant Child one day will rise
And shall the breadcrumbs follow,
Guided by flames neath southern skies
In murky swamps to wallow.

Grim horrors shall beset the three
The three without their master.
Yet this is how the end must be
To thwart the dread disaster.

"I'm sure you can mark the likeness to your own situation."

She hung her head.

Three? Without their master? Could it mean... surely not... Sholeena too?

"So it's like that, is it?" said Roy in a sudden temper. "The fey thought it foolhardy for two so young to seek out the faerie king's lair. Your own words. So how is three, (even younger, I might add) a better idea? And guided by a prophecy? Fie on such prophecies!"

Roy wasn't berating the duchess. Not really. Nor did she take it so. With graceful forbearance, the lady kept a stoic mien and let his anger run its course, his words crashing against her as the sea rages against the shore. She then took refuge behind her platitudes.

"The despairing seek hope from any source. I have only made possible what the seers have foretold and given you the answers you sought. What you choose to do with them is yours to decide."

She folded her hands in her lap and stared upward as though seeking the moon's advice.

"Well, you know my position, Roy," I put in. "But I'm not liking that bit about there being three of us - nor will Mistress Julia, I imagine."

After a lengthy pause, the lady spoke once more.

"I will have words with Julia," she said softly.

Before we could depart, the lady asked me: "Have you, perchance, a scrap of parchment and some ink?"

"Yes, your grace," I said, producing such from my bob forthwith.

Accepting them, she continued. "I should like to leave a note for Baba, thanking her for the use of her hut."

As she composed the brief missive, Royland stewed in silence. I considered how to thank the good lady for her own assistance. Though our future course seemed bleak, it was gracious of the famous woman to have lent us her aid.

"It was kind of you to have them awaken the trapper," I declared.

"He's a buffoon, but I didn't like the way they were treating him anyway."

"What will the queen demand of you for freeing Rip?" I asked.

"I shall assume his obligations," she replied as she dipped the quill in the ink pot. "Each year before the court convenes, I shall present myself at the pitch. I may be getting old, but If I can't beat a leprechaun at ninepins, then it's a sorry life I've led."

Quite apart from her noble status, the woman was extraordinary. I no longer had to wonder why the elves called her 'The Bright One.'

CHAPTER FIVE

The Homewrecker

"Adventures are never fun while you're
having them."

~ C.S.Lewis ~

I was going to be alone again. As I sat down next to the village pond, the bright-scaled fish drifted lazily by, so close I could've reached out and snatched one up. But these fish weren't for eating. The elves kept them just to look at. I envied these fish. Before Master Jordan took me from my village, I too always had friends to swim by my side.

I slid my feet out of the confining boots and let my toes fan out before plunging them in to savor the water's cool caress... Ahh. I was always happy to escape my leather prisons for a time. They were necessary for walking on the stony ground that even the elves used for their pathways. They also served another important purpose. They helped me to fit in.

The elves were much kinder than the men of Conclave had been. They saw me as different but didn't call me any bad names and poke fun at me for no reason. Of course, Lucas had always been nice. And Roy just ignored me, the same as he did

99

everyone else. At least he was even-handed with his indifference.

One of the koi swam up to nibble on my toe. I let him. He was only exploring. It kind of tickled.

And now they were both going to leave.

I felt the sunlight on my skin. I closed my eyes and tilted my face up to catch even more of it. As my breathing deepened, the laughing voice emerged from a different pond, my pond within.

"You could go with them," he suggested.

In this place, the light was more subdued. It was always raining, or just about to be. Filbert leaped high above my inner pond and came splashing back down, showering me with his splatter.

"But it's dangerous, Filbert," I moaned. "Our master said so."

There was a swirling motion, and Filbert's fins flashed back into view.

"She also left it up to you," he reminded me. "She wouldn't have done that if it weren't very important..."

When Mistress Julia called me down to talk about it, she had been so hesitant. All the while, the two boys had fidgeted in their seats. I could tell they were tired from being out all night again, drinking and dancing with the faeries. I wished they'd thought to take me along. I would've enjoyed the drinking part, at least. It seemed they'd gotten all their questions answered.

I was shocked to hear the prophets had said things about me too. My people always knew how to read the signs and portents. They foretold when fishing would be poor or when bad weather was coming. But they never told us what a particular person might do.

Even Mistress Julia believed it enough to let Roy and Lucas go wandering off on their own. Only very senior journeymen were supposed to be allowed to do that. She would justify this break from their training as teaching them in the 'Elven way.'

She would release them to take their *Hop leng poH*. And me too, if I wanted. All of them looked relieved when I said I probably wouldn't, like they didn't really want me to anyway.

Lucas had looked so sad.

"What are you suggesting, Filbert? Do you think I should go?"

Deep down, I knew I was just talking to myself. It was a part of myself that had, until recently, been quiet. It had spoken to me only with feelings, small urges that I could never explain. Now my other awakened self had a voice (and many strong opinions). Mistress Julia told me that by the time a person becomes a master, she and her homunculus work together so closely that they are one again. 'Re-integration,' she called it. But for now, I liked the little fish and valued his advice.

"If one must swim into dangerous waters," he counseled, "it's best not to do so alone. Your friends need you. Do you think those two city dwellers can make their own way through the dangers of a swamp? You've seen how poor a swimmer Lucas is. Of course you can stay safe here. But how will you feel if *they* don't come back?"

He was right.

I'd just been remembering how nice it was having friends to swim by my side. Since coming to Conclave, Lucas had always stuck up for me. Maybe this time, *I* needed to be the helpful one. The fairy prophets might be wise. Sometimes, a danger shared is a heartache spared.

"Thanks, Filbert. I think I know what I must do."

"Anytime," he agreed as he prepared to dive. "You know where to find me."

And with a swish of his tail fins, he was gone.

***

We walked out past the edge of town, Royland, Lucas, Hazhi and me. Our traveling cloaks flapped about us in the stiff breeze. Lucas led the way, being best acquainted with the way to find the glade. The somber sun of midday beat down upon us. But our shadows soon faded and thinned as from the west an ominous bank of clouds came rolling in. The scent of rain was on the breeze and something else besides. It was the sharp tang that sometimes you could smell before a storm.

"Quite unseasonable weather," Royland remarked.

"Yep," returned his cousin, looking back over his shoulder. "Isn't this supposed to be the dry season?"

Hazhi paused to peer back at the village. A look of concern crossed his face.

When we'd set off, the boys had been surprised to find Hazhi was to join us. When they pressed Mistress Julia about it, she said that 'three without their master' was bad enough. It didn't have to mean without any adult presence. 'But it's dangerous,' Lucas had argued. 'You forget, dear boy,' Hazhi had answered, 'that danger is my middle name! (or near enough, given some cultural latitude).'

So it was all four of us who passed into the linden wood to find our guide. The wind soon lost its teeth. We had the trees to thank for that. I could see their tops bending and swaying, but it was almost windless down here on the ground.

Up ahead, Lucas paused, then led us toward the low-burning campfire where sat the old woodsman.

"Rip?" said Lucas, disbelievingly.

Though seated, I could tell the man was tall. He could likely meet Royland eye to eye, maybe even looking down on him a little. He lacked the long white beard they had said he had. Instead, there was a neatly trimmed goatee in its place. His eyes were close together and his nose stuck out too far, just like Lucas and Roy and all the others I'd met beyond my home. His hair was slicked back. It was so streaked with gray you could hardly tell it had once been brown. And a grimace soured the man's face.

"The name's *Van* in case you forgot," said the man, slowly rising to his feet. "Who's the elf and this fine young lady?"

"He's Hazhi Dia Quobias, and the lady is our fellow journeyman, Sholeena. I thought you'd be waiting for us in the glade."

"Well, I woulda, but the glade ain't open just now. The faeries shut her down since the gathering. Most of 'em's still sleeping it off, I guess, so I pitched my camp right here nearby."

"How far is this place you're taking us?"

"Couple'a days, give or take. We can set out at once, I reckon. The rain makes no nevermind to me. Funny clouds up there today. Came out of nowhere; they did. Have you ever seen the like?"

"I have," said Hazhi, whose face had gone ashen.

He looked like he would say more, but then decided not to. As Van put out his small fire, scattering dirt atop its ashes. I shifted nervously. Lucas looked over at me and smiled encouragingly. Royland bent down to tighten his boot lace. I was worried about all the walking. I was wearing two thick sets of stockings. Boots gave me blisters on a long hike.

"We're heading east to a tricky little ravine not many know is even there," said Van. "I left Master Hans and his lady fair at the mouth of that ravine where Tinatia told him to go. First stop, though, is the top of that rise yonder."

He pulled on his pack, took up a long walking stick, and headed directly off.

"I'm told a mite has changed since first I went to the glade. It still puzzles me how that could be. 'Twas a dastardly trick that was played on me by Sean or whatever his name truly is. I know I took a nap or two on that long night while we played. But never did I suspect the whole world had moved on as I dozed. In truth, I awoke a time or two to hear some fairy voices speaking unguardedly. I discovered that rascal of a leprechaun is not named Sean at all. His true name is Rumple-something-or-other. I'll tweak him right proper with it the next time we meet if I can recall the rest."

The man's long strides set a grueling pace as we tried keeping up behind him. Not in the least was he winded by his efforts. In fact, he started whistling a tune as he went.

"You're going to have to slow down," complained Hazhi before five minutes had passed. "As an elf of the wood, I can, of course, keep up, but these young ones aren't used to so strident a pace."

I was glad he had said it, for I didn't like how fast the man was walking. But watching the elf, I saw his face had reddened. Unlike with my folk, this didn't mean he was angry. I think he was just out of breath.

"Hazhi's right," I said with sympathy. "My legs are sore already. And you'll have to carry me if you keep running ahead like that."

The trapper paused and looked flustered. He scratched his chin and spat. But when he turned, he set off with a slower gait. This was much more pleasant. That is, until we got to the base of that hill. Even walking slowly uphill was tiring, but especially on me. The mounds we had back at Indigo Bay were tiny little things with gentle slopes. Not like this monster. I bit my lip and struggled to keep going. At the top, I collapsed at once to rest.

It never did rain on us in spite of the wind lashing past. From up here atop the rise, we could see that the clouds were all gathered above the town from which we'd come, like sheep huddled in their pen. We could make out occasional flashes of lightning followed a few seconds later by rolling peals of thunder.

"Well, I'll be jiggered," declared Van. "I've never seen the weather gang up on a single village before.

"I have," said Hazhi once again. "On the night my daughter was born, the winds wracked our village in just such a manner. I suspect Sithia's labor has begun."

Royland stood staring in fascination at the clouds off in the distance.

"Then you must go to her!" Lucas exclaimed.

"I was supposed to see you safely to Ki bodey and introduce you to Master Shon... " the elf hedged.

"We'll be fine on our own," declared Lucas. "Goodman Winkle can show us the way."

"Your wife and daughter need you, Hazhi," I added.

"Well, make up your mind, man," said Van. " Are you in or out?"

"I... suppose I should head back," said the elf wearily.

We sent him off with our good wishes. Once Goodman Winkle had gotten 'the lay of the land,' the four of us headed back down the hill and were properly on our way. I found walking downhill much more to my liking. And I even came to appreciate the man's whistling after a time. The storm in the distance made me wonder what my own birthing labors would one day be like. That was no mere tempest in a teapot brewing back there. I prayed silently that the little one would arrive safely.

***

Three days later found us still struggling along. Goodman Van led the way, and we followed as best we could. It surprised the old trapper when, on the first night, Lucas had produced two large tents from his side satchel, poles and all. I remember being cross with Lloyd for always calling me 'Mudslide,' but I'd long since forgiven him for this. I was very grateful now for the iron cook pot and other things his enchanted pocket let us have without needing to lug them around on our backs.

Roy kept the bugs off us. Lucas swept the plants back where they grew too thick. And I could always locate or make fresh water. Though I still didn't like hiking, I was getting used to it, and Van said we were making better time than he expected, given our leisurely pace.

So it was on this third day he announced our goal was in sight. An unexpected and foreboding dip in the land led down to what appeared to be a dead end at the base of a cliff. Once we'd scrambled down the treacherous scree that littered the steep slope, however, we discovered a narrow crevasse one could squeeze through. According to our guide, it led into a secret ravine wherein stood a mysterious tower that had been Hans' and Gretta's destination.

"Here's where I left 'em," declared the old trapper. "I'll take my payment now and be on my way."

"Aren't you coming in with us?" asked Lucas.

"That wasn't part of the deal," said Van. "I confess I was a mite curious. I peeped in from the edge before, but your grandpappy once told me this was a special place of punishment used by the fey. And I've had my fill of *that*."

Royland untied his purse strings and handed Van the promised amount, thanking him and wishing him smooth travels. Before he left, Lucas had confirmed our directions.

"So when our business is done here, we're to head east toward that mountain in the distance and circle round it to find *Venghom Ki-bodey*?"

"That's right, young'un. You can't miss it. There'll be smoke curlin' up from chimneys and the like. That elf fella said you was to meet Shon at the tavern there. Best of luck to you."

And with that, he was off.

I lined up behind the two boys, and we crept into the narrow fissure at the cliff's base. Royland entered first, slouching low and crab-walking within. He was followed by Lucas. I had to use darksight to follow them into the gloom. I wondered what we might find at the tower Van had described. From the way he had talked, it sounded like it might be a fairy prison of some sort. I fished out my knife and kept a close watch over my shoulder. Mother once told me it's the shark you don't notice that's the true threat.

There was only one incident as we cautiously crept through that cleft. A family of badgers had taken up residence in the abandoned crevice and claimed it for their sett. On espying them, Roy released a brief burst of flame that sent them scrambling out a side-tunnel which we carefully avoided as we passed.

At the far end, I stepped out from behind my two companions, blinking in the afternoon light. We were in a small canyon bordered on all sides by rocky bluffs. The little valley was pleasant to look at. Warmed by the surrounding stone and sheltered from the wind, it was replete with honeysuckle still in bloom, and butterflies flitted about. Though nothing specific pricked at my mage sight, the place reeked of enchantment.

At its center stood the tower. It was thin and round and made of a stone so pale as to be almost white. It drew one's eye ever upward along its spindly height. It was so slender, it seemed a stiff wind could blow it over, but we'd soon find out that this was not the case. So tall it was that its sharply pointed cap seemed poised to pierce the sky. No openings were evident until near the very top where it bulged slightly outward. A single arched window overlooked us from on high.

"How tall do you reckon it is, Roy?" Lucas whispered.

"I'd estimate at least seventy feet," answered Royland without pause.

"I'm not doubting you, cousin, but isn't that rather impossible, especially given there are no walls to buttress it?"

"I would have thought so. Yet there it stands."

"What do you suppose Master Hans hoped to find here?"

"I don't know and refuse to speculate. We won't find out by gaping at it from here. Let's go and see."

But if the two thought the mystery would up and reveal itself when we moved closer, they were soon to be disappointed. After weaving through the underbrush, we stood at the tower's base and gaped at it a while from there instead. No doorway, stair or ladder did we discover even after having walked all around it. Nothing stuck out to our mage sight either, except a low pulse of enchantment that pervaded the whole thing. It tickled and teased us with hints of its purpose.

Lucas was rubbing at the back of his hand. He startled when he realized he was doing so.

"It's fairy magic," he announced.

Roy stepped back and glared up at the tower.

"Open sesame," he intoned in an ominous voice while waving his hands in supplication.

Lucas snorted.

"Worth a try," said Roy with a shrug. "Clearly, we must get to the top."

"Well, according to my earth sense, this thing is solid all the way through. Any ideas?"

"Levitating someone is out," muttered Roy. "The range is too great for something that heavy."

"Mistress Julia could just fly to the top," I put in helpfully.

"Well, she isn't here," Roy returned, staring at me in annoyance. "Have you any aeromancy skills you've not told us about? No? I thought not."

"Leave her alone, Roy," said Lucas. "I asked for ideas."

"Okay then," said Royland. "Perhaps we could transform ourselves into butterflies or construct a catapult and launch ourselves up there."

"Sarcasm doesn't become you, cousin. Look. I have several coils of rope in my bob, more than enough to reach the top. What I don't have is a grapnel, which we likely *could* levitate to that height. And I doubt we could jerry rig a trustworthy one out of cooking implements and the like... Wait. Sholeena, you're a genius..."

I didn't know what Lucas was on about, but I liked the sound of that last part.

"What are you thinking?" asked Roy warily.

"When Sho and I first saw Mistress Julia fly, I asked her whether anyone could do it. She told me there was more than one way to peel an onion. She said our gifts could confer 'many enjoyable forms of movement' or some such. All the while, our master was playing with a daddy long-legs. I think she was suggesting something."

"That would be just like her," said Roy. "She never comes straight out and tells you something, does she? She prefers you get there on your own. Given what you just said, I'm reminded of your performance at the menhir on the night of our initiation."

"What of it?"

"Afterward, I heard some of the masters remarking on how much you resembled a great spider, with all those vines curling out from your back. Do you think you could repeat that performance?"

My head was spinning from their excited back and forth. The two had grown up together, and both were obviously very smart. As a result, they almost knew each other's thoughts and spoke in a rapid shorthand that left others to flounder. It didn't help when they used big, rare words I hadn't learned yet. I remembered that night, though. Lucas *had* looked like a big spider...

"You're going to climb up there!" I announced.

The two looked over at me as if just remembering I was there. Royland rolled his eyes, and Lucas grinned and slowly nodded.

"If you recall, it took a great amount of power for me to do that," said the nice one. "I'd been storing up energy from my weeding for days."

With a wave of his hand, Royland indicated the fields surrounding the tower.

"I see a feast of honeysuckle all laid out before you, cousin. I hope you brought an appetite."

***

Around us, the ground lay blackened and shriveled. By my mage sight, I could perceive six flailing vines protruding from the boy's back. With his satchel slung over one shoulder, Lucas began his ascent. Haltingly at first, but with ever-growing confidence, he skittered up the smooth stone wall just as a bug ascends the bole of a tree. Roy and I watched in fascination.

I used to wonder why a mage couldn't levitate herself. After all, I had often levitated objects weighing more than a person. When I'd asked my app-master about it, he'd seemed confused. His answer wasn't really an explanation. It was more like a demonstration. He bade me reach back and grab myself by the shoulders. 'Now,' he said, 'straighten your arms to lift yourself from off the ground.' I told him that was ridiculous. He had only smiled and advised me to quit asking such silly questions.

As Lucas neared the top, a humming sound was heard. There were a tense few moments when a hive of hornets up in the eaves disgorged a seething black mass. This swirled and swarmed about, descending toward Lucas, who promptly flattened himself against the wall to cling there, helpless. But then Roy stretched out his hand. Under his stern glare, the cloud of tiny warriors withdrew, leaving my friend (mostly) unscathed. Completing his climb, Lucas heaved himself over the open window's lip and disappeared within.

My hands and arms had become tinged with a nervous green while I waited for the boy to reappear. I couldn't help myself. Roy crossed his arms and wet his lips but said nothing.

Then a big coil of knotted rope came arching out the window. It uncoiled as it fell, and we stepped back as the excess came spiraling down to plop down at the tower's foot. Before he'd gone up, Lucas had assured us he had more than an ample supply of rope in his bob. It was still surprising to me the little satchel could contain such a bounty. I silently thanked Lloyd once again for his kind and helpful gift.

Roy drew the rope taut and tested his weight upon it. This stilled the dangling line. It must have met with his satisfaction because he placed both feet on the wall and started his climb at once. And there was Lucas, leaning out high above, waving us up.

The stones were a little slippery under my booted feet, and I dared not look down. I was okay, and the ascent proceeded smoothly until I was about halfway up. It was then my arms began to tire. Lucky for me, I found it easy enough to shift my feet down to stand swaying upon a knot for a time until I regained strength enough to renew my efforts. Roy was doing the same, but not nearly so often as I. It was thus we finally arrived, panting and heaving at the opening we had sought. The boys gripped my shoulders and hauled me over the sill.

When at last I stood surveying my surroundings, I was unimpressed. The place reeked of abandonment and far worse.

We were in a circular room about eight paces across.

The large double window through which we'd entered may once have been glazed, but only one of the panes for such now hung ajar in the weathered opening. It now gaped, hollow and empty, letting in what little light pierced the flapping tatters of what had once been curtains. To this, Lucas had added a lantern he'd lit and rested on a table near the room's center. Various furnishings may have once been elegant, but now stood in a state of disrepair verging on decomposition. There was a dresser, a trunk, an empty bookshelf, and a chair whose cushions had seen finer days. Cobwebs abounded, and the place was sore in need of some sort of predator to reduce the population of dust bunnies which swirled around in the draft. There was an upper deck accessible by a rickety wooden stairway we were to learn contained only a single bed whose stained mattress crawled with vermin.

The only intact feature was a small stone fireplace. It directly faced the window, and rust was evident on its grate. It was upon this that Royland's eyes became riveted. Lucas soon stepped up beside his cousin, and both stood transfixed. Not to be left out, I wriggled in and invoked my own magesight to see what was so interesting.

"This is indeed the place," Royland remarked.

"Yep," Lucas confirmed, "that's their enchantment all right."

I could make out a vague hint of magic in the stones surrounding the grate, but it didn't strike me as all that potent. It was just a little whiff of pyromancy from long ago.

"Well, fire it up then," I exhorted them.

The boys set aside their packs and hung their cloaks over some pegs on the wall. As they settled themselves on the modest hearth, I cleared a space before it and spread my own cloak over the grimy tiles of the floor. On it, I squatted down with my legs crossed and prepared to watch the show.

Roy ignited a magical blaze just above the grate. It was immediately enveloped by swirling misty vapors which resolved into a sphere that hovered there like a cork bobbing on a pond.

"Still with us, I see," observed the man whose face smiled out from the hovering ball.

Just over his shoulder, a young woman was bending near to peer out at us as well.

"I can't actually *see* you, of course, but if you are hearing this, I imagine you found the fey amenable, and you've managed to get up here somehow. Gretta and I have only just enjoyed a most exhilarating climb to achieve these lofty heights. The brownie who traded us that magic bean should be commended. It performed admirably, twining up the tower's side and providing ample handholds for our lively ascent.

"We found the tower to be abandoned and in disrepair. According to legend, it was once inhabited by a young maiden who had earned the wrath of the fairy queen herself. When her illicit dalliances with the fairy king were laid bare, the damsel was spirited away to this very tower to dwell for years in lonely captivity.

"For his flagrant infidelity, Queen Tinatia cut off Orenob's beard as he lay sleeping. This robbed him of half his powers. Furthermore, she cursed his face to break out in blemishes before removing herself from his castle and his life. Thus began the great division among the faire folk. The faeries who sided with the queen have called themselves the seelie fey ever since."

The woman behind Hans leaned in closer and whispered something in his ear.

"I was just getting to that, my love," said the man aloud. "You may be wondering: 'What has all this to do with our quest?' Well, I'll tell you then.

"Orenob had been most enamored of the young maiden's lustrous golden tresses. During her time with him, he had used his considerable fey powers to cause them to grow even thicker and more quickly than normal. Therefore, not many years after her confinement, Rapunzel was able to use her long tresses as a rope to descend from the tower. At its base, she severed the braid and absconded with a prince of some distant kingdom.

"On returning to check in on the damsel, Queen Tinatia was outraged to find the tower empty and the long plait dangling from out of its open window. She rolled it up and packed it away in a trunk atop the spire. And here it has lain ever since, waiting for Gretta and me to claim it. For you see, Orenob's lair is also said to lie atop a spire, a sinister spike rising high above the mires over which he rules. And with the proper enchantment, Rapunzel's braid will make the perfect implement with which to surmount it!

"And so, fellow travelers, we wish you the best of luck on the roads ahead and --"

"Tell them of the next marker, dear," interrupted Gretta with a playful smack to the back of the man's head."

"Ah, yes," said Hans, after flashing her an indignant glance. "From here, Gretta and I have decided to head farther east. We shall record our next message at Eagle's Keep. I misdoubt me any enemy of the kingdom will have the temerity to seek it out within the duke's own stronghold! We shall be staying in the mage's quarters there, but you'll find our upcoming report in a far humbler nook."

And on that mysterious note, the sphere faded to black. After a moment, it burst back into a red ball of flame, which slowly fizzled to nothing.

Lucas was the first to speak.

"A seventy-foot long braid of hair?" he exclaimed. "That wouldn't have been my first guess as to what they were after."

Royland said nothing. He seemed sad. I wanted to comfort him, but he didn't like to be touched or looked at directly. He kind of made *himself* lonely. I rolled back up to my feet and bent to retrieve my cloak. I gave it a shake to dislodge the lint clinging to the outside. This sent the bunnies all scurrying for cover and raised a cloud of choking dust. Roy covered his nose and glared over at me.

"It's getting a bit late," said Lucas. "Why don't we set up camp right here? It seems secure enough."

"Pull up the rope, then," said Roy.

"On it," answered his cousin, already striding toward the window.

They were at it again. Talking in half-sentences and leaving me out. While Royland fiddled with the flue, making sure it would draw properly, Lucas began stacking firewood from his bob on the small hearth. Poking around, I found an old broom leaning up in a corner and started clearing a space where we could lay out our bedrolls. The ancient bristles of the broom's brush deteriorated as I did so, adding many shards of their length to the pile of debris I was collecting. I covered this mound of dreck with the remnants of an old rug I peeled up from the greasy floor by the dresser. It would have to do. Sleeping outdoors would have been just as untidy, but the earth and leaves would have seemed fresher somehow. No one claimed the nasty bed up in the loft.

"Tomorrow, we head east to *Ki-bodey* to meet with Shon," declared Lucas. "He should be able to guide us safely to the border of Eagle's Keep Duchy."

"I wonder what the humble nook there shall reveal," said Roy, staring pensively into the lambent light of our fire.

***

I awoke in the stillness of the night. I'd been dreaming about swimming in shoals off the Indigo Bay. Just as in the best of such dreams, there had been no need to breathe. In the dim, blue-tinged waters, I was surrounded by schools of minnows and angelfish. And the halodule grass waved all about, tickling my limbs as I swam through it.

But a nagging feeling began gnawing at my serenity. There was a *wrongness* just up ahead. I couldn't put a name to it, but some instinct was screaming I'd better heed the danger. I swam urgently up to wakefulness. As impressions of the disturbing dream faded, both sets of eyelids snapped open wide, and I sat up with a gasp.

It came to me that I was in the tower. Safe. High above anything which might threaten me. Yet my pulse was racing, and I was having trouble setting aside the feeling of disquietude. The room was dimly lit by the fire's glow. A rattling sound caught my ear, causing me to spin about and face toward the fireplace. There sat Lucas on its hearth, rummaging within his pack. Various items lay strewn on the floor about him, and he seemed very intent on his search. What was he doing?

Nearby lay Royland, soundly asleep. Perhaps I should rather think 'soundlessly asleep,' as the young man's pillowcase was active, muffling any noise near his head. Thus, a ruckus such as Lucas was raising wouldn't likely disturb *his* slumber as it had mine.

Turning once more to regard the younger cousin, I saw he had stilled. Peering into his 'bob' he reached within it and fished out a stick. It was a shaft of wood about as long as a person's forearm. Its smooth, round surface reflected the soft, orange glow from the grate. Was he... sniffing at it? With a snarl, he snatched the stick back from his face and appeared poised to set it atop the flames.

"Lucas?" I said.

Startled, he turned toward me, thrusting the stick behind his back.

"Sho...Sho-LEE-na?" he replied.

"Why are you up so late?" I asked. "What is it you're doing over there?"

"Thirsty," he mumbled.

Then he cleared his throat and said more naturally, "I was thirsty."

His reassuring smile was anything but. The stick slipped from his hand to roll across the hearth and clatter to the floor.

"Well, that's easy to remedy," I declared.

I reached over and unclipped the waterskin from my pack. Rising and stretching, I sauntered over to sit beside Lucas near the fire. I had to step carefully to avoid some of the clutter. There was a leather-bound book, several bottles of colored liquid and even a full stoppered waterskin. Odd. I eased myself down, unstopped my own waterskin and offered it to him.

He accepted it awkwardly, lifted it up and swallowed a swig.

"That's nice," he said, wiping his mouth with the back of his sleeve.

Just then, a log resettled, sending a cascade of small sparks dancing above it.

When I turned back toward Lucas, I found him leaning close to me making a strange face. He grabbed me roughly by the nape of my neck and pulled me closer still. His lips parted as his mouth sought mine.

It's not like I hadn't thought about it. Despite his pinched face and pointy nose, he'd always seemed so nice. A girl could do worse. But it shouldn't be like this. I had learned from Royland that Lucas was helplessly smitten with a girl from their hometown. If I ever decided to 'canoodle' with a boy, I'd want to be his only one, not some convenient hussy out on a hike. Here and we'd just heard that sad story about Rapunzel and how she'd ruined the fairy queen's marriage with her improper ways.

I raised my hands between us and thrust him back, flustered.

His eyes flew open wide. And his look of fascination and hopeful leer were soon replaced by an expression I'd never before seen on Lucas, an angry sneer of contempt.

"You're an ugly toad anyway," he spat.

And, rising, he stalked back over to his bedding. I was stunned. As he settled there without another glance my way, I blinked back the tears that threatened to spill over onto my cheeks. The fire warmed my back and side, but I felt a coldness wash over me. My shoulders lowered, and my chin drifted down to rest upon my chest.

"You know that wasn't Lucas," murmured the voice.

It wasn't his usual, laughing voice.

I let my mind sink down to the consoling depths of my inner pond. Filbert swam in agitated circles upon its surface, one bright fin sticking up out of the water.

"I knew something was off with him," I moaned.

"Clearly, it was the boy's homunculus," said the fish. "You know it's been at odds with him ever since its emergence. It governs his sleep as all we homunculi do.".

"I thought of that, Filbert," I returned, "but that doesn't make it any better. It means there's a part of Lucas, deep down, that really feels that way."

"What he said doesn't necessarily express his true feelings. The unconscious can be a funny fish (case in point). You rejected him, so he lashed out. What you *should* take away from this is there's a part of Lucas, deep down, that wanted to *kiss* you..."

After a time, I returned to the world without. Though his cruel words still whispered in my heart, it was time to get on with life.

I picked up Lucas' bric-à-brac and stuffed it all back in his satchel. I moved my mat over closer to the fire and tried to snatch what rest I could before daybreak.

***

"Sholeena? Sholeena?"

I awoke to the shaking of my shoulder. When I opened my eyes, Lucas' smiling face swam into view. I flinched back, alarmed.

117

"Rise and shine!" sang the boy. "It's the early catfish that gets the sludge worm!"

Royland was frying some eggs, and most of the boys' gear was packed up and ready to go. My arms felt a little stiff and sore from yesterday's unaccustomed climb. Though part of me was still angry with Lucas, I knew it wasn't really his fault. And he had a hard mission to complete. Helping him was why I'd come. And if his homunculus was still giving him trouble, he needed his friends more than ever.

"Awww," I cooed. "You tortured a metaphor for me."

Lucas snorted and shook his head in disbelief. Just this past spring, Lucas had been my language tutor. Back then I'd been very awkward with speech, and he'd taught me many strange words and concepts. I think it still amazed him how quickly a Paluda can learn stuff. Good. I dug out my mess kit and hurriedly approached Roy before all the good ones were gone.

A Paluda's colors changed to reflect her mood. It was like breathing. It happened automatically, but you could also do it on purpose, either to deceive or to avoid upsetting others. I had given my skin a faint orange tinge to mimic happiness. But there was no fooling Roy. As he deposited the eggs on my tin plate, Royland stared me right in the face and frowned. But just as he was incredibly perceptive, I found he could be trusted not to betray one's secret feelings. That, or he just didn't care enough to remark on them.

Climbing down was much easier than climbing up had been, at least for Roy and me. We didn't even have to use the wall. Lucas, however, still had to retrieve the rope and spider crawl down after us. He had to blacken another whole swath of honeysuckle to make up for the energy he'd spent. The butterflies were going to be unhappy about this.

So, in the morning light, we marched toward that lonely mountain in the distance. It seemed to be just across the next field, but it would likely take all day to reach its base. Mountains always seemed closer than they were. That is until you were right on top of one. Lucas prowled slightly ahead with his crossbow out and at the ready. Roy went next, and I brought up the rear. I unsheathed my knife and held it just in case.

But little of note happened that day, and as the sun fell lower in the western sky, we sought about for a suitable campsite. It was a secure little clearing with a cluster of boulders far from any running water. No animals should disturb us if we built our fire properly and kept it stoked throughout the night. Pitching our tents, we set to work on our other chores. We had only a cold meal to avoid broadcasting food smells.

"... I don't see why not," said Lucas. "You definitely have the time *now*. Besides, I've already managed to perform an enchantment on my own."

'Then you shouldn't need me to show you," Royland reasoned.

"It's just that I need to learn how to give an object a *permanent* enchantment."

Well-familiar with the debate by now, I hunkered down to listen.

"Why?"

"It's something I need to do."

"That would be an answer to 'what,' not 'why.'"

"Just show me one time. Harden my crossbow."

"It's already made of witchwood, Lucas. Nothing's going to break it."

"I just need to see how it's done so I can do it for myself. The object I have in mind must be enchanted by my own hand."

Royland suddenly wheeled on his cousin.

"So, you *do* intend a talisman, then!" he accused.

(You owe me a worm) said Filbert. (I told you Roy would wheedle it out of him)

"I do," his cousin admitted, directing his gaze downward. "When you showed me how to form a conduit, you cited Narfaggle's Law and explained how a conduit could be established from a primary affinity to an enchanted object. I made sure to look it up later on."

"I might have known you wouldn't let it go. You know, they call *me* compulsive, Lucas. But when it comes to obsession, I think it's *you* who take the cake (and various other dessert dishes as well). If you've read up on it, then you are aware a talisman should be attempted only by a seasoned master. Not by a jumped-up journeyman for a lark."

A girl could learn many interesting things just by listening to these two bicker. I heightened my camouflage, curled up my toes, and listened harder.

"They say the same thing about grand workings, Roy, and yet I managed one as a mere apprentice."

"And it nearly killed you, if I recall."

"It would have been worth it. Desperate times, cuz. Times like now. I can't explain it. I just... need this."

Roy cocked his head, as though sensing the truth in the statement. Was that sympathy creasing the man's brow? Who'd have thought it? After a long pause, Royland spoke.

"Give me the crossbow."

The relieved smile that widened Lucas' face would have almost done a Paluda proud.

"Sholeena, I know you've been listening," Roy added. "Go and fetch us some water."

Honestly, that Royland never missed a beat.

When I got back, he and Lucas were seated across from one another on a spread-out blanket with the bow resting between them.

"So, you know how to empower an object," he was saying. "To make it permanent, an extra twist is required, but there's a cost. When you teach an object to power itself, it continuously draws magic from the surrounding environment, rather like the pull of a grand working. This is why mages don't carry many enchanted items on their person."

"Explain," said Lucas.

"It might seem like carrying a bunch of ready magics around would be a dandy idea. But do you recall how it felt to be next to Westarbor's Gates after Master Chadwick had enchanted them?"

"Oppressive," said Lucas ruefully.

"That's because they were drawing all the magic from their surroundings. Normally, when a mage like you or I work magic, it depletes our magic centers somewhat. When we rest, we replenish these energies. Were you to deplete your reserve then rest near those gates, your magic would restore itself much more slowly, if at all. The same holds true for smaller magic items. You can carry a few around on your person without much consequence, but these add up. Imagine several dozen little leeches draining all the power from around you and nibbling at your own magic center --"

"I get the picture, Roy. No need to go on so about it."

"I just want you to understand you should use caution when deciding how much power to invest in a given object. Generally, no more than is needed to perform its task is wise."

"So noted," said the boy earnestly.

"Watch carefully now. I only intend to do this once."

As Royland stretched his hands toward the crossbow, I saw with my mage sight a myriad of tiny specs stream forth to bathe it in a glittering array of his 'hive mites.'

"First, the empowerment," he said.

As he chanted 'inexsuperabilis permanens lignea' over and over again, more and more of the little devils streamed forth and were absorbed into the wood.

He paused.

"And then the twist."

There was a flicker. It happened so quickly that I could scarcely perceive what happened. Reality bent in an odd way, and Roy's magic center rattled and throbbed, hurling its mites willy nilly in a diaspora of whirling cinders. These formed a cloud above the crossbow and were rapidly drawn within.

"...and, Bob's your uncle (and my father, incidentally)."

Lucas sat staring in wonderment, mesmerized by the weapon that now lay darkened and faintly flickering in our mage sight.

"It'll settle down in a minute or two," Royland continued. "After that, I doubt even a blacksmith could put a dent in it. There. I kept my part of the bargain. Now show me the item you intend to enchant."

Still sporting a look of amazement, Lucas produced the stick I'd seen on the prior night and placed it before his cousin. It gleamed in the moonlight and almost looked to be enchanted already.

"What's this?" asked Roy as he reached out to take it up.

"I got it from Hazel," Lucas replied. "When Holly's acorn dropped, this was attached to it. She called it 'the umbilicus of a dryad's first birthing.' She claimed it 'contains much power,' but so far it seems a fairly ordinary stick."

"Are you sure she wasn't just having you on?"

"I don't think so, Roy. It calls to me, like it *wants* to be enchanted. Sometimes I just stare at it, and it gives me a happy feeling, but it longs to be something more. It's like when I know a plant is content or needs watering or whatever. It's not a feeling I can express to any lacking my affinity."

Again, Royland scrutinized his cousin's face. What he found there seemed to satisfy him.

"I'm not sure mixing our magic with that of the fey is such a good idea," he said. "But I can see you're determined. If you're to do this, cousin, then you must do it where Sholeena and I can observe and render aid if you get into trouble."

He was including me? Why Royland, it's almost like you have regard for another human person. He stared over at me and snorted. I knew he couldn't really read minds, but his perception of a person's attitude was uncanny. I oranged to recall Lucas sometimes called him the 'thought sheriff.'

"Well, what was it Baron Downham liked to say?" returned Lucas with a sly grin. "There's no time like the now."

And with that, he set his crossbow aside and indicated Roy should place the rod before him. We gathered close and waited with bated breath for our friend to attempt this newly learned sorcery. Steadying his breathing, Lucas began to incant.

"inexsuperabilis permanens lignea... "

Roy and I watched as Lucas drew out and gathered a tangle of vines from his magic center. It was a verdant meadow with a little hillock at one end. The vines erupted from random locations across the entire field. There was also a little stick man running frantically about. Serves him right, the nasty little thing.

The vines twisted and merged into one another in a whirling bit of fusion, spiraling together to form a single, large vine. This came twining down Lucas' right arm, eventually emerging from his palm to spear the shaft of wood. More and more twisted greenery slithered forth and entered the stick, seeming to be devoured by it. Lucas shuddered in the throes of ecstasy.

A nimbus of green light wreathed the would-be wand. And from its far end, the vine emerged at last. But was it the same vine? It slithered and flexed in an almost serpentine manner as it cast about. Then it stabbed the ground past our blanket's edge and went snaking off toward the woodland beyond.

By this point, Lucas was looking pale and drawn, and his magic center was nearly spent. Yet still the savage investment of power ground on, wringing the last of the magic from the boy.

"Enough, cousin!" shouted Roy. "The twist! The twist! You must do it now!"

But Lucas was unresponsive. His face had gone slack. His hand was locked into a rigid claw, out of which his withering vine protruded. Roy reached over and began slapping and shaking his cousin, but it was to no avail.

"We must help him," I cried. "Leave off, Royland. Join with me instead."

I had been part of a joining only once before. It had been a desperate gamble to drive out a possessing fey spirit from a master of conclave. I'd had no practice since, but Filbert and I had done some reading on the topic. I knew how one should commence, but I had no spell for what I intended. Drawing upon my studies of the old tongue, I invoked a joining just as Lucas had wrought it on that day, improvising the needed words.

"Commodare eum potentia," I whispered, 'lend him strength.'

The waters of my pond swirled up at once to envelop both Lucas and Roy. This formed the most basic unit of communal magic, the triad. Thankfully, Roy held up his end, but I sensed from my place as conductor that Lucas was adrift. His power was rapidly ebbing. As my waters and Roy's mites swirled in to fill this void, rather than being renewed, the drain only continued.

We had bought a reprieve for Lucas, but had I doomed us all?

I sensed the verdant energy emanating from the tip of the accursed stick burrowing through the earth into the grove of trees beyond.

One by one, those trees seemed to awaken and though the night remained silent, I sensed bursting from them a song. It was the song of life and growing. It was the joy of sunlight and the patter of cool rain. It was the shade of leafy boughs and the soft crumble of moss at one's roots. It was all of these things and more. And I swore in that moment that if I had to die here, I'd die happy for having heard it.

But what was this? A trickle of relief?

Just as the sea reared back betimes from the shore, the tides had turned. All of Lucas' energy came flowing back, suffused with the joy of that song. He shook himself and blinked his eyes, even as a gasp of relief escaped my lips.

"And then the twist," he muttered.

His green field heaved and shuddered, and his vines fell limp and spent. The last of them were absorbed into the talisman, which now shone like the noonday sun.

Roy staggered to his feet and shuffled over to his cousin, wroth written plainly on his face.

"You can just never do things by halves, can you?" he complained. "Almost killed us again. Well? What have you to say for yourself?"

Lucas muttered something indistinct.

"What was that?"

"And Bob's my uncle," Lucas repeated, speaking a bit more clearly.

"Unbelievable," grumbled Roy. "Why do I even bother?"

At this, he pivoted and sulked back to his tent, leaving me to watch over my exhausted friend. Lucas mumbled something else, closed his eyes, and was soon fast asleep. I was alone again.

"Filbert," I said. "I hope I'll always have you to talk to."

"Alas," replied the fish. "Such is not meant to be. Once we start completing one another's sentences, you'll know that re-integration has... "

"No? ... commenced, then," he finished.

And my heart knew peace. Whatever my problems were, my little fish could always find some way to make me laugh.

CHAPTER SIX

The Fox

"I have noticed even people who claim everything is predestined, and that we can do nothing to change it, look before they cross the road."

~ Stephen Hawking ~

Dear Lucas,

I just received your missive the day before last. Lynette nearly swooned when its seal was broken. It served her *right* for leaning in so close. Please resist the urge to go completely native. (I'm trying to envision you with a ponytail, and the picture isn't flattering.)

I understand you have a great many irons in the fire, as the smiths are wont to say. Life moves apace here as well.

The new mill is nearing completion on schedule. Your father and Gregor send their regards. Your uncle and his wife have departed the mill and taken up a farming tenancy once again. It's the old Henderson place just across from the Cunningham's dairy farm. For their part, Andrew and Helen have taken in a group of young ladies who were orphaned during the siege. They're teaching them to milk the cows, their own children having moved on to other responsibilities.

It was Marjery Cunningham who brought us your news from fair Lorédon. Her brother, Drew, has set his cap for the first griffin flight to Fairglen on Todd. The king is most eager to greet the strange animals that have so transformed commerce in his kingdom. The other girl, Nellie, is grounded at present. Her bird, Blynken, is brooding over our first clutch of griffin eggs!

You might be interested to know the House of Straw has been repurposed. It's been set aside as a sanctuary for Westarbor's tame griffins. 'Tis managed by Rupert Cain and is now known as 'Griffin Isle.' Sir Harrison makes regular runs out to it. We're building a lighthouse, a proper dock, a stable for the animals, and barracks for the soldiers who are to watch over them. Father says we must safeguard these vital new assets of the barony.

We've also received some thrilling news from the capital. For Prince Henry's eighteenth birthday, the king has announced a grand ball in his honor. The peerage from all throughout the kingdom have been invited to attend. The royal heir is presently touring the kingdom, but on his return next summer, the date will be set on which he will be made a crowned prince.

The court is rife with rumors that a new Duke of Northford will be raised up during this same gathering. And father is in the running! Due to Baron Stein's poor health, there's no surfeit of candidates for the position. Unless his majesty opts to place a complete outsider in charge of Northford Duchy, most believe it's down to either father or Guy Lord Downham. Stars preserve us all from the latter choice!

I believe it was the poet, Sextus, who first wrote 'absence makes the heart grow fonder.' I imagine he must have known someone like you. For across the many leagues which separate us, your missives can still pluck at my heartstrings. I always find ought to keep me occupied, but often of late, I feel I'm just marking time. 'Tis as though gray clouds hover o'er me since the day you left. And Westarbor has become a more dismal place for want of your laughter.

Regarding your unconscious will, I know little of such matters, but I shall add it to the long list of concerns I have for my protector. I can assure you such worries already figure most prominently in my nightly prayers. I implore you to exercise the utmost caution in your most recent endeavors. Keep yourself safe and convey my fond wishes to Royland as well.

Your Lady to Serve and Protect,
Megan Arenson
Daughter of Westarbor
Seer of Truth and She who frets o'er headstrong errant journeymen

I finished reading the letter for the third time. It was sheer good fortune we'd checked in at the hostelry before it had been sent on to Palm Springs. The good citizens of Ki-bodey had been all abuzz with tales of the second griffin flight to touch down in the village square so soon on the heels of the first.

"That letter must be pretty interesting," Sholeena remarked to Roy. "It's like his eyes were glued to that parchment."

"Not necessarily," returned my cousin, taking a casual sip from his flagon. "I told you he was smitten."

We sat amid the bustle of what passed for a village tavern, surrounded by the chattering elves. From the hub-bub of nearby exchanges, I caught tantalizing snippets of conversations, but nothing coherent. I felt rather conspicuous. The three of us stood out from the other patrons. But here is where we were to meet our guide, so here is where we remained. We had claimed a table near a side wall plainly visible from the entrance. By this late hour, we were quite deep in our cups, for it would have been impolite to hog a table without ordering. As I nursed the bitter ale, I mused aloud, not for the first time, about our appointment.

"I wonder what's keeping Master Shon. You don't suppose he's come and gone already?"

"Doubtful," said Roy with maddening calm. "He'd have surely left word with the barkeep. Perhaps *we* should do so and retire to our rooms."

"It's still a bit early for that, cousin. Mayhap we can pass the time with a game instead. What say you to another round of 'I spy?'"

Royland only groaned and rested his chin on his fists.

After a brief pause, Sholeena chimed in brightly with: 'Would you like to hear a riddle?'

The Paluda girl was looking a little wobbly, and her speech was slurring a bit more than was usual. I don't think she was used to fermented beverages. But unlike Roy, over-consumption seemed only to make her cheerful rather than morose.

"Shoot," I said.

"What'sh black and white and red all over?"

I puzzled on this for a time. My own drinking may have dulled my wits somewhat because a ready answer eluded me. A great many things could fit the criteria she'd set.

"A skunk on the target range?" I hesitantly put forth.

Sholeena shook her head in negation.

"I haven't the foggiest notion," said Roy. "Tell us, then already."

Smiling, she indicated the parchment on the table before me.

"A missive from Lucas' shweetie!" she snickered.

Caught quite off-guard, I chuckled. And even Royland smiled in appreciation.

"Look at you!" I praised. "Already poking fun at our homophones."

Sholeena discolored and said in all seriousness: "I shwear I didn't mean anything... vulgar."

The laughter this elicited from Roy and me drew many a curious glance from the tables nearby.

It was at this time an elven woman stepped toward our table from out of the crowd. She peered at each of us and then looked about as if seeking someone else. Finally, she spoke, addressing Roy.

"Are you here to meet with Master Shon?" she inquired.

"We are," replied my cousin. "Has he arrived?"

"Cholith Depa Shon sends his regrets," she said with a slight bow to the three of us. "A matter has arisen in the southern reaches, and he will be unable to assist you. I am his *ghojawus*, his journeyman. He sent me in his place."

Her dark, almond-shaped eyes flashed from beneath delicate long lashes as she regarded us. She seemed young, but I'd been fooled by this before. I'd have to reserve judgment until I learned more about her.

"Well, I'm called Royland Wagge, and these are Lucas Harper and Sholeena Blorlafargalish. We are *ghojawi* to Puquabeth Chosha Julia. We require a guide to take us safely to the border of Eagle's Keep Duchy. Please be seated that we may discuss it further.

"*Jhivath shohvath batlaponia noba*," said she, sliding into the empty seat beside Sholeena. "I am named Hazhiwab Ghosha Bitig, but you may call me Splash."

If memory served, her name would mean something like 'Laughter of the rushing river.'

"*Sowee batla shey jhey*," I put in. "Are you a water mage, then?" I guessed.

"I can see why you might think so," she answered in fluent Ostenian, "but no."

And with a small shrug, she failed to elaborate.

Introductions having been accomplished; we began making our plans.

Of the three Elven masters, Shon was the most junior, being only a hundred and forty years old. He patrolled the southern reaches of Lorédon, beating back various incursions from the south. Splash had become his journeyman after her apprenticeship under Mistress Julia at Conclave some thirty years ago. The woman was well on her way toward earning her own mastery as a therianthrope. Her totem was the fox.

On hearing of our quest, the elf grimaced.

"You would do better to return to Conclave and take the eastern road, then proceed south into E.K. The southern route is nearly impassable these days. Due to its many dangers, the merchants have long since given up on maintaining it."

But Royland insisted on taking the old south road.

"There's something on it I need to investigate," he explained.

Indeed, despite the Brubakers' mentioning their next report would be awaiting us at Eagle's Keep, there was another red dot on Grandma Gretta's scarf midway to it. And my cousin was nothing if not painstakingly attentive to such details.

Eventually, it was agreed that Splash would guide us to the border along that route. Tonight, she would share Sholeena's room and in the morning, after a hearty breakfast, we would all head out.

***

"Will you please quit waving that thing around, Lucas?" said Roy. "It's becoming annoying."

The branch bent gently forward, clearing the way before me.

"I can't help it," I replied. "It's as though I have a dryad root of my very own. Besides, all the stylish fairy godmothers are sporting wands this season."

Royland groaned.

"Well, if you ever affix a glittery star atop your talisman, I shall disavow you as my cousin," he muttered.

I heard Sholeena's breathy chuckle from farther back. In deference to my cousin's admonition, I holstered the wand and instead took up my crossbow from where it hung from a cord on my belt. I was supposed to remain vigilant and alert for danger.

Splash led the way as we snaked along through the wilds, seeking the old south road. She had cautioned us that from here on out, the way was rarely patrolled. The elf preceded us by about twenty yards, acting as an advance scout.

On first sighting my crossbow, the girl had looked dubious. Her own preferred weapon was a more standard bow. Like all things Elven, it was finely crafted. I was told it was made from yew wood; difficult to obtain in these sad times. Although smaller than the longbows favored by Osten's knights, it had a similar draw. Instead of a single, long frowning curve, it bent back up at each end rather like a handlebar mustache. I was told this was done to avoid having the string slip off an end when it was fully drawn.

Before we had set out, Splash let me try a few shots with it. Drawing the string back hurt my fingers, and the young woman's laughter assured me my technique was atrocious. Returning the favor, I offered her use of my witchwood special. At first, she was perplexed by the absence of any means to crank it back. I obligingly wound it using my special talent. Setting a bolt into its flight groove, she loosed at the fence post that was our target. Unlike my amateurish effort, she did manage to strike the post, but the shot arrived several inches above her mark. My crossbow was wound so tightly that there was far less of an arc than one might expect. Moreover, as the tip of the bolt bit home, sinking deep into the wood, a shower of splinters rained out to either side. And the blow had imparted to the post a distinct wobble. Her face betrayed no surprise, but her almond-shaped eyes lingered on me assessingly as she returned my instrument.

Splash, too, had been full of surprises. Once we had departed from Ki-bodey, the girl had shucked her boots and headed into the wilderness unshod. As a therianthrope, she was the master of her own body and could grow thick pads on the soles of her feet. With her hair lashed into a rough ponytail, I noted another startling transformation as she marched ahead of me. Over time, the girl's already pointed ears had drifted gradually upward, rising to rest atop her crown. By then, they were covered by a velvety reddish fur tipped in black. Though generally front facing, they swiveled about from time to time.

So merrily we marched along, the three without their master having become, for the nonce, four without their *masters*.

Suddenly, from up ahead, the Elven girl stilled. Her hand came up signaling for us to halt and be silent. I repeated the gesture for those to the rear, whose shuffling strides soon ceased. I heard the twittering warble of finches in the distance, underscored by the squabbling of jays. The woodland seemed peaceful. And yet our guide stood motionless as she scented the breeze. It could have been the angle, but it looked as though her muzzle had elongated somewhat.

It flitted by so fast I could scarcely discern its form ere it was gone.

Its wings made a low buzzing hum as it squirmed through the air to disappear into the trees on our left. As quick as thought, Splash nocked an arrow and sent it whizzing after. With a wet scrunching sound, the buzzing abruptly ceased. Cautiously, she ducked beneath a protruding branch and stepped beyond my line of sight. By the time I'd crept up and navigated the same obstacle, I spied the girl about six paces ahead, examining her kill.

Skewered to the bole of a linden tree was the carcass of a horrid creature I'd once heard described by Master Pete. It was a black thing about as big as a good-sized bird, but there the similarities ceased. It had a single bulbous eye that put me in mind of a bug's. And rather than feathers, its skin was a glossy membrane stretched over a framework of skeletal ridges. Four bat wings protruded from its shoulders. And from behind, it trailed a whip-like tail sporting a barb like an arrowhead midway along its length. This member still twitched and spasmed as a grayish-white fluid oozed down from its side. This frothed and sizzled on meeting the open air, eventually hardening and darkening to the yellow-brown of amber.

"I must have nicked one of his venom sacs," the Elven girl remarked as I approached.

"Is that a Cyclochiroptean?" Roy asked, stalking up from behind us.

"We call them *waminbodocha*," she replied. "But yes. These one-eyed bat things are fairly recent. They're spreading like a wildfire. And where there's one, there are bound to be others. I think we need to backtrack a bit and bypass this valley altogether. Once I've delivered you to the border, I'll report this sighting and we'll send in some specialists to purge the cluster."

"The tail is a lot like a shtingray," said Sholeena, leaning in to inspect it.

"Our *puachoqua* have noted that resemblance. And though the venom differs, it's said to be well nigh as painful."

"Well, lead on, then." I said. "I don't fancy making camp near a nest of *those* things."

And off we went, retracing our steps. The cyclos had put us another day behind. But apart from the silent urge that drove us from within, we had no particular schedule to keep. As Roy was fond of saying: 'Prudence is the better part of wisdom.'

It was several more days before we gained the high south road, or rather, the tangled mess that remained of it.

***

"So how much father do you reckon it is to the next marker, Roy?"

We were huddled around my cousin at the first camp we had made since achieving the roadway east. Just as Splash had warned, the road was in a dismal state of disrepair. It was deeply rutted and overgrown, and in places had washed away entirely. Still, it lay fairly straight and true and should run all the way to the border with Eagle's Keep. Royland had once again unrolled his scarf and was puzzling over it in the morning light.

"Well," he said with some reluctance, "It's a knit stitch and three pearl stitches farther on. If this is to scale, that's about seven miles, as near as I can tell. This marker is smaller than the previous two, and after that, the terrain gets all wonky."

"Do you recognize any landmarks down here?" he asked of our guide.

"Nothing leaps out at me," replied Splash. "I think I see trees and rivers and such, but it doesn't jibe with anything I've seen on my patrols."

"There's another little one on the edge down here," put in Sholeena.

"That's no help," said Roy. "It's way on the other side and many leagues away. We'll just have to see what's there. Perhaps the message will clarify what comes next."

My cousin stepped off to retrieve his waterskin. As he hoisted it up and drank, Sholeena began fiddling with the scarf. As Royland strode back over, annoyance was evident on his face. He came up short when he understood what she was doing. The girl had folded the scarf over on itself so that the two small red dots touched. They combined to form a full-sized mark. Moreover, the terrain features matched up rather convincingly.

"Oh. I see it now," exclaimed Splash. "That must be the Singing Green Mountain up ahead and the road continuing past."

The scarf was now shaped like the letter 'L' just as our southward trek had turned east. Roy quickly located a second pair of smaller dots. The first was just past Eagle's Keep, and another was on the opposite edge farther on. Shouldering Sholeena aside, Roy made another fold, and the 'map' reversed yet again to stretch southward once more.

"Well spotted, Sho," I praised. "You just cut leagues off our journey.

"Eight," declared Royland. "Only eight more markers to go then."

Poking him gently in the ribs, I gained Royland's attention and steered him aside by his elbow. All the while, he kept trying to stare back at the new route the folds in his garment revealed.

"What?" he snapped when I shook him.

"You need to show Sholeena more respect, cousin."

"She obviously had a good idea," he begrudgingly returned.

"Then you should say so. Everyone deserves some encouragement. It's only civil."

"State the obvious. Got it," he said absently. "It fascinates me how Gretta could have double reverse-knitted an entire map from memory alone. Forgive me if I seem a bit distracted."

"It *is* rather astonishing," I admitted. "It puts me in mind of something *you* might do if you were so inclined. You're a genius, Roy. Maybe you have that in common with your grandmother. But sometimes you treat people as if they don't matter. Intelligence doesn't make up for poor manners, nor does it negate the need for empathy for others."

"She just saw it differently and made a lucky connection."

"Isn't that what intelligence is? The ability to recognize patterns and make leaps of logic? Luck may have played a part in it, but just look at how quickly she picks up languages."

I turned to indicate where the girl stood chattering away with Splash in Elven.

"I admit I was a mite hesitant for Sho to come with us, but I'm beginning to think we're very lucky to have her here. Just promise me you'll try to be nicer toward her."

"I'll... try" said my cousin.

I gave this reluctant declaration good odds of success. For I'd never known Royland to fail at anything he honestly attempted.

We set off with high hopes of reaching the next marker by mid-day. Little did we suspect the difficulties that lay ahead. The mountain loomed, but seemed to draw no nearer despite our steadfast and vigorous pace. It was several hours later when we noted a change in the land about us. The vegetation was defoliated and barren. My vertiginous sense throbbed in sympathy with the surrounding denuded plants, each of which sported numerous stinging cuts. Parched by the sun's radiance, partial leaves skittered along the ground, some still attached to their withered stems. It was as though autumn had come full on, heralded by madmen with machetes. I was the first to give voice to the dread that slowed our faltering steps.

"What could have done all this?"

Surveying her surroundings, our guide cast about, her lips forming a tight line. She strode over to a wounded clump of ivy clinging to a tree nearby. Fishing about in it, she drew forth a small brownish, papery lump and examined it closely. Her fox ears flattened as she grimaced.

"Blade moths," she declared. "Three days hatched is my best guess."

"Can they hurt us?" asked Sholeena, going a bit green.

"Oh yes," said Splash. "They're a most pernicious blight. Keep your eyes on the horizon upwind of us. When swarming, they go where the wind carries them. Also, watch for places to shelter, caves and the like, if there are any to be had. You don't want to be caught out in the open if any should fall upon us."

Having issued us this caution, she urged us to resume our march. The roadway proved wide enough to accommodate two abreast. Splash and I struck out in the lead with Roy and Sholeena close upon our heels. As instructed, I kept a wary eye to the north from which wafted what wind there was.

Nary a crevice, gully or cave did we spy before all went grievously amiss. The open ground o'er which we trod stretched ever onward before us. It was thus with no small amount of trepidation that we received Royland's grim news.

"To the north!" he shouted. "A dark cloud arises!"

Swiftly facing about, I strained to confirm my cousin's sighting. As usual, he was correct.

"Remain very still," Splash advised. "They might pass us over."

"And you might want to rethink your color scheme," she added to Sholeena. "Green attracts them."

With a grim nod and a toss of her head, the wide-eyed Paluda girl shifted her hue to an angry red. Roy might stand a chance at convincing some moths to move away. As a therianthrope, Splash had informed us she could toughen her skin to almost that of a rhino. But I didn't like my own chances within a swarm of the destructive pests. Nor would mastery over vegetation provide me with any kind of effective barrier. Thinking quickly, I assumed my earth-shifting stance.

"Terram aratro!" I intoned.

Just as with the grave site back at Gentle Repose, I felt a great strain in my lower back and loins. The firmly packed earth of the old road was even harder to penetrate, but desperation now drove my effort. A droning sound arose. The cloud from the north had blackened half the sky and continued in its swift advance. When its shadow fell over us, there was a deep trench about eight feet in length with mounds of loose earth on either side. It would have to do. I crawled in, exhausted and spent.

Roy leapt down, and Sholeena squeezed in between us. Last to enter was our guide.

"We need some sort of lid," hollered Roy as the humming sound increased.

Rooting about in my Bob, I pulled out the canvas from one of our tents. Working in concert, we stretched it open above our heads and scrambled to hold it fast about the edges of our trench. I think we managed it only just in time because 'twas then the impacts began. It was like a hard, pelting rain. I could feel it through the canvas where it bulged above my head. A weight pressed down as even more amassed.

Next, and to my horror, I began to see many slits of light pierce our impromptu barrier. The canvas was being rent and slashed by these terrible creatures! Had I just dug my own grave? Here in this darkened trench, would we suffer a painful death from a thousand cuts? I silently pleaded with the creator above to spare me from such a horrific demise. And I recalled with better appreciation what Sir Fletcher had once told me. There are no atheists in foxholes. But even as I resigned myself and prayed my soul was ready for redemption, my cousin offered a ray of hope.

"Repellere insectorum!" he all but shouted in my ear, and his magic streamed upward *en masse*.

The weight on the canvas abated, and the impacts became much less frequent. I could tell, however, that this reprieve was but temporary. For no sooner was our burden lifted than still more bugs arrived to cluster and congregate on the depressingly thin ceiling above. I felt a sharp stab in my scalp where it pressed against the canvas, and a thin trail of blood dribbled down into my eye.

Grimacing and fervently repeating his mantra, Roy then did the most heroic thing I had ever seen him do. Throwing his leg atop the lip of the trench, he pressed past us and rolled out from under our cover. The rest of us scrambled to reseal the breach even as I mourned my poor, soon-to-be deceased cousin. Over the ear-piercing hum that had come to dominate our darkened world, I heard his defiant cry.

"Calidus ignis ardentis!"

And just as when the sun came peeping out from behind a cloud, a ruddy light flared into being, painting our tattered canvas barrier in all shades of orange. The weight pressing down on us lifted once again, and still more of this rosy salvation shone forth. It was then a great grinding, popping sound began. It buzzed like the tormented screams of the damned. Cautiously I peered without, enthralled.

And there stood Royland beneath the largest ball of magic flame I'd yet seen him produce. It hovered there like the sun. And into this pulsing, angry ball of fire, the blade moths swirled and drifted. A tornado of such whirled into it to be scorched and ejected. Where this vortex of death touched the sphere, brief yellow flashes of light danced on its surface to the accompaniment of buzzing pops.

I stared in wonderment as the minutes dragged on. My cousin used his gift to funnel the wretched bugs to their fiery doom as the sky to the north cleared and brightened. Ever southward, the dark cloud drifted. When at last all was clear above, three of us emerged from our huddle beneath the battered remnants of canvas. There stood Roy, covered in minor cuts and abrasions but smiling, nonetheless. His patchwork cloak hung shamefully down over one shoulder, its tattered remains riddled and rent. He took one look down at me, shrugged and said: 'I guess we're gonna need a new tent.'

I hugged my cousin. As he squirmed and withdrew, his gladsome grin gave way to a scowling pout. With the toe of his boot, he scuffed at the pile of insects he had slain. I could tell it was hard on Royland. He had a great empathy for bugs. Under more ordinary circumstances, one could truly assert he would never hurt a fly.

***

It took us a while to repair the road I had ruined and start back on our way. It was therefore nearly nightfall when we arrived at the base of the mountain. Up to this point the road (what remained of it) had run arrow straight, but now it curved off to the south to detour around. We sighted many secure spots to set up camp and investigated several caves where we could find cover should this be required again. We chose a spot near one of these we found to be unclaimed. Having only the one tent, it was decided that two would sleep while the other two remained alert. It was to be me and Splash standing the first watch.

Royland was disgruntled. He had wanted to seek his grandparents' message straight away. But since the hour was late, and we needed to establish a secure camp before the fall of night, we had dissuaded him from this. He was, at present. stewing in the tent and preparing to set out at first light. Mayhap daybreak would see my cousin properly gruntled once more.

"Well, that was an exciting day's journey," I declared. "It'll take more than a few bugs to deter the likes of us."

"I don't know, Lucas," grumbled Sholeena. "If it's all the same to you, I'm going to go ahead and count that as one of the 'grim horrors' that shall beset the three. I can scarcely wait to get all those out of the way."

141

And with a broad yawn, she wished us a peaceful watch and slipped into the tent to join Royland.

Count on Sholeena to find the humor in such a situation. Her quip, however, reignited my musings on the matter of the prophecy. It had indeed promised us grim horrors. We were undoubtedly being 'guided by flames' and were inarguably 'neath the southern skies.' But since we hadn't yet wallowed in a murky swamp, did that mean the three of us were safe until after such a time? Hmmm. Still, it would be best not to take any chances. Prophecies could be tricky, as the Brubakers had found to their detriment. And this one still had Suzie as a backup.

My magic had mostly recovered thanks to the thriving plant life all around. In that barren strip that had been mutilated by the moths, there had been little to work with. But as we traveled east, we passed at last from out of the blighted area. And here, amid abundant greenery, my wand had worked its magic. Before times, I could draw the life force from a plant to restore my magic center. But thanks to my fey-touched talisman, I could now connect to the intricate network of roots below. It was slow and fussy work, requiring great concentration. But I was able to draw a trickle of energy from the forest as a whole. No single plant need suffer to restore my strength. Still, I was loath to use this gift very often. I could sense the health of the land, and overall, it wasn't ideal. The Bright One had spoken truly when she'd said the land might be failing.

I settled with my back to the fire so as not to blind myself to any dangers which might lurk. My darksight was active, and my wakefulness spell had been cast. I doubt the fox-shifting elf sitting nearby thought I'd be any good as a sentry. Or perhaps as a mage she had a mind open to the possibilities.

"I met her once," said Splash, breaking my reverie.

She too was seated but faced in the other direction. Between us, we commanded a considerable view all around.

"Who?" I asked.

"Your grandmother. Abigail. She was a nasty piece of work. You're not like her at all."

I'd almost forgotten how old the elves were, even the youngest of them. It figured if the 'girl' had apprenticed at Conclave thirty years ago, then she may have known Grandma Abbey. I tried to recall her, but all that came to mind were some of her house mates from House Owl, none of whom were elves. No. Splash had lived at Julia's estate up on the hill. As an apprentice, it was unlikely she had mingled much with the aspirant journeymen.

"Thanks. I think."

"Why do they call it the singing green mountain?" I mused aloud. "I mean, I get the green part. It's well forested all the way up to the tree line. But singing? Unlikely."

After a minute, my companion spoke.

"Not many can hear it," she said softly.

"Can you?"

There was a pause.

"It's quiet now. But when I adjust my ears, I can sometimes make out a low rumble in a tone so deep that humans and even the elves cannot perceive it."

"Of what does he sing?"

"That, I cannot say. Others hear it more clearly. It is said that the oreads speak directly to the heart of the listener. As dryads are to trees, oreads are to the mountains. Only rarely does one reveal his aspect, but you'd better pay heed when one does. They speak of the turning of the world, of the grinding plates that Gaia set into motion long ago. These collide with one another, raise mountains and sometimes cause great upheavals ere they settle.

"It requires much patience to speak to an oread and listen for his reply. I understand the very prophecy you follow took several years to reveal itself in full. Stone is patient, and slow to speak, but it does so from the accumulated wisdom of many centuries."

I had encountered some of this in my studies of geomancy, but ne'er had I heard it expressed with such passion. Though outwardly vigilant, I found I'd been lulled into a meditative state by the woman's words. And there, within my inner garden atop my hill of earth, I heard it.

It wasn't a sound I could properly describe. It was more a vibration I could feel deep within my bones. And it occurred to me at once that I wasn't hearing an oread at all. This heartfelt rumble was coming from within. If the oread was singing, my little hill was singing back! It sang not in words I could follow. It rumbled and growled and roared. I quivered atop it caught helplessly in the throes of this speech that was not.

I sped up my breathing to extricate myself from the disturbing meditation. But I soon found myself drawn back down. My little hillock would have its say. As the ground atop my inner hill twisted and scraped and swirled, flinty chips flaked off to reveal a rugged face. Its eyes rolled about, finally fastening on me as I quivered there. Its lips parted, and a single word rang forth.

"Brother," it rumbled before the eyes fell closed and the face crumbled away.

I found myself once again seated with my back to the fire. Splash was squatting down before me, peering into my eyes.

"Is ought amiss?" she whispered urgently.

"I... thought I heard something," I whispered in return. "I'll be fine."

After a time, the shifter girl resettled, and we silently resumed our watch.

***

The sky was barely brightening when Royland and Sholeena roused us from our slumber. Well, it was chiefly Roy, eager to be off. The sun was not evident as we lay in the mountain's shadow. Blearily, I rubbed my eyes and began making ready for the day. Last night's impromptu meditation seemed but a dream, and a most disturbing one at that. Had that really happened? Harboring some apprehension, I decided to take a look within.

144

There was my tranquil green field. To one side stood the little hillock representing my earth affinity. No strange face marred its rugged uniformity, and no cryptic words did it utter. All was peaceful. But what was this? At the field's far end, I spied activity. Not content to relinquish his nighttime vigil, the scarecrow stalked among a cluster of vines I had not grown. I adjusted my perspective, drawing nearer.

"Hello, he who shall remain nameless until such time as he agrees to behave properly," I greeted him.

The scarecrow looked up and scowled at me. Then he shrugged and returned to his digging. What was that long pole he held in his stick-like hands? How had he manifested such an item? I moved closer still, willing the vines to part, but they resisted. How was that possible?

"Hey. I'm talking to you. What's that you're doing over there?" I shouted.

The nameless scarecrow looked up at me once again, smiling.

"Farming," he said.

I examined the nearest vines and verified they were not under my control.

"Well, you need to stop that. Your nighttime duties are done. Go back to sleep and leave off whatever *this* is."

Still smiling, he brought the pole upright. It was topped with a curving steel blade. It was a harvesting scythe he had somehow managed to manifest! He swung it downward in a long, sweeping arc. Then he bent and began grubbing about on the ground. When he stood, he held a severed vine oozing dark fluid.

"Thirsty," he said. "Hungry *and* thirsty."

With that, he brought the fruit of his labor up to his lips and sent it wriggling down his throat.

"*I'll* show you thirsty," I declared sternly.

Usually, I controlled the reality within my own inner realm. It was, after all, a space created and governed by my imagination. Perhaps a mage's magic center was real enough, but how he envisioned it set the tone for what happened there. My self-image here included clothing and most of the items I carried in reality. Over time, I had discovered I could manifest other simple items at need.

This time, I desired something specific. I halted the meditation. Returning to my bedside and locating my fey wand, I gripped it tightly before easing back within. My homunculus awaited me there amid his patch of rebellious vegetation. Willing the wand to life, I plunged a vine-like root into the 'ground' at my feet. I then began absorbing all the energy from out of my metaphorical field.

For a miracle, it worked.

The defiant weeds soon began to wither and shrivel for lack of any sustaining force. When they'd all been purged, I returned the energy. I tested raising up new vines, and all heeded my will.

If a canvas sack with eye holes could pout, I was now looking at it. With a vague shimmering, the scarecrow vanished back to whatever abyss he haunted during the daytime hours, and I was left alone. Bravo Lucas, I thought. You're still the master of your own imagination. Bully for you.

I reemerged to find my cousin holding the tent flap open and peering within.

"Get up lazy-bones," he admonished me. "We're burning precious daylight. What's keeping you?"

"I was just doing a little pruning on my inner landscape," I returned. "Nothing to concern yourself over."

I really should have confided in Roy. I should have told him of the disturbing mess that had become my inner life. But he had enough on his mind of late, having just nearly died and all. Besides, it had been more than a month and a half since I'd begun having trouble with my homunculus. Taming it was a journeyman's first task, and it was supposed to be a simple one.

Quite frankly, it was getting a bit embarrassing. The others needed to know they could depend on me.

"I'll be right out."

As I dressed and made ready, the doubts continued to nag at me. I was a good person; wasn't I? Why then was this task so difficult? Was I, deep down, so stubborn and intractable? Could Roy have meant it when he claimed my dangerous obsessions 'took the cake'? Was he right?

***

We attended to our morning ablutions, packed our gear, and struck the camp. Rather than returning directly to the roadside, we took some time to look around. With magesight, we surveyed our surroundings, alert for the telltale glimmer of enchantment. It was a tiresome couple of hours as we slowly made our way around the base of the peak, casting all about.

"Here's something," said Sholeena.

But it turned out to be only a broken spear that lay discarded by the roadside. The shaft was ensorcelled with a hardening spell which had obviously proven insufficient. Whatever mishap had befallen its owner was now lost in the mists of time. Clearly, there was a story here. But it wasn't our story, so we moved on.

"Over here," shouted Royland excitedly.

I stumbled through the underbrush to arrive at my cousin's side. He was at the base of a cliff face, examining some marks that had been chiseled into the stone. 'H.C.B.' they read. And sure enough, just below these markings lay an old enchantment, the nature of which was familiar. As the others gathered near, I used my wand to clear a space before it. The ground flattened somewhat, and the vegetation curled back to make way as best it could.

"What's 'H.C.B?' asked Sholeena.

"It's my grandsire's monogram," replied Royland. "It stands for Hans Christian Brubaker."

"Let's activate the enchantment then," said Splash. "I must confess, I'm eager to see how these 'marker' spells work."

We shucked our packs and made ourselves comfortable as Royland prepared his fire spell.

"What's a mono-gram?" asked Sholeena, elbowing me gently in the ribs.

"It's the first letters of each of one's names," I answered.

"What does the middle one mean?"

"It's his Christian name."

"I know it's 'Christian,' but what does it *mean*?"

"No. I mean, 'Christian' is his middle name. Don't your people have such?"

"No. We don't need any," she said with a slight frown. "My mother's name is 'Blorla,' and my father was 'Fargal,' so I'm just Sholeena Blorlafargalish. See? Simple. Not like you people and your fancy ways."

It was useful information. I'd have to remember this tradition of appending a truncated family tree to one's name if ever I should meet another Paluda.

"Hush now," said Splash. "I think he's ready."

Royland stood staring at us, demanding our attention. Once we'd quieted, he invoked the flame. The familiar mist drifted down from the engraved letters, and we were once again confronted by the smiling face of Hans.

"I *do* hope you find *this* one," he began, waggling his eyebrows up and down. "I know I said the next would be at Eagle's Keep. But Gretta and I just couldn't wait to share the news."

The man's jubilant expression deepened as he leaned in closer, grinning from ear to ear.

"Gretta is with child!" he declared. "After we return to Conclave, our Robert shall have a baby brother or sister. The blessed event is still about six or seven months off, as near as we can tell. Plenty of time to complete our mission before Gretta grows too gravid to navigate the spire."

"Speaking of that," said the man in a more sober tone, "the enchantment of Rapunzel's braid is complete. It makes an ideal implement for climbing. Gretta and I tested it on this very cliff face. At our command, it snakes upward, fastens itself securely, then coils tight, drawing us up after. Then it flips end over end to repeat the performance.

"It will require some further practice, but with the aid of this enchanted artifact, we shall doubtless arrive atop the spire fresh and ready to confront the demon who rules over it.

"That's all for now. You'll hear from us again at Eagle's Keep. Till then, may the roads rise up to greet your feet and the wind be ever at your back."

Royland sat down, stunned by the news he may have an aunt or uncle he had never known. His flaming sphere fizzled and disappeared with a faint popping sound. I knew that concern for the child's fate was even now sweeping through my cousin's startled mind. Had the child survived, it would be twenty-something years old by now, more like an elder sibling than an uncle or an aunt.

My cousin wasn't one to weep, instead becoming sulky and withdrawn. Over the years of our association, I'd come to recognize the subtle signs which signaled his sorrow. These were all now painfully evident as Roy sat staring sightlessly at the base of the bluff. He didn't seek to be consoled, for such was not his way. But one certainty leapt to the forefront of my thoughts as I watched him wrestle his demons. Fairy king or no, I wouldn't want to be Orenob when next my cousin came to call.

"Seven," said Royland with savage indifference. "Just seven more markers to go. And then shall come a reckoning."

***

The four of us leaned back from our empty tin plates. This was to be our final meal within the borders of fair Lorédon and the last night we would spend with Splash. Our guide had informed us that the border lay only a few miles down the road. I released a belch as quietly as I could.

Sholeena stared over and grinned. The Paluda girl made no such pretense of politeness when seeking gastronomic relief. She even made a game of it, proudly loosing such guttural utterances with gusto. Back at Conclave, Sholeena had been so unsure of herself. Troubles with language and societal norms had tormented her and made her timid. But here in the wilderness and among friends, the girl had relaxed, and her confidence was growing by the day. I liked this more carefree Sholeena, but hoped she would soon learn to temper her tendency toward the gauche with a more ladylike behavior.

"So, can we expect guards at the border?" asked Royland.

"We do have some scouts picketed hereabouts," answered Splash, "but I doubt you'll encounter any. The soldiers of the south have better things to do than collecting tariffs. Besides, the merchants haven't moved along this road for decades. My people have likely noted our presence already. The *tammanegha* of the *watheesh* are only seen when they wish to be. I doubt even *I* could sneak up on one."

"No. I think I can safely leave you here. I must return to my master. I am certain he is missing my assistance in keeping the southern reaches clear."

"Well, *we'll* certainly miss your guidance," said Roy, filling the awkward silence that had descended. "Please convey our thanks and best wishes to your master."

"At times like this," I began hesitantly, "it is customary among my people to make a parting gift; something to commemorate the time we spent together. I've not known you overlong, but one thing I will remember is your amazing skill with archery."

From within my cloak, I drew forth the small bundle I'd prepared.

"These are bowstrings I fashioned with my own hand from some linen I grew and spun. You'll find them very difficult to break. They have to be to stand up to the tension of my crossbow. May they serve you well and deliver your arrows straight and true."

I thought it a rather eloquent gesture, but Sholeena was not to be outdone.

"I made you something too," she announced.

So saying, she stood and retrieved a small waterskin from her pack. It was a typical bladder made of sheep or goat hide with a tote string and a stopper.

"It refills itself as you walk along," declared the grinning Paluda.

Inspecting it with a more critical eye, I caught the faint glimmer of enchantment that surrounded it.

"Where does the water come from?" I asked.

"There's water hiding in the air all around us," said Sholeena with an upturned palm. "Where do you think rain comes from?"

Splash looked honored indeed. She inclined her head and accepted.

"Made it yourself?" Roy muttered. "I take this to mean you enchanted it. And when, pray tell, did you learn to do that?"

"My good friend, *Royland*, taught me," she said, walking over to hover above his shoulder. "Now Bob's *my* uncle too!"

Royland groaned.

"I implore you," he said. "Do not misinform our master that I'm instructing others in the arcane arts."

"It'll be our secret," said Sho.

Then, quite unexpectedly, she flung her arms around his neck, ambushing him with an affectionate Paluda hug from behind.

It was a moment or two before I could again speak in a steady voice.

"Don't worry, Roy," I added. "I once heard your father remark that three people can keep a secret perfectly well..."

It hung there for Roy to finish for himself.

"... if two of them are dead," he avowed. "Yes. I know. Let's hope it doesn't come down to that."

That was the last we saw of Splash. Not one for long goodbyes, she gathered her few belongings and departed in the night. I'm pretty sure we left her with the impression that humans are a bit mad. But I like to think we'd acquitted ourselves fairly well on the road thus far.

CHAPTER SEVEN

The Chirurgeon

"Is there no balm in Gilead? Is there
no physician there?"

~ Jeremiah CH 8 v 22 ~

We emerged from the forest to find the rolling plains stretching out before us. We needed no marker stone to inform us we were entering a new duchy. Yet there it stood, just to the right of the road. Its pointed pyramidical cap proudly proclaimed the precise point of demarcation. The heavy obelisk of gray stone was a familiar sight throughout the realm of Osten. Such were set and maintained along the borders by his majesty's adjudicators and survey teams. It was considered a high crime to move or deface one.

No. Where the forest ended began a field of stumps running north to south. The ambitious woodcutters of Eagle's Keep had harvested the trees for timber right up to their duchy's edge. But they dared not step foot within the lands claimed and cultivated by the elves. So the border was plainly evident where the linden forest sharply ceased.

The road continued on, running slightly uphill. And in the distance, squatting atop the rise, we spied a lone tower belching smoke into the overcast autumn sky.

We'd yet to break our fast, hoping to do so at the first inne or accommodating farmhouse we might find within the civilized lands which lay ahead. So we marched up the rise toward the lonely tower, uncertain of what welcome it might provide for weary travelers.

Though the landscape was bleak, the increased visibility was comforting. For it left no place for would-be assailants to lurk. I let my shoulders relax and shortened the cord on my belt. The comforting weight of the crossbow now rested against my right thigh opposite the case of bolts lashed to my left. Roy led the way, his lanky strides setting a slow and steady pace. I strolled after with Sholeena shuffling along by my side.

"Hail the tower!" shouted Roy as we crested the rise.

On receiving no immediate reply, Roy moved up to the stout, iron-banded door and rapped upon it.

It was several moments before the door creaked partway open, preceded by a clunking sound.

He was a burly man with a short scraggly beard wearing a chain mail shirt that appeared to have been hastily donned. His thumbs were hooked in his broad belt, on which was secured the haft of a heavy flail. Its spiked iron head hung from a short chain and rested against his chausses. He cocked his head to one side and looked us up and down.

"Travelers from the Elven lands by the look of ya," he said by way of greeting. "But yer ears be rounded proper. What's your business in the E.K. then?"

"You have the right of it, sergeant. We are recently arrived from Lorédon. We are students there. Our master granted us leave to travel and see some of the world before resuming our studies. I am Royland Wagge. This is my cousin, Lucas, and the young lady is Sholeena."

I had to hand it to Roy for recognizing the rank insignia. I confess I didn't know what those squiggles meant. They all looked quite similar to me.

"Did you hear that, Brian?" said the sergeant. "They're here for a vacation. Oh, that's rich."

The door opened wider to reveal another man. He was leaner and had the slack-jawed look I'd come to associate with the dimwitted. But the man held a fully drawn crossbow at the ready, rendering rather moot the precise status of his intellect. Brian smiled with half his face.

"Scholars, then, are you?" continued the first man. "And what, pray tell, do you study?"

Roy glanced back at us before answering.

"Magic," said Roy, cocking his brow. "We are three journeyman mages come to pay our respects to the duke and to visit with our brethren stationed at his castle. We thought we might trouble you to share news of the road ahead and aught you might know of the dangers thereon."

My cousin's revelation hung there before the astonished men. The laughter had fled their faces and the sergeant's hand hovered nearer to his weapon. I'd had my doubts about Royland as our spokesperson, but he was doing surprisingly well. Using his talent to read people, Roy was playing them like a fish on a line. I wondered how long he could keep it up. I reckoned my cousin had nearly used up his entire daily allotment of words.

"I take it you can prove what you say?"

"I have letters of introduction from our master. But these are sealed missives to be presented at Eagle's Keep itself. Would a demonstration of our magic suffice, sergeant...?"

"Von Holstein. Thaddeus Von Holstein," he grunted. "And this is my corporal, Brian Pendleton. At ease, corporal. Sure. Show us some magic, then."

Roy turned and stalked off about ten paces. Would he conjure another ball of flame? That was one of the flashier spells he knew. But no. I soon saw Roy settle into his familiar old shielding stance.

"I stand ready," said Roy. "If you will order the good corporal to loose a bolt from his crossbow at me, I will show you how such an attack is quite useless against mages of Osten."

That even had a bit of dramatic flair. Good for him. I wasn't worried in the least that my cousin might be injured. Back in our practice yard at Fowler Ranch, I must have tried a thousand times to penetrate Royland's blue kinetic shield. It wasn't until I'd gotten my witchwood bow that my efforts had met with any success. Even then, it was a contest.

At the sergeant's nod, Brian loosed.

In that instant, the dim blue circular disc snapped into existence. The bolt halted in mid flight and fell softly to the ground at my cousin's feet.

After that, the two men became most accommodating. They told us about the surroundings and even invited us inside to share a modest meal with them. Thaddeus assured us there was no inne or settlement within easy walking distance. Most of those who had populated the duchy's western border had fled north long ago, abandoning their fields and tenancies.

The two had been sent to man this remote outpost far from the center of things, and only rarely saw another human soul. The meal was filling but basic, consisting chiefly of field rations. Since the war had depopulated the area, there was precious little else to be had. We soon bade the two watchmen farewell and traipsed on in the mid-morning light. Roy hoped to reach civilization as soon as possible. Camping on the open plains was dangerous this far south.

***

For three days and two nights, we trudged wearily onward through the desolate countryside of E.K. Whereas in Lorédon the land had been clearly ailing, in these human lands, bereft of the caring ministrations of the elves, the landscape had grown downright dreary. The western plains had given way to brushy scrubland that stretched eastward as far as the eye could see. At least we had encountered no major threats thus far. It was my understanding that Duke Gaulle maintained a network of

156

outposts, patrols and pickets along the southern border to thwart any obvious attempt at incursion.

Although the border was well-patrolled, no defense was perfect. And over the years, the farmers and other inhabitants of the region had suffered enough hardships and setbacks to send them fleeing north toward safety. We had passed more than one abandoned farmstead on our trek and had even made camp at several of them. It was sad to see the once-productive fields lying fallow and given over to scrubby growth.

It was toward another abandoned farmhouse we were even now making our way. Perhaps it would prove suitable for this evening's rest. With my wand, I was parting the weeds of the overgrown lane leading up to the weather-beaten shack.

"I shpy with my little eye, something that starts with 'H,'" prompted Sholeena.

The game had been going on for some time now. We found it kept the Paluda girl distracted from our miserable march and provided an acceptable alternative to her moping.

"Is it that hawk circling above the barn?" Roy promptly inquired.

"Yes," she grumbled dejectedly. "I shwear you must be cheating somehow. Your turn then."

But before my cousin could offer one of his offbeat brainteasers, there was a disturbance to the left of the overgrown lane. On hearing the rustling sound so close by, I hastily holstered my wand and scrambled for my crossbow. Alas, before I could ready it, the creature was upon me.

It was hairy and brown and stood nearly as tall as my waist. With its head held low to the ground, it rushed me from out of the weeds. I felt the impact like a tree feels an axe, both shins flaring in twin points of pain. My legs flew back, and I sprawled atop the creature. It bucked and heaved. I felt a stabbing pain in my thigh, and a queasy feeling overtook me as I was hurled from off the creature's back to lie battered upon the ground.

It turned, snorted, and pawed at the earth in preparation for another run at me. Still in a daze, I stared up at the creature from where I lay amid the broken weeds. My muscles tensed as I prepared to make a desperate roll to the side. But this would be difficult, for I could no longer move my right leg. I saw my death approaching on cloven hooves.

Then suddenly, Sholeena's knife embedded itself to the hilt in the creature's left eye, even as I heard my cousin cry: 'gloriabitur securis!'

The pig managed a high-pitched squeal that ended in a gurgling squawk as Roy's force axe spell lopped off its head. Momentum carried the beast still kicking to within arm's reach ere it collapsed and skidded to a stop, disgorging a jet of crimson splatter upon me and all the surrounding soil.

I was still gathering my wits when Sholeena fell upon me. She was turning me over and pressing something hard against my thigh. Pain erupted from that spot, which had been numb until but a moment before.

"We must stop the bleeding," she shouted.

I felt sick.

My vision was blurring and my shallow breaths seemed insufficient for my body's demands.

And there was Roy's fuzzy outline, standing over me and handing Sho his belt.

"Not too tight," he cautioned as the darkness crept over him. "It needs to bleed a *little* lest it become infected."

"Get more rags. We need something to... "

***

A sharp bump jarred me awake. I felt the sun on my face and a scraping vibration scuffed at my shoulder blades. My right leg throbbed with a dull ache. As the cobwebs cleared from my thoughts, another bump made me wince in discomfort and caused my eyelids to flutter open. It occurred to me that my feet were higher than my head. Shouldn't it be the other way around? I was staring into a clear blue sky. I wanted to roll to my side, but my arms were lashed firmly to my sides.

"Wha...?" I croaked.

Immediately, the scraping ceased, and my legs were lowered to the level of my head. A shadow soon fell over me and the empty sky above was filled by the silhouette of a frowning Paluda face.

"He's awake," she announced.

"It's high time," said Roy.

"Wha...?" I repeated groggily.

"Water?" asked Sholeena.

At the mention of water, I was seized by a great thirst. My gummy tongue failed to salivate, and my head pounded in sympathy. I tried forming words with my parched lips but had to settle instead for an urgent nod. By this time, Roy had approached and stood staring down at me while Sholeena unstopped her waterskin.

I felt the dribble of cool relief on the back of my tongue. Then I was seized by a sudden coughing fit. However much it might seem a good idea, one oughtn't to inhale one's water. Too soon, Sholeena withdrew the welcome draught.

"You must take only small sips until you're stronger," she said.

My throat felt raw. Slowly, my last conscious moments paraded in bits and snatches through my befuddled mind.

"Was that a... pig?" I finally put forth.

"Indeed, it was, cousin," answered Roy. "Not your proudest moment. Despite our worry for you, Sholeena and I have already agreed that doesn't count as one of the 'grim horrors' that shall beset us."

Turning to Sho, he said, "Let's stop here for a bit and see about redressing that wound."

Sholeena loosed the ropes that bound me securely to the makeshift travois they'd created from our tent poles and canvas.

"Do you think you can sit up?" asked my cousin.

"Of course I can... "

But it was then a trembling shook me as another bout of dizziness descended. I felt weak, and the pounding in my head took on a new urgency.

And there was Sholeena, wrapping her arm about my shoulders and gently easing me upward.

"Slowly," she soothingly advised.

"Yes. Best to take things slow," added Roy. "You lost a lot of blood. Sholeena said it would be best to keep your feet elevated above your head and to cleanse the wound often lest it go septic."

Sholeena turned toward Royland, her frown deepening.

"Roy wanted to put maggots on you," she accused. "But I wouldn't let him."

"How... how long since the attack happened?" said I, taking care to speak clearly.

"It's been nearly three days, now," Royland supplied.

Standing was difficult. My right leg would bear no weight. But Royland helped me to my feet once I'd explained my predicament. I hadn't shat for days, and now that I was upright, I felt an urgent need. Roy helped me over to the side of the road where grew a sickly-looking tree. In truth, he half-carried me there. With my butt planted firmly against the bole of the magnolia, I loosed the pressure that had built up in my bowels while Roy stood nearby, studiously looking the other way.

I considered the ode that future bards might write of the epic battle. 'Twas by a mighty pig that Lucas the Just was laid low! The demon swine did best him after a fearsome struggle.' And had I actually died, I shuddered to think how the stonecutter at Conclave might have memorialized it on my marker. But wise folk knew that feral pigs were in some ways far worse than wild boars. A wild animal would usually shy away from the presence of humans. Formerly domesticated swine, however, had no such compunctions. In fact, in their tiny minds, they actually associated humans with food.

"Pulver in ventis," I incanted once I'd finished.

It was a dandy little spell Master Chadwick used to shed the mud from his boots back at Fowler Ranch. I frowned and repeated the incantation but couldn't seem to raise my magic. Growing agitated and grabbing up a handful of magnolia leaves, I tidied up as best I could in the old-fashioned manner. We made our way back to where Sholeena was establishing a temporary camp. My wand. I must find my wand. Roy eased me down onto the travois, and I lay there, panting.

"Do you feel strong enough to eat something?" asked the Paluda girl.

"Not yet," I replied, "but I'll take some more water if you please. Also, please fetch me my wand; I need to check on something."

As I slaked my thirst, one small sip at a time, Roy and Sholeena regaled me with recent events. In addition to the one I'd had the misfortune to stumble upon, there were several families of feral swine running about the abandoned farm. After my mishap, my two companions had barricaded themselves in the barn and seen to my care. By nightfall, a fever had set in and they feared moving me. Roy retrieved the beheaded swine and was pleased to find that Sholeena was a passable butcher. He slow-roasted what meat she could salvage using his magic flames, and the two had eaten 'high on the hog' ever since. They assured me they'd saved some prime cuts for when I'd recovered enough to enjoy them.

My friends had been sick with worry when I failed to regain my senses. Yesterday, when my fever finally broke, they had seen fit to strike out in search of a more civilized area. They hoped to find there a healer or proper physic. Taking turns at pulling my travois, it had been slow go.

It was patently obvious that I was in no fit shape to walk as yet. After this break, we would resume our trek with me playing the part of a helpless burden. But there was something I needed to check up on first. I told my companions I intended a meditation to renew my flagging strength. In truth, I feared something more sinister was afoot, but there was no use worrying them further just yet. Gripping my wand tightly, I envisioned my inner garden. The last thing I saw as my breathing deepened was the thought sheriff peering at me, his troubled brown eyes narrowed with suspicion.

Within, I found the chaos I had feared. Looking down from above, I could see my field was divided. At one end stalked the scarecrow. He had renewed his farming efforts in a far more ambitious manner than previously. His rebellious weeds now covered the entire field, save for a small stretch at its near end. The clear area was separated from the main field by two long ridges of stone that shouldered out from my hillock of earth. It was as though the little hill had sprouted arms which protectively embraced the remaining open swath. It was here I chose first to alight.

I climbed the rocky ridge to peer over at the doings of my errant homunculus. I was pleased to note that the leg I imagined for myself was healthy and able to bear my imaginary weight. I considered the hill, recalling that night under the singing green mountain. It had spoken. 'Brother,' it had said. Was it (he, it was definitely a 'he') speaking to the oread? Or was he referring to *me* as his brother? I'd never heard of anyone else having two affinities. Was it possible I had two homunculi as well? If so, it appeared they were working at cross purposes here.

"Thanks," I told my hillock, just in case. "I'll take it from here."

I slid down the ridge and struck out into the defiant field. I was soon face to face with my nemesis.

"I see you've been a busy little farmer," I bristled. "I believe I told you not to do this."

"True," he replied. "But I never agreed. What's more, you've left me in charge for a long time now. How do you like what I've done with the place?"

Something was different about him. It wasn't just the snark. I'd buy that as an echo of my own patterns of speech. No. It was something else. Then it hit me. The eyes. From his formerly hollow eye sockets, two human eyes glared out at me in challenge. I took a step back.

"Well, I've returned now," I said. "So you can just sod off. As to all this, you know I prefer a fallow field until such time as our magic is required. It's much more peaceful that way."

And, pointing my wand at the ground between us, I sent a root plunging into the field and set about absorbing all the magic sustaining the fickle flora. As before, the weeds withered and the scarecrow scowled. It took a bit more effort to sweep clean the entire field, but I continued until every last one of them was gone. Their master soon followed them into oblivion.

I returned to the world without, where my leg still hurt, and my shallow breathing still left me feeling woozy. With a feeble hand, I holstered my wand. When we set out once more, it was Sholeena who led the way and Roy who pulled the travois behind.

"You should try to rest, Lucas," said Sho. "Getting more sleep won't do you any harm."

If only she knew.

"I spy," said I, "with my little eye, something beginning with a 'C.'"

"Is it yet *another* cloud?" Roy dutifully asked.

"Yep," I replied as we bumped along. "Not much else to see from down here."

***

Thus, we wended our way eastward several more days. Thankfully, we were beset by no 'grim horrors' while I was indisposed. My two companions plodded along without complaint, but I knew the chore of hauling me along was wearisome. I used my wand at every opportunity to siphon a bit of life force from the surrounding plants. They had little to spare, but I judged my need sufficient. Although this restored my magic and eventually healed the minor bruises and abrasions I'd suffered, such transfers only slightly aided the more severe wound I'd taken to my thigh. The tusk had pierced me very nearly to the bone, and only time would mend it fully.

Nevertheless, by the third day, I struggled to my feet and attempted to walk on my own. With the aid of a long stick Roy had fashioned into a crutch, I hobbled along as best I could for part of each day. It was even slower than simply letting my friends drag me on the travois, but I needed to work my muscles and to begin rebuilding my strength. It was during one such episode that we encountered the hunters.

From the road to our rear came the sound of hoofbeats, heralding the arrival of fellow travelers. I turned about, leaning heavily upon my crutch. After a moment, I sighted two men. They rode sorrels and were armored in brigandine mail. I looked over at my cousin, who shrugged. From the look of them, they were either impoverished knights or the servants of a wealthy one. I was given little time to consider the matter as they cantered swiftly up the road, raising a cloud of dust behind.

"Clear the road. Make way!" one hollered on their fast approach.

We quickly complied and were standing on the berm below them as they drew abreast. The two were armed with sabers which remained thankfully sheathed at their belts. The red-haired one moved to the fore and squinted at us while his companion stood warily back.

"I see you bear arms," he said. "And one of you is wounded. Are you deserters, then?

Royland said nothing. I knew him to be focused on the men's intentions. And Sholeena had reverted to her former shy manner, standing well back to our rear. So it fell to me to make the introductions.

"Indeed not, good sir," I answered. "We are but travelers on our way to Eagle's Keep."

"And what is your business here, I wonder? There's a war on, you know. How came you to lurk upon this particular stretch of roadway?"

The man's flat, even tone bore no malice, but his choice of words certainly smacked of suspicion. As I opened my mouth to reply, he held up his hand. Making a peculiar gesture, he signaled to his confederate, who wheeled about and trotted back the way they'd come.

"No matter," said the first man. "Our master will soon arrive. Should he deign to have words with you; we'll sort out the truth of the matter. If not, you are to stand well clear of the road until our party passes."

That forestalled any further pleasantries. The man then sat his steed in silence, watching us closely and making no move to leave. Roy hovered close and whispered in my ear.

"He's not too fussed about us, cousin. He's just doing his job."

He could have fooled me. There was something vaguely threatening about the man's aura, and his unblinking stare was a tad intimidating. A few minutes later we heard voices of men conversing, the creak of leather and the clatter of steel as a column of men approached our position.

They were led by a knight. I knew him to be such a man by the heraldry he bore. Even from a distance, I could make out the simple pattern emblazoned on his shield. In the early days of heraldry, very simple bold shapes were painted onto a knight's shield. These could be easily recognized at great distances and thus served to identify him on the battlefield. As more complicated designs came into use, these simpler shapes were set apart in a separate class known as the 'honourable ordinaries.' One might think a more fanciful design would indicate a high station, but quite the reverse was often true. A simpler lay-out was indicative of a very old household of Fairglen. Such designs were jealously retained by their descendents.

Though not presently armored for battle, this fellow bore this shield like a badge of honor. Azure, a blaze Or; it was (a simple gold slash dividing a field of blue). His lance was held upright and the fine silks matching his heraldry proclaimed to all that this was a man of consequence. Supporting this proclamation was the mount he rode. He was a large, grey beast of a type I was to learn was bred in Freemark. The breed was called 'Andalusian' and he was stunning to behold. His equine majesty was matched only by the steed of the man's squire. For the lad that rode beside the knight sat upon a Friesian horse no less elegant.

The knight and his squire led a column of men. Some were mounted riders. There were also archers and other men afoot. These were followed by a train of pack animals laden with equipment of various sorts.

As this procession approached, I puzzled on its nature. It was too large to be a single lance and yet too small to be a proper company. And though the men we'd first seen wore military attire, many others did not. I reckoned there were perhaps a score of them. I stood by the roadside, puzzling thus with my fellow journeymen as the unusual entourage approached. It was customary for travelers to share news when they met on the road. Would they ride on by?

I'd been standing much too long. My leg felt as if it would let me down soon (and not gently either).

When the knight drew abreast, he signaled for a stop and turned to peer down at us. His retinue drew to a halt behind him. As the dust settled, a fat man on a donkey plodded up to join the knight. His plain brown robes and shaven tonsure marked him as belonging to some priestly order. He dismounted clumsily. The knight stepped down to join him with a grace that affirmed his well-muscled nature, as did the squire, with similar ease.

"You must be the three 'suspicious individuals' my outriders reported. You don't look to pose much of a threat. From your attire, you are no mere peasants. Moreover, your clothing has a distinctly foreign line to it. Tell me, from whence came you, and what is your purpose here at the war front?.

I could ask him the same. Moreover, I wanted to ask whether he was in the habit of accosting every traveler he came upon and rudely interrogating them. But a man like this would never suffer such a stain on his honor. He would be compelled to seek satisfaction. I knew well by now that 'satisfying his honor' would usually entail beating the tar out of the smart-mouthed journeyman who besmirched it. So I kept a civil tongue and answered the man politely.

"We are mages, good sir, and are recently come out of Lorédon."

His entire demeanor shifted at this. The mages of Osten stood outside the usual feudal hierarchy, but we were afforded an unofficial rank, very similar to that of a knight. Some masters were held even a notch higher in esteem. Of course, a new journeyman wouldn't be. But we hadn't yet revealed our standing within the guild. The priest, or whatever he was, beckoned to the knight and whispered something to him. Whereupon the knight cleared his throat and began anew.

"Let's start over, shall we?" he asked rhetorically. "Allow me to introduce myself. I am Sir Charles Stapleton, of the Fairglen Stapletons. Perhaps you have heard of me?"

His statement hung there unanswered, and the man looked disappointed as the three of us exchanged blank looks.

"It's surprising if you haven't," remarked his squire, filling the gap. "My master has made quite a name for himself on the tourney circuit."

It was surprising to *me* that the lad had spoken out of turn and that his knight didn't admonish him for the lapse. If Derrick had ever interrupted Trenton's discourse so, he would be rebuked for the breech of decorum. But Sir Charles only smiled, saying 'indeed.'

I'd never been a great fan of jousting, but judging by the admiring smiles of his men, I imagined their master placed quite highly in the lists.

"This is my squire, Kendrick," Sir Charles went on to say. "We are on a hunting trip, of sorts. And this rather drab fellow is Friar Wallace. The good friar is my spiritual adviser and attends to our soul's needs. And may I ask whom I am addressing?"

It always baffled me that direct questions were seen as rude, whereas it was considered the height of politeness to ask if one could ask them.

"Sir Charles, I am Lucas Harper, a journeyman serving Mistress Puquabeth Chosha Julia of Lorédon. These others are likewise journeymen to my master. I present Journeyman Royland Wagge and Journeyman Sholeena Blorlafargalish."

Royland bowed when introduced, and Sholeena managed a sort of curtsy. I hoped the good knight didn't find my manners lacking, but it was all I could do to remain propped up by my crutch.

"As to our purpose here," I continued, "we are pursuing our training according to our master's wishes. A part of this entails a journey to Eagle's Keep. As you can see, I have recently suffered an injury. My fellows and I are, at present, seeking a hospital or proper physic."

"Hey, *I've* heard of you," chimed in the squire. "You're that fairy boy they've been going on about at court!"

"Well, I wouldn't put it *that* way," I muttered. "But essentially, yes."

"Pray tell us, then," the young man continued. "How did you hurt your leg?"

"We were attacked by a pig," I confessed.

Some chuckles of wry amusement arose from the gathered men. I suppose they'd been expecting a more grandiose explanation for my infirmity. Still, I thought it unkind of them to laugh at another's misfortune. I'd heard of adding insult to injury but blushed to be experiencing it firsthand.

"It was a very *big* pig," I added testily.

More chuckles erupted at this until one among them objected.

"Tis no laughing matter," said the man with some heat. "My da was gored by a tusker once, and it weren't a pretty sight. The poor old sot was laid up for a whole fortnight; he was, with me and me poor mum havin' to attend his every bodily need."

This sobered the others somewhat. They stood staring about ashamedly in the wake of their confederate's outburst.

It was then that Friar Wallace stepped closer to Sir Charles and muttered something in his ear.

"It so happens," declared Sir Charles, that Friar Wallace here, is a skilled battlefield medic and chirurgeon. As a courtesy to the mage's guild, the worthy friar would offer you his services. Do you accept?"

I knew that some of the mendicant orders practiced other professions. Some were lawyers, vintners, or even shoemakers.

"This is *most* agreeable," I exclaimed. "Of course I accept, and gladly."

To the others, Sir Charles announced: "We shall make a brief camp here and tarry to share news while the good friar ministers to our ailing countryman. For does not the code enjoin us to 'protect the weak and defenseless?'"

The men snapped to at once, clearing an area and retrieving gear from the pack animals.

***

"Fetch me my medicinals," said the friar to a lackey.

After but a brief delay, the man returned with a small black bag with a wooden handle. It hinged open at the top to reveal a clutter of glass bottles, rolled-up strips of cloth, jars of unguents and various accoutrements.

"Hmm. Let's see what we're up against," he said cheerfully.

Friar Wallace pulled back the bandage to reveal the angry mess that had once been my inner thigh. I felt a tearing sensation when the cloth separated from my flesh, taking with it a goodly portion of the clotted scab. A fresh pool of bright blood welled up to trickle over the inflamed area. I inhaled sharply when he dabbed at this with a damp cloth and bade me to lean farther back.

I was glad for the privacy screen that had been erected. I took firm control over my voice lest any mewling whimpers escape to earn me a reputation as a simpering poltroon. After cleansing the wound most thoroughly, Friar Wallace bade me to press down firmly on it with a wad of linen. I heard the clink of glassware as he rummaged within his bag. The friar's search soon produced a small jar with a broad lid. Its label read: 'Balm of Gilead.'

"This is healing astonishingly well for so deep a wound taken only... five days ago; did you say?"

"Four and a half," I answered tersely.

"I'm a fast healer," I added.

"Still," said he, "it could use a few stitches if you want the muscle to knit properly. It's lucky for you that pig missed your femoral artery (and some other important bits that lie adjacent, eh?)"

I only grunted in response to the man's jocular remark. I didn't find such a thought funny in the least.

"This will ease the pain somewhat and help you to relax," he explained.

He scooped up a dollop of the milky white substance with two fingers and smeared it liberally over the wound. The balm emitted a pleasant scent akin to that of poplar trees in the springtime. The man's assurance was instantly affirmed. I felt a soothing coolness overtake the ache and fill me with a sense of well-being. But I paled on sighting the large fishhook he next withdrew from his bag. Producing a bobbin of coarse white thread from the same source, he leaned in close and squinted as he threaded it through the eye of the oddly bent needle. I tensed when he came at me with it.

I had to look away when the needle pierced me, but it wasn't so bad. If I thought of something else, I could almost ignore the scraping sensation as he laid a line of stitches into my raw flesh. His hands were gentle, and I sensed his subtle skill with this grim task. In a trice, it was done. And though the lesion still throbbed and burned a bit, I felt a rightness where before there had been only affliction. The friar reapplied fresh linens, wrapping them tightly about my injured member.

As I lay back on my mat, I considered my good fortune. In but a handful of days, providence had provided the very succor my companions, and I had sought. In the absence of prompt medical attention, I knew a person risked permanent impairment from so grievous a wound. Moreover, the practice of medicine had become remarkably advanced since the days of our primitive ancestors. I was only too grateful to live in such enlightened times.

"Rest and plenty of liquids," said the friar. "You may work it gently, but do nothing strenuous for a few days more, lest you undo my good work."

"I thank you, Brother Wallace," I humbly muttered in reply.

By now, I was no stranger to setting up a campsite, but the elaborate preparations that went into establishing this 'temporary' one were quite above and beyond my expectations. Sir Charles took his ease while his lackeys all scurried about. As always, care for the animals came first, or rather, second only to the knight's comfort. The two splendid stallions of the knight and his squire were led away and picketed separate from the lesser horses in the entourage. Groomsmen and some of the other men were sent to gather wood for a fire, doubtful of what could be had in the scrubby basin in which we lay. One of the men at arms seemed to be in charge of the effort.

"Sir?" said Sholeena, approaching him shyly and speaking for the first time.

He glanced testily at her, but then his brow smoothed and he addressed her in genteel tones.

"Yes, miss? Is there aught I can do for you?"

Taking another step forward and presenting my bob, she withdrew from it a stout log.

"We've firewood aplenty, if it would be of any help..."

The man gulped and stared at her agog.

"We've clean water aplenty as well," she offered. "I can fill yon trough for your animals if you would like."

"Capital!" exclaimed Sir Charles, stalking up behind the man and clapping him on the shoulder. "I suggest you accept, Lars. Had I wondered whether these three were truly mages, this marvelous demonstration has surely put any such doubt to rest. I shall accompany the good lady mage. Lady Sholeena, was it? Let us be off to the watering trough. I would fain witness this miraculous feat."

The knight offered his arm, and Sholeena meekly took it and was led away. As his man-at-arms stared in bafflement between the log and my satchel, I heard the knight's cheerful voice trailing off.

"... I hadn't previously had occasion to consider how useful traveling with mages could be. Can you perchance..."

"Take whatever you need," I told Lars. "They're in that side-pocket. The one with the brass buckle."

But while Sholeena quickly became the toast of the camp, my cousin remained aloof, lurking about its edges and observing the men. When I was alone, he approached to kneel by my side. Making a pretense of checking my bandages, he caught my eye and muttered softly.

"Have a care, cousin," he said. "These men are not at all what they seem. That friar, in particular, is a man of secrets."

He said no more and moved off when we were approached by a pair of men sent to move me nearer to the fire. We all enjoyed a peaceful meal and a pleasant rest, sharing tales of our respective travels. Sir Charles and his men claimed to be a simple hunting party. Being in the vicinity, the knight had taken a notion to visit his brother, who was stationed at the war front. They were making a short side-jaunt to Eagle's Keep for this purpose. For our part, though we didn't share our mission, we stuck chiefly to the truth. We were three mages given leave by our master to travel about and see the world a bit before returning to our studies.

I was surprised at how swiftly Sir Charles had warmed to our company, given his initial stuffy welcome. I suspected Sholeena had something to do with this. I noted his thoughtful smile whenever he regarded her. All too soon, the meal was done, and it was time to move on.

"Since we are in no particular hurry," said the knight, "and are headed for the same destination, I should like to propose that we travel together to the keep."

I had secretly hoped for such an outcome but was a little put off by Royland's sudden frown.

"It's a kind offer, Sir Charles," I said and meant it. "But wouldn't we just slow you down?"

"Tis of little consequence," he replied. "My happy reunion with Sir Stanley can wait another day or two, and the horses could do with a more restful walk for a time."

'Sir Stanley Stapleton' struck me as a strange name for a knight. I should like to hear how Sholeena would manage it when they were introduced. Taking my amused grin as acceptance, the knight nodded and turned to his men.

"Strike the camp!" he commanded. "I should like us to be well underway and several leagues nearer to the keep ere darkness overtakes us."

"You two," he said to a pair of men who sat nearby, "may help Lucas back to that stretcher conveyance and carry him in the vanguard."

"No need," said the squire. "He shall ride upon Fearless, whom I will lead at a gentle walk. In this manner, we can make better time."

A hush fell over the men, and all looked in astonishment at their knight, who seemed perplexed.

"Very well, sire," he sputtered.

Friar Wallace looked at Sir Charles, agape.

Recovering his composure, the knight grinned sheepishly at us.

"I mean, very well squire. Have it as you will. For does not the code enjoin us to 'show charity to those in need?' Let your humility serve as a lesson to us all."

And with that, the men leaped back into motion once more.

When all was in readiness, Kendrick led his spirited charger to the head of the company. I had given him my scent and stroked his mane for a time before two men helped me to mount. Straddling the beast stretched my stitches a bit, but I'd be damned if I would submit to riding sidesaddle. A little discomfort would be preferable to the ridicule *that* would likely engender. As the day wore on, however, I would come to regret this hasty decision.

As night began creeping up from the east, the outriders returned to report that a suitable site had been discovered for our first night's camp. Some of our fellows were even now clearing an area just a short distance ahead. According to my aching thigh, the sweet relief this promised couldn't come soon enough. I sensed from Fearless a similar anticipation as he picked up his step toward a rubdown and a fresh bag of oats. With his master guiding him by the leads and despite his spirited nature, Fearless had in fact provided a gentle ride. Rightly had the worthy steed earned this reward for his day's labor.

I winced as the men eased me down. My thigh ached and throbbed. It ascribed a whole new meaning to the phrase 'saddle sore.' The men of the hunt all marveled anew when Roy unpacked our tent from my bob.

Sir Charles was heard to remark: "Now *that's* a handy haversack."

Sholeena endeared herself further to Sir Charles and his men when they tasted their water ration that night. The Paluda girl had used her gift to freshen the casks. Over the years, the water here in the south had taken on a strange taint. It was believed to be a sign of the encroaching dark magic from the southern mire. Its bitter tang had crinkled many a nose and lay unpleasingly upon the tongue. After Sholeena's treatment, however, the crisp, clear taste was most refreshing. Nor was there a dearth of such. Our water mage had replenished all the stores. There was even enough for washing and other luxuries.

Royland continued to sulk.

***

And so, the days wore on, each delivering us nearer to the duchy's namesake. Here on its outskirts, we began to spot signs of more recent habitation. We were even overtaken by a patrol. It was the familiar group of six riders that those in the E.K. termed a 'six-pack.' They stopped briefly to share news with Sir Charles, then continued on their way.

At least we encountered no aberrant threats from the south. That is, until the third day. For it was then Sir Charles' outriders returned to report a problem up ahead. The advance scouts had come upon another abandoned farm, this one a fruit orchard. On closer inspection, they found it swarming with cyclochiropteans, known to thrive in such environs. Rubbing at his chin, Sir Charles pondered this a moment before sharing his decision.

"We shall set up camp here. Lars and I will ride ahead with a crack team of archers and purge the vermin. We shall make of them a gift for the duke upon our arrival."

"Kendrick," he added almost as an afterthought, "I should like you to stay here and see to our guests until the bloody deed has been carried out."

"I understand," the squire acknowledged.

He seemed a bit let down by the pronouncement.

As all made ready to depart, I was surprised to see the friar was to accompany them on his fat donkey. When I asked about it, Kendrick informed me that Brother Wallace would insure anyone stung received prompt medical aid. It seemed the friar had a supply of a new antitoxin said to be proof against the cyclos' venom if promptly administered. He looked eagerly forward to a field test to see whether it would prove efficacious.

Roy too, opted to join the men, whether out of boredom or a sincere desire to be of help. I didn't worry for my cousin; he could take care of himself. Rather, I worried for the rest of us. I'd been told that the blade moths which were plaguing Lorédon rarely strayed this far east. But it had been comforting to know Roy could deal with them should they do so.

I slid down from Fearless (a feat by now I could accomplish unassisted) and hobbled over to take my rest by the bundle of sticks marking where the fire was to be lit. While others set to their various tasks, Kendrick handed his horse's reins off to a groom and came to sit by my side. Despite his steady kindness to me over the past several days, we'd rarely spoken. At first, I'd been gritting my teeth over the injury. And when we camped at night, Sir Charles usually dominated the conversation.

I could tell the young man was disappointed about not being included in the hunt. Thinking to repay his kindness, I sought about for some topic to distract him.

"So, Kendrick," I said, "how is it working for Sir Charles?"

He looked at me askance.

"It is well, I suppose," he said with a furtive smile. "What do you make of my knight?"

"He seems an honorable sort, if a bit bombastic."

The lad grinned.

"Just so. He is both of those things, and I thank you for your candor."

"By this I'm certain you mean my bluntness."

"And if you don't mind my asking," I asked, "what's with that friar you have in tow? In Fairglen, is it the habit of mendicants to wander about the countryside in the company of knights?"

"It is for *this* one, at least. Brother Wallace is a special case."

"One wouldn't expect a man under a vow of poverty to be so rotund," he further mused. "By the look of him, I don't imagine he's missed many meals. The men call him 'Brother Walrus' behind his back, for the way he wattles about when not sitting on his fat ass."

I smiled; his pun reminded me of my old master.

"For all that," continued Kendrick, "he's a capable man. He serves his lord well and can be a dangerous fellow in a fight."

Of that, I had no doubt. I knew that most friars were sworn to shed no blood and eschewed the art of swordplay.

Nonetheless, the cudgel he bore looked serviceable enough. And whatever else the corpulent friar might be, he was a damn fine healer.

"What did Sir Charles mean when he said he'd make a gift of the cyclos to the duke? Have they some special use?"

"Not that I'm aware," said the squire. "Oh, his grace's alchemists are experimenting with the venom sacs, seeking some use for them in the war effort. But naught has come of this as yet. The vile things vitrify rapidly when exposed to the open air. No. Sir Charles will doubtless collect all the tails from the vermin and present them to his grace as proof of the purge. Duke Gaul once offered a bounty of half a shilling per tail spike, thinking to inspire the peasantry to eradicate the creatures."

"What happened?" I asked.

"The bounty proved to be counterproductive. His grace called it off when he discovered some scurrilous knaves were actually breeding the creatures in their orchards to collect on it."

I shouldn't be surprised. It would take an entire bushel of apples to fetch a half a shilling. It only made sense that the villeins would soon grasp the potential and seize on such an opportunity. It might not be patriotic, but serfs were nothing if not practical. Short-sighted, perhaps, but practical.

I sighed. Reaching over to the bundle of sticks before me, I muttered 'digitus flamma.' This caused a small flame to lick out from my index finger, igniting the dry wood.

"It must be a fine thing to be a mage," said Kendrick wistfully.

"It's not as easy as it looks," I assured him. "It takes a lot of hard work and study to develop one's potential. And in truth, many tasks one can perform by magic require more energy than simply doing it the old-fashioned way. Still, when it works, it can be gratifying."

Smoke issued out from the spreading flames and began to form a column rising straight up and bending slightly eastward with the breeze. I retrieved a log and set it atop the stack. Before long, servitors brought victuals and a skin of good wine. We shared many tales about our respective (and very different) upbringings.

I soon surmised that Kendrick was raised among the high nobility. He didn't share his surname, but I suspected he must be from a prominent family. Perhaps this was why Sir Charles was so lenient in disciplining the young gentleman. I, in turn, spoke of growing up in Westarbor. Kendrick was very attentive, asking many probing questions.

Eventually, our conversation turned to political matters. It wasn't my favorite topic, but it was in this realm the squire could truly hold his own. He was fascinated to hear my ideas and made many astute observations of his own. His command of the facts was notable, and he even managed to change several of my own long-held beliefs with his arguments. I always enjoyed a good conversation with an equal. Few of my contemporaries save for Roy fit the bill, and my cousin shares ideas as a miser shares his gold. None of the squires I had met previously had been intellectuals. But Kendrick impressed me as such with his witty and open dialog.

"So," said he, passing me the near-empty wine skin, "if you could change any law in the kingdom, what would it be?"

"Honestly?" I asked.

"No, lie to me, you blackguard. Of *course*, honestly."

My head was feeling light from the wine we'd consumed, but a clarity came over me as I pondered the question.

"It wouldn't be a single thing," I said carefully. "People need to rely on the law as fair and just. It would discomfit them if things were to change willy-nilly. No. It would be many small things done gradually, over time."

"Give me one example," said Kendrick.

"If *I* were king," I said blushingly. "I would start by relaxing the sumptuary laws."

"What?" the squire exclaimed. "If anyone could dress in whatever manner they liked, how would one assess a man's worth? Commoners could prance about posing as noblemen without consequence. It'd be chaos."

I'd quite forgotten that nobles could be prickly about their perks.

"Not all at once, Kendrick. Hear me out. I know what of I speak. In the first place, not everyone can afford to wear finery. Many are struggling merely to survive. But I've heard the grumbling when a fellow is denied the prospect of wearing a fine shirt to his wedding because it would be 'above his station.'

"Just imagine a kingdom in which everyone could know the pride of striving for betterment. Where the people see that their lives and those of their children can be better if only they put in the hard work. If a farmer can afford a slightly finer suit for his Sunday best, then bully for him. Let him buy it. It will only benefit the clothiers and the cloth merchants. Commerce would boom, uplifting everyone. It would lead to a cultural renaissance wherein all aspire to be the best that they can be."

"And what of the king?" asked Kendrick. "Seeing as, by definition, he cannot 'better' himself, would he not soon be fending off rivals left and right?"

"The king who brought about such change would surely have the love of the people. In Westarbor, the baron encourages all his people to improve themselves and their lot as best they're able. In return, the people adore the man because they sense he's on their side. Order is maintained."

Kendrick swallowed the last dregs and re-stopped the wineskin. He belched politely, then smiled and swayed to his feet.

"Well, my idealistic friend," he said, "if ever I should have the king's ear, I will let him know your opinion on the matter. I shall send a servant to collect our plates. Rest well, Lucas. We are only a day's travel by horse from the keep, and Brother Walrus informs me that you should be able to walk the remaining distance. For what it's worth, I should *like* to live in the world you describe."

He was right. In addition to the friar's gentle ministrations and despite daily pummeling by the saddle, my wound was healing nicely. It helped that each morning I'd been leeching strength from the surrounding greenery. This blighted land had little enough to spare, but with each draw, I felt more fit to move under my own power.

"You're right, of course," I said. "I shall always remember your kindness. I hope I can one day repay it."

"Well," he said, stepping closer, "there's one way."

"What is it?"

"You can tell me what you three are really doing out here. I sense you have a good heart, but you're a poor liar. I like to think I've earned a bit of honesty."

"I can tell you this much. What we do, we do for the sake of all in the kingdom. More I cannot say, but rest assured it is important and for the good of all. Only Lady Brighton and a few others know of our quest, and it's best that it remains so. I'm sorry I can't say more. Some deceptions are necessary."

"The duchess?" he mused. "Interesting. But it is as you say. Sometimes deception is necessary. We all have secrets, and not all are inimical. We shall speak no more of this."

And with that, he stalked off.

I stared into the fire and felt its warm radiance tighten the skin of my face. It was only mid-afternoon, but I fancied a nap already. I saw Sholeena pitching our tent with the help of several eager young lads. I roused myself to meander over for a little lie-down. Tomorrow would be a long day. I should heed the squire's good advice and 'rest well.'

***

In the morning, I roused myself. Sir Charles and his squad of archers had returned yesterday evening, but I hadn't even bothered to attend the evening meal. I had slept straight through the night, untroubled by the revelation I'd be walking from here on out. My thigh was a bit stiff, but the puckered edges of the jagged scar now lacked the red swelling which had heretofore made it sensitive to the touch. When last I'd removed my bandages, I'd opted to leave them off.

The camp was stirring. The soft clatter of men moving about invited me to come without. First, however, I needed to attend to my depressing morning task. With a frown, I unholstered my wand and sought within. Since last I'd thwarted his attempt to farm my inner field, I'd not seen the scarecrow. But I could sense his skulking withdrawal each time I awoke, and his leavings lay about. Once more, I cleansed my inner field. Only a weed here and there did I find. But remnants from my nightly haunt lay scattered in my mind.

That duty done, I arose and stretched. Fully rested, I was eager for the day.

When I emerged, I found Royland there with Sholeena standing beside him. Roy handed me a trencher and bade me to break my fast quickly. They'd eaten already. Loath to disturb my rest, they had been waiting patiently to pack up our tent. Sir Charles and his squire had retired to their pavilion tent to make ready for the day, and their men were equipping themselves strangely.

What was this? The men had changed their tabards. All now stood wearing purple and gold livery, colors reserved for the royal house of Osten itself! And prancing up to the fore came Fearless, led by a groom bearing the same. Sewn upon his quilted barding lay a symbol known by all. Twas the royal seal itself thereon emblazoned. I reeled in astonishment. Could this be true? It must be. None other than the Ostens would *presume* to wear these symbols of the realm. Twas death to any lesser man who would dare to counterfeit them.

And out from the pavilion came first the knight, Sir Charles. He was fully outfitted in gleaming armor and grinning ear to ear. Gods, the man cut a fine figure.

"Gentlemen and lady, it is my supreme honor to present his royal highness, Henry, Prince of Osten."

Upon this introduction, Kendrick stepped out in full regalia. Well, he didn't have a scepter or crown or any such, but he may as well have had. All bowed their heads, as so too did I. Sholeena managed her sort-of curtsy. Glaring over at me, Royland smacked the hat from off my head.

"The prince would have it be known that all here are forgiven any improprieties or liberties taken with his person during the time of our ruse. In his tour of the kingdom, his highness thought it best to travel incognito, the better that he might assess his people's true feelings. His advisers thought this a prudent course as well. To minimize any danger to his highness from any enemies or malcontents, he's been posing as my squire.

"Those of you in the royal retinue have played your parts well. But now, as we approach the stronghold of Eagle's Keep. We must lift the veil of secrecy that the prince may ride forth and be accorded all proper respect on meeting his grace, the duke. Thus, all proper behavior and deference due his highness is hereby restored. Now, before we set out, I believe the prince wishes to share a few words."

With a clanking sound, Sir Charles retreated a few paces and nodded to his charge. Kendrick scanned the assembled men. Prince Henry, I corrected myself. I still couldn't help but think of him as 'Kendrick', a habit that might land me in the stew if I wasn't careful.

"All may rise," he began.

Roy and I straightened.

"A fellow of my recent acquaintance may have put it best when he said: 'Some deceptions are necessary.' As Sir Charles reminds us, all royal protocols are henceforth reinstated on pain of our displeasure. So, strike this camp and make yourselves presentable. Tonight, we arrive at Eagle's Keep."

To murmurs of "yes, your highness' and 'at once, my prince,' the men shuffled about. But the prince had yet to release them. Prince Henry caught my eye, his face deadpan.

"To our unwitting guests on this leg of our journey, I bid you *adieu*, for we must set out posthaste. Our advance scouts have already ridden ahead to announce our arrival. I trust you will arrive safely at the keep in a few days' time and look forward to meeting you again one day. This audience is dismissed."

As the prince stepped over to pat his horse on the muzzle, his men all fell swiftly to their tasks. Roy and Sholeena began striking our tent, but with nowhere near the efficiency of the prince's men. I stood in stunned silence. How had I not seen it? How had *Roy* not puzzled it out? Had I really been lecturing royalty on how to run the kingdom? 'If ever I have the king's ear,' indeed. Here and the young man standing before his mount would one day have both of them.

Later, as we ambled down the lonely road, I asked Roy why he hadn't figured it out.

"I knew something was off about Kendrick," he said grumpily. "But I was more focused on the friar. I think he was deliberately goading me the whole time."

"Did you ever figure him out?"

"Oh. Yes. I have now."

"Well?"

"I believe he's in his majesty's spy network, the brotherhood of the board. You know, like Taylor and that jester fellow from the caravan."

"Really? He could have fooled me."

Royland squinted over at me and failed to take advantage of the opening.

"*I* met a *prince*," said Sholeena.

CHAPTER EIGHT

The Scribe

"Oho!" said the pot to the kettle;
"You are dirty and ugly and black!
Sure no one would think you were metal,
Except when you're given a crack."

"Not so! not so!" kettle said to the pot;
"'Tis your own dirty image you see;
For I am so clean – without blemish or blot –
That your blackness is mirrored in me."

Anonymous poem from
St. Nicholas Magazine in 1876

On the second day, we saw it. I believe it was a Tuesday, but I confess I'd quite lost track. In the distance, we beheld a shining city on the hill. The stronghold of Eagle's Keep roosted proudly atop a rocky plateau, the dimensions of which would rival a small mountain. Farmsteads lay all about us. None of them stood abandoned. Though it would be winter in Westarbor, the sun shone down on these southern lands as late crops were harvested by the bustling villeins. This near to the keep, none feared the depredations of the enemy, and the patrols were frequent.

We were stopped many times and questioned about our business here. The patrolmen seemed especially twitchy and terse, what, with the recent arrival of the prince and all. They glared at us suspiciously when we told them of our intention to visit the keep, but then they left us to be on our way.

It still vexed me that I hadn't realized I'd been rubbing shoulders with royalty. All the clues had been there, after all. The very name, Kendrick, means 'royal power.' It also derives from Mackendrick, meaning 'son of Henry,' a transparent ruse indeed. I considered just how many extraordinary people we'd met on our journey thus far: a fairy queen, an elven duchess, and now even a prince of the realm! A part of me had to wonder whether the king himself was lurking up the road ahead, just waiting to spring out at us when we least suspected. But no such fanciful musings could have prepared me for what was actually to be our lot.

"Hold up a minute, cousin," said Roy. "I see a copse of trees up ahead. Since we're in sight of the keep, perhaps it were best if we freshen up and don some finer attire for this last leg. We don't want to arrive as beggars."

That made sense. Mayhap the patrols would cease their glowering were we bedecked in finery more befitting to mages. Royland's cloak, in particular, smacked of seediness. Despite our best efforts to mend it, the garment had looked patchwork and tattered ever since the blade moths had worked it over. So we stopped and took it in turns to ease our bladders and freshen our garb before walking the final distance.

At the keep, or rather, in its shadow, we found a long line of wagons waiting to be admitted. Each was being carefully inspected before being allowed within the citadel's lower walls. The place was enormous, far grander even than it had seemed at a distance.

This was no simple motte and bailey keep, nor even the city on a hill it had first appeared. Rather, it was a city 'in the hill.'

Much of it had been carved from the very stone of this great outcropping and rose in terraces high above. The open area around its base was encircled by forty-foot walls. This comprised but a small fraction of the entire stronghold, the bulk of which lay burrowed deep into the mountain itself. Pennants flew proudly at even intervals at each tier. They bore the distinctive symbol of duke Gaul, the black eagle on a bright golden field of Or. And higher still, atop the very mesa itself, stood the castle proper. Doubtless, one could see for miles from out of the narrow windows piercing its lofty stone walls.

An enemy would have to be mad to assault so formidable a fortress. I could certainly see why our current enemy chose to fight a war of attrition rather than confront us directly. Sadly, this tactic was proving troublesome for the duke. Years of relentless battering had driven away many folks from the duchy's outskirts. And though the nearby lands seemed productive enough, they were scarcely sufficient to meet the needs of so mighty a fortress. According to Master Pete's reports, frequent shortages plagued the duke, ameliorated only by the constant influx of goods from neighboring duchies. Should the king ever withdraw this aid, one had to wonder how Duke Gaul might fare on his own.

"State your names and your business here at the keep."

I blinked.

We had reached the head of the line, where a stern-faced guardsman stood before a group of others. He was staring at us expectantly.

"We are three mages come to visit our brethren here, sergeant," said Roy. "I am Royland Wagge. My confederates are Lucas Harper and Sholeena of the Paludaria."

Just then, a monk in a familiar brown frock sidled up from among the men and beckoned to their leader. It wasn't Brother Wallace. This fellow was much slighter of frame and looked to be younger. But his garb and shaven tonsure marked him as being from some similar order. His eyes flitted to us and back as he whispered urgently into the man's ear.

"Ah, yes," said the sergeant, "it seems you are expected."

He turned to the contingent of guardsmen and indicated two of their number.

"Take them to lift five," he said with a peculiar emphasis. "They are to be taken directly up to tier four."

The two men grew round-eyed as they acknowledged the command and scurried to obey.

"See that they receive a proper welcome."

Roy's pensive gaze lingered on the sergeant before stepping toward the open gates. The men of our escort took up station, one leading the way and the other falling in at our rear. Their hands hovered near their weapons as we were hustled forward through the narrow streets.

"Next," barked the sergeant.

***

The town of Stronghold was all stone and timber. Land was at a premium here. And the tall, narrow buildings crowded close together, separated by the narrow streets and alleyways. The rare bits of greenery I spied were sad little things growing in pots on some of the balconies above, and my vertiginous sense hungered for the lack. Beside me, Sholeena shuffled along, wide eyed with wonder. Ahead of us stalked Roy, peering neither left nor right.

Having traveled outdoors for so long, it took my nose some time to adjust to the closeness of human habitation. The smell of smoke and the odor of refuse and other rot combined to form a stench to which only city-dwellers were accustomed. I knew Meadowfork had such a smell. But in the small hamlet, it had been much less intense, and one hardly noticed if one had lived there long.

It was with no little amazement that we approached the lift. Our escort marched us up to a sheer cliff. At its base rested a cage of wooden slats resting atop a wooden platform the size of a wagon's bed. Beside this was a great wheel made of wooden planks and beams. It put me in mind of our mill wheel, except that the spokes were all on its inner side. And, apart from its central axle, the inner area was hollow and empty like a great open jar laying on its side. The lead guardsman stepped up and directly into the cage, indicating we should follow.

Gingerly, Roy stepped onto the platform as well, as did the rest of us once he'd moved toward the back. The guard to our rear addressed two burly men who sat nearby.

"On your feet, miscreants," he said. "Marco and I need to deliver these three up to tier four."

At this, the frowning men walked over to the wheel and stepped within. At our guard's signal, the two began walking along the wheel's inner surface, and our cage began to rise. For the stout ropes ascending above us had grown taut. Turned by the wheel, they hauled us upward. At each level was an opening in the face of the cliff. Moreover, as we passed each of these, an unmoving arm sticking out from our cage caused a bell to be rung. As the fourth of these sounded, our upward movement ceased, and our platform sat slightly swaying at the end of its tether. When the lead guard shoved home a beam to lock firmly within the stone, the swaying abruptly ceased. Our cage had come to rest directly alongside a broad set of reinforced doors.

I smiled in appreciation. It was a feat of engineering worthy of our own Javier Lewis.

"We are arrived," said Marco. "At this time, we must ask you to surrender any weapons you might have on your persons and give your rucksacks over to Barnaby for inspection. We can't be too cautious during the royal visit. I'm sure you understand."

Reluctantly, we complied. I wondered what Barnaby would make of the void pocket on my bob. But then, as Roy handed the man his backpack, he said an odd thing.

"Friend," said my cousin with a frown, "do what you are here to do."

The words were familiar. And as I puzzled over just where I'd heard them before, a hatch on the door to the right slid open up at head height. Peering out was an unfamiliar man. He had a salt and pepper beard and a broad-brimmed gray hat. Held to one eye was an ocular exactly like the one the king's emissary had used at Conclave. He stared at us through it with his other eye squinted shut.

"Well done, men," said the bearded man to the soldiers.

At this, the other door swung inward to reveal three armored men with weapons drawn.

"Take them," he said, "and separate the short one from the others. Best you come along peacefully, now. You've nowhere to run."

Royland stepped forward to be immediately seized and restrained. Sholeena backed into Barnaby, only to be shoved roughly forward into the waiting arms of two others. Why was *I* always 'the short one?' Sholeena had barely an *inch* on me; two at best.

Resigned to but baffled by our confinement, I let myself be guided firmly from the lift by our erstwhile 'escort.' The priestly fellow garbed in gray led us down a dimly lit stone hallway. We soon arrived at a small room wherein several heavy doors stood ajar. Roy and Sholeena were ushered through the first, and I was thrust unceremoniously into another. Without a word, the wary guardsmen closed the door behind me, shutting out the little light by which I had managed to glimpse the windowless cell.

"Digitus flamma," I murmured.

This caused a small flame to lick forth from my index finger. I wished I had studied Lorraine's gift more carefully when I'd had the chance. She could make patches of heatless light, which would shine for a time without further empowering them. As it was, I had achieved only a temporary solution to my sightlessness.

By the light of my little flame, I made my way over to the chair in the room's center. It was a sturdy piece, and I found it to be bolted to the floor. The only other items of note were an empty wooden crate and some kind of cloak which hung from a hook above it. I eased myself down onto the hard planks of the chair and extinguished my flaming finger.

I sat in darkness, pondering my predicament.

Although I'd hardly been expecting a hero's welcome, thus far I found the duke's hospitality somewhat lacking. Whatever could have set them against me so? The man in the gray hat had singled me out from the others. Moreover, he'd been peering through one of the conclave's oculars when he'd made his grim pronouncement. I knew the purpose of these recently devised trinkets was to detect fey energies and thus identify when a man was possessed by a wight. I'd helped bring about their development myself. Could my own aura bear the taint of the fey? Such was not the case when Cassius McClure had examined me back at the academy. But I *did* possess several other fey marks and items that could have triggered the device. Perhaps being new to such detection, this was all a mistake, and the overzealous guardsmen were merely being cautious. That must be it.

I fervently hoped Roy and Sholeena were receiving better treatment. I knew Roy could handle himself, but the Paluda girl was likely terrified by our detention. And what would the guardsmen make of her strange camouflage that would undoubtedly arise from *that*?

Calm down, Lucas, I told myself. You're among countrymen here. I'm sure the precautions they're taking here are well-reasoned and all of this will be sorted out in its own good time. Still, they could have at least left me a chamber pot.

***

I couldn't say how much time had passed before a slim ray of light pierced the gloom from a slat high up on the door. This meager light soon diminished as the opening was obscured.

"Stay where you are," came a voice from without and the rattle of keys could be heard.

I was momentarily blinded when the door swung inward. Two guardsmen stepped into the room, followed by the man in gray. Just behind the man was the friar I had seen down at the gates. He followed the other meekly, clutching an iron cross that hung from a chain about his neck. In his other hand, he held the handle of a small bucket from which a shining thing protruded.

The leading guardsman bore a lantern, which he set down in the room's corner, causing eerie shadows to dance about on the ceiling.

"Secure him," said the man in gray.

I remained silent and compliant as the guards stepped forth and shackled my wrists to the arms of the chair. In the darkness, I hadn't noticed the manacles that had hung from each by chains. They bore various symbols and runes but looked serviceable enough despite the decorations.

"You may leave us."

My new host seemed to be a man of few words, a habit I intended to emulate. I sensed this was no time to give free rein to my smart mouth. Such had led me only to grief in times past. Though I had many questions I longed to ask and many outraged exclamations begging me for release, I would bide. Surely what these men would have of me would be made clear soon enough. I watched with trepidation as the two guardsmen silently withdrew, alleviating the overcrowded confines of my cell.

"We shall begin with a simple test," said my jailer. "Brother Parvus, if you will."

The humble friar stood tremulously forth and muttered: "We drive you from us, whoever you may be, unclean spirits, all satanic powers, all infernal invaders, all wicked legions, assemblies and sects."

At this, he withdrew from his bucket a tiny mace or scepter. With a flick of his wrist, he splashed me with the contents of its hollow head. A clear liquid splattered across my forehead to dribble into my eyes and down to my chin.

"Hey!" I exclaimed.

The chains tethering my wrists grew taut as I sought unsuccessfully to wipe away the offending splatter.

"Mark you, brother," said the man in gray, "how he flinches from the touch of holy water. Now I ask you, demon, what is your name?"

"I'm Lucas Harper of Meadowfork," I sputtered. "All you had to do was to ask."

"Do not seek to mislead us, spirit, for we have divined your true nature. I ask the name of whatever foul creature possesses this boy. Spare us your feeble attempts at deceit. I see you shall require some further persuasion."

Brother Parvus dipped the aspergillum back in the bucket in preparation to douse me a second time.

"Wait," I hastily put forth. "There's a very simple explanation for what you may have seen."

"Go on," said the man in gray.

"The faeries have marked me that I may attend their gatherings. Not the enemy fey, but our allies, the *seelie* fey!"

"Marked you how?" he asked.

"What may I call you, sir?" I asked in turn.

"If a good Christian name doesn't burn your tongue, you may address me as Inquisitor Mattius," he said testily. "Now answer the question, creature. Marked you how?"

"Twas from a kindly dryad of Conclave I received it, inquisitor. It graces the back of my hand. The king himself is aware of it. He named me the envoy to the seelie fey. The Duchess of Lorédon herself bears a similar mark. I have seen it."

I was unsure whether I was doing her grace any favors by revealing this, but I thought a bit of name dropping couldn't hurt my cause.

Brother Mattius glared at me suspiciously and drew forth from his pocket my fey wand.

"And what mischief, pray tell, do you intend with this? Have you come to do harm to our prince, or merely to infiltrate the capital to spy upon us?"

I wasn't sure how to answer that. The choices he offered didn't include any with an innocent intent.

"Neither, inquisitor," I assured him. "We came only to confer with our fellow mages here and to pursue a private pilgrimage, having to do with a journey taken long ago by members of our order."

Then I saw it. A flicker of doubt passed over the man's aspect. Turning to the friar, he said, "What say you, Brother Parvus?"

Tightly gripping his cross, the younger man stepped nearer. His eyes grew wild as they bore into mine.

"Most cunning serpent," he spat, "no more shall you dare to deceive the human race, persecute the Church, torment God's elect and sift them as wheat. God arises; His enemies are scattered and those who hate Him flee before Him. As smoke is driven away, so are they driven; as wax melts before the fire, so the wicked perish at the presence of God."

"It would seem that Brother Parvus doesn't agree with your plea of innocence," said Mattius. "Here is what shall happen, then. You will strip off your clothing, don these penitent robes, and we shall bring you before the full inquisition where you will beg for mercy. Anything you'd care to confess now will be considered in your favor..."

But before any of that could happen, there came a pounding on the door. It soon swung ajar to reveal a man dressed in the attire of a nobleman. It was Lars, Sir Charles' henchman from the hunt.

"... make way," he was ordering the guardsmen who sought to deny him entry.

Turning to the door, Mattius addressed him angrily.

"Who are *you*, and by what authority do you disrupt the servants of his grace?"

"I am Lars Templeton of Ayrshire, squire to Sir Charles Stapleton of Fairglen," he proclaimed. "As to the latter part of your inquiry, I've been sent by Prince Henry himself to remove this man from your custody. The prince, whom even your master is sworn to obey, has vouched for the three you are detaining. You are to release them at once."

Brother Parvus retreated to the room's corner. But uncowed, Mattius drew forth his ocular and peered at Lars through its lens before lowering it and replying.

"In that case," said he, producing a set of keys, "I see no choice but to grant you his parole. But have a care, squire. Brother Parvus has detected a dark stain on this boy's soul. If any harm comes from his release, let it be upon your head."

He unshackled my wrists and indicated I was free to take my leave.

As I passed through the doorway to join Lars, I was relieved to note the other door was open and unguarded. I heard a voice from within.

"Queen me!" shouted the triumphant Paluda.

"I believe the proper phrase is 'king me,'" muttered my cousin in reply.

Looking in, I saw the two sitting across from one another at a small table on which a game was in progress. Roy was just placing a red checker atop another on his side of the board.

"Well, I'm a girl, so mine are all queens," his opponent declared.

Fascinated, I watched as Royland surveyed the situation. Then, lifting a double black checker, he made a swift series of double-jumps all around, clearing six of Sholeena's pieces from off the board.

"Very well, then," he said. "The queen is dead. Long live the king!"

Sholeena's skin took on a bluish tinge as she gaped at her few remaining pieces.

"I yield me, sir," she said in resignation. "Oh. Hey Lucas, have they finished questioning you, then?"

"Well, for now at least," I mumbled, "thanks to Lars here."

"Come with me," said the squire. "I'll fill you in on aught you need to know."

So the four of us departed the quasi-dungeon where suspected malefactors were detained. I was no worse for wear but a bit less sanguine about our prospects.

***

"I apologize for my late arrival, Lucas," said Lars as he steered us along. "I'd have gotten here sooner, but this place is a maze of corridors. A rabbit warren has fewer ways to get about."

I could see what he meant. In the short time we'd been following him, I'd already gotten turned around.

"I think I know why they singled me out," I said rather charitably, I thought. "It was an understandable mistake."

"I was all set to greet you up on tier five, but your lift never arrived there."

"What's on tier five?" asked Sholeena.

"Oh. The mage's quarters, the better guest rooms, the duke's grand audience hall, and the like."

"Is that where we're going now, then?" asked Roy.

"I'm afraid not," said the squire. "When the TSA sent word of your detention, the duke changed his plans for your stay here."

"But we've been cleared by the prince's own word," I argued. "What is this TSA?"

"The Theological Surveillance Authority, or 'TSA', is a group formed by the local clergy to safeguard us from infiltrators and heretics and the like. According to the mages, that Brother Parvus fellow has a wild talent to spot fey magic. And since Conclave sent us the oculars, they've taken it upon themselves to mount a watch on all citizens and travelers. The duke is understandably suspicious. One of the first infiltrators they ferreted out was a close adviser of his, an old and dear friend. When he was discovered and taken into custody, the man hung

196

himself before he could be questioned. A black smoke was seen exiting his cell."

"That's terrible," I decried.

"Unfortunately," Lars continued, "as a direct result of this, the duke takes very seriously any recommendations made by his clergymen. I'm afraid you and your friends won't be permitted anywhere near the prince during his stay here. It's a pity. We'll be enjoying a welcoming feast this evening, and his highness was most eager for you to attend."

"Well, where *are* you taking us, then?" asked Roy.

"Tier three, that is, if I can find the blasted stairway down. Normally, you'd stay in the mage's quarters, but, sadly, more basic accommodations are the lot of those under suspicion by the TSA."

It galled me to be so mistrusted. But perhaps this was for the best. After all, hadn't Master Hans indicated the next marker would be found in a far humbler nook? The problem would be where to even begin our search. Eagle's Keep was an anthill of tunnels and chambers too large by far for a swift inspection. It might take us weeks to search out the next message. And I was loath to do so under the distrustful scrutiny of his grace's ecclesiastical minions, who seemed to bear a grudge against me.

"Ah, here we are," said Lars.

At the end of the hall before us, a stone stairwell descended. The flickering wall-mounted candles which had lit our way had grown sparse, and only a faint light could be seen from down on the next landing. I was sure it took an entire crew of chandlers to keep this place well lit. And I couldn't imagine the number of bees it would take to provide all the wax. Peering at one of the ensconced candles with mage sight, I detected the faint glimmer of pyromantic enchantment like we used at Conclave. My spirits fell once more as I considered the daunting task which lay before us. How were Royland, Sholeena and I ever to find the fourth marker amid the many similar enchantments gracing Stronghold? There must be some way. Surely, Royland's grandparents wouldn't have set us an impossible task; would they?

Dispirited and exhausted, we finally arrived at our quarters. They were a set of rooms off a stone hallway where craftsmen and laborers were housed.

"It's not much, but at least it's a place to lay your head," said Lars as we surveyed the cramped surroundings.

We were thankful to have a secure place to sleep and told him so. Having discharged his duty to us, the faithful squire promptly took his leave. He needed to prepare to attend his master at the feast. The three of us began unpacking our gear at once. We quickly agreed our search could wait until after a good night's rest and a proper planning session.

When laying out our bedrolls atop the simple straw mattresses, Sholeena discovered a folded missive bearing a waxen seal. She delivered it to me because my name was written on its front. The intact seal bore the royal crest of Osten, but no enchantment was visible to my mage sight. Roy and Sholeena huddled around me with interest when I broke the seal, unfolded the missive, and began to read it aloud.

To my stalwart, onetime traveling companions,

I was startled and no little displeased to hear of your discomfiture upon arrival at Stronghold. I had looked forward to resuming our acquaintance with further discussions of the kingdom's welfare and your role in it. His Grace, Lord Gaul, feels it would be best that I distance myself from your company during my stay here. I have done what I can to assuage his grace's wary misgivings and have secured for you a reprieve. You will be molested no further and free to go about your business unhindered. Know, however, that you will be watched throughout your visit. If ever you are in Fairglen, feel free to call upon me, and perhaps then I may satisfy my curiosity over what you misfits are about.

Your Liege and Future King,
Henry, Son of Raymond,
Prince of Osten

Despite the daunting search that lay before us, it was clear that we must start if ever we hoped to succeed. We didn't want to arouse suspicions. So, since I was the primary focus of their distrust, it would be my job to distract the TSA while my companions began our search in the guise of normal daily activities.

Toward that end, Sholeena would begin by laundering our clothes and bedding, a task long overdue anyway. The primary scullery for Stronghold was down on tier two. While there, she would surreptitiously scan all fireplaces and ovens which might be the humble nook we sought. Roy, along with my bob and the bulk of our funds, would make a shopping trip down on level one. There, he would purchase a new tent to replace the one the moths had shredded. He would then set about restocking our provisions for the next leg of our journey while keeping an eye out for his grandparents' enchantment. For my part, I decided to explore the monastic library up on tier four. Where better to direct the hounds than back to their very own kennel? Besides, I liked books.

The library, when I eventually found it, was actually quite small. When I'd first ascended back to tier four, I noted with chagrin several tonsured men in brown frocks who seemed to be following my movements. When I stared at them, they turned away and pretended to have a conversation, but they soon followed if I again began moving. I thought about asking them how to find the library but decided instead to amble about with my mage sight active to get a sense of the surroundings.

The ornate double doors stood ajar, and within I could see a lighted space. It was plain and drab for the most part, but to my right and centered on the southern wall was a stained-glass window depicting an angel. He stood within a Gothic arch with wings outspread, his flaming sword held point down. This room must lie at the outer part of the mountain, for natural light streamed down through the panes of glass to paint the floor below it in striking hues.

Seated at a long table nearby were several more tonsured friars. All had their backs to the window, and before each rested a slanted but mostly upright rectangular plank of wood. Silently, they were scratching away with styluses (styli?), oblivious at first to my entrance. As my eyes adjusted to the bright light, I was surprised to note the friar farthest to my left was Brother Parvus himself. He was engrossed in his task, and a frown of concentration marked his features. I moved closer. And when the man looked up, he seemed disconcerted by my presence.

"May I help you?" inquired a man who approached from the rear of the room.

"Ah... yes," I said, looking about.

Apart from those that lay open before the monks, I saw no books on display. The room had, however, many tall cupboards lining its walls. I had heard that the monks kept their books under lock and key, but I had imagined chains like those used at the academy at Conclave.

"I am visiting here for a time and had heard this might be a place to obtain a supply of parchment, Brother...?"

"Hewitt," returned the man.

And with a rueful smile, he continued.

"I'm afraid you heard wrong, young man. Parchment is passing scarce here in the E.K. Very few ranchers remain. There's a thriving cross-trade for sheepskins from Freemark, but most of these are reserved for military correspondence. Of what remains, we've barely enough to continue the Lord's work. I could offer you a sheet or two that are too small for scripture work, but the price for such is two shillings per square."

I was dumbstruck. That was damn near a half a crown for a square less than a page in size! At that price, a book of a hundred pages would be worth a duke's ransom. I needed to replenish my writing parchment, but such outrageous sums were well beyond my reach. I took a different tack.

"Well, then," I began haltingly, "have you any used parchment? Perhaps some initial drafts with too many mistakes or old correspondences that are no longer needed?"

"Perhaps..." he returned with a doubtful, sidelong glance. "There are some palimpsests we use for practice. What would be the point of such?"

"I'll give you a groat for one. There's something I'd like to try."

Brother Hewitt bunched up his lips and nodded. I untied my purse strings and counted out four pence into his upturned palm. Then he turned and led the way to one of the cupboards. The other friars at their scriptorium had by this time returned to their work, scratching away at their boards. Brother Parvus, however, sat motionless, reproaching me with a black look.

Brother Hewitt retrieved from a stack of pages a sheet of parchment containing all manner of writing. All of its margins were filled, and layer upon layer of ink in different hands and calligraphy covered both sides. I took it over to a table near the back wall and seated myself far away from the others. Back at Conclave, I had once seen Edgar perform a simple spell to remove a name from "Genealogy of the Gift." I had witnessed the spell with my mage sight active and thought it might come in handy one day. How did it go again? Ah, yes.

"Scripturam vim extermina," I incanted while pointing to a word on my parchment.

The ink in that area faded to blank. Got it in one, I thought happily. It didn't require much power, but I'd only cleared a small spot. I thought it would require many repetitions to scrub the entire sheet clean, but that was a small price to pay for savings of, what was it? one and two-thirds shillings? I gleefully set about repeating my success. Curious, Brother Hewitt stepped nearer to peer over my shoulder.

"What's that you're doing there?" demanded the astonished friar.

"Just a little trick I picked up from a fellow scholar at Conclave," I replied.

After observing my efforts for a while longer, he then asked: 'Can you do one for me?'

Although normally a charitable sort, I stifled my first impulse to consent. I had an idea.

"Well," said I, "This taxes my powers somewhat. And seeing as you can charge folks two shillings for a blank sheet, perhaps I should get a shilling if I erase one for you. Half seems fair; don't you think?"

The custodian's lip twitched up in a smile, and with his eyes alight with avarice, he began to haggle like the most miserly of merchants I had ever met. Eventually, he beat me down to a groat per page. But I held out for a banality as well. For every six sheets I cleared, one would be mine to keep. It took me all afternoon, but when I'd finished, my coin purse had fattened considerably, and a full stack of blank parchment sat at my elbow. They still had some bumps and ridges where the oak gall had bitten in a bit, but by and large, they'd make passable writing parchments.

Standing and stretching my back a bit, I collected my things and made ready to depart. The light had diminished from the south-facing window. The sun's rays slanted in from the west, projecting a slender angel on a cupboard to my left. The other mendicants had all departed. Only Brother Parvus remained. I approached him. And as I did, his hand strayed to the iron cross, which still hung about his neck.

"May I see what you're working on there?" I asked.

His eyes locked with mine and a slight smile tugged at his lips. He swiveled the board about to face me. On it was a beautifully rendered page. Against a stark white background, the letters were drawn in the exquisitely exacting lines of calligraphy pleasant to behold. The first two letters were enormous and were composed of tiny angels crouched in various poses. Their raised halos were burnished in gold leaf. I was stunned by the beauty of the single page Brother Parvus had spent his entire day perfecting. I was somewhat less pleased when I read the verse of scripture it illuminated.

 anyone worships the beast and his image, and receives a mark on his forehead or on his hand, he also will drink of the wine of the wrath of God, which is mixed in full strength in the cup of His anger;

and he will be tormented with fire and brimstone in the presence of the holy angels and in the presence of the Lamb. And the smoke of their torment goes up forever and ever;

they have no rest day and night, those who worship the beast and his image.

So much for making friends, I thought.

***

We met back in our rooms, the other journeymen and I. Sholeena and Roy had nothing significant to report. Each had covered only a small portion of their respective levels, and neither had sensed the specific enchantment we sought. Their search was hampered by the pyromantic candles placed all about and by other enchantments as well. Sholeena had grown quite excited on encountering magic that some wizard had placed on a baker's oven, but it turned out to be only a cleaning charm. I reclaimed my bob from Roy and placed the stack of parchments within. Tomorrow would be more of the same.

On learning of my dealings with the librarian, my companions urged me to return there. We could use the coin, and my remaining in sight of our watchdogs seemed to give them comfort. Neither Roy nor Sholeena thought they had been followed. So on it went, day after day. So far, however, the sole result of all our efforts was my coin purse growing a bit heavier. I never made as much as on that first day, for the wily librarian continued to reduce the price he was willing to pay. As he explained it, my new sheets had put a glut on the market. With the surfeit of parchments now available, he was unable to charge as much for a sheet as previously. 'Supply and demand,' he had called it. I simply thought of it as a good thing never lasting.

So it was with some surprise that on the fourth day I walked in on an argument.

"I tell you, there's none to be had," said Hewitt.

Before him, Brother Parvus was wringing his hands and looking rather agitated.

"But you had stacks of it only yesterday," he bemoaned.

"I did," replied the glum custodian, "but the duke and his scribes conscripted every bit of it. Moreover, our coffers are all but tapped out. The money we'd hoped to raise from it won't be forthcoming."

"But the "Morgan Crusader Bible" is nearly complete," moaned Parvus. "Brother Hamish, Brother Humphrey and I have all but completed the book of Revelations. We had hoped to see it done and bound, so we could present it to the bishop by Martinmas."

"Well, I'll speak to the duke's men again," said Brother Hewitt, "but you shouldn't get your hopes up. The shortages grow ever worse, and the steward is practically at his wit's end."

Clearly grief-stricken, the brown-frocked servant of the quill trod dejectedly back to his seat. I moved over to my accustomed place and started laying out a few items from my bob. I retrieved the stack of pages I had earned thus far and sorted through them. Most were ordinary parchments. Some were dog-eared or had small tears or other imperfections, but a few were of the finer vellum the monks used. I separated these from the lesser parchments and soon had a tidy stack of eighteen.

Pushing my chair back, I arose and approached the unhappy and idle trio in the scriptorium. They marked my approach through narrowed eyes. I laid the stack before Brother

Parvus saying: 'Take them. A gift. Consider it a donation from one who admires your exquisite work.'

Eyebrows arose all around, but Brother Parvus made no reply. He ran his hand over the smooth surface of the topmost unblemished sheet, then stared up at me searchingly. Nodding once, he distributed the largesse among his brethren and set promptly to work.

My own work slowed after that. Brother Hewitt was nearly out of palimpsests. After erasing the last of them, I entertained myself with a beautifully bound philosophical work by Cicero. In it, he proposed that an ideal government was one formed by an equal balancing and blending of a monarchy, a democracy, and an aristocracy. In this ideal mixed state, he put forth that the royalty, wise aristocrats, and the ordinary folk should each have a role. I found his arguments compelling, if a bit naïve. They assumed that all men were of good intention; that tyrants and oligarchs would willingly set aside their lust for power in favor of the common good. It had astonished me when Kendrick (or Prince Henry) had called me an idealist, for I'd always thought I had a more cynical turn of mind.

Of course, Cicero's wistful writings hadn't saved Reme. Reme fell, after all. It was said that far across the sea to the east lay the land of our ancestors. Legend had it that a great city was founded there by two brothers raised by wolves, Romulus and Remus. As was inevitable, the two fought, and Remus slew Romulus and named the city 'Reme.' This Reme grew into a mighty empire that spread across the continent and then evolved into a republic, bringing many cultural benefits and scientific advances to its people. But just as all good things come to an end, Reme grew corrupt. And like a dying animal, it fell prey to scavengers in the form of barbarian hordes and mythic creatures.

Our ancestors fled the collapse of Reme to these shores, where they met the elves, dwarves, and other goodly races. Fairglen and other human capitals were established by men and eventually coalesced into the Kingdom of Osten. It is a kingdom where, if we aren't very careful, this history may repeat itself. I was thankful that our forebears brought with them the writings of

Cicero and others. If our current leaders hearkened to the lessons of the past, perhaps Fairglen might be spared the fate of Reme. What I didn't quite ken was how our language had changed so much. We still retained the 'old tongue' that was spoken by the Remans, but Ostenian standard bore little resemblance to the speech of our forebears...

So engrossed was I in such musings that I failed to mark the passage of time. As darkness settled over the chamber, Brother Hewitt's approach startled me from my reverie. He was closing up and had come to reclaim the tome and shoo me on my way. I thanked the man, departed hastily and hustled toward our rooms. Roy and Sholeena would doubtless be growing concerned by now.

On entering our chambers, I found the two talking excitedly.

"Lucas!" exclaimed Sholeena. "You just missed him!"

"Missed whom?" I asked.

"Not twenty minutes ago," said Roy more soberly, "a footman arrived bearing a message --"

"He was dressed all in red and had a note for us on a silver tray," interrupted the Paluda girl.

Royland waited to see whether she was done, and the girl subsided.

"It was the livery of Conclave; that of our own guild," Roy explained. "He brought us an invitation."

"Who sent him?" I asked as Royland handed me a note.

"Best you read it for yourself," he replied, forestalling Sholeena's attempt to tell me.

I moved closer to the lantern to regard the writing.

Greetings, fellow mages,

I was initially most pleased to hear of your arrival and had prepared a hearty and proper welcome. Imagine my disappointment to discover you had somehow earned the duke's displeasure. I have been petitioning his grace that you may at least be present for one of my reports. It would be an exciting addition. And it would add some human interest to what is otherwise a dry recounting of the war's stalled progress and the duke's need for various materials.

Good news! His grace has finally relented. Please send word if you will be able to attend tomorrow's 'briefing up on the battlement.' I'm certain the good people of my audience would be most gratified to hear how you are getting on and your plans for the upcoming days. I shall order an escort should you answer in the affirmative.

God willing, I shall greet you on the morrow. Until then, stay safe and pray for those who keep you thus,

Peter Redmond Doyle

That was Master Pete alright. I noted with wry amusement that his overused tagline was present even in his written correspondence. I felt I already knew the man, though we had never met. I had been privy to many of his daily reports to Conclave when I'd sat in proxy for Master Chadwick there. His twin, Redmond, had the uncanny knack of channeling his brother's speech and gestures over any distance. Thus, Master Pete spent twenty minutes at noon each day summarizing conditions here at the war front for the conclave of wizards.

"What do you think?" asked Roy.

"I think we need to consider most carefully what we will say and what we should not."

"I agree," said my cousin, "but since you weren't here, we sent word back with the footman anyway."

"We said yes!" Sholeena exclaimed.

***

The wind caught at my cloak in sudden gusts, heightening my sense of vertigo as I peered out upon the land. The pair of guardsmen who'd escorted us here had stayed back in the tower, and Master Pete was nowhere to be seen. So, we stood alone on the battlement of Eagle's Keep, high atop the mountain citadel of Stronghold. I was right. You *could* see for miles from up here.

Sholeena was shivering behind a merlon and trying not to look down. Roy was watching the eagles, which were the keep's namesakes, fly in lazy circles above us. The watch fire stood unlit next to a sundial they used to mark the hours. We were on the north wall of the keep, far across from the mews where the duke's great birds roosted. As I understood it, Master Pete needed to face north when he gave his report because his brother, Redmond, would be in the assembly hall facing in the same direction. Were he to stand facing south, the masters would receive his briefing while staring at Redmond's back.

"Hello, journeymen!" came a jovial voice from the east tower.

And from the narrow doorway beneath its conical cupola strode Peter Redmond Doyle, so resembling his brother that I had to do a double-take (as it were). Smiling and waving, he stepped out upon the parapet and approached us. His billowing robes were at once pressed flat against him by the buffeting wind. Roy took the lead, nodding and declaring, 'well met.'

Introductions were made all around while Master Pete repeatedly inspected the sundial. When the shadow on the dial pointed directly at XII, Royland asked why we weren't getting started.

"We've a few minutes yet," Master Pete declared.

He went on to explain that his brother would begin channeling him from Conclave at precisely noon. But since the sun traveled across the sky from east to west, and Conclave was to the west of here, it wouldn't be noon there for several more minutes. Experience had taught him and his twin to make allowance for this celestial phenomenon. It made sense, but I'd never before had occasion to consider that it might be a different time of day somewhere else. What a wonderful world we lived in. There was always something more to learn.

Soon enough, Master Pete straightened and turned his regard northward. With a toothy grin, he addressed his invisible audience.

"Greetings, Conclave," began Master Pete, pausing for effect.

"The skies above Eagle's Keep are clear today, if a bit windy. The duke sends his regards and wishes to thank the conclave for continuing its unwavering support of the war effort. He especially looks forward to the arrival of your new healer. It is his grace's understanding the girl's a miracle worker who has nearly eliminated the plague from Deerfield. We are sore in need of such. The men out at Redoubt are beset by all manner of vile illnesses of late. I suppose they don't call them the Black Plagued Marshes for nothing."

Pete paused again to deliver one of his signature smiles. Could it be true? Were they sending Bella down here to tend to the sick?

"We are dispatching fresh troops and transferring and hosteling the sick or wounded here at the keep in a steady rotation, the logistics of which are quite daunting. But his grace remains determined to maintain our forward base while planning bold strikes deep into the enemy held land. Mayhap one day we can discover where the blackguards are hiding and actually do them some harm."

He puffed out his chest, raised a fist, and struck a noble pose. It occurred to me that Master Pete thoroughly enjoyed his reports.

"Yesterday, I promised you a special treat," he went on to say. "Here with me today are three of our number who left the conclave some months ago on a sojourn to become the first non-elves to be instructed in Lorédon. I know that if we were physically present, you would give a warm welcome to Royland, Lucas, and Sholeena!"

Sholeena waved. My face split in a grin when Roy began scolding her.

"They can't see or hear us, you know," he muttered.

"Royland," said the wizard, "is there anything you'd like to tell the folks back home?"

"Not really," he replied.

Master Pete frowned briefly at my cousin, but then his smile snapped back into place as he faced front.

"Royland would like to express his fond regard for all the good people of Conclave and his hopes for a swift triumph in the war," he reported.

"Have you aught to add, Lucas?"

"Uh... Oh, yes. I want to thank Lloyd Bridges for the void pocket he provided us. It's been a godsend. And I hope the fairies aren't getting into too much mischief."

Master Pete did a more reliable job of faithfully relaying my own message.

"Last but not least is Miss Sholeena," he said with a playful tilt of his head. "I'm certain the masters would like to know what gave you and your confederates the notion to traipse all the way here into the middle of a war zone, a dangerous trek fraught with perils. What say you?"

"Um, well..." said Sholeena as the color drained from her face.

She glanced over at me with a look of panic, then continued.

"We thought the soldiers could use some cheering up!" she choked out.

"Ah," said Master Pete. "The young lady said they wanted to inspire the soldiery to be of good cheer, the better to overcome the enemy and their diabolical plans. Well said miss! But I'm afraid our time is nearly spent. In addition to the items I listed yesterday, Stronghold is running low on clean linens and will take any you can send. The infirmaries are full to capacity. Medicinal herbs are also in short supply."

"God willing, I shall report again tomorrow at this same time. Until then, stay safe and pray for those who keep you thus. Peter Redmond Doyle, signing off."

He maintained his pose for another few seconds and then sagged with relief.

"That went well, I think," said the wizard, leaning against a merlin.

The shadow of an eagle passed over him, interrupting the light.

"Why are you really here?" he asked. "And why does duke Gaul think so ill of you?"

He spoke in more sober tones than the voice he used as a war correspondent. Were our deflections that obvious?

"I wish we could tell you," I returned. "In part, it's a private matter, but more rightly, it's a dangerous secret best shared among as few as possible."

"Now you've got me intrigued, journeyman. Perhaps I can guess it. Now, why would three new journeyman mages leave their master's side and travel..."

Just then, there was a clunking sound to my right. I whirled about to face the noise. But it was only Sholeena. The Paluda girl was messing about with the logs of the watch fire, one of which had rolled loose. She stared over at us excitedly.

"H.C.B!" she announced. "That's his monogram, right? H.C.B?"

***

Royland and I rushed over at once while Master Pete looked on, bemused. In his haste, my cousin nearly shouldered Sholeena aside, but then he caught himself.

"Pardon me," he mumbled, and waited for her to give way.

"I think I see it," he went on to say as he rummaged among the logs. "Well done, Sholeena."

The Paluda girl beamed.

My cousin began handing me logs which I carelessly stacked nearby. Soon I could see them as well. They were the same chiseled letters we'd seen carved into the cliff face. And just below them lay the enchantment.

"We need to do it now, cousin," I advised. "The duke won't permit us up into the keep unescorted. This may be our only chance."

The guardsmen who comprised our escort were by now peering out from the east tower and looked ready to emerge.

To Master Pete, I said: 'Master, we need to find something here. If you'll be patient, you'll soon learn something of what we're about. Can you keep our escort from growing too nosey?"

"I've heard about you," he replied. "They say you three laid out Gunther. I'm sure the prat had it coming. And you befriended the fairies and fought off a goblin invasion, to name a few others. Whatever you're cooking up next, I think I'd like to see it. Count me in."

"Here now, what's this then?" shouted the soldier stalking toward us.

Putting on his best game face, Master Pete intercepted the man.

"I was assured I could have an exclusive interview with these three uninterrupted, corporal. We've finished today's report, but I need to gather more information for tomorrow's. We need the logs for... well, never mind why we need them. Suffice it to say it's important to keeping the goodwill of the conclave. How much harder would it be to prosecute this war lacking our continued support."

"Well I..."

"I *suggest* you return to the tower and wait until our

business here has concluded. I'll alert you when I'm done with these three, and you can deliver them back to the lower levels. Those are your orders, are they not?"

The corporal straightened and nodded, waving the other man back as well.

"And close the door," Pete shouted at their retreating backs. "You're distracting me from my work."

"That was amazing, master," I muttered.

"You just have to know how to talk to soldiers," he returned with a grin.

By this time, Roy had the firebox emptied and was ready to stoke it with his gift. The three of us looked on as he invoked a magic flame. We huddled close so as not to miss a word. The face of Master Hans soon swelled up to fill the sphere. But he wasn't smiling as before. He looked troubled, and a gasp emerged from Master Pete as he observed fire speech for the first time.

"Hello again, future unnamed person, if indeed you are a friend and not one of the fiends sent to spy on us and unravel our plans."

This wasn't an auspicious beginning. Where was that chipper attitude that had so characterized the first of the markers we'd found?

"We've discovered that dark minions of the enemy are capable of possessing a man and subjugating his will. We had thought Stronghold to be a safe haven, a place where we might place Gretta's talisman for those that follow. But now we know that minions of the enemy can walk these ramparts with impunity in the guise of the most trusted of men."

"Heed me well. If you be one of these, know that you shall never puzzle out where the next markers lie. But if you be of true heart, then we must set before you a test. For you see, we have marked a weakness in our foemen, the unseelie fey. Though blessed with language skills that surpass all others, the faire folk cannot read. Therefore, to follow us further, you must first solve a puzzle of words that Gretta has cleverly designed. Hear then her first clue."

At this, Hans withdrew to be soon replaced by the countenance of Gretta. She too was of a most somber disposition. She peered out and said the following:

"Many birds besides proud eagles soar above this keep.
Not all reside in aeries or within his grace's mews.
Seek the cock that never crows nor even makes a peep.
And cardinals will point the way when you, in turn,
have shared the news."

"As this one ushers in the day
While the night owl takes roost to slumber
The golden path won't lead you astray
If you follow the words without number."

"What could it mean?" muttered Master Pete as he stared in bewilderment at the collapsing ball of flame.

But I was already digging out parchment and ink from my bob. If this was a word puzzle, then the exact wording would matter. Roy was staring upward at the eagles still circling above. My cousin was doubtless already working out the answer. He never forgot such details, but I wanted to write it all down while it was fresh.

"Perhaps we should return to our rooms and think on it," said Roy.

I gazed up at my cousin and marked something peculiar.

"I think not," said I. "We must strike while the iron is hot, as the smiths are wont to say."

"You've an idea?" he asked.

"No. But I spy, with my little eye, a cock that never crows."

Following my gaze upward, my cousin then spotted it as well. Affixed high atop the tower adjoining the battlement was a wrought iron weather vane. It featured a rooster perched on an arrow. This rotated and swiveled to indicate the direction of the wind.

"We must get up there," I said.

"Was that Master Hans?" asked Peter.

"It was," answered Royland. "Did you know him?"

"I'm afraid not. He was before my time. The man was a legend. You're his spitting image, though; I must say."

"He was my grandfather."

"And Mistress Gretta looked so young. I did meet *her* a few months back. She was in the infirmary. Poor old dear wouldn't utter a word."

Roy's face got that pinched look again. He didn't need to say it aloud. I could read it in his expression. 'Six. Just six more markers to go...'

"We can discuss it later," I snapped. "We need to examine that weather vane atop the tower. You keep the hounds at bay while I climb there."

Master Pete gaped up at the sharply pointed cap surmounting the tower in question with a look of disbelief. Sholeena, too, looked a little green.

"You stay here and help Master Pete, Sho," I said. "I'll go up and lower a rope for Roy."

I only hoped I had enough magic to spider up there. It was about thirty feet, less than half of Rapunzel's tower. What I hadn't accounted for were the treacherous conditions of the wooden shakes that shingled the sharply angled roof. They were brittle and a bit slimy from mold. They would soon need replacement. Nonetheless, I managed the climb, as did Roy after a few minutes of effort.

We regarded the ironwork as we clung to the uneven tiles.

"I think I've got it worked out, Lucas," said Roy. "The cardinals that will point the way aren't birds. They're the cardinal directions, like on a compass. We can 'share the NEWS' by turning it first north, then east, west, and south."

"Just do it, Roy. I can't hold us here forever. I'm starting to lose my grip."

Looking below, I saw Master Pete having an animated discussion with Sholeena, Roy, and Lucas. I recalled that Master Pete was a light mage like Lorraine. He was maintaining semblances of us to fool the guards should they decide to check up on us. Roy and Lucas weren't moving or saying much, but Sholeena appeared to be having a good time.

As Royland turned the weathercock for the fourth time and pressed down on it, a circular cavity beneath it opened. Reaching in, Roy retrieved a longish bundle wrapped in oilcloth. He almost dropped it, which would have been a tragedy, when a sudden gust forced him to grip the base of the weather vane more securely. It was time to head back down. After Roy had descended the knotted rope with his prize, I detached the rope and skittered down with the last of my flagging strength. And viola.

When we returned to the others, ghost Royland and Lucas faded away to haunt the battlement no more.

"*Now* we can go back to our rooms," I said. "I think we've pushed our luck with the guards to its limits. We thank you, Master Pete, but it's time for us to depart."

The man nodded, but his face bore a vaguely dissatisfied look.

"I shall report on your antics here today neither to the conclave nor to the duke. I sense your mission is both vital and secretive. But when all's said and done, I think you three will owe me an explanation over a stiff drink at a tavern. Though in truth, I've found our reckless adventure quite exhilarating. Farewell for now. Don't be strangers."

"We'll stay safe," I said.

"And we'll pray for those who keep us so," added Sho.

***

Back in our rooms, Sho and I watched as Royland carefully

216

unrolled the bundle. First, the oilcloth was removed. Likely this wrapper was merely a precaution to waterproof whatever lay inside, but nothing should be overlooked. My eyes first fell on the wand that was revealed. It was nearly the length of my own, but its enchantment was markedly less potent. Moreover, atop its head perched a carved wooden eagle. The detail was exquisite. I could almost imagine it taking wing.

But more interesting at the moment were the letters covering the inner surface of the oilskin. They were written in a tidy script that covered the cloth. Roy spread it out and read it aloud. This was chiefly for Sholeena's benefit. Although the Paluda girl could read, she wasn't yet very proficient at it, and many of the words confronting us now would be challenging for her nascent skills. It said:

When I'm ill, you are my solace.

I am near to a raging fire.

My report, endures flawless

speak civilly and without ire

Consider the phrase betimes it is mulish

hereafter swimming abaft. is most foolish

EAM MALF SUIT NUN ETIRE AUQ

Immediately, I marked the capitalized letters running down the left-hand side. Whatever could 'WIMCE' mean? The concluding line reminded me of the old tongue, but its meaning was sheer nonsense.

"Her malf has not been auq?" I said aloud.

Royland grunted.

"Another puzzle," he said. "Perhaps it relates to the second verse Gretta gave us in her clue. Do you still have what you wrote down of it?"

I produced the parchment on which I'd scribbled her words, and again Royland read it aloud.

"'As this one ushers in the day' - that would be the rooster on the weather vane. 'While the night owl takes roost to slumber' - same time, dawn. 'The golden path won't steer you astray, if you follow the words without number.' Any ideas?"

"Maybe the golden path is the path of the sun as it crosses the sky?" said Sholeena.

Roy looked at her appreciatively.

"That may well be," he said.

"There's a stained-glass window of an angel in the monastic library up on level four," I put forth. The sunbeams trace a reverse picture of it across the floor and up the shelves as the day progresses. I didn't notice whether there were any owls or other birds on it, but there could be. And where better than a library to find 'words without number?'"

"It's certainly worth checking out, as the librarians are wont to say," quipped my cousin.

So we rolled up the wand and its wrapper in Royland's scarf and took ourselves to the library.

We entered at about midday. The monks were all at their scriptorium, scribbling away contentedly. Behind them, the window cast its kaleidoscope of light upon the boards of the floor. I checked, but no birds were portrayed in the colorful panes of glass. Brother Hewitt soon arrived to greet us.

"I see you've brought some friends today," he said. "I'm afraid I have no more used parchment with which to barter."

"That isn't why we're here, brother," I replied. "Would it be all right if the three of us sit at the back table as we try to work something out?"

"As long as you're quiet," he cautioned, eyeing the others assessingly.

While my companions made base camp at the table in

question. I drew brother Hewitt aside to ask a few more questions. He had never heard of a 'WIMCE.' Then I asked him the name of the angel depicted in the glass. It was the archangel, Michael, he informed me, the one who led God's army when Lucifer was cast down. Nor did his flaming sword have a name apart from 'the sword of Michael.' I had hoped to find some sort of bird reference to confirm our hypothesis. Finally, I asked him what was in the cabinet where I'd seen the angel come to rest.

"Books," he replied.

"May we peruse them?" I inquired.

He looked at me askance.

"If you're extremely cautious," he finally agreed. "Some of them are originals, and many are quite fragile."

He produced a key and unlocked the cabinet in question. I retrieved a stack of books from its upper shelf, thanked the man, and brought them over to my companions. Whereupon we each began leafing through various volumes, uncertain even of what we sought. Most were prayer books, commonly called 'Books of Hours.' But there were also books about political philosophy, poetry, epic journeys and battles and even a large, full-color bestiary that kept Sholeena amused. Words without number, indeed.

"This is getting us nowhere," sighed Roy as he closed the bindings on yet another tome.

This caused the trio of monks to look over at us again in disgust.

"Keep it down," shushed Brother Hamish, "Some of us are trying to work over here."

The monks sat in such silence that one could easily forget they were even there. Both Roy's scarf and the oilskin lay open on the table before us. We had examined them repeatedly for clues to the task Gretta had set for us. Roy shot brother Hamish a black look before turning to me and whispering, 'In what manner should we follow words without number? What could it possibly mean?'

It was at this point Brother Parvus lay his stylus aside, arose from his stool and paced over toward us. I was made a bit uneasy as he hovered there, glowering over my shoulder. After a minute, he spoke.

"May I see that?" he asked, indicating the oilcloth.

Was that politeness? From Parvus? I nodded assent, and he took it up, examining it closely.

"I believe I can be of assistance, if after that you promise to take your wagging tongues elsewhere."

"By all means," said Roy. "We'll take any help we can get."

Parvus grunted and strode back to his easel, bearing our precious clue. Roy grew agitated when the friar began dipping his stylus in his ink pot and making a series of horizontal marks on its surface. But he soon returned and laid the modified verse before us. He had underlined some of the words. Reading only these, It now read:

When you are

near to a

report,

speak

the phrase

hereafter abaft.

EAM MALF SUIT NUN ETIRE AUQ

"These are the words without number," he said simply.

I stared at the cloth in befuddlement for a moment, but then I caught on. Words without number clearly meant those lacking the numerals like 'I', 'V', and 'X'. Also 'D', 'L', 'C', or 'M'.

"Now honor your promise and leave us in peace."

With that, he pivoted and stalked back to join his silent brothers.

"What's 'abaft?'" I asked Roy when we were headed back down the stairway to tier three.

"It's a nautical term," Sholeena supplied, surprising us once again. "It means toward the back of the ship or behind it."

"Could it mean reversed or backward?" asked Roy with sudden excitement.

"Sometimes it does," answered Sho.

My cousin stopped right there on the landing, retrieved some ink, and began making more marks on the cloth by the light of the candles there. Then he held it up for me to inspect.

"What do you make of this, cousin?"

Reversed, the last line read: QUA ERITE NUN TIUS FLAM MAE. It meant something like 'Where will you be?' Then, all at once, the solution struck me. Translated from the old tongue, 'quaerite nuntius flammae' meant something else entirely. 'Seek the messenger of the flame' It read. Of course, Royland had already worked it out, but it was nice to know I was no more than a step or two abaft of him.

It occurred to me I should liked to have known Gretta when she was younger. Her artful obfuscations were perplexing, but always made sense in the end. I could definitely see where Royland got his genius. No fairy alive could have puzzled that one out. Terwilliger certainly couldn't have, and he was the only fairy I knew who could even read.

***

Roy wanted to invoke the wand straight away, but Sholeena and I convinced him to wait. It was late in the day, and in all our mucking about on the battlement and in the library, we'd missed the midday meal. My stomach was urging me to take a pause, and my magic center was throbbing with the ache of overuse. So, we returned to our modest quarters and partook of a cold repast from our stores there. In the afterglow of this modest feast, a great lethargy came over me, and I implored my cousin to hold off until morning.

Deep within the bowels of Stronghold, there was no light to mark the dawn. The distant tolling of the morning bell was just fading as Sholeena shook me awake. Roy was still splayed out on his mattress, snoring silently into the shroud of stillness wrought by his enchanted pillow. I threw my shoe at him to startle him awake. Though I longed for a hot meal, I knew such would not be forthcoming as I watched my cousin hastily make ready for the day.

He gripped the wand with excitement and took a deep, calming breath.

"Quaerite nuntius flammae," he commanded it.

Sholeena and I stared wide-eyed as the magic manifested. By our mage sight, we saw the eagle on the head of the wand become animate. The carving remained still, but from it, a spirit eagle emerged, flexing its tiny wings and launching itself toward the door. From behind it fell glittering sparkles, painting the floor with a glowing golden trail. When it encountered the planks of the door, the spirit eagle sailed right through, not hampered in the least by the obstacle. With a puff of golden glitter, it disappeared from our sight.

We hurried after. This must be the golden path to which Mistress Gretta had referred. Roy opened the door, and the pathway lay clear before us. Eschewing my mage sight, I could detect not a glimmer of it, but when I again attuned myself to mystical energies. I saw the path running straight down the hallway until it passed from our view around a bend.

Once more we followed, with Roy taking the lead and Sholeena and I trailing behind. It was hard keeping up with my cousin. In his eagerness, his lanky strides ate up the distance in a walk so brisk it might be mistaken for running.

"Slow down, Roy," I groused. "We've no idea how far it is. The locals will think us mad if we go dashing down the halls."

As I may have mentioned previously, Stronghold is immense. Its tunnels ran haphazardly throughout. A veritable maze of corridors, storage rooms, and living spaces, it was designed by the duke's ancestors to withstand a prolonged siege. And few save for the city planners knew its full extent. After what felt like hours of trudging through tunnels, we could see the trail's end.

It was in a deserted stretch of the corridor down on level one. No candles lit our way, and Sholeena, marching to our rear, now bore a lantern. The pathway ended in an alcove. From the grit present on the floor, it hadn't seen a dust mop in ages. Within it stood a stone urn that looked too heavy to be readily moved. Peering over its lip, I saw it contained naught but the dust of time. No eagle was evident, but the golden path clearly ended here, and on the wall above was the sparkle of an enchantment nearly too faint to be seen.

Sholeena set her lantern down on the roughhewn stone floor nearby. Roy sheathed his wand and prepared to cast his spell of fire.

"Congratulations!" beamed Hans, peering out from the orb. "If you are hearing this, you have doubtless passed Gretta's little test. If not, you might want to have a look up on the keep's battlement."

I seated myself on the floor and stared in rapt attention as Master Hans continued. The by now familiar orb bobbed above the urn whence had issued the revealing mists. The golden path had rapidly faded on the commencement of the good master's speech.

"From here on out, the way grows more dire. We head south, right into the teeth of the enemy's strength. Hopefully, for you who follow us, the matter will be resolved, and the way will be clear. But remain vigilant. The Black Plagued Marshes contain many dangers of their own. Strange creatures have always prowled about it even prior to the stirring of the enemy's hand. And not the least of these dangers are the dire maladies said to overcome those who dare set an intruding foot in these lands. Take precautions if you would follow us further. Tis said that he prepares to fail who fails to prepare."

The wizard smiled and nodded his agreement with his overworked aphorism.

"Several explanations have been put forth by our healers as to why these environs are so deadly to men. The first has it that the bites and stings of insects and other creatures are responsible. Others contend the brackish water of these fetid fens contains some toxin fostering illness. Regardless, Greta and I intend to guard against both.

"Although hydromancy is among the least potent of my gifts, we intend to make our own drinking water on this trek. Know that even boiling the tainted swamp waters is not proof against the sickness. Also, as a Willoughby, Gretta has cleverly enchanted our cloaks by her entomancy to repel vermin that might seek to infect us. I suggest you take similar precautions.

We will leave a further record of our progress every couple of days. If you are in range of one, the golden path will show you the way. I'm still uncertain why the oracle bade us to leave this record, but Gretta and I imagine it is for the annals of posterity. One day, I hope we can meet, and you can tell me what you think of our historic journey. Until then, pleasant trails, my friend."

The orb returned to its fiery state, then gradually dwindled to nothing.

"So, was that number five?" I asked aloud. "Do only five more remain?"

"No," Roy returned. "On the scarf, there's only a single mark at Eagle's Keep. That still only counts as one."

We retraced our steps as best we could, losing our way only a few times. It was decided we would set out in a few days' time. We bought new cloaks for each of us. On Sholeena's advice, these were a drab olive in hue with mottled patches of brown and gray. They were designed to blend in with forested surroundings and render one less visible in such. Royland affixed a minor enchantment to each that repelled insects.

Sholeena assured us she could provide as much clean water as needed. We filled my bob with as much of everything we could think of which might prove useful. By Wednesday morning, we were ready to go.

***

One more incident of note occurred ere we departed from Eagle's Keep. It happened just as we exited the gates. As when we had arrived, the sentries were present, inspecting and questioning the newly arrived. The queue to exit was a much simpler affair, just a cursory nod as we passed. The royal visit had concluded several days ago. The prince and his entourage had set off for Freemark, the next leg on his grand tour of the kingdom, so security was a bit more lax.

Nevertheless, among the assembled men was Brother Parvus, scrutinizing those who would gain entry. On spotting us, he stepped over.

"Hold, if you will, journeymen. I would have words with you."

We moved a bit further down the lane and waited for the man to catch us up. He nodded briefly to the others and then turned to stare directly at me, a placid look of calm upon his pale features.

"I know we had a rocky start," he began. "And I wouldn't be surprised if you doubt my intentions, but know that I seek only to share the gift bestowed on me by my creator. As his humble servant, it is incumbent upon me to warn you of the danger."

Well, cheery as ever, I thought. I nodded my understanding and waited for him to continue.

"There is a darkness attached to you, journeyman."

"Not just the mark on your hand," he quickly forestalled. "That fey magic is, as you say, likely something harmless. Rather, it is a dark stain that gnaws upon your very soul, though I now suspect it doesn't own you completely as yet. Beware its creeping."

What could I say to such an ominous warning? Every

response that came to mind sounded trite or dismissive. So I opted for silence, nodding my acceptance of his words.

"Would you accept a blessing, journeyman?"

Again I nodded.

Gripping his cross in his left hand, he pressed his right to my forehead as he gave voice to his benison.

"Unclean spirit, whoever you are, I command you along with all your minions now attacking this servant of the lord. By the mysteries of the incarnation, passion, and resurrection, depart him! Begone, Satan, inventor and master of all deceit, enemy of man's salvation. Nor be emboldened to harm in any way this creature of God, other innocents, or any of their possessions. The sacred Sign of the Cross so commands you. The blood of the Martyrs and the pious intercession of all the Saints so command you. May the good lord look with favor on this child of light and speed him on his way."

"Amen," I muttered, sensing he was done.

The sun rising in the east shone brightly in our eyes as we headed down the road toward the trail. We hoped to make it to Redoubt in a couple of days. It was the most forward outpost of our countrymen and a rallying point for the duke's forces assaulting the south. Reaching it would put us most of the way to the next marker. Thereafter, we'd be on our own behind enemy lines.

"How do you do it, cousin?" asked Roy as we ambled along.

"Do what?"

"Connect to people like that. I'd swear that Brother Parvus is actually rooting for you now. Wasn't he trying to arrest you, not five days ago? What's your secret?"

"Persistent politeness and empathy for others can often work wonders," I replied.

But in my heart, I knew dread. What was this darkness Brother Parvus had seen in me? Could it be related to my misbehaving homunculus? And if so, what should I do about it? I shoved these questions aside, as I had so many times before. It was a nice day, and these were matters best left for another.

I'd never been a particularly religious sort. And all the strange trappings of faith were sometimes baffling to me. I knew they gave others reassurance. But I assumed the creator just wanted each of us to muddle through as best we could with the gifts he'd given us, helping one another along the way. During Brother Parvus' rant, I'd detected not a flicker from my mage sight. And yet I felt fortified, as though a sweet breeze had cleansed me within. I felt as if a higher power was on my side, and it gave me solace. Whatever hardships lay ahead for the three of us, it was comforting to think we mightn't be *entirely* on our own.

CHAPTER NINE

𝔗𝔥𝔢 ℭ𝔞𝔭𝔱𝔞𝔦𝔫

"It matters not how strait the gate,
How charged with punishments the
scroll; I am the master of my fate: I
am the captain of my soul."

~ William Ernest Henley ~

The head of the trail had been easy to spot, and it seemed well-traveled at first. The scrubby growth had been cleared away in a broad lane stretching southward that bore the imprints of many a hoof and boot. The first day was a tedious hike on a well-marked trail where our greatest challenge was the boredom it engendered. By midday, we had passed the final marker stone and crossed over Osten's border. But no sudden change in the surrounding landscape heralded our advance into the Black Plagued Marshes. Instead, more gradual changes ensued.

As we traveled farther south, we began encountering muddy stretches and an occasional pool of standing water. The path we followed ceased running true south. It meandered about to detour around such obstacles. The wetlands grew ever thicker with insects, the buzzing and chirping of which became a constant backdrop to our sodden footfalls. Even the air seemed thicker and smelled somewhat of rot and decay. By nightfall, the ground had grown spongy with moss, and stands of tupelo trees cast their long shadows as the sun settled slowly in the west. We set up camp beside a cluster of these.

"When can you make the golden path, Royland?" asked Sholeena once again.

"I doubt we've gone even two leagues as yet," said Roy. "The next marker is at least four miles past Redoubt. And that's still about a day and a half father on. Ask me then."

On the morning of our departure, Roy had invoked his wand several times. On each occasion, the little eagle had emerged and flown back toward the keep. But on the third attempt, it had ceased to do so. From this, my cousin surmised that its effective range was somewhat less than two miles.

"I'm glad we haven't discovered any grim horrors yet," I put in.

I draped my cloak over the canvas of our tent. So far, Roy's enchantment had been doing a good job of repelling the pests, but I thought a little extra protection couldn't hurt. Back at the marketplace in Eagle's Keep, one of the merchants had been touting the benefits of 'Simon Strangelove's Miracle Elixir.' Most had thought him a fraud. But, being familiar with the product, I'd bought out his entire supply. I slid the small crate out of bob and unsealed a bottle. By its pleasant, minty scent, I recognized it to be the genuine formula. After slathering it liberally on my face and arms, I offered some to my companions.

"Well, don't get too comfortable, Lucas," said Roy. "You're on the first watch."

"Remind me never to play rock-parchment-scissors with the thought sheriff again," I grumbled to Sholeena.

The land still seemed rather barren of animal life, but something else was making me uneasy. Within the moisture all around us, the plant life was thriving. Although hale and vigorous, I detected from my vertiginous sense an unwholesomeness. They were like the tainted weeds the scarecrow had raised in my inner garden. And though they would bend to my will readily enough, I sensed in the nearby plants a strange reluctance. It was as if they were only humoring me and silently smirking at my efforts.

As we settled into our billet and prepared to find rest, Sholeena drew our attention to some markings on one of the tupelos. They were deep gouges in the bark slightly above the height of my head. According to Sholeena, this was how a bear marked its territory.

"I thought bears lived in forests," Roy put forth.

"Bears can live anywhere," returned Sho. "In Indigo Bay, we have them, though it's usually just the little black ones. Maybe its just some different thing that's *like* a bear."

I shuddered to think what kind of aberrant thing might serve as a bear analog here in the Black Plagued Marshes. I knew that even black bears could get pretty big. And though the claw marks would indicate a creature that stood only slightly above my waist at the shoulder, the thing probably outweighed all three of us combined. And those gouges were pretty deep. It was a shame none of us were trackers. We had no idea how old the marks might be.

After assuring myself that no large creatures lurked among the cluster of trees, I invoked darksight and prepared for my first night's watch.

***

Heading farther south, the trail became much less distinct. We found an occasional boot print, indicating that we were headed generally in the proper direction, but these became fewer and farther between. The spongy moss o'er which we trod was quick to erase the imprints of our steps, and the sun was becoming more difficult to spot. Trees now grew all about us. Their branches hung thick with moss, and their boles were barely visible through the obscuring vines and dense tufts of boscage.

It was a good thing for us that the men of Duke Gaul kept the trail well blazed on their frequent supply trips between Eagle's Keep and Redoubt. We were reassured each time we found a bit of colored cloth tied to a branch. My cousin had taken up a long walking stick. He used it to probe the ground ahead of us. For the thick mat of moss grew just as readily on the surface of stagnant pools as it did on the sodden muck that passed for soil. Sholeena had a good instinct for finding firm footholds, but Roy or I would occasionally make a misstep, earning a soggy boot as our reward.

It was nearing midday when we encountered the bear. It began with an ominous rustling sound from the bramble ahead and to our left. Recalling the incident with the pig, I swiftly cocked back and loaded my crossbow, backing up to assure a clear field of vision. When the creature emerged, we were ready. The great shaggy black beast came ambling out from the thicket ahead, swinging his pointed muzzle first left then right. Then he bawled out a throaty challenge and stood fully upright.

Having no hope of outrunning the creature, I loosed the bolt from my witchwood bow. His threatening roar became an agonized bellow as the bolt pierced the bristling fur below his neck. Spinning about, he dropped to all fours and loped away with an unsteady gait. I loaded another bolt and made ready to pursue.

I wasn't much of a hunter, but this much I knew. I didn't fancy having a wounded creature wandering about nearby. Such animals were unpredictable and prone to lashing out. Best we follow and learn of its fate, perhaps delivering a finishing shot or two. So, cautiously, we followed the blood trail on the ground. Not a half an hour later, the bear was found.

He lay in a thick patch of unfamiliar vines where, undoubtedly, he'd stumbled with his last remaining strength. His sides heaved like great bellows, and his back leg twitched and spasmed. Raising my bow, I granted him the final mercy with a shot placed directly in the base of his skull. He lay still.

My companions and I waited in silence as we surveyed my grizzly kill. I needed to retrieve my bolts, but wanted to make certain the creature was truly dead. It turned out to be a lucky thing we had waited, for soon we spied a subtle creeping movement near the carcass. My vertiginous sense began to throb, and as we watched, the vines slunk forth to encircle the bear. Moreover, their roots became untethered from the ground, rearing up in serpentine fashion to plunge into the still warm remains. They first penetrated its eye sockets and mouth, slithering deep within. Then, thrashing wildly about, they rooted anywhere else they could find purchase, raising weals, burrowing beneath its hide and splitting its raw flesh asunder.

We gaped in horror as the vines consumed our erstwhile ursine adversary.

"Run!" shouted Roy, freeing me from my frightened stupor.

Wait, I thought. I should be the *last* one to fear plants! I planted my feet, drew forth my wand and leveled it at the ground before me as the vines reared up in a vaguely bear-like manner. But try as I might, I couldn't connect to them. They were no longer rooted to the forest floor.

"Gloriabitur securis!" shouted Roy as the thing shambled nearer.

And force axe lopped off one of the creature's legs. It stumbled, granting me time to withdraw a bit farther. But as I turned to put more distance between us, its arm swept down to scoop me up. On contact, the vines began to constrict, binding me tight. They sought to enter my mouth as I uttered my terrified mantra.

"Ambulare interitus," I croaked.

Whereupon the weeds touching my person began to blacken and wither. I felt the rush of green energy fill my magic center, but it was foul, like an overripe fruit that soured the stomach and made one feel unclean. The rot and decay crept up the creature's arm, defoliating the vines and making them brittle until at last I fell from its grip. The thing loomed above me, fifteen feet tall if it was an inch, glaring stupidly at its stub of a missing arm. The leg that Roy had severed had nearly grown back whole.

"Calidus ignis ardentis!" came my cousin's clarion call.

And a great fire formed in the belly of the beast. It pawed at the air in ursine fashion, then silently sagged into a scorched heap. I picked myself up and hobbled toward Roy, who was still feeding the flames with a vengeance.

"Where's Sholeena?" I asked.

"I'm here," she said, stepping into view from out of the trees.

Her camouflage cloak worked surprisingly well, and the mottled green patches of her face and arms were only just forming a fleshy outline. Roy didn't stop until the entire grove of vines had been reduced to a smoking, charred mass. At its center lay a grizzly lump, unrecognizable as the bear it had once been. He was no longer very fuzzy; was he?

It was our first encounter with strangle vines. Regrettably, it wouldn't be our last.

***

It is said among woodsmen and hunters that sometimes you get the bear, and sometimes the bear gets you. I was just thankful our recent encounter had been of the former variety.

"I just felt so useless," Sholeena groused yet again as we marched along.

Since the encounter, the girl had been sulking. We tried telling her she wasn't expected to overcome such hideous creatures on her own. Her magic wasn't suited for such. We valued her contributions and were doing very well as a team. But she remained disconsolate.

"Have you considered that spell you used to dehydrate the nettles back at the créche?" I asked. "I'd wager those vines would get rather brittle lacking their water."

"I hadn't thought of that," she said more brightly. "Royland's fire would make much quicker work of them if I dry them out first. I'm just glad that bear showed us which plants to avoid. We didn't have strangle-vines where I grew up."

And so we marched along, wary of the vegetation growing all about. It was several hours more before we spotted another stand of the carnivorous creepers . It was a fair distance off from the trail we trod, but we paused, intent on purging it from the land.

"Omnino siccis plantis," the Paluda girl intoned once she'd moved as close as she dared.

With a steaming haze of mist, the plants began to wilt. As their leaves shriveled and the green of the vines' casings turned to brown, numerous purple flowers began to blossom along their length. It was a rather beautiful display, and we marveled at this unexpected outcome. One by one, these began opening, each disgorging a bevy of seedlings which drifted upward on fluffy white pappi. Apparently, the dying plant sought to propagate itself as a dandelion spread its seed.

"Arescet et mori," I said, adding my own spell of withering to the mix.

At this, the villainous vines and their abundant blooms began blackening and shriveling still further.

"Calidus ignis ardentis," added Roy, almost as an afterthought.

When the dried and shriveled growth was touched by my cousin's magical flame, they went up in a fiery burst that tore through them with a rapidity that would have done a dragon proud.

"Well, that was easy," said Roy. "I confess clearing that first patch took nearly everything I had. Despite my being descended from a Brubaker, my Willoughby gift isn't ideally suited to pyromancy."

"You could have fooled me," I replied. "I find even 'digitus flamma' difficult to maintain."

"Yes, well, to each his own, cousin. From here on out, we should focus on such teamwork. Hopefully, in this manner, the three without their master can rise to meet the challenges before us."

We continued on with Sholeena now in the lead. Perhaps due to her savage upbringing, we found the Paluda had an instinctive knack for orienting herself in these natural surroundings. She rarely made a misstep and was the best at spotting the colored bits of cloth which blazed the trail. Following in her footsteps, we made much better time than when Roy or I took point. Despite the tendency of my mind to wander, I tried my best to keep my eyes peeled for dangers. The constant droning of the swamp didn't help.

So I was somewhat surprised when Sholeena drew to a halt and bade us both be still. I wanted to ask what was amiss, but my friend seemed to be listening very intently, and I didn't want to distract her.

"Level out the ground here, Lucas," whispered Sho.

Confused and curious, I nonetheless silently heeded the command. Tapping into my earth affinity, I caused the mud to shift and flatten for as far as I could reach.

She began moving again, this time toward a stand of trees on our right. Crouched low, the girl glided through a wet stretch and slipped within the shade of the trees, with Roy and I sloshing after.

Though many kinds of trees grew in these swampy environs, tupelos were the most numerous. Their trunks grew very thick at their bases. As the dry season was well underway, the water level was several feet lower than its highest point. This was evinced by the muddy brown color on the banks of the standing water and by the network of exposed tree roots. It was beneath one such cage of roots my companion was now slithering.

I was wading up to my knees in stagnant filth, but I followed, nonetheless. Sholeena waited until both Roy and I were huddled near.

"Aquam claram," she muttered.

This caused the brown water we'd churned up to clear and settle, rendering the pond placid and pristine once again.

"Someone's coming," hissed the girl. "And they're being very shneaky."

"How so?" whispered Roy.

"They're communicating with bird noises. I heard them closing in behind us. But they're the wrong birds for this place and season."

So we sat crouched within our cave of roots, pressed up against the banks of a stagnant pond, waiting for whoever was stalking us to appear. It was uncomfortable and wet. I knew the Paluda girl could dry our outfits once we'd emerged from the filthy mire, but I imagined the stink would remain. I pulled my variegated cloak tighter about me and remained very still.

Though it felt like hours, it was likely only a quarter of one before we spotted movement to our left. It was a man creeping along from the way we'd come, stopping now and then to peer ahead or examine the ground. He wore no livery, this man. His plain brown clothing blended well with his surroundings, and on his face were smears of mud that looked to be intentional.

When he'd nearly reached the spot where we'd angled off, he stopped and cast his eyes all about. Then he lifted his head, pursed his lips and chirruped out a warble as pretty as any robin calling his mate. He paced carefully around the spot and dipped the toe of his boot into the water of the pond. This immediately stirred up a cloud of brown grit as the scum on the water's surface rippled outward in small circles.

Before long, three others arrived, marching down the trail in loose formation. These men wore leather armor and carried spears. I breathed a sigh of relief. From their attire, I judged these were men of Osten. I considered hailing them as they approached their scout, but decided to observe for just a bit longer. The scout spoke in a low voice as he gestured toward the ground, then shrugged in bewilderment. I could make out snatches of his quiet report to the man I assumed was their leader.

"... three sets of boot prints, one extra-wide... a dwarf maybe..."

"???"

"... dunno. It's as if they just grew wings and flew off from here..."

"!!!"

I stared at my companions and nodded. As I prepared to break the silence and move out into the open, I was interrupted by a sudden shrill warbling from Sholeena. The four men whirled about, their gazes sweeping our general vicinity before locking on our position. The jig was up. We sloshed out from our place of concealment under the watchful scrutiny of the patrolmen, one of whom was bent over with laughter.The other three had weapons drawn and very serious miens indeed.

"You fellows hiding over there," he said. "Keep your hands in sight and come out slowly. Is that all of you?"

"All right," said I, sloshing closer. "And yes, it's only we three."

"Identify yourselves and explain your presence here."

I explained that we were three mages of the conclave traveling to Redoubt. We had hidden because we didn't know who was stalking us. The man's name was Tim Hodges. He and his men were charged with patrolling the trail from the south road down to Redoubt and keeping it clear of threats. They'd been following us since discovering our first night's camp. On hearing we were mages, the men seemed relieved. There were two masters stationed at Redoubt whose services were highly valued. They were less pleased when I informed them we wouldn't be staying long. Nonetheless, they offered us an escort there. If we set off at once, we might arrive by nightfall. We accepted, of course.

We asked for a short break, so Sholeena might dry out our clothing and equipment. Soggy socks would have been most disagreeable on a half day's march. While we were tidying up, Tim turned to his tracker, a man named Richard Chapman. The fellow was still grinning ear to ear and shaking his head from time to time.

"What's got you so amused, Dick?" the patrol leader asked.

"The girl," the man replied, glancing over at Sholeena.

"Explain."

"Well, as you may know, for our signal, I use a robin's spring mating call, as it's unlikely we would hear such in the marsh in wintertime. But when she revealed their location, twas with the female robin's response call. Sort of an in-joke among us naturalists. Methinks the lass must have a rare sense of humor."

If only he knew the full of it.

***

When we approached Redoubt, the first thing I noticed was the open space. We had made good time, and several hours of daylight yet remained. Stepping out of the dense vegetation, we arrived at a wide, cleared area leading up to a gentle rise. It wasn't much of a hill, but it was notable for its elevation above the surrounding wetland.

Straddling this barren slope was a great rectangular palisade made of stout logs about twenty feet in height. These were pointed at their tops to form a zig-zag battlement of sorts. Behind it stood men whose heads and shoulders could be seen. Clearly, a wooden parapet ran along the wall's inner side, providing cover for those crouched behind it. Corporal Hodges had dispatched a man to forewarn them of our coming, so the wall was fully manned on our approach.

From the corner of the structure, arising higher still, was a lookout tower sporting a peaked roof. Atop this, a gold and black banner perched stirring gently in what passed for a breeze on this stifling, stuffy day. The fortress was primitive but looked impressively solid. Earthen ramparts lay around it, and an incline led up to two massive wooden gates, presently closed.

"Hail the Redoubt!" shouted the corporal. "Squad Six would enter with three visiting mages."

"Advance and be recognized," returned a voice from the tower.

We moved closer and stood for inspection. The man in the tower was familiar to me. Though we'd never met, his portrait hung in the hall of masters back at the conclave. I was uncertain what welcome to expect, as I'd had several altercations with his son. Moreover, the man was an autonomist, a faction not presently in great favor there.

"Welcome Squad Six," said the man after surveying us coldly. "You may return to barracks. As to your... visitors; they are to be taken directly to the captain. He'll know what to do about them."

We were subjected to many a silent stare as one of the gates was swung wide.

Not quite a full regiment, the Seventh Expeditionary Force, had initially been led by one of the duke's knights. The man had also held a commission as a full colonel of the duke's militia. But the word was he had fallen ill about a month ago and had not, as yet, recovered sufficiently to resume his command. Redoubt was therefore run by a newly promoted captain who had heroically led them to victory when the shambling mounds had first attacked.

Muddy, sweaty, and stinking of swamp water wasn't the first impression I had hoped to make. But I shouldn't have worried. For it turned out that Roy and I had hitherto met the man. As we were hustled across the compound and taken to headquarters, we found him seated at a table there poring over a map.

"Harold? Harold Hunt?" I said, surprised.

"Actually, it's *Captain* Hunt now," he returned. "Hello Lucas. Roy. Have you fought off any more bandits lately?"

He bade the astonished patrolmen to go get cleaned up while he 'renewed some old acquaintances.'

"And have Corporal Clark report here on the double," he added.

When I'd last seen Harold, he had just reenlisted in the Osten militia when it mustered in Deerfield, just south of the caravansary. Harold had been a roustabout for Master Ross, the boss of the Tomcats. He'd left us to serve the kingdom's need for reinforcements here in the south, resuming his former rank of lieutenant. It appeared he'd come up in the world since.

We introduced him to Sholeena. Harold poured us each a glass of some rotgut usquebaugh they brewed out here in the swamp. He assured us it would grow hair on one's chest, whereupon Sholeena set hers pointedly aside.

"I haven't much time to reminisce," declared Harold. "I've got a meeting with the mages and my second officer about an offensive we're planning. So let's cut straight to the chase. What are you three doing out here, and how can I help?"

Harold looked troubled when we shared our intention to travel farther south. He looked aside and bunched his lips.

"I'm not saying no, but I'd advise against it. There're things out there in the swamp at night that'd make a strong man die from fright."

"Grim horrors?" asked Sholeena.

"You bet, miss. That and then some. What could be so important?"

"Well," said Roy, "we really can't say, but for Osten's sake, we must risk it. May I show you something on your map?"

Harold nodded assent with a furrowed brow.

Roy produced his scarf and spread it alongside Harold's map of the area. Indicating a spot on the map, he asked, "What can you tell me about this area?"

"That's Rockridge," said Harold, leaning closer. "It's a stony outcropping about five miles south and east of here. It was one of the sites suggested for Redoubt, but the bog surrounding it was deemed too treacherous."

"That is where we must go," Roy declared. "It needn't be right away. We'll take a few days to prepare."

"Look, I can't emphasize it enough. It's dangerous out there. Though the enemy hasn't done anything overt as yet, hostile creatures prowl all around. You should really reconsider. Who authorized this, anyway?"

"I'm afraid our mission must remain secretive. We would consider it a personal favor if you could just put us up for the night and ask no more about it."

"I could maybe spare a man to guide you there," Harold offered after a thoughtful pause, "But it'd have to be kept out of the daily reports. With luck, you could make it there and back in a single long day's hike. We could call it a routine scouting expedition."

Royland frowned as he considered.

"A guide would be most welcome, but I doubt we'll be returning. It depends on what we find there."

A knock was heard from the open door and a man stepped briskly in. He was a thickset fellow with a bushy brown beard so dark as to be almost black. With his shoulders pulled back and with eyes straight ahead, "Reporting as ordered, Captain," he said.

"At ease, Corporal. These three are Royland, Lucas, and Sharon...?"

"Sholeena," I supplied.

"Corporal Clark here is my staff clerk. He'll find you a place to sleep and show you to our mess. I'll come and join you there after my briefing."

Taking that as a dismissal, we funneled out the door and into the compound beyond.

"I've never seen Harold so hurried and tense," I murmured to Roy as we ambled along.

"The captain has a lot on his mind," said the clerk. "You can call me Dave, by the way. We don't stand much on rank out here. I'm afraid what serves us as mages quarters is fully occupied. You'll have to bunk in the barracks. The young lady, however, must have private accommodations."

The bunkhouse was built along the eastern wall. It was a long building filled end to end with rows of canvas cots. On many of these reclined sleeping men. We would soon learn they slept in rotation. At each end of the building and in its middle, ladders ascended to hatches. These led up onto the battlement above, the palisade of which formed part of our ceiling. It was an efficient design, but I didn't imagine the tread of heavy boots would be very conducive to sleep.

"Squad Four is on a long supply run," said the corporal. "You can rest here this night and perhaps tomorrow as well."

He indicated two cots on which we could rest our packs. He then asked Roy and I for assistance hauling one of the other cots outside. We followed him to a ramshackle building near the end of the row.

"Miss Sholeena can stay here," said Dave. "It's not much, but at least it's private. Is this acceptable, miss?"

"It beats sleeping outside, Corporal Dave," she replied. "What's this normally used for?"

The man looked abashed.

As Roy and I trundled Sholeena's cot into the rickety shack, the clerk spared us a whole history lesson.

"Originally, this was to be pens for the livestock. Upon our arrival, we brought a number of goats and chickens with the goal of providing some fresh milk and eggs for our soldiers. Not two weeks later, the goats all sickened. Even feeding them exclusively on imported grains couldn't revive the ailing beasts. Not long after that, a malady ran through the chicken population. Before it was discovered, it had laid low half the camp. Those who'd eaten of their tainted meat or eggs suffered the trots for days on end. A new supply schedule was hastily organized, and now regular runs back to the E.K. provide the bulk of what sustains our force."

"Nowadays," he continued glumly, "the men use this space for a bathhouse. But they won't be needing it anytime soon. Our water rations are so severely curtailed that there's barely enough for drinking. And there won't be any more until Squad Four returns next week."

And sure enough, gathering dust in the room's corner was a collapsible canvas washing tub. I had noticed the pungent reek that had pervaded the bunkhouse but had thought it impolite to mention it. I was, after all, a mite over-fragrant myself, having sloshed all day through the muddy mire. Sholeena smiled, and I could sense her thoughts immediately. This is how Royland must see us all the time.

"Corporal... Dave," I said. "I know you wanted to take us to the mess hall next, but I think we'd like to tarry here for a bit and get settled in. Could you come back for us in an hour or so?"

"I suppose that would be alright," the man agreed.

"And could you, perchance, bring us some empty barrels?" chimed in Roy.

***

When Roy and I met Captain Hunt in the mess hall later that night, it was in clean clothing and smelling fresh. Harold was smiling and looking rather excited. Sholeena's bathhouse had caused quite a stir. Men were even now lined up for a chance at a good scrub. Corporal Dave had stayed with her to keep things orderly.

After his meeting, Harold had brought with him the two master wizards stationed here. Harland Reznic was the master I'd seen in the tower on our arrival. His son had been Royland's head of house back at Conclave. If I understood it aright, his affinity was for the direct application of force. He could levitate and move objects far more readily than most and was considered to be strongly gifted. The other man was Dominik Cooke, a geomancer responsible for the earthworks hereabouts. Redoubt rested on firmer ground due to his diligent efforts at draining the nearby swamp and shaping the earthen ramparts to buttress the fort atop the hill. Both had been stationed here for nearly a year now and were due to return to Conclave on the next rotation.

The mess hall was closed, but since the briefing had run late, Captain Hunt had it re-opened. The five of us sat sharing a pot of tea while enjoying a native dessert. It is said that rank hath its privileges.

Ideally, while in the Black Plagued Marshes, one should eschew all native foods. But as a practical matter, experimentation had proven some to be safe enough. It being late autumn, or what passed for such here in the south, the tupelos hung heavy with esculent berries. These small purple fruits were easily collected, that is, if one didn't encounter any cyclos nesting among them. Each had a rather large pit in its center, and the oily flesh was a bit sour on the tongue. But with a little work, they made a tasty pie filling.

"I expect the bathing will continue long into the night," said Harold. "Not to mention the laundering of bedding and the like. I understand the girl can render cloth all but dry in a trice."

"She can," Royland confirmed. "But now that the bathhouse is in use again, where will Sholeena sleep?"

"She can sleep in the mage's bunkhouse," said Master Cooke. "Harland and I will both stand the watch tonight. The morale boost she's given the men is worth far more than a missed night of sleep."

"That's easy for *you* to say," Master Reznic put in grumpily. "It was *your* watch anyway."

"It's the *least* we can do, Harland. And never let it be said that Dominik Cooke didn't always do the least he could do!" he added with a wry grin.

"We were fine when we could at least catch some rainfall," said Harold, "but it hasn't rained in more than a fortnight. That's the dry season in a swamp. Muddy sewage all about us, and not a drop of it potable."

"Yes," Master Cooke agreed. "It's been depressing to see the water everywhere but have scarcely enough to wet one's whistle. Though both Harland and I can make small amounts of water, your friend is clearly a gifted hydromancer. It's sheer good fortune to have her visit us at such a time."

"Sholeena likes to be helpful," I said. "It's likely she'll exhaust herself filling up your stores. Enjoy it while you can. We need to leave fairly soon."

Master Cooke looked troubled by this.

"What *is* this mysterious mission you're on?" he asked. "How can your master condone your gallivanting into such dangerous environs?"

"Suffice it to say that she does," Roy answered tersely.

"It's irresponsible," declared Harland shaking his fork at me for emphasis. "A dereliction of her oaths. She should be here *with* you."

I waited for his outburst to subside before answering.

"I wish she were, but she can't be, for reasons we're not at liberty to divulge."

"Don't look at *me*, Harland," said Harold. "They're not under my command, nor are we even in Osten, where martial authority might sometimes come into play. They seem set on this crazy journey, and we've just got to respect it. It's been a long day. Think I'll turn in."

"Aren't you getting a bath?" asked Master Cooke.

"I can hardly wait for my turn at a bath and a shave," said Harold. "But the men come first. We ask a lot of them, and it goes down easier if they see I won't ask for what I won't endure myself."

And it occurred to me then, that when done honorably, rank also had its share of responsibilities and drawbacks.

***

That night, I was awoken by a voice from within. It started as a rumbling the grating of which penetrated my sleeping mind. In the darkness of the barracks, I could sense no disturbance among the other sleeping men. And yet the phantom sound didn't relent when I rolled to face the wall and squeezed my eyes tighter shut.

"Arise, brother," rumbled the voice. "An ill wind blows."

I scratched absently at the back of my hand. Then I sat up, and my eyes snapped open wide. All about me remained peaceful, but my fey mark was throbbing, and an uneasiness furrowed my brow. I felt the scarecrow take his leave as my waking mind took up the reins. It hadn't been he who had spoken. By the time I'd settled my breathing enough to peer within, my inner garden and its adjoining hill lay tranquil and still withal. But the vague sense of dread persisted.

"Visio tenebris," I muttered, softly invoking my darksight.

As quietly as I could, I laced on my boots and headed for the ladder at the barracks' northern end. By my mark I could detect a fey presence, but the sense wasn't directional. It was more akin to scenting a cloying odor. Nonetheless, it seemed to grow stronger in this direction. I climbed the ladder to the opening above and peered along the battlement. All was peaceful here as well. I could see the sentries standing their silent watch. Several of those nearest marked my presence with a swift glance before returning their gazes to the moonlit marsh.

I clambered the rest of the way up to stand behind the east-facing parapet. Its pointed timbers provided cover up to my chest. The grinning moon shed a gentle radiance upon the clearing out to the darkened tree line. Beyond even this, the predawn light was overcoming the stars as it painted the horizon in shades of gray.

To my left, another ladder stretched up to the lookout platform where the mages kept watch. And peering over its edge was one of the masters, his pale face indistinct. Doubtless, they had marked my emergence from the barracks below. I hesitated, then mounted the ladder's rungs. As I climbed, I focused on my fey mark, which continued to pulse and throb.

On gaining the platform, I was met by the questioning gazes of both Master Cooke and Master Reznic. A low railing enclosed all four sides of a platform about eight foot square. There was barely room to stand beneath its low peaked roof. A bench straddled its center where sat Master Reznic. His colleague stood pacing nearby.

"You're up early," remarked Master Cooke. "Curious about the watchtower?"

Again I hesitated.

"There's something out there," I whispered.

"Where?" asked Master Reznic, craning his neck to peer over the railing.

"I can't *see* it, but it was somewhere out that way," I said, pointing to the north. "It's fey and approached very close. Now it's moved some distance off. I feel it still watching us, and it seems... malevolent."

It had taken me some time to make this determination. It was hard to explain. Up to this point, the fey I had met had imparted more wholesome feelings to my mark. From this thing, whatever it was, I sensed a spiteful glee and a brooding expectation.

"Perhaps you're imagining things," said the seated master.

"You know I can sense them," I returned. "And some of the faire folk can cloak their presence even from our mage sight."

"Well, be that as it may," sighed Master Cooke, "you say it's withdrawn now? Surely that means... wait. What's that?"

He was pointing to the tower's base. Master Reznic rose to a crouch and stepped over to join him.

"Visus aquilae," he incanted softly, swiping his hands across his eyelids.

"I see it now," he said. "Rouse the camp. We're about to have company."

Master Cooke reached up into the eaves to retrieve a long, curved cow horn which hung there. I moved to peer over the railing myself. As the first rays of dawn lit the field, I spied several lumpy bundles below. The one nearest was the easiest to make out. It was the bloodied carcass of a creature resembling a deer. Other similar decaying piles had been laid out every hundred feet or so, presumably out to the tree line.

From behind me the horn sounded in two deafening blasts, each of which rose in tone near its ending. It sounded very like the horn Sir Fletcher had used at the battle of Tillerson Ranch. But its proximity caused me to flinch and drowned out all other sounds for a moment. I stood dazed in its aftermath. I felt a hand on my shoulder and turned to find Harland Reznic muttering something at me.

"Humans fret although, useless, fear and bafflement," he said.

"WHAT?" I returned, confused.

"I said, YOU MUST GET BELOW, LUCAS. CLEAR THE BATTLEMENT!" he shouted angrily, pointing toward the ladder."

Chagrinned, I nodded, stepped over, and began climbing down. What could it mean? I supposed I should return to the barracks, but how? Men were even now pouring out from the hatch below. On reaching the palisade, I encountered men trying to come the other way. I stepped aside so as not to hinder them. This forced me out onto the barracks' slanted roof. I felt my boots sink into its thick, springy thatch. As even more men mounted the wall, I finally gave up on that way down and sought another. I sat and slid on the seat of my britches to the roof's lower edge. There, I hung from the eaves and dropped the remaining distance to the ground.

Even here within the compound, I felt I was in the way. Men scurried all about hastily donning their uniforms as the camp came swiftly to a state of order. Roy was peering out from the doorway of the barracks. Across the way, I saw Sholeena emerging from the mage's shack, casting her wide-eyed gaze all around. We moved to join her when she waved us over. We had to duck past a group of men who were handing long shafts of wood up to the men on the walls. I saw no bows in evidence and had to wonder why. I was later to learn such weapons were ineffective against the foe we faced.

"I mark four from the north," came a shout from the tower, "and more are on the way!"

And out from the command bunker strode Harold Hunt, attended by men bearing crates. I wanted to help, but didn't know how. Those around us all stepped with a purpose and seemed to have the matter well in hand. Best for now just to stay out of their way.

Captain Hunt ascended to the tower, and the mages climbed down to the battlement. Master Cooke positioned himself at the center of the north wall, and Master Reznic took up station on the northern corner of the east-facing palisade. A silence swept over the camp. We waited a tense few moments until another call rang down from above.

"Light 'em up!" bellowed Harold.

At this, Master Cooke let loose with a roaring ray of flame just as the head of an enormous creature hove into view. It was like that bear creature my fellows and I had fought, but much larger. It was made of writhing vines and shambled forth to stand head and shoulders above the twenty-foot palisade, dwarfing the men thereon. Its vines singed and blackened where Dominik's fire played across its chest. It flinched and reared back, only to step forward once more. It extended an enormous arm, sweeping it toward the defiant defenders.

It was then that the poles were raised in unison. They put me in mind of the long, forked shafts the men of Westarbor had used to shove over goblin scaling ladders. Each ended in multiple tines which caught in the snarled mass of vines comprising that massive arm. One man toppled from off the wall, but the others held, grimly straining against the beast and pinning fast its limb. Dominik's flame intensified and smoke issued forth as the creature's head became ablaze. It sank from our sight, and the arm withdrew.

No sooner had I marked this than a second creature lumbered into view. This one arrived at the eastern end of the north wall and was met by Master Reznic. He, too, sent a gout of crimson mage fire at the beast on its approach. It was an impressive effort. I'd once seen Master Chadwick scorch a Mygalom with this spell, but the effort had taxed him dreadfully. As a water mage, fire was my app-master's least potent element. Nonetheless, any mage could do it. Ideally, there should be a pyromancer on these walls. As we had only a geomancer and a dynamancer, I wondered how long they could hold out.

"Seven," shouted Harold from the top of the tower. "The final count is seven! Last one's a little bugger, though."

The men around us let out a gasp, then hunkered back down to their tasks. It seemed that when it came to shamblers, seven wasn't considered a lucky number, size notwithstanding.

"We should help," said Roy to Sholeena and me.

"If they'll let us," said I in reply.

We began making our way toward the ladder to the northern wall. But even as we did, a further command rang down from above.

"Break out the hellfire gourds!" cried the captain. "Release them only on my command."

While the two master wizards became engaged with another pair of the beasts, a third arose. Forming a long set of 'arms' from its amorphous mass, it latched onto the tower and began to climb. Then down from above came a small packet. It fell directly upon the creature, splattering it but having no other immediate effect. When the creature was midway up, however, it became wreathed in wispy white vapors. Then it suddenly burst into bright flames. It shuddered and thrashed, still clinging stubbornly to the tower's beams. Finally, it sagged limp and fell away to smolder and burn below.

I topped the final rung with Roy and Sholeena close upon my heels. The battlement was a chaos of pole-wielding men and angrily shouted orders. I would have expected bestial roars from the attacking behemoths, but all I heard from them was the crackling of flames as they writhed in silent agony. Here at the western corner opposite the tower, we three gained a foothold well back from the struggling defenders.

I saw Dominik looking grim, but still spewing his fire in irregular, sputtering bursts. His men had pinned the ropy limbs of the creature he battled. Meanwhile, the 'little one' had nearly closed the distance to the wall directly behind it and another loomed large beyond that.

"Hellfire. Now!" came a shout from the tower. "Target the smaller one first!"

It was small only in comparison to its fellows. It still stood half again as tall as the bear creature Roy and I had bested. A man stood forth, cocked back his arm, and flung his gourd in a high arc. When this met the advancing abomination, it burst open to bathe him with its contents. And as the misty vapors again issued forth, the creature recoiled in torment.

The final beast veered away from it, lumbering toward our position instead.

"Omnino siccis plantis," shouted Sholeena, extending her palms toward the brute.

I heard a crackling noise, as the shambler's leading leg faded from green to brown. His next step sent him spinning to one side as the brittle limb gave out.

"Good one, Sho," I praised.

Another man stepped forward with a gourd, but before he could launch it, the creature's elongated arm shot out to sweep the battlement. The exhausted men managing the poles were caught off guard by the sudden maneuver. I flinched to see two of them snatched up and tangled in its grip. With horror evident upon his face, the man with the gourd hurled it at our flailing opponent.

"Levare et colligentes!" cried my cousin.

And to my astonishment, the gourd halted in mid flight, reversed course, and drifted back into Royland's waiting arms. He turned his sorrowful brown eyes upon me expectantly.

"We can't let them burn," he exclaimed.

I knew what my cousin wanted. Could I do it? It had worked on the bear, but that was done in desperation. With no further time to consider it, I placed a shaky leg atop the palisade and leaped from the wall, trusting to a twisted mesh of vines to cushion my landing.

I clung to the creature's shoulder and felt its vines wrap about me tight. Soon the roots would be seeking my flesh. It was larger than the bear. Stronger too. As it constricted about me, I put my final breath to good use.

"Ambulare interitus," I wheezed.

And where the vines touched me, they shriveled and decayed as a rush of green energy joined my own. Before long, I could breathe again. Soon I was slipping down the creature's side as the vines constituting its arm fell limp and separated from the main body. We landed in a heap, the two soldiers and I. I struggled to stand erect. One of the men was staring about wild-eyed with fear. The other lay unconscious nearby.

We rushed to drag the insensate man away from where the creature thrashed. We were nearly trod upon by a massive 'foot' which suddenly turned brown and crumbled away. Bless you, Sholeena. And after a nightmarish few minutes of heart-pounding terror and running, it was done. All seven of the beasts lay scorched and unmoving. The gates were thrown open so the two wounded soldiers and I could be reunited with our triumphant fellows.

***

Nearly there, I thought. The swamp seemed subdued as we made our way through the slimy muck and clumps of sedge. From up ahead, we heard robin song. Tilting her head back, Sholeena warbled a reply in kind, then led us onward. At least the insects were leaving us alone. The marsh was teeming with them, but thus far Roy's enchantment was keeping them at bay, or at buzz or whatever. I even saw some of them skittering across the surface of the water. It mystified me how their little feet could hold them high and dry. I wondered whether I could do the same, but Royland had assured me I was far too heavy. Only something as small as a bug could successfully glide atop the 'surface tension.' Still, wasn't magic supposed to be able to break such rules? After all, a stone shouldn't be able to float in mid-air, yet this was the first spell I had mastered. Roy had only grimaced and told me I was free to try it.

"There's a hazardous area directly ahead," said Sholeena. "Dick says we need to go around it to the right."

"What? Again?" I complained.

For a mere five miles, this was turning into a tediously long hike. Captain Hunt had warned us the treacherous bog surrounding Rockridge would prove challenging, and now I had no cause to doubt him. Thank the stars Harold had given that Richard Chapman fellow leave to guide us there. But after that, we'd be truly on our own.

The Captain had been only too happy to provide us with a guide, though he still questioned the wisdom of our trek. The shambler attack a few days prior was the largest that Redoubt had suffered to date. According to Harold, the creatures usually arrived in ones and twos and were easily dispatched once the proper tactics had been developed. The captain was most concerned that enemy fey were now guiding the monsters by laying out a trail of carcasses for them to follow and feed upon. This also seemed to bolster the size and ferocity of the aberrant beasts. He regretted having to break out his secret weapon so soon.

The gourds contained a mixture of volatile liquids the Remans had termed 'Greek fire.' This substance burned at an extremely high temperature and stuck to whatever it splattered upon. Better still, it ignited on contact with water and burned even when (especially when) wet. Its making was a closely guarded secret of the Farax Navy. On the king's recommendation, they'd sent several cases to Duke Gaul to counter the new threats we were facing. Harold preferred to call them 'Hellfire Grenades' because the hardened gourds that kept them stable were shaped rather like a pomegranate. And because he thought the phrase to be more descriptive and intimidating.

Turning a corner, we emerged from a densely wooded area. Ahead lay Rockridge, its stony prominence jutting above the surrounding marsh. The sun was a little past its zenith, just about as we'd expected. Dick was waiting for us on a dry hillock before it.

"Well," he said, "this is the place. Not sure what you're looking for here. It's just a barren bit of rock."

"We thank you," said Roy. "We'll take it from here."

"I'd stay and share a meal, but I want to get back before dark. It can get a mite spooky out here when the sun goes down.

If you want to check it out quick, I can wait and take you back," he offered.

"Thanks, but no," returned Roy. "We've another journey ahead of us."

"Have it as you will, then. I'm sure this little girlie can keep you lot in line. A regular little marsh marm she is. Schooled me in a few things already."

"Oh, and another thing," he announced. "There's something the captain wanted me to tell you. He said to keep yourself safe... and to pray for us that keep you thus. Said it might give you a belly laugh."

And with that, he turned and headed back the way we'd come. I turned to regard the ridge once more. Roy retrieved Gretta's wand. When he invoked it, the tiny eagle darted from its head and soared toward the prominence. The glittering trail this produced was barely discernible under the noonday sun. But soon we were wending our way ahead and wondering what we'd find.

CHAPTER TEN

The Chieftain

"If you're going through hell, keep going."

~ Winston Churchill ~

Despite Dick's dire cautions, the night was progressing peacefully. I sat atop the stony bluff, surveying the surrounding marsh. Roy had relinquished his watch some time ago, but hours yet remained until the dawn would release me from my own vigil.

Master Hans' message had been brief and perfunctory. He simply reported his and Gretta's arrival at this outcropping after a few days' march. Apparently, a will-o'-wisp had led them on a merry chase about the bog. It had taken them a while to overcome its beguiling allure. I knew my fey mark afforded me some protection from such mental intrusion. But I made it a point to instruct my companions in the spell of liberation I'd learnt this past spring.

Rockridge had proven remarkable only for its elevation. It was just a barren stretch of rocky ground jutting up above the wetlands. Its only inhabitants were small gray salamanders.

These skittered about from rock to rock on our approach. They resembled lizards, but Sholeena assured us they were actually amphibians, more akin to frogs. I was loath to touch one. Some newts were extremely toxic. But those, Sholeena explained, usually advertised this fact by their bright colorations. Little gray ones like this relied instead on their camouflage and were quite harmless.

After a belated midday meal, we opted to set up camp here. It seemed secure enough.

I tilted my head back and regarded the stars.

"Can you feel it?" said a voice from within, the clarity of which caused me to startle.

I deepened my breathing and sought for my magic's source. As my inner field swam into view, I marked the lanky figure seated cross-legged at its center. His straw hat was canted back, and he stared upward toward the sky of our inner realm. Above, the field of stars shone down from this hazy window to the world without.

Though still slender, and somewhat knobby-kneed, the scarecrow had filled out since I had last regarded him. In one smooth motion, he pushed up from the ground and turned to face me.

"Feel what?" I asked, uncertain.

At this, the scarecrow smiled, stalking a few steps nearer. It was a wholesome grin, friendly about its edges. But I remained wary. Sholeena had once shared with me a piece of wisdom her mother had imparted to her. 'When a shark shows you his teeth,' she had advised, 'do not mistake it for a smile.'

"We are stronger, you and I," he replied. "In this place, so close to the origin, the plants are suffused with Gaia's own vigor. We grow more powerful by the day."

I had no way to measure the truth of this declaration, but our green field did seem a bit larger and perhaps more... intense?

"So I was thinking," he went on in a laconic drawl, "why should the two of us be locking horns like two bucks fighting over a doe? We'd do much better helping one another and working together toward our goals."

Finally! I thought. Was this not the very point of raising one's homunculus?

"What do you have in mind?" I cautiously asked.

His smile broadened, and I could now make out a row of regular teeth beneath his papery mask. Had he always had such? I couldn't recall.

"Give me leave to farm one small corner of our garden. And in return, I will advise you throughout the day and lend you my strength when it is needed. It is, after all, in my own interest to keep us safe from the dangers which threaten."

"What about the moral code I've tried to impress on you? Do you agree to abide by its strictures?"

He hesitated, peering thoughtfully upward.

"You hold the upper hand for now. I will submit to your judgment when such matters arise. But I reserve the right to argue my case against such when time permits. I've noted you have a nasty habit of acting against our own self-interest at times."

"How so?" I inquired.

"You imperiled our own life when you leapt from the wall onto that vine creature. Better to have burnt it down from the safety of the parapet."

We spoke for a time more, the scarecrow and I. Though well matched in intellect, we held very different world views. He seemed a more selfish, narrowly focused version of myself. He was also more impulsive, seeking immediate benefit and gratification. This, rather than considering the long-term consequences of actions he would take, especially as they related to the needs of others. I had spent my life subjugating my baser impulses and learning to be a good person. It was interesting to witness this inner struggle personified.

Eventually, I acceded to his terms, and we shook on it.

As we did, there came an ominous rumbling from my inner hill, causing the scarecrow to glance that way in irritation. His hand was warm and smoother than I'd imagined. I wondered what he'd meant by 'lending me his strength,' as though it were separate from my own. I suppose I'd just have to wait and see.

I emerged from the meditation with a relieved sense of accomplishment. There was still a long way to go, but I felt we'd taken the first steps along the road toward lasting inner peace. If this kept up, I might soon be able to grant the fellow a name. I considered several as I huddled atop the hill, awaiting the first light of dawn.

***

"This is fascinating," said Roy, leaning in closer.

We had encountered a line of greenery marching along the ground and up and down the trees before us. Bewildered by the line-dancing leaves, we'd halted our southward advance and stood gaping at the spectacle. Roy had cautioned us to stand well back as he sent out his hive mites to investigate.

"I sense these are not the ordinary variety."

No kidding, I thought.

On closer inspection, we'd discovered these leaves weren't skittering along under their own power. Each was borne by an ant engaged in a peculiar sort of harvesting activity. There were many thousands of them, by the look of it. Though most were no bigger than a typical ant, among them wandered a few nearly as large as my fore-knuckle. These, my cousin had informed us, were the soldiers guarding the tiny workers whose scissors-sharp jaws were defoliating the neighboring forest. Thus, an unbroken river of pilfered foliage ran east to west for as far as the eye could see. We would need to cross it if we wanted to keep on a straight track south.

Sho and I quickly grew bored, while my cousin stared as though spellbound.

"*We should simply burn a path through these pests and be done with it,*" declared my inner voice.

I was fairly certain that wasn't the proper answer to the dilemma. Such a plan certainly wouldn't meet with *Royland's* approval. But I didn't want to be overly dismissive of the scarecrow's advice. At least he was talking to me now. I acknowledged the destructive impulse with a grunt and took a sip from my waterskin.

"What do you think, Royland?" asked Sho.

"Hmmm?"

"How will we get across? The next marker should be just up ahead now. We want to get there by nightfall, right?"

How like Sholeena to coax Roy from one of his obsessions by triggering another of them. At once, my cousin's eyes became focused, and a look of determination lowered his brow. I could almost see the wheels turning in his mind.

Stepping back, my cousin sent out still more of his swirling magic specs. These fanned out and descended to the ground before him. And where they touched, I marked a shifting in the leafy dance. A set of open spots took shape, the lines bending to form them.

"Step only where I step," Roy cautioned, leading the way into the field of gyrating greenery.

Sho moved carefully forward, doing as we'd been bidden, and I took up the rear. Before us, the pattern continued to alter even as the lines behind me resumed their erstwhile march. We were deep among the skittering ants before I saw the squirrel, or rather, what remained of it. Crawling all over its lifeless form was a swarming mass of the soldier ants picking its carcass clean. Only by its fluffy tail could I discern its nature. Evidently, the unfortunate creature had somehow aroused the ire of the tiny warriors.

I gulped and resolved to remain on the straight and true.

About twenty minutes later, I was most relieved to step clear of the final few insects and resume a more natural stride.

Since leaving Rockridge, we had encountered many such obstacles to our progress, but none had proven too challenging.

There'd been blood leeches nearly the size of eels in a stream we'd had to ford. But Sholeena had alerted us to this danger and showed us how best to avoid them. The Black Plagued Marshes did indeed play host to a wide variety of odd creatures. But none, thus far, had arisen to the level of the 'grim horrors' we'd been promised. Two more markers had come and gone. It wasn't until the fourth day that we arrived at a barrier which might prove impassable.

We emerged from yet another dank mire fraught with cattails. Just beyond a tangled stand of tupelo trees hanging heavy with moss, we espied a broad, flat expanse of marshy grassland stretching out as far as we could see. At first, I thought this was good news, until I recognized the nature of the 'grass' in question. The waist-high field of grassy terrain was, in fact, an enormous stand of stranglevine which sprawled out far into the distance. Within it lumbered shamblers of every description, their writhing shapes mimicking the forms of the animals they had trapped and consumed. According to Roy's scarf, it was directly through this horrific hedge that we must wend our way. Perhaps there was some way to circle around it, I thought doubtfully.

Roy climbed a tree to get a better view of the situation. He returned, shaking his head and with a pained look on his glum features.

"It stretches out both east and west beyond my line of sight," he reported.

"Well, it can't go on forever," said Sho. "How far can you see from the top of a tree, anyway?"

"I'd estimate about nine miles from fifty feet up," answered Royland without pause. "That's a good day's hike, maybe two through this muck."

"*I have a suggestion,*" whispered my inner voice.

"Let me guess," I thought back at him. "We should burn our way straight through it."

"*No indeed, my mistrustful master,*" he replied with mocking respect. "*The poor things are only thirsty. Let me talk to them, and perhaps we can come to an arrangement.*"

I didn't see what harm could come from just talking, so I told my companions there was something I'd like to try. I approached the edge of that fatal field considerably closer than perhaps was prudent. And as I did, the part of my mind that commanded plants uncoiled as if of its own accord. I felt the scarecrow 'speaking' to them soothingly and cajoling them into performing various acts.

While rooted to the ground, these behaved much like ordinary plants and heeded our will. But experience had taught me that once untethered or attached to a corpse, these vines would be beyond my control. The scarecrow put the nearest of these through a series of movements: swaying gently in place, flattening out, and forming a few simple shapes.

"*I see,*" said the scarecrow as if to himself.

I could sort of make out what he did, but there was a nuance to it I couldn't quite fathom.

"*Now hold out our arm, Lucas,*" my homunculus urged me.

"Why?" thought I in reply.

"*These vines need to taste the blood of a creature in order to take its form. Fear not. Once attached, we shall feed it with our magic rather than our flesh.*"

I didn't like the sound of that one bit. His assurance put me in mind of the fable of the scorpion and the frog. Now, I trusted the scarecrow about as far as a child could throw an ox. But, whatever his intentions, I knew he'd never betray his own self-interest. And whether he liked it or not, this depended on my own physical well-being. Our fates were linked.

I took a steadying breath and held out my arm.

One of the larger vines reared up at once, untethering itself from the soggy ground. Its dripping rootlets glistened as it struck, quicker than thought, just as a snake strikes its prey. I blenched to feel it take root right there in a blister beneath my skin. But all the while, the scarecrow compelled it, barring it from rooting further and feeding it with our gift. After a time, it hung there slack, waving about as a contented cat swings its tail.

"On to step two, then," said the scarecrow with glee. *"Continue feeding it our magic. I'll go attract some others."*

"Wait!" I cried. But he was off.

As other vines uprooted themselves and slithered toward me, I became uncertain. Was I to host dozens of these creatures? Was I to become a human pin-cushion?

"What are you doing, cousin?" hollered Roy, with concern evident in his voice.

"I'm not entirely sure," I shouted back. "Just stand well back. It'll be all right."

("I think," I did not add.)

When the other vines struck, it was not upon me they feasted. Instead, each bit into the first vine which still dangled from my forearm. A third wave of them clamped onto these, and so it progressed. Each subsequent group of vines attached themselves in a network of tendrils snaking all about me. And the draw upon my magic increased. Initially, it had been but a trickle. Now, however, though still manageable, it placed a substantial burden on my garden's resources.

"That should be plenty," said my papery-faced counterpart, having returned his attention within. *"Keep feeding them, or it all goes south. And I mean that in the figurative sense, not the literal."*

It was then I felt a shift. It was difficult to find my bearings at first. My vision exploded suddenly outward. And rather than standing, I found myself to be seated and bent over forward. As I raised my 'head,' my 'eyes' revealed the truth. My body now consisted of writhing vines, just like those of the shambling mounds we had fought. Turning, I spotted Roy and Sholeena standing to my rear and looking up at me with alarmed expressions. They looked tiny.

I lowered a 'hand' to the ground, palm-upward, and beckoned to them with the other.

Sho moved forward, but Royland caught her arm and roughly hauled her back. The two exchanged some angry words

I couldn't quite make out. Then Royland stepped hesitantly to the fore. He poked at my 'finger' with the toe of his boot. I felt this with a faculty that was similar to touch, but it came to me through my vertiginous sense. Roy glowered up at me, then cautiously mounted my outstretched hand. When no harm befell him, he waved Sholeena over to join him there.

Once the two were securely settled, I cupped my hand and lifted them up to peer at them more closely. Judging by their expressions, I feared my attempt at a reassuring grin had fallen short of the mark. So, I deposited them on my 'shoulder,' nearly fifteen feet above the ground. As I grew more accustomed to my enlarged verdurous form, I began to make out their voices.

"I'm sure he's alright, Royland," said tiny Sho. "He's going to give us a ride through the field."

"He could have forewarned us of his intentions," Roy muttered darkly.

'No, he couldn't have,' I failed to say. I guess the writhing vines constituting my shambler anatomy weren't quite up to the task of vocalization. So instead, I raised a huge hand up before them and made a thumbs-up gesture. And with that, I stretched and began testing my newly formed legs. It felt like moving through molasses, but each lumbering stride cleared eight or ten feet. This was actually a superior pace to anything we could accomplish on our own six legs.

So, keeping the bright afternoon sun to the right, we all headed south - in the literal sense, that is.

***

I think the scarecrow was right when he said we were getting stronger as we traveled south. A month ago, I could never have sustained so large a network of vines. What had he said exactly? The 'origin' was suffused with Gaia's power or some such? Well, whatever it was, it wasn't going to be enough.

As I trudged through the weary miles in the vast field of stranglevines, the drain on my magic was steadily shrinking my reserves. I had staunched the loss somewhat as I refined my technique. The trick was not to feed them too much. No sooner would that single vine attached to my forearm become energized than the ones attached *to* it would siphon it off. They, in turn, would be leeched dry by the third tier and so on. Eventually, however, some at the periphery of the network would become sated. At this point, they would drop off to take root in the soil below, flower, and eject their seeds. New vines would join us to replace them in some fashion only the scarecrow seemed to fathom.

At first I was afraid to encounter the other shamblers ambling about. But now I knew they would ignore me. Evidently, they don't attack their own kind (a useful trait for any successful species).

I'd even managed to learn a few new tricks. From the shoulders of the amorphous manlike blob I'd become, I'd extruded a pair of pauldrons. These now served my companions as high-backed wicker chairs in which to ride in comfort. Though squeamish at first, the two had come to trust my vines wouldn't tear into them. They sat swaying gently upon these perches as the shadows began to lengthen. I sullenly managed my power's outflow and focused on what Roy had to say.

"...this is clearly the epicenter of the stranglevine infestation. Should we make it back to Osten alive, we must warn the duke. This place could use a good clear-burning, and soon. Elsewise, these pernicious things may spread all across the land."

"Filbert says it'd be better to find something that eats them," said Sho. "You'll never find all the places the wind takes those seeds."

The fish had a point, I thought.

Since brokering our agreement, I'd given the scarecrow leave to cultivate one corner of my inner field. We'd paced it off, and he'd never since strayed from his designated area. As I plodded along in the world without, I spared some concentration to visit him there.

"I'm running low on magic. I'll need more if this trek is to continue. You promised you would 'lend me your strength when needed.' I'm feeling such a need."

"*I used up much of* mine *establishing the network,*" he replied. "*It's recovering now, but it's a slow process. Why don't you tap into old grumpy over there? He's your other self, after all.*"

By this he meant the hill which lay adjacent to our field. I'd long since learned to form a conduit to my store of earth power to share it with my inner garden. It was an excellent suggestion, but one I'd hoped to keep as a last resort. I'd never before heard my secondary affinity referred to as 'old grumpy.' But I'd seen evidence of a personality emerging there, one not very well-disposed toward the stick figure before me. But if *he* was 'my other self,' then what was the scarecrow?

"*Or perhaps we could have the vines consume the passengers and use* them *as fuel,*" said the scarecrow with a wink.

"*Just kidding!*" he guffawed. "*They may still be of some use to us. But you should've seen the look on our face. It was priceless!*"

I didn't care for his cruel brand of humor. Just kidding, indeed. But was he? I knew the creature to be capable of extreme selfishness, but this went well beyond the pale. If this crinkly faced hyena was indeed a reflection of my unconscious thoughts, it occurred to me that I didn't like myself very much. I turned on my metaphorical heel and retreated toward the hill.

I formed the conduit and instantly felt the rush of energy replenish my verdant grove. Was it only my imagination, or was the hillock now glaring down at me unhappily? The impression dissolved as I returned my attention to the massive beast I'd become. It was still slogging along through the carnivorous grove. The vines seemed content as they sipped at my renewed strength. Would it be enough?

The hour was late when I noticed the change. The moon had arisen, and by its pale light, I saw the shadowy but welcome forms of trees ahead.

I'd been running on embers and sheer willpower in equal measure for what felt like hours now. So my heart leapt in triumph when finally my massive foot fell upon open ground. My inner hill had shrunk alarmingly after imparting the last of its stored energy. The trickle that remained had been barely enough to sustain the march. I'd grown fearful the network of vines in which I was cocooned might turn to other sources of sustenance. But now, at last, I might be shed of the wretched things. I stepped a few more paces and came to a rest, thankful for the spongy bed of moss on which I trod.

First things first, I thought, awakening from the stupor into which I'd sunk. My companions sat dozing in their chairs. The gentle rocking as I'd trudged along had lulled them to sleep hours ago. I'd missed their chatter on the last dreary leg of my lumbering trek. But I honestly couldn't blame them. The hour *was* late. I'd taken the precaution of wrapping each within a loop of vine to hold them securely in their seats. I supposed it was fitting payback for the time they'd spent lugging me around on the travois.

I released the vines that held them fast, scooping each up as gently as I could. Their tiny bodies squirmed when they startled awake, but they soon relaxed and I eased them to the ground. Sholeena headed directly off to relieve herself while Roy tried invoking his wand.

***

Avoiding stands of stranglevine and various venomous vermin, we traveled as directly southward as we were able. As it was overcast, the occasional glimpses of the sky above proved unhelpful in this endeavor. My father had once told me that moss grew thickest on the sides of the trees which faced north. But according to this rule and the fuzzy trunks I could spy nearby, north lay in every direction at once.

Roy puzzled over his scarf, but no landmarks leapt out at him. And the tiny eagle on the head of his wand had long since ceased pointing back the way we'd come. Only two more markers lay ahead. And I know my cousin both longed for and dreaded to hear his grandfather's final words. Despite the many twists and turns we were forced to endure, Sholeena steadfastly led the way. She was softly whistling the merry marching tune she had learned from the trapper.

Through the thick foliage, the Paluda girl led, occasionally becoming lost to our view. My pace faltered when, on the second day, the whistling ceased and an eerie silence ensued. Where but moments before, Sholeena had been, not a branch stirred to mark her passing. Only the buzzing of the insects replied when softly I called out to her.

Then suddenly, there arose a great clamor directly to our rear. Something large was crashing through the brush. And along with this tumultuous clatter, a piercing howl was heard. My cousin and I exchanged a swift glance. Then as one and without a word, we fled forward and away from the sound. Alarmed, I sped recklessly ahead to distance myself from that which pursued us, with Royland hot on my heels.

I wondered if climbing a tree would be best. But without knowing the nature of our stalker, my feet opted for distance instead. Bursting through the boscage, we came tumbling out into a small clearing. Before us stood a line of spear-wielding men awaiting our emergence. They wore drab colors, and each sported a brightly painted, scowling wooden mask. Could these be the dark druids my countrymen so feared?

From the bushes to our rear, three others soon emerged, jabbing with their spears and denying us any hope of retreat. I saw my cousin tense, preparing some defense. His slender fingers splayed out, no doubt to ready some dire spell. I raised my bow; certain I could thwart at least one of our attackers. But then, ere I could loose, Sholeena appeared suddenly beside me, grabbing at my elbow and sending my shot skittering astray.

"Stand down!" cried the Paluda.

Having spoiled my one chance at mounting a defense, the girl looked guiltily over at me, even as our foemen fell upon us. Rough hands soon held me fast. Sholeena and I were dragged forcibly over to where Royland now lay on his back in the dirt, a spear held close by his throat. Two more of our attackers crept up from the rear; some sort of net was spread out between them.

"We yield, we are --"

This earned me the butt of a spear to my gut. When I doubled over in pain, I was cast down to sprawl atop my cousin. Sholeena made no move to resist as she was prodded onto the pile. Soon a weighted net of strong ropy cords was cast over us and pinned down at each corner by the spear-wielding men. Scowling from their frightening masks, they jabbered among themselves. Doubtless, our fate was being decided. But I could discern no glimmer of their intentions from their foreign words and wooden faces.

Perhaps Royland could sense some hint of their mood as he lay there, silent and still. But even if he was so inclined, he wasn't sharing his thoughts at the moment. Fear of reprisal by our captors had taken his tongue. Huddled close, we took solace in the fact that we still drew breath.

"*Well, isn't this a pretty pickle?*" the scarecrow grumpily mused. "*We could have killed* one *at the very least...*"

I glanced at the Paluda girl shivering there beside me. Why had she halted the battle? She'd always been stalwart and true. She must have had a reason. It'd better be a good one, I thought to myself as my outrage flared up anew.

Relieved of our packs and other gear, our arms were bound behind us. And we were prodded along through the swamp. Our masked escort surrounded us on all sides. The threat implied by their sharp spears discouraged any discourse. Nonetheless, I found an opportunity to whisper to my cousin as we navigated a tricky bit of shrubbery.

"Any ideas, Roy?"

Looking about warily, he mumbled his unhelpful, sarcastic reply.

"Try using your politeness on them, cousin..."

Eventually, we arrived at a clear stretch of slimy muck leading up to the shore of a lake. Our captors paused, and several of them forged ahead into a tall stand of cattails, parting them and urging us forward once again. The water came up to our knees as we sloshed our way unhappily forth, followed by our well-armed guides.

The lake ahead was expansive and broad. Its waters looked cleaner than most. It lacked the covering of duckweed and patches of brownish scum prevalent on other ponds I'd seen hereabout. Its tiny rippling waves lapped gently against the rough-hewn raft of logs to which our captors led us.

A fresh jabbering arose among the men, and several glanced our way. They seemed to be arguing over how to proceed. But before they'd resolved the matter, Sholeena spoke up in a guttural voice.

"Hindi sila marunong lumangoy tulad namin," she said. "Mababaw ang kanilang hininga at maikli at mahina ang kanilang mga daliri sa paa!"

All turned to regard Sholeena whose skin had begun blending into her surroundings. She was staring at the ground submissively. After a brief pause, one of the men came over to loom above her.

"Pagkatapos ay sasakay sila sa balsa," he proclaimed, "parang mga sanggol!"

At this pronouncement, several of the others colored slightly. Whereas before, these men had a ruddy hue, their skin tone now shaded into orange. Could they be of Sholeena's folk? I would have laughed aloud had I not sensed his joke was somehow at our expense.

But in spite of my relief that we at least had a way to communicate with our captors, their kinship with Sholeena did nothing to ease the chafing of my wrists. We were herded onto the raft and made to sit among our packs and those of the others. I noted their wide-set eyes and flattened faces as each removed his mask and stacked it on the raft as well. Then one by one, they stepped out into the waters of the lake and slipped away with nary a splash. Several swam alongside us, towing the craft.

Rocking gently, we glided along, our fate now in the hands of these web-footed strangers.

***

I stood with my back against the post to which I'd been bound. It was hot. It was humid. At least there were no bugs. This, despite the fact that our wide-eyed friends had relieved us of our cloaks. Roy stood nearby, similarly trussed up. Wrapped in a cocoon of hempen ropes, we must've looked like a pair of spring lambs ready to be turned on the spit. Sholeena sat facing us with no such restraints upon *her*.

"Who are these men?" I asked her once they'd left us there alone.

When our raft had made landfall, we'd been hauled to our feet and marched to the village center. It was a quaint little cluster of rickety straw huts. These encircled a stone statue of some sort. It vaguely resembled a woman with her arms upraised.

"I think they must be one of the lost tribes," reported Sholeena in a hushed tone.

"Lost tribes?" I prompted her.

She crossed her legs and rested her chin on her fists, gathering her thoughts.

"Have you heard of the war of the sea kings, Lucas?"

"I have not."

"Nor have I," put in Roy.

"It began long ago, before even your kingdom was formed. It was fought for possession of Indigo Bay. The Farax Pirates sailed down from the north, seeking to extend their rule. They were opposed by the men of Freehold, a colony in the south. You now know this as the Duchy of Freemark. Neither side seemed to know or care that my people were already living there in peace. They called us the 'muck-savages.'"

"Who won?" I asked.

She began scratching absently in the dirt with a stick as she considered.

"No one," she replied.

"What do you *mean*?" asked Roy. "Surely *someone* had to come out on top."

"A third party soon entered the fray," said Sholeena with eyes downcast. "The merfolk used the chaos to occupy several of the Indigo Isles, laying claim to new fishing grounds deep within the bay. They formed a loose alliance with several of the lords of Farax and claimed this for their service."

Sholeena was interrupted by a clanking from across the way. Looking over, I saw a group of Paludas were rummaging through our packs. One had discovered my tin cowbell and was ringing it experimentally. I don't think they'd found the void pocket as yet, but it was only a matter of time.

"*Then* what happened?" asked Roy.

"Eventually, a peace was brokered. Our tribal lands were restored to us. No one really wanted the swamplands where we mostly lived. But we were now hemmed in on both sides, and some of our hunting grounds were taken. Worse still, the sea people refused to depart from our fisheries."

She cast her gaze downward, and her eyes took on a far-off look. When she continued, there was bitterness in her voice.

"The merfolk are a vain people, prone to cruelty and very jealous of their territories. If a Paluda was found fishing beyond the reef, they would drag him down to the depths to see how long he could hold his breath. A few returned to tell us of this vicious practice. What little safe forage remained to us was not enough to feed the people. There was hunger. There was want. And there was resentment, both for the sea people and for *your* kind as well."

"That's *awful*," I whispered.

"A great *pagtitipon* was held to decide what to do about it."

"A pagi-what now?"

"It means an assembly of all the Paludaria. I think you would call it a 'folkmoot.' Each tribe sent their *pinuno* and honored elders to this great gathering. There they argued... debated? over what would be best. We knew we must act as one people if we were to secure our future. Many wished to wage war against the sea folk. But most thought this foolish. The merpeople could simply retreat to deeper waters to regroup and come against us in great numbers. Others wanted to take up arms and reclaim the lands to the north or south. But wiser heads prevailed."

"How so?" prompted Royland.

I heard a great gasp from the men plundering our packs. And sure enough, there stood one of them, pulling a tent pole out of my bob while the others gaped in open amazement.

"It was decided," continued Sho, "that some of our tribes would seek elsewhere for a land to welcome them. We had heard of a great marsh which lay many days' travel to the south. According to the stories we'd heard, it was lush and green, full of abundant life, and fed by many waterways. The soil was deemed too wet for your folk to farm, so all of it lay unclaimed. Perhaps there, our people could thrive."

"You mean the Black Plagued Marshes," I put in somberly. "How'd that work out for them?"

"Six tribes of my people set out for the south. The Paludaria was much reduced. Many of their elderly and very young ones were left behind with the three tribes that remained. All knew the journey would be hard, and its outcome uncertain. Nevertheless, within a fortnight, the great Paluda migration was underway. Not many returned, and those few who did brought discouraging news. The great swamp was not the peaceful place we had hoped. It was a land of only death and sickness. The creatures that called it home were numerous, fierce and aggressive. Many of our people were lost. But there were always rumors that some had survived and made a place for themselves and their families. And it must be true... for here they *are*."

Sholeena spread her palm and indicated the village that surrounded us. Her skin had taken on the bluish cast, denoting sadness or solemnity. I'd rarely seen that shade on Sho. Her eyes squinted shut, and we were all silent for a time, pondering the tale she'd shared. I relaxed to hang listlessly in the ropes binding me to the post as the afternoon sun bathed us in its brilliance. I could hear the soft clatter and exclamations from those still examining our belongings. According to Sho, we were on an island. No creatures should molest us (apart from our captors, whose intentions remained distressingly unclear).

***

"Kahit na hindi ka namin kilala, mukha kang isa sa aming mga tao. Sino ka?"

I awoke from an unpleasant doze. Sholeena was standing up and facing away from me. Beyond her was gathered a group of villagers. In their midst was a wizened old coot wearing a fancy headdress. It was he who had spoken and now stood silent, awaiting her reply.

"Ang pangalan ko ay Sholeena Blorlafargalish," answered Sho. "At ako nga ay taga Paludaria."

The man considered this. I didn't know what yellow denoted, but that was the color of his skin as he issued his next stern declaration.

"Kailangan mong kumanta para patunayan ito sa amin."

Sholeena blushed. That is to say, all color faded from her as she took on the hue of her surroundings. Gathering her courage, she pointed up to where the sun hung above the horizon.

"Napakahusay," she replied. "Tatawagin ko ang pagpapala ng buwan kapag bumaba ang araw mula sa langit."

At this, the man harrumphed, turned, and shuffled off. Those with him broke into a subdued babble of their strange speech as they, too, departed.

"What was that all about?" I asked the girl once they'd left.

"They do not recognize me but can see well enough that I look like them. The pinuno says I must *sing* to prove I am of the people. I told him I would invoke the moon's blessing."

"I hope their tune is the same as ours," she added nervously.

We hadn't long to wait. When the sun crept near the horizon, several women of the village arrived to escort Sholeena

275

over to the statue, before which the entire village was now congregating. One young Paluda dragged a pair of drums to rest nearby. Each was the size of a small barrel. He also had a framework of wooden slats. These made tinkling noises when he struck them with his sticks. And there, dangling off to his left, hung my cowbell. Oh well. Finders keepers, I suppose.

I squirmed within my bindings and managed to gain a better view of the proceedings. Royland did likewise. The women had covered Sholeena in a flowing smock that could almost pass for white when compared to the muddy brown of the others. Atop her head, a garland of lilies was rested. I marked her struggling to suppress the green hue from her features.

The chieftain, who Sholeena called their 'panuno,' stepped up alongside her to address the crowd. He spoke in a somber voice for a time in words I failed to fathom. He indicated Sholeena, then spread his open palm toward the sun saying, 'Magsimula!'

Upon this pronouncement, the drummer began pounding out a booming introduction. One! Two! One-two-three-four! Whereupon, all the men of the village blatted out two long, mournful notes. After a short pause, they began chanting in unison. It was a deep-throated, rhythmic chorus sung to a simple melody. The words were complete nonsense to me, of course, but I found the deep resonance of their blended voices strangely compelling. After several four-beat measures of this, they broke into a higher-pitched refrain. Their lamentation filled me with sorrow.

When they repeated their chorus, the drummer began laying into his stretched hides in earnest. His booming strikes fell in counterpoint to the men's doleful chant. Bum-baba-Bum baba-Bum! Bum! Bum! On the refrain, he switched to striking his makeshift marimba, its tinkling notes trilling above their voices with perfect synchronicity. I doubt even Royland possessed such a mastery of rhythm, though I'd bet shillings to pumpkins he was itching to try.

Then all fell silent. The sun was halfway gone. And by its ruddy light, Sholeena stepped forward, raising her arms in a benediction. Her posture was the same as that of the statue before which she stood. Her voice, when it rang forth, was astonishing to me. It was a clear, mature alto that could melt one's heart by its sweetness. It swelled to form a different melody. Its lilting rhythm was akin to, but somehow softer and lighter than, the men's energetic chant. It spoke to me of peaceful longing. It trilled upward, then swooped back down to a stuttering conclusion. She followed this with the same two haunting notes with which the men had begun.

Immediately after this surprising solo, the chorus swelled anew. While the men resumed their chant, all the village women echoed the tune Sholeena had sung. The two melodies blended together, vying for dominance in a strange, auditory tug-of-war. All the while, the booms and trills of the drummer fell in elegant counterpoint to the whole. Finally, joined as one, the men and women of the tribe sang those two long, eerie notes, adding a third, even longer note to conclude the piece. The last glimmer from the setting sun faded, leaving only its rosy afterglow on the horizon.

By this failing light, I saw the chief turn toward the gathered crowd. He posed to them a question in a stern, commanding voice. A hearty cheer went up. And though their babbling voices were foreign, it was clear they indicated joyous acceptance. From within the impromptu ovation, a chant emerged and gained in strength. Sho-lee-nah! Sho-lee-nah! Sho-lee-nah!

Evidently, our friend was being welcomed by the tribe. Bully for *her!* Perhaps now she could put in a good word for my cousin and me...

But even as I thought things might be looking up, I saw Sho herself looking up. She had turned her back to the crowd and stood staring at the statue looming above. She must have said something to the chief, for he was gaping at her, a look of purple amazement on his bewildered face. She pointed over at us and spoke to the man once more. At their pinuno's signal, the crowd soon quieted, and two grim-faced men were dispatched toward Roy and me. I breathed a sigh of relief when they proceeded to untie us.

***

As the last rope loosened, I took a stumbling step forward, only to fall flat on my face. My hands tingled and burned as my circulation resumed, and I couldn't feel my feet at *all*. Rolling over, I sat up, and the Paluda helped me up to sway unsteadily in the half-light. Noting my mishap, Roy was more cautious, clinging to his pole until he could feel his lanky limbs.

Over before the statue, some men were igniting a vigil fire. A plume of smoke was just beginning to curl above it. The rest of the villagers sat huddled around in rapt attention as their chief told them a story. That must be what was going on. With gestures to the sky or out toward the lake, he held them enthralled, his voice rising and falling in a dramatic cadence. As we approached, I saw mothers holding their round-eyed youngsters. Who knew Paluda kids were so cute?

Sholeena moved over to meet us, and our escort stepped away to rejoin their fellows. Sho was still draped in ceremonial garb. It looked quite fetching on her. And although my blood was now flowing aright, and the tingling had all but ceased, I still felt oddly feeble. Roy, too, looked crankier than usual.

"What's going on, Sho?" I asked. "What did you tell that old man?"

Sholeena's grin broadened a notch.

"I told him we are powerful magicians and can make the statue speak if he gives us some time."

Roy and I exchanged a look.

"Sonomancy?" muttered my cousin.

"Better than that," said Sho. "Come and see."

She led us up to the statue. It stood about ten feet tall to the top of its crown. The arms rose up beyond that. While the chief continued to recount his tale, I examined it. When I invoked my magesight, I was nearly blinded by the thing. Magic emanated from it in pulsing waves that swept past me all around. It was no wonder I felt weak; the thing was undoubtedly sucking the magic right out of me. This could be a problem.

"It's enchanted," I said unnecessarily.

Both my cousin and Sholeena stared over at me with identical acerbic smiles. It should have been patently obvious to me long before this. But I'd had quite a lot else to be processing up until now.

"It's entomancy," declared Royland. "I had wondered about the lack of insects on this island. This thing is repelling them strongly, forcing them out nearly to the lake's edge, unless I miss my guess."

"That's not all," exclaimed Sho. "Look at the pedestal it's resting on."

And there, carved into the stone pretty as you please, were the letters: HCB. I knew we'd been close to the ninth marker before our capture, but who knew we'd find ourselves practically sitting atop it? I wish Roy had his wand to confirm this.

"Here are your wands, by the way," said Sho, producing them and passing them to us. "I told the pinuno we needed them to awaken the statue spirit."

Well, that was easy, I thought, mentally adding: 'I wish I had a sack of gold coins and an arrow that can slay the faerie king.' Sadly, none of that materialized. Either the wand had been a coincidence, or my wishes were all used up. Still, it cost me nothing to try. I shook myself and watched as Royland invoked his wand.

"Quaerite nuntius flammae," he commanded it.

Whereupon the tiny spirit eagle sped straight to the statue and was promptly absorbed. It shed but a single puff of golden glitter. This drifted down to the ground, emitting faint sparkles.

"Tell the chief we're ready," said Roy.

Sholeena thought it best we should make a grand show of invoking the marker. So once the chief had made his announcement and while Roy prepared his fire spell, she and I droned a nonsense verse I'd taught the children back at the crèche. We waved the wands around for good measure.

"Marezedotes andoezedotes,
andlittlelambszedyvy akidlledyvytoo!"

"Marezedotes andoezedotes,
andlittlelambszedyvy akidlledyvytoo!"

Up streamed Royland's little sparks of light to form a ball of magical flame between the statue's outstretched hands. It was larger than his typical sphere. Up rose the swirling mist from the statue's base to gather around the flames, subduing them. As the overlarge face of Master Hans formed upon its surface, a gasp went up from the assembled villagers.

"Welcome, fellow visitors, to the humble village of Nayon. If you're hearing this, either you've met its inhabitants, or they've passed from this world. Gretta and I stumbled upon this island quite by accident..."

At the word 'Gretta,' the villagers all began making a strange one-handed gesture, muttering 'ang Garetta' among themselves in voices filled with wonder.

"We were fleeing some sort of gigantic aggressive armadillo that walked upright. Its shell had proven nigh impenetrable and even resisted my fire. So we opted for the better part of valor. Hoping the thing couldn't swim and praying nothing more dire awaited us there, we leaped into the lake. It was our good fortune to be found by a group of Paluda fishermen. They gave us quite a start, I daresay."

"Paluda," chanted the villagers, then stilled to listen on.

"They took us to their island, rather forcibly, I might add. As luck would have it, Gretta knew a smattering of their language from the time she spent stationed in the Far East. In pigeon-Paluda, she managed to quell their initial hostility. I think the ice-breaker was when she managed to convey she was with child. Though highly suspicious of outsiders, the women of the tribe would never allow harm to an innocent.

"Eventually we determined this was some wretched remnant of a tribe who had dared the great swamp, (or malaking latian, as they name it). The tribe was dying out. They were beset each night by creeping flesh-eating beetles that burrowed up from below. The things were photo-sensitive, disappearing to lie dormant by day. The group was only surviving by huddling around a vigil fire all throughout the long nights.

"Ere we departed, Gretta suggested a way we could help them. I was eager to move on, but we tarried for a time. Gretta performed a grand working to enchant their protective idol. Henceforth, it will drive away any insects in a large circle around the village. It works, too, if the lack of mosquitoes is any proper gage. I worried about my beloved performing such a large-scale magic in her delicate condition. But Gretta was adamant. 'No small act of kindness is ever in vain,' she insisted."

Hans smiled as if at a fond memory.

"Now, as to our quest and the continuance thereof. We believe we are getting close. According to the Paludas, The great spire lays about a three days' slog to the south and just a bit to the east of here. We'll leave our next report when we are in sight of it. Until then, happy trails, my friend. Say goodnight, Gretta."

At this, the enormous face of Gretta swam into view. And when it did, many of the older villagers stood to their feet.

"Good night, friends," she sang, "or magandang gabi, mga kaibigan, as the natives say!"

"Magandang gabi, Garetta!" the villagers all hollered back.

When the sphere finally darkened, many whispered conversations arose among the villagers. There were also cries of Sho-lee-nah! Roy-land! Lu-cash! Well, I could live with that, I shuppose.

***

The next morning, we prepared to set out once more. We'd stayed up late into the night conferring with the chief, with Sholeena acting as our translator. The tribe had flourished after the Brubakers had passed through and eliminated the bug problem. I asked if the beetles still presented a threat beyond the borders of the protected island. It made my skin itch to think of being eaten in my sleep by burrowers from below. But, no. We were assured this pestilence, too, had passed some years later only to be replaced by a plague of blind frogs and several other horrors. The one constant in the Black Plagued Marshes was change; it would seem.

The small community had no dealings with 'the big chief who sits atop the skinny mountain.' His minions would occasionally drop by to play tricks on them, but for the most part left the village alone. I had to wonder why the demon hadn't placed any major obstacles in our way as yet. My fey mark hadn't detected any faerie presence since the attack on Redoubt. The way Terwilliger had carried on about Orenob, he had eyes and ears everywhere. Duchess Brighton had made similar remarks. Perhaps he was hoping the swamp itself would put an end to us. I wondered whether this casual indifference would continue when we invaded his own backyard.

We asked about the dark druids. According to the chief, this group was only loosely affiliated with the king of the spire and his minions. They dwelt farther to the north, beyond the strangling field through which we'd come. We must have somehow missed them, for which I was not the least bit disappointed. So, looking forward, it was time to make some kind of plan. The faerie king would be no weakling. We had no idea what his powers might be. Up until now, we'd been focused only on completing the journey itself. I hoped that Roy might have some ideas.

Breakfast was unusual, but very welcome, nonetheless. It consisted of some small savory meat pies. According to Sholeena, the Paludas collected cattails that grew by the lake's shore. Their roots were ground into a fine powder which could be baked and used much like flour. I didn't ask about the filling. It had a strong fishy aftertaste, and I expected a full list of its ingredients might spoil my appreciation.

Before leaving, I spent some time repacking and reorganizing my bob. At their chieftain's command, the Paludas had returned all of our gear and equipment. It lay in an untidy heap before their stone idol. We hadn't time for a full inventory, but all the essential items seemed to be present. As I was stowing the final few knick-knacks into bob, I paused.

Sholeena and Roy glanced up curiously when I stood and strolled over to the young fellow lugging his drum toward a hut. I stepped in front of him to gain his attention. As he rested his burden, I retrieved the cowbell from an inner pocket of my cloak and presented it to him. I'd only been keeping the thing because it reminded me of Gregor, who'd gifted it to me back in Meadowfork. I could easily obtain another one day, and perhaps the young drummer would use it to spread a bit of cheer among his fellows. From across the decades that separated us, Gretta's words from the prior night had touched me. 'No small act of kindness is ever in vain,' she had said.

I could see in the boy's eyes the truth of her statement as he grinned and accepted. Who knew how many lives would be touched by this small gesture? It was through Gretta's own act of charity that we'd won our freedom, after all.

"Salamat," said the smiling boy.

"*Now you're just being insufferably maudlin,*" grumbled the scarecrow.

CHAPTER ELEVEN

The Verdant Child

"When life itself seems lunatic, who knows
where madness lies?... Too much sanity
may be madness, and maddest of all is to
see life as it is and not as it should be."

~ Miguel de Cervantes~

Peeping from out of the thicket, we watched him creep ahead. The river was quite shallow here, a crossing he had purposely sought. The slow-moving waters fell gently over a protruding lip of rock. This two-foot drop bordered a broad, still stretch of murky brown one could hardly tell was flowing. Below it lay another great pool. But at the rim, we were told, a lucky fellow might just manage to wade across.

The Paluda guiding us had bidden us to hang back. This 'Ilog ng Luha' (river of tears) marked the southern-most border of the Paludas' hunting grounds. It was home to many vicious predators who lay there in wait for animals seeking to slake their thirst. Not the least of these predators was the dreaded Galamay Palaka, an enormous frog who could swallow you whole. Beyond the river began the fetid fens, a stinking mire most creatures had the good sense to avoid. But alas, it was there where Royland's scarf had insisted we must go.

Low to the ground, bare-footed and shirtless, Blandor inched his way forward. Even though we were looking straight at him, he blended so well into the terrain it was difficult to mark his progress. According to Blandor, the great frogs were attracted to movement of any kind. They lay mostly submerged, with only their googly eyes poking above the water's surface.

From behind the cover of a smallish boulder, Blandor flashed us the signal. We were to ready ourselves to move. He was unstopping a waterskin and preparing to make his throw. When I'd asked about the thing, Sholeena had called it a blood lure. She went on to inform us it was used when fishing to attract certain creatures, or sometimes as a decoy to draw predators away.

Blandor's toss was impressive for a man lying nearly flat on his stomach. It sailed in a high arc to land in the lower pool with a mighty splash. It disappeared for a moment, then came bobbing back to the surface. Caught by the current, it went bobbing off, oozing a scarlet trail. All was silent for a moment; and then all hell broke loose.

First, several logs which had been lying up against the banks detached themselves and made for the disturbance. Behind each, the water churned, and I caught glimpses of sinewy tails thrashing. Each made a beeline toward the lure, closing in upon it from all sides. But then, my eyes were drawn to the upper pool from which was emerging the head and shoulders of an enormous, slimy toad. It was easily the size of a shambling mound, even when half-submerged. And from its shoulders protruded a row of puckered tentacles, like those of a squid, writhing all about. Its broad mouth gaped wide. It seemed to scent the air. Both bulbous eyes, each as big as my head, swiveled around then locked straight ahead.

As water cascaded down from off the massive creature's back, great waves went out in ringlets from where it arose. But this was as naught to the surge that followed when into the air it leapt. Fifty feet through the sky it sped, trailing a gushing stream of water.

The reptiles, intent on the blood in their midst, were thrashing about the bobbing lure. Snapping at it, they were oblivious to the impending threat from above. Galamay Palaka plummeted atop them. And where it landed, the water exploded outward in all directions. For seconds thereafter, the splatter rained down, and an enormous wave went surging forth. Its wake sent several of the hapless reptilians tumbling up onto the banks. But many others were snatched up by flailing tentacle arms. They twisted and snapped in a futile attempt to extricate themselves as each was drawn upward to be dropped or flung into Palaka's broad, open maw.

During this frenzy of motion and death, we hoped we might make our way speedily across. When I arose to do so, however, Sholeena seized my arm.

"Wait," she commanded. "Hold tightly to this," proffering me the end of a rope.

I'd almost forgotten *that* part of our plan. Those rocks would be slippery and treacherous. Bootless, the Paluda girl was confident of her footing. Moreover, if one of us should fall, the other two could haul him back up or tow him along in their wake.

I gripped the rope firmly and followed the girl out onto the open bank. The water at the drop-off was nobbut ankle deep and flowed sluggishly over its lip. But still I felt its relentless tug whenever I sought to place a foot. Sholeena had been wise to insist on the rope, for the stones were slippery indeed. We paced along calmly despite our sense of urgency, choosing safety over speed. I tried to ignore the furious commotion below as I held tight to the safety line. I hoped against hope that a large pair of eyes wouldn't spot us and deem us a tastier prize.

I saw Roy arrive on the far bank and nearly lost my footing as I watched him turn to anchor our line. A minute later, we were hustling toward the welcome concealment of the weeds beyond. I paused to look back, hoping to catch another glimpse of the havoc we had wrought. But the sight was already lost from our view. A Silence had reclaimed the scene, broken only by the restlessly lapping waters of the upper pond. Sholeena again seized my arm, dragging me into deeper cover where Royland sat staring about with relief etched upon his weary features.

I reckoned we'd gotten off easy, based on the descriptions we'd heard of other grim horrors lurking hereabout. I'd no idea, for example, what a 'frumious bandersnatch' might be. But I was glad we hadn't encountered one, given the haunted look they'd brought to the Paluda chief's eyes.

***

It was in some ways easier to march through the Fetid Fens. Visibility was good, and the ground was mostly clear. Apart from the occasional clumps of trees which grew on hillocks all about, the primary flora were sparse growths of stinging nettles, easily avoided. My chief complaint was the stench that arose, becoming ever more obnoxious the further we marched along. It was the same foul odor I'd smelled on two prior occasions. It was the feculent stench that had accompanied Orenob's image when he'd been summoned to the standing stones. I took this as further evidence we were drawing nearer to the faerie king's lair.

I paused, then angled off to the right. My two companions followed without comment. The Fetid Fens played host to another danger, which I was well-suited to counter. The ground from which the nettles sprouted was, for the most part, firm. But here and there, they instead grew atop a soupy muck that could suck an unwary traveler straight down under. These quagmires weren't easily discerned by sight from the firmer ground around them. But with my earth sense, I could suss them out readily enough. Sholeena, too, could spot them. So we took it in turns to lead the way around such obstacles.

"I think we should break for the midday meal," suggested Sholeena with a sigh.

The sun rode high in the overcast sky. Peeping out now and again. With our zigging and our zagging and our tired bootsteps dragging, it was getting tough to tell which way was south. But still, we plodded on. And since the morning sun was gone, I sought a spot to rest and stuff my mouth.

Wait.

Why were my thoughts all spinning about and making rhymes again? Surely there wasn't a dryad grove here in the midst of the Fetid Fen. This was no forest. There were no proper trees. No dryad would dwell in environs like these!

"Um...Roy?" said I, halting in my tracks. "Do you sense something strange nearby?"

He stared at me as if I'd grown two heads and said simply: 'Why?' in reply.

Once I'd explained my suspicions, he became much more engaged. He cast all about, squinting his eyes, eventually shrugging and shaking his head. Sho, too, came up empty. Mayhap we should try to employ the direct approach instead.

Well, thought I, it can cause no harm to at least give it a try...

"*You don't know that,*" the scarecrow said. "*Perhaps it were best to give it a rest and let the sleeping fey lie.*"

Ignoring him, I issued the standard request.

"May we speak to the Mistress of the Glade?"

My question hung there, expectant. Then my fey mark began to tingle and burn as a glowing patch of greenish light came rippling into view. It was oval-shaped, six feet in height and wide enough for two. And when its wavering surface solidified and cleared, a most convincing forest in this window had appeared. I believed it but an image hanging in mid-air. But from it, I felt an invitation that verged on a command. It was daring me to step within. A challenge was at hand.

The others looked to me questioningly. I shrugged at them in reply. Narrowing my eyes and lifting my chin, I strode to the fore and stepped right in. And as I passed beyond and through the strangely glowing disc, I hoped I wasn't mistaken to have taken so frightful a risk.

***

We stood in a ring of hawthorn trees. Their thorny trunks and branches spread above. Beyond them lay a forest most fair with butterflies and birdsong. And the sky was a clear cerulean blue one rarely ever saw. A gentle breeze was wafting by, fragrant and refreshing. We had but a moment to take this all in before we heard the voices.

"Are these... humans we see gaping at us with open mouth o'er lowered chin? The Glade of Endless Summer is a faerie place. Who allowed such filth to enter in?"

"The little one has a fey mark, mother, and asked most properly. By our custom, we must honor such, as I'm certain you'll agree."

"So, it was you, Katrina. I might have guessed. You were always the most impertinent of my brood. But beware smiling strangers. They present many dangers. And their seemingly civil manners are often misconstrued."

The center-most tree was massive, a good two yards in girth. And her mighty roots bulged out all around to straddle the loamy earth. She must be ancient, this hawthorn tree. I had thought all dryads were oaks. I supposed a wider variety must exist among these goodly folks. I sensed the five hawthorns confronting us were solid and just as real as you might please. But the fictional forest surrounding them was naught but an illusion. I smelled the faint taint of the fetid fen wafting along on the breeze. And I strove to find my tongue to explain the reason for our intrusion. (A little flattery mightn't hurt either.)

"Mother dryad," said I, "we admire your grove and are awed by its splendor and elegance. We've journeyed far to seek the spire. Do you know aught of it, perchance?"

Then from one of the younger trees stepped out a slip of a girl whose eyes were wide with curiosity. She had the slender figure a dryad's aspect seemed to favor. Her skin was a darker shade than those I'd met before. And, like an elf, her ears were pointed, sticking out from her silky green hair. Most striking, however, were the long, dark nails extending well out from her fingertips. And when she spoke, her fulsome lips revealed pointy teeth, like those of a cat.

"The little one is cute, mama, and he speaks with such charm and wit. We've had so few visitors here of late. May we play with him for a bit?"

The others also began peeping out from within the boles of their trees. I thought perhaps I'd made some progress toward befriending a few, at least. But the stern voice of their matron soon forestalled my premature elation.

"Hush, daughter, and stay well back from these creatures, whose honeyed words oft hide their sting. What mischief do they intend at the spire, and what would they have of our king?"

"We bear you no malice. We're friends to your kind, but your king sends his minions to vex us. His swamplands creep near with each passing year. And we fear he might mean to annex us."

Whew. Rhyming was exhausting. But I needed to keep it up. The others were depending on me.

"See," said the youngest. "He says he won't hurt us. I'll make him swear a vow."

Turning to me, she said quietly: "Do you cross your heart and hope to die?"

Her emerald green eyes bore straight into mine, and I felt the rush of her compulsion. I struggled hard against the urge to complete the childish oath she would have me take. With her long, pointy nails and her branches bristling with thorns, I knew she possessed the means to seal such a deal. Her seemingly innocent desire to 'play with me a bit' took on a very different meaning. I was loath to invite a poke in the eye, stabbing in to mar my features. I held my tongue (barely) to avoid such a fate. Fairies are most literal-minded creatures. The child pouted prettily.

"Answer me truly, mother dryad," I panted once I could again breathe freely. "Are you and your daughters of the seelie court? Or are you the unseelie?"

And from within the towering tree, her voice rang down to answer me.

"I dislike this term: 'unseelie.' 'Tis a misguided label at best. Our servile sisters who dwell in the north... ah... but I have digressed. Say, rather, we are the *true* fey, unspoiled by the touch of man, living by the ancient ways, set down in Gaia's plan."

I took that as a simple 'yes,' her other blather being quite a mouthful. I'd stick with 'unseelie,' thank you very much. And as I listened on, my hope for peaceful discourse grew more doubtful. (I learned she didn't care for human beings overmuch.)

"Your people are a pestilence, who live by the sword and the axe, burning the bones of our fallen to warm their wretched shacks. We are well aware of you foul upstarts. Our king told us we should expect you. No clemency will *your kind* find in our hearts. We stand by our king and reject you!"

"Steeped in blood is your history. Is it any wonder we shun you? Nay, it is no mystery. In vile butchery, none have outdone you. For you kill all you touch, however much, you fail to understand it. And none doth say to such slaughter: 'Nay!' None of your ilk countermand it. In the taking of life and the giving of pain, you humans are unsurpassed. But our king's unrelenting and steadfast campaign, shall end your reign of terror at last!"

Such vehemence.

"Then we shall go," I offered. "Please show us the door. We'll find the spire on our own and trouble you no more."

But I found it was far too late by now to bow out quietly. The dark dryad had it in for us. She stepped out from her tree, to stand among her children. She arched her brow and glared at us before resuming her rant once more.

"Speak to me not of peaceful leave-taking. I feel you're no friend to the fey. You think to afflict us with odious queries and then be merrily on your way?

"Our king is wise and mighty. Such antics as yours won't alarm him. He fears no powers you might possess nor those of *any* who'd harm him. He's made of this world a paradise for those who serve him well. Look ye about at the wonders he's wrought, the marvelous home in which we dwell.

"Look ye and despair, for this shall be, the last sight given unto thee. You'll bring no mischief to fret and beleaguer our royal lord in his majesty. Proudly we who serve the king rise up, the wicked foemen's plans to foil. 'Tis only death for those like thee. We'll use your bones to fertilize our soil!"

And upon these words, her ropy roots surged up from the ground below, grasping at our ankles and holding us fast. Royland and Sholeena had up until now seemed content to bide and let me make our case. But now they were shouting and thrashing about as we all became rooted in place.

"Let me go!" shouted Sho.

Royland looked grim. And I pulled loose my wand from its sheath. But I doubted I had much of a chance to thwart this attack from beneath. Pitted against an ancient dryad standing in her own grove, my pale mockery of a dryad's power would sorely insufficient prove. It'd be like trying to dig through stony soil with just a rusty spoon. Possible, but unlikely, and it wouldn't happen soon.

'He never succeeds who ventures not,' I thought with a mad turn of mind.

"*Hold!*" interrupted my inner voice. "*I said I would aid you if danger arose, and this seems more threatening than most. Let me have use of our voice to speak. Quickly or we're compost!*"

Rather than die with such a reckless rhyme on my lips, I relaxed my throat muscles and handed him the reins.

"Hold, harridan," the scarecrow spat, our voice dripping now with disdain. "Ere I die, let me clarify something for you."

(I was eager for him to explain.)

The dryad paused. She seemed shocked by our rudeness but was also curious about what I had to say.

"The king is not a friend to you. He's trapped you within an illusion. But I shall disabuse you from the throes of this delusion. In the seeming of your dreaming, all within looks fit and hale, but the land lies sere and barren when you look beyond the veil."

At this, I felt welling up from within me, a torrent of magic. The power was my own but different somehow, shaped by a spell unknown. And where it touched, the dryad's veil of seeming was undone. The fantastic colors faded from the sky, and about us the landscape lay muddy and bleak.

"Look ye and despair? Well, turnabout is fair. And fair is not the word that I would choose, to describe the swampy land fraught with naught but grit and sand and occasional pools of slimy, bubbling ooze. Your king has betrayed you. The forest is dead. He's given you only illusion instead."

And from the dryads who stood there in startled disbelief, came the chorus of their weeping and despairing wails of grief.

"*Now! While they're distracted,*" said the scarecrow in my mind. "*Use that wand thing of yours to free us!*"

So I did just that. And we ran.

Hawthorn trees differed from oaks. And though they could grow quite old, even the eldest of them rarely topped thirty feet. Would Holly's rule of thumb for a dryad's reach hold true for this clade of tree as well? But my feet decided to abandon the math and simply start running like hell. Sholeena couldn't run as fast as Royland or I, and Roy couldn't sense the sloppy pits of quicksand. So, despite the scarecrow's urging, I held back, and we sprinted away at the best speed we could jointly manage.

Nothing pursued us, and when we finally felt we were well in the clear, we paused to catch our breath. We could still hear the tree sprites wailing in the distance.

"Did you have to be so harsh?" I asked of my homunculus, saddened by the dryads' keening lamentation.

"*You wanted to live, didn't you? You heard what she said. We were to be tree food before I intervened. And that creepy little one wanted to poke out our eyes. Leave it to Lucas to sympathize with our captors. I hate it when you get all weepy over stuff like that. They got what they had coming. Or they 'reaped just what they'd sown,' as the farmers are wont to say.*"

"I suppose you're right. I just hate seeing creatures suffer. And in case I didn't mention it before, thanks for your help... Reginald."

"*I... see,*" said the scarecrow. "*That was no random pick. That name means 'the ruler's adviser,' to the best of my recollection. I suppose by this I am meant to infer that you are the ruler in question?*"

"And don't you forget it, Reggie," I smilingly confirmed.

***

So, he knew we were coming. I shouldn't be surprised. Why, then, did he send no imps to bar our path? Did Orenob think so little of us? Or was he merely biding his time and waiting atop his spire to smite us? We would soon find out, in any event.

The stench bubbling up all around us had intensified. We could even see it now. A low-lying green mist swirled about our ankles, and a thin haze hovered in the stagnant air. I wished I could have spent more time with Mistress Julia. Doubtless, her aeromancy could have shown me a few ways to filter out such an odor.

"Quaerite nuntius flammae," Roy called out for the thirteenth time.

Unlike his prior dozen attempts, this one bore fruit. The tiny eagle from the tip of his wand sailed forth into the tainted sky. We quickly lost sight of the soaring bird.

"Finally," said Roy with a sigh.

So, the tenth and final marker was now but two miles off. We picked up our steps in excitement and scanned the horizon ahead. I recalled from the prior marker what Master Hans had said. His next message would be recorded when the spire was in sight. Our hearts beat with anticipation as we hustled ahead in the failing evening light.

It stood there in the distance like a slender finger pointing up. My studies of geomancy had a name for such a formation. They called it a 'butte,' I think. Personally, I preferred the Paludas' description: 'skinny mountain.'

Royland stared, deep in thought, at the smaller arrangement of rocks to which the eagle's glowing trail had led us. Although eager enough to get here, he now seemed halting and uncertain. I, too, was distracted. At the edge of my inner vision, too dim to be seen directly, were flickers of a once-familiar sight. Back at Westarbor Keep and then again at Aeriston Mine, I'd encountered a strange phenomenon that was called a 'ley line.' It was a river of geomantic force running deep beneath the earth. Touching it but once had awakened my secondary affinity and given rise to my inner hill.

From Grandma Abbey's memories, I knew that harnessing the incredible power of a ley line was only possible for a geomancer, and that to do so was an extremely hazardous undertaking. Among her final words to me, she had claimed that each time she had done so, she'd left a bit of her humanity behind. That Orenob's lair sat atop one could be no mere coincidence. I shuddered to think our dreadful adversary might have this, too, at his disposal.

The night had come full upon us by now, and the stars were out. We could make out only the strongest of these, feebly twinkling above the hazy mire. The steaming tar pits surrounding us bubbled and expelled their gasses. We'd had to veer from the golden path many times to work our way around them. Was this natural? Or was it some byproduct of the faerie king's use of this 'heart of the swamp' he possessed? Who could say, save the king of the fey? We'd just have to ask him about it; I guessed.

"No sense putting it off any longer, cousin," I said to my hesitant friend. "It's time to see what the Brubakers have to say."

Sholeena stepped up near him to rest a hand on his shoulder. And he didn't move away. Pressing his palms together, he sighted along his thumbs and uttered the by now familiar incantation. A ball of fire blossomed above the depression in the rocks where the eagle had come to rest. And as it was enveloped by swirling vapors, a haggard face was soon revealed. It was Master Hans, but looking like we'd ne'er seen him before. His brow was lowered in sadness o'er his sorrowful, pale blue eyes. And where once had rested a lively smile, a frown tugged at the corners of his lips.

"Greetings, future traveler," he said half-heartedly. "It's been a long and difficult road up till now. I hope you who follow us have had a gentler journey than have we. Tomorrow will see us at the spire and up to the fate awaiting us at its top. Gretta is scouting the way ahead even now, and I thought in her absence I'd take this opportunity to have a private word with thee."

He looked down for a moment, collecting his thoughts.

"It occurs to me," he continued with a slight catch in his voice, "that there may be another interpretation of the words given us by the oracle."

As his words hung there, his eyes flashed up to meet mine squarely, as if he knew precisely where I stood despite all the years separating us. And in them was a sadness so profound that it twisted my heart within my chest. He knew.

"I suspect this dire alternative hasn't escaped Gretta's notice, either. She is most astute and well versed in the art of word play. Neither of us has yet found the heart to broach this unthinkable possibility. And so we laugh and feign certainty in the success of our venture.

"And yet, here on the very eve of its culmination, I feel I must tell *someone* of the fears that haunt my heavy heart. It is you, dear listener, I would choose as my confessor, that I might enter into battle fully shriven of any doubts which might stay my hand from the deeds which must be done.

"I would ask that you pray for us, but I know not whether the all-knowing can respond to such appeals from across the veil of time. Therefore, I pray for *you* instead. I pray that you now live in a kingdom bereft of the foul manipulations of the demon of the spire. I pray that by the time you are hearing this, all has been resolved in favor of Osten; and you may live happy lives by our sacrifice. And most fervently, I pray that Gretta, at least, will be spared should our efforts prove insufficient. I hope you may one day hear her laughter and come to know the gentle radiance of the soul that lies within her. I will do all in my power to see that this is so. If only one may return, I pray that it is she."

"Amen," I said, (twenty-six years too late to be of any use.)

Again, his head lowered and a brooding silence ensued.

"But soft," he muttered, "my love approaches even now."

And into the scene stepped Gretta.

"Started without me?" she asked testily, in a falsely offended tone.

"Nearly done, my love," he answered with counterfeit cheer.

"Did you remember to mention where the final marker would lie?"

"I'm certain he, she, or they can guess. But why don't *you* tell it, my dear?"

Gretta harrumphed and stepped in close.

"Circumstances permitting," she announced, "the eleventh and final marker will be placed atop the spire itself. In it, we shall joyfully relate the triumphant conclusion of our mission!"

But was that apprehension haunting her eyes as she blithely went nattering on?

"You've done very well to follow us thus far. Hans and I look forward to meeting you one day and hearing the tales of your own journey. Until then, fare thee well and may your footsteps be guided by the creator's grace!"

The sphere went dark.

As my eyes adjusted to the faint light that followed, I heard muffled sobs from just off to my right. It was Sholeena looking bluer than I had ever seen her, her shoulders shaking with undisguised grief. But when I glanced over at Roy, his face bore no frown, only a sober look of peace. As I watched, a wistful smile even crept up from beneath.

"Aren't you sad, cousin?" I asked him. "I should have thought these grim revelations would depress your spirits and sour your mood. They certainly have mine."

Ordinarily, Roy wasn't one to waste words. But my cousin surprised me this night. He spared us a soliloquy so impassioned in its nature that we wouldn't soon forget it. I sensed my cousin, in this rare instance, was finally speaking from his heart.

"They *knew*," he breathed in a wistful voice, the wonder of which was apparent. "Don't you see, cousin? From almost their journey's outset, they knew of the danger and went anyway. To be sure, I am saddened by the events which took place. There will be no eleventh marker. What is done is done. What happened here cannot be changed. But their intent made all the difference in the world.

"I am no longer ill-disposed toward the oracle. She offered them a great gift. She gave them a choice. And rather than despair, they chose their duty, and hope. They were heroes, after all, not some hapless dupes of a careless fate. They chose instead to be champions of the kingdom, willing to risk all for the good of those who follow.

"And though my own fate is uncertain, I intend to do the same. The prophecies don't reveal what might become of us when the deed is done. We've wallowed in the murky swamp and faced the grim horrors therein. A final test to prove our resolve awaits us. I'd wrestled with the implications of whether we should take this final step, trusting to a higher power to see us through. But now I am decided. I, at least, shall go. My grandparents chose hope. And, as the eldest son of their line. I shall gladly do the same to honor their memory."

I stood there, stunned. Who knew my cousin could or would ever wax so eloquent? I tried hard to burn his answer word for word within my mind. When next I had the chance, I would have to write it all down. Such a speech from Roy was one for the ages. And if I should live so long as to publish my memoirs, his stoic sentiment would figure most prominently in its pages.

***

That night, as I slept, a lucid dream disturbed my somnolent slumber. I grasped at once it was something apart from my usual drowsy drifting. It put me in mind of the horrible visions Grandma Abbey had once sent to plague my sleep. It had the same sharpness that I recalled from such. Every detail was crisp and clear, with colors even more intense than those from the waking world.

I was sitting at the base of a craggy hill. I couldn't speak or move at first. I looked to the summit of the thing from which was falling an avalanche of flinty chips and earth. These crumbling lumps slid down and clattered, finally coming to rest. And from where they'd splintered off appeared a face up at the crest.

I'd seen this face but once before when the singing green mountain had given me a vision. At the time, he'd said but a single word. He'd named me his 'brother.' On the craggy face above, a toothy smile soon formed. I sensed this was meant to be reassuring, though it would have seemed menacing to most.

"Brother," he addressed me in a gravelly voice well-suited to his aspect, "our time is short, so listen well."

The paralysis gripping me began to ease, and I felt it turn loose of my tongue. I believed I could move and speak freely now. But the earthy creature before me had asked for my attention. So I hunkered down and listened.

"The one you call the scarecrow is no friend to thee or me. Do not let him beguile you. He is our enemy. He suppresses our true nature, supplanting it with his own. In truth, he's a wicked changeling sent by the unseelie throne."

"How so?" I asked. "He dwells within our own magic. Surely, he is my homunculus."

With a creaking rumble, the face rose slowly upward, shedding more stone to form a massive rocky head. And I could see broad shoulders beginning to protrude.

"He was implanted many years ago when your grandmother got with child. Like the cuckoo bird who places her own egg in another bird's nest. He would have overtaken your mother had her magic not been suppressed. And when she died, the creature fled and came to rest instead in thee. He lay there sleeping until such time as your magic would awaken.

"Have you not often wondered how your verdant powers came to be, descended as you are from a more normal geomancer? 'Tis the power of the foul usurper given unto thee, overlying and suppressing ours. That's the proper answer."

He made a convincing set of arguments, this creature who I assumed was my inner hill.

"If this... usurper... owns the power of my garden," I asked, "then why does he bargain with me?"

"He might have overcome your mother much more easily. His essence was watered down when it passed on to you in the womb. In some ways, you've made his powers your own. He also failed to reckon on the fey-touched wand you wield. He was furious when the power of that talisman was revealed."

"How can you possibly know all of this?" I asked with sudden suspicion. "For all I know, you could be some vile sending of the demon who sits atop the spire. How am I to know *what* to believe?"

"You feel in your heart the merit of my words. For they are your own unconscious thoughts and beliefs. I only give voice to them. Ever since the friar's warning, you have suspected the truth. But you've been a bit preoccupied with our journey, and so you left it to *me* to mull over."

"Why didn't you tell me all of this sooner, then?"

"I didn't want him to hear us talking so. Please forgive my hesitation. He's far stronger than I and a danger to us. I was studying the situation. I considered many ways we might communicate unheard. Only recently did I discover he can't hear us speak within your dreams. So here we are at last out from beneath his watchful eye. I feel I know you, Lucas, though we've not spoken directly overmuch. I should. I *am* you, after a fashion."

At this, he lifted a rocky arm free from the side of the hill and jabbed a stony finger at me.

"So my advice to us is this," he said. "Lie low and do not let the scarecrow know we suspect. And by no means trust him or grant him any more power. I..."

"Lucas? Lucas?"

It was Royland shaking at my shoulder and cajoling me awake.

"It's time for your watch. Sholeena and I need our beauty sleep."

"Speak for yourself," muttered Sho.

I felt the scarecrow's slithering withdrawal as I again took up the reins of consciousness. All was in order in our inner garden. Not a leaf was out of place. But I shuddered to think that Reginald might be a changeling, merely posing as my homunculus. Here and I had thought we were finally seeing eye to eye. Hadn't I enough to worry about with daylight drawing nigh?

I crawled out of our tent and added a few more sticks to the fire. Invoking my darksight, I sat and regarded the spire off in the distance. I could trace its faint outline against the greater blackness of the sky. What perils awaited us at its summit? I'd know soon enough, but I couldn't help but wonder.

***

Once again, I felt the supple vines bulging from my back. They were stronger than ever before. It barely took any effort at all to flex them and heave us upward. I'd grown more accustomed to the six-legged crawling motion required to maintain a firm grip on the stony face of rock I climbed.

We'd already ascended to dizzying heights. I felt the weight of my comrades hanging from the stout rope tied firmly to my belt. I doubt I could have managed it without my inner hill's help. For he was making handholds as we went, dimpled into the very stone of the spire. They were spaced like the rungs of a ladder, which Sholeena and Roy could climb. Not easily; they still needed me to tug them up the steep incline. But now and then, we could pause to rest and cling there for a bit before ascending again.

More than halfway up, with an eternity still to go, we happened upon a narrow ledge where we could rest more fully. We were on the spire's shady side, out of the morning sun. We hoped before having to deal with its heat, our tedious climb would be done.

"My arms are aching, Lucas," said Roy as we rested on the shelf. "How are *you* holding up?"

"Better than I expected. My vines seem more than up to the task, but I worry for my inner hill. Working rock is taxing, and I haven't had much practice at it. We may need to rest more often if he shrinks any further. I hope his stored-up strength will hold out until we reached the top."

"Him," Roy mused. "You call it a 'him.' Does this mean he's a second homunculus, after all?"

"Something like that," I muttered in reply.

Sho said nothing. Of the three of us, she had the most trouble with heights. Moreover, her feet weren't well-designed for climbing. Her elongated toes fit into the toeholds readily enough and were surprisingly strong and agile, but they were slender digits more suited to swimming. She looked exhausted.

Back at our previous camp, we'd suggested she stay behind. She'd done her part and more. Now that the prophecy of the three had been fulfilled, we thought she might want to circle back to the Paluda village and wait for us there. But Sholeena wouldn't hear of it. 'You've gotta be sure, right?' she'd said. I blamed Royland's inspiring speech from the prior night. Ever since, the girl had steadfastly insisted that she 'was a hero, too.' I didn't know what use she might be in a fight with the faerie king, but I had learned on this journey never to count her out.

What amazed me most of all was that we'd met no opposition as yet. None. We were clinging precariously to the sheer face of a cliff! What time would be more ideal to swoop down and send us plummeting to our deaths? It was as if Orenob actually wanted us to reach the summit. The thought gave me shivers.

"*Count your blessings,*" said Reggie, testily. "*And commence climbing again.*"

I'd almost forgotten the scarecrow was present in my mind. He'd been oddly silent all morning, not offering the smallest bit of advice or snide commentary. With a sigh, I extruded our vines and readied myself to continue our ascent. I pictured Royland's grandparents swinging along up here at the end of a long braid of blond hair and almost chuckled. Had they even made it up to the top?

***

A few yards from the spire's peak, we paused for a final rest. We wanted to be at full strength and readiness when we arrived at the top. The wind whistled by. At this altitude, it blew in strongly from the west. No other sound did we hear from the lonely summit above to give us any clue to what awaited. At least up here the awful stench was somewhat more subdued, or perhaps I'd just gotten used to it.

I readied my crossbow and loaded an iron-tipped bolt specially crafted to use against the fey. I looked down at Roy, and he nodded. He'd readied his shielding spell to protect me when over the spire's lip I crested. I counted silently to three, then madly scrambled upward.

Tumbling over the edge and frantically casting all about, I came up to one knee and sighted on the only figure looking back at me. He was definitely a faerie, or so my mark informed me. He was tall, but somehow smaller than I'd expected. The overlarge visage he'd projected to his minions at the standing stones had led me to expect some sort of a giant. But in truth, he was no larger than a typical man, if a bit over-muscled. His face was fair and elegant but marred by puckered boils. And on his head rested the thorny crown that I remembered.

All this I took in at a glance.

My finger tightened on the trigger, poised to let my quarrel fly, but something stayed my hand. He made no move to defend himself. Nor did I sense any imminent threat of magic from this man. I knelt there, hesitant, as Roy and Sholeena clamored up to my rear.

And then he laughed.

It was a booming bellow full of merriment one wouldn't expect from such a villain. Had the faerie king gone mad?

And then he spoke.

304

He spoke in a voice rich in its timbre, with noble overtones. Each word fell delightfully upon my ear, making me yearn for the next.

"So, lacking provocation," he observed, "you fail to loose on an otherwise unarmed fellow. I rather wondered whether you would."

I waited for the other shoe to drop, but he seemed to have concluded.

"Why aren't you rhyming?"

Again, he laughed.

"You came all this way, and that's the first question you would put to me? Rhyming is for toadies and lackeys, a way to pay respect. A king needn't bother with such paltry pleasantries."

My ears burned with shame.

"Podagra flammae!" cried my cousin, stepping out from behind me and spewing out a roaring cone of flame.

These flames passed directly through the king, causing him no harm. He merely smiled at my cousin, then vanished.

"That's more like it," said his voice from just off to our right. "I prefer a man with spunk and the courage of his convictions. Well-done, young Brubaker. You remind me of your grandsire. Hans also shot first."

And another image of Orenob came wavering into view. Was this one real, or but another shade?

"Not to be boastful, but I think you should know, you haven't a prayer against *me*."

"There's where you're wrong, slayer of innocents," exclaimed Royland, apoplectic. "We do have a prayer. It is one uttered two generations ago, demanding your annihilation. Over the years, it has grown in strength while passing down my family line. It rages in my blood and calls for yours."

"Yes. Yes. Very poetic. I was told you had a first-rate mind beneath all your sour-faced brooding. Did you anticipate some glorious battle to be waged atop the spire? If so, I will gladly oblige you. We can get to that later, if you *insist*. But first let us converse for a time with more civility. Have you no *questions* for me? Has climbing up the side of the spire exhausted your curiosity?

So firmly had the king's presence riveted my attention that I'd scarcely been aware of aught else. I marked for the first time the full nature of my surroundings. The barren berm on which we stood was a level stretch of natural rock. But behind the man with whom we spoke, lay a garden in fulsome bloom. And nestled in its midst stood a number of monolithic stone slabs resting in a rough circle. It strongly resembled the standing stones at Conclave, differing only slightly in detail.

Sholeena looked confused. What the hell, I thought. Weren't we getting off track here? This wasn't only about vengeance, after all.

"Perhaps we should hear what the king has to say," piped up Reginald.

Just great. As if I needed his two farthings just now. Royland had the best mind among us, but this situation was obviously too personal for him. *I* needed to decide, and *quickly*, how best we might proceed. Keep Orenob amused and find out what we can about the heart of the swamp while he was feeling inclined to play host. I still had the feeling he *wanted* something from us. Let's play out this farce to see where it may lead.

"Very well. We accept," I affirmed, glaring at Roy to quell his passion. "Let's exchange words."

"Then let us adjourn to the garden. I find it a peaceful place to reflect."

At this, he turned on his heel and headed toward the plateau's center. As he did, bright red flowers burst into bloom alongside the path he trod. I think they were called 'hibiscus.' Megan would've known for sure. He led us along this crimson path to arrive near the stone formation. Were we to battle him here, at least there'd be plenty of vines for me to use.

"Where are your minions?" I asked on an impulse.

"My... minions?" he said with an amused smirk I was learning to dislike. "You mean my subjects? I assure you, there are no 'darlings' among them. They're a rough-and-ready band of misfits who remain loyal to their original sovereign rather than that usurping former queen of mine. To answer your question, I sent them away. There are private matters to be conducted among us today."

That was odd.

Sholeena turned a nervous green on preparing to enter the conversation.

"If I might be so bold as to ask, why were you unfaithful to your queen?"

She had come a long way, but Sholeena could still be awfully blunt. Though couched in good manners, the nature of the question itself was most indelicate. But once again, Orenob only smiled. He picked a nit from his vest before answering.

"Apart from the typical tawdry reasons, Rapunzel was an early experiment of mine. I was new to the heart of the swamp and wanted her to bear me a daughter to become the verdant child. It was only bad luck the queen found out about it and went stomping off in a snit."

Alarm bells were ringing in my head. This was the very topic I'd hoped to explore. How could I get him to tell us some more?

"Such matters, after all," he said, "are what brought you here. Are they not?"

"They are," I admitted warily. "What is this 'heart of the swamp?' and what has the verdant child to do with anything?"

"There. You see?" said the ruler, "You needed only to ask it of me. The heart of the swamp is a relic rare, passed down from ancient times. It's part of a set we call 'Gaia's regalia.' Among its sister pieces, there is a belt known as 'the heart of the mountains,' a cloak called, 'the cloak of the wind,' and several other such. None have been seen in modern times except for the one I bear."

He stepped deeper into the tangled growth surrounding the standing stones. And as he did, the vines bunched in, snuggling closer to brush against him like loving house cats. Turning to face us, he continued.

"As to the Verdant Child, Lucas, he has everything to do with my vision for the world. Only one possessing a human soul can utilize the magic fully. Long have I sought to create such a one to be my successor. Up until now, my efforts have been for naught. Imagine my glee to recognize in thee the very fellow I'd sought!"

"You wanted the heart of the swamp? Come stand before me, and I'll give it thee freely, without any reservation. With no boons owed and no vows taken, you may do with it then whatever you may."

It seemed too good to be trusted. Where faeries were concerned, there was always a twist or cost. But could I squander the opportunity to retrieve the very item we'd come here to fetch? I looked to my companions as I teetered on the decision's edge.

Sholeena seemed doubtful, her skin a pale yellow. I knew well what that meant by now. But my cousin seemed conflicted. Fully fixated on our foeman's face, he stared at him with naked disbelief. Sparing me but a brief glance, he muttered his advice, his words filling me with relief.

"He means what he says; every word of it true. And yet I mistrust the fiend."

That decided me. If despite his hatred, Royland certified the offer was genuine, that was more than good enough to act on it. I stepped cautiously forward into the garden, using my gift to part the leafy growths.

I stretched out my hand to the king of the fey. He gazed at me solemnly. Then, with both his hands, he lifted the thorny crown from off his head. He looked no less regal without it. His curly brown locks hung free, swaying gently at the wind's command. Proffering me this treasure, he placed it in my outstretched hand.

Then, from Orenob, there followed a great gasp. Could this day get any stranger? He fainted dead away, and a fit of shaking gripped his limbs. He lay atremble there amidst the weeds.

I could do nothing but stand there watching. For I felt a new commotion boiling up from within. My hand was tightly clamped onto the crown I'd been gifted, and I couldn't put it down. The trap had been sprung. I felt myself being drawn downward involuntarily. I arrived in my inner garden with the scarecrow hovering over me. I was caught in the twisted vines that grew at the scarecrow's end of the field. I tried prying them back from where they ensnared me, but I couldn't make them yield. Was this a betrayal, then?

"Why?" I asked as I lay there.

"You were always fated to serve me."

And he stripped off the papery mask from his face to reveal the aspect beneath it. It was a visage well-known, for it was my own. And a shudder ran down my spine. As I struggled against my bindings, he bent low and placed this pallid mask of a face to cover mine.

"Now *you* can be 'Reggie,' and I'll be *Lucas* and live in the world without. What fun I shall have reigning over it and spreading my swamps all about!"

"What do you think gives you the right," I asked him indignantly, to impose your will on another so, much less the entire mortal sphere?"

"Power, my foolish former master. Think on it as you lie here feeble and weak. 'Might makes right.' It is often said by those who power's favor seek."

He spared me a gloating grin which I am sure had never before graced our face.

"Our friends are growing concerned for us, and I must go reassure them or deal with them in some other fashion. So I must leave you now and ascend to my proper destiny. Don't bother getting up. I know the way. I can see you're quite tied up at present. I'm off. Don't mind me. I've places to see and Lucas to be."

And with that snarky, insincere farewell, he vanished from the garden and left me there.

Well, I'd been here before, I thought. Several times too often, actually. My mind had been violated so frequently I was considering the benefits of putting in a turnstile. Through the eye holes of the mask now covering my face, I peered over to regard my inner hill. It was worn nearly flat from carving all those handholds into the side of the spire.

"Don't look at *me*, brother," grumbled the hill. "I *tried* to clue you in."

***

Once again, I lay staring up at the sky of my inner realm. Upon it, I could perceive the farce playing out in the waking world above. There was Royland, staring curiously at me. And there was Sholeena, crouched over the prone figure of Orenob and cradling his head as he spasmed. I cried out to them. But only one could hear my pleading wail of warning. (Well, two perhaps, if one counted my inner hill, who now lay flattened and sulking.) In my own voice, I heard the scarecrow addressing my companions.

"I can't understand it," he lied. "After handing me the heart of the swamp, he simply collapsed."

"Perhaps it's some reaction to relinquishing the artifact's power," Royland mused. "If you ask me, It couldn't have happened to a nicer fellow."

"You're terrible," exclaimed Sho. "Help me to hold him still lest he do himself an injury."

"Why would we want to do that?" I heard myself ask. "We've got what we came here for. Let's leave him to his fate and plan our next move."

Both Roy and Sholeena looked shocked at this. And though the Paluda's attention lay elsewhere, Royland peered over at us with the penetrating gaze I'd come to know so well. I lost sight of him as the scarecrow turned our head aside. That's it, Roy, I thought hopefully. The scarecrow may have deceived *me*, but good luck fooling the *thought sheriff.*

310

"Though in this instance I happen to agree," said Roy most thoughtfully, "such a sentiment is rather unlike you, cousin. Are you certain you're feeling all right? And since when do you leave a preposition to dangle so? Perhaps you should give me that crown that I may stow it away more safely in my pack. Its energies seem to have unwholesome side-effects."

Our gaze drifted down to the thorny crown still clasped tightly in our hand.

"No need," said my sly usurper. "It's where it needs to be. Not without good reason did the faerie king entrust it to me. My verdant power can hold its baleful influence in check."

"I'm afraid I must insist," said Roy more sternly, lowering his pack to rest between us and working open its fastenings.

The scarecrow frowned in resignation and moved as though to comply. But I felt our muscles tense in preparation. As he crouched before my cousin, he let his magic fly. All about me, his spindly vines surged up at his command. And using them, he drew to his cause the local vegetation.

Vines from the garden (the actual one) came surging up to snatch up both my cousin and Sholeena, coiling tightly about them and dragging them deeper into that verdant grove. Their reflexive struggles were as naught against the sudden and unexpected onslaught. He bore each to the base of one of the standing stones and lashed them firmly there in place.

"Ah, well," he sighed. "I always knew I couldn't fox you two overlong. Strange that it was a slip of grammar that gave me away so soon. Best I make a clean break of it, anyway. Just sit tight, and you may help me celebrate my coronation. As I return to the loving arms of the artifact that spawned me, I find these lofty heights most apt, a fitting venue for my elevation."

I felt my arms uplifting the crown to rest it atop my head. Its magic nearly struck me blind as it penetrated my frightened mind. A horrid buzzing overcame me. And the scarecrow danced in ecstasy as we were penetrated by tendrils of its ancient power.

"*At last!*" exclaimed a new voice that swirled within my skull. "*Lord Oberon was powerful, but this one will do nicely in his stead. Well done, changeling, or should I call us 'Lucas' now?*"

"*Nay, mistress,*" answered Reggie, in a voice that was somehow deferential despite its smugness. "*It's time to reclaim your place of prominence in the world. Not since the great flood have you been so properly awakened. We should reclaim your true name, Rhea, that the earth may tremble at your memory.*"

I wished they would take their gloating chatter elsewhere. It was getting quite crowded in here. As if in response to my idle wish, their attention was soon drawn outward. The two arose to see about a ruckus from above.

"You're not Lucas!" Sholeena was shouting. "He'd never treat us so! What fiend are you that possesses him? I'll drive you out with the magic Lucas taught us! Cogitationes liber--"

Her spell was choked off in mid-incantation as a set of vines wound tight about her throat, causing her eyes to bulge out in alarm. I knew our magic didn't actually require verbalization. I hopefully awaited the strength that might allow me to free myself, but such was not forthcoming. Chuckling, the scarecrow explained.

"Naughty girl," chided Reginald. "That will avail you not. I am no mere possessing spirit. I am Lucas now, so entwined within his soul that such murmurings would only strengthen me as well. Moreover, you'll note your magic fails to answer to your call. The stone to which I've bound you muffles any magic near to it. You and your sour-faced friend will find it will permit only the smallest of cantrips to find purchase no matter how fierce your concentration.

"Nonetheless, I tire of your wearisome prattle."

I looked on with horror as Sholeena's struggles to draw breath became more feeble. Eventually, she went still, and her face faded from angry red to blue. She hung there, limp, beginning to whiten.

He then turned to Roy, who remained silent, staring as if lost into the distance.

"And what of you, Royland?" asked the scarecrow in confusion. "No fiery retort? Not that it would help you anyway, your magic being similarly stifled. Still, I would've expected you to struggle more. Being a clever lad, mayhap you are resigned to your fate. You disappoint me."

Turning from him, the scarecrow withdrew my fey wand from its sheath. He sniffed at it, and I felt my nostrils crinkle in distaste.

"Well, we won't be needing *this* any more," he declared, tossing it carelessly aside.

Again, I turned to my inner hill.

"Can't *you* do anything?" I whispered frantically. "He's killing Sholeena!"

"I cannot, brother," he mind-whispered back quite dejectedly. "Not only have I spent all my power, but he has pierced me with his roots, siphoning off what little I can recover."

I winced.

It was the very tactic I had used against the witch when her rocky tors had imprisoned me. I found it ironic that this time it was I cast in the role of geomancer while my adversary controlled the greenery. Nor was I empowered as the witch had been.

The ley line!

"Rockytop," I whispered urgently. "There's power aplenty lying at the spire's base if we can but reach it."

He must have kenned my meaning at once. I was to learn later that by granting him a name, however inadvertently, I'd deepened our bond. I saw my homunculus straining to arise from our inner hill, only to fall back in defeat.

"What's that you're doing down there?" said the scarecrow from above, drawing my bindings painfully tight. "Cease such struggles. You haven't a chance at escape."

Fortunately for us, it was then that Orenob began to stir. I suppose I should rather think of him as Oberon, now that the accursed artifact had revealed his true name. He rose shakily to his feet and staggered toward us, his wroth writ large on his fuming face.

"Creature," he addressed us. "Long have ye held me in your thrall. And though I now be well shed of thy yoke, I take umbrage at thy hideous possession. I shall repay each second of my imprisonment with torments to equal your transgression. Ye'll wish ye'd ne'er been created, much less so affronted a king of the noble fey. So swears Oberon the mighty, who is privileged to meet out thy judgment this day!"

Bully for him, I thought. And though I feared for my own physical well-being, I was thankful for his timely intervention. But as he lunged forward, the scarecrow only laughed, summoning his vines once again.

"A pretty speech," returned the scarecrow. "But even in your younger days, you'd be no match for the likes of me, now that I've been elevated. And in your weakened, barely recovered state, it's not even a contest. You surely should have waited."

With the faerie king conscious and on the attack, the vines had stopped strangling me. Unfortunately, the rhyming was back, I noted most unhappily.

The scarecrow had entangled the king and stood there chuckling with glee as he lifted Oberon bodily up and battered him against a standing stone. The spire rang from the fearsome blows that bludgeoned the hapless monarch back to insensibility. And just like that, the urge to rhyme, again... departed me.

But the scarecrow wasn't finished with the bloodied ruler. He hurled his insensate form away and toward the spire's edge, his toss falling short by only a bit. My lips drew down in a disappointed frown as the fey king's bruised and battered frame flopped onto the berm, rolling to a stop just shy of the brink.

While all this was happening, as distracting as it was, I marked some movement from the Paluda girl. The vines still wound about her tight, biting deep into her throat. From the whitening of her skin and the protruding of her tongue, I had feared Sholeena might be dead. But down below her waist, from her upper thigh and calf, several of the vines had been severed and lay slack. She was pushing the toe of her still-bound boot into the heel of the other, freeing her foot from its confines. What was she doing?

"And just what do you think you're doing, girl?" said the scarecrow, echoing my thought.

Sho's eyes snapped open wide.

As her foot slipped fully free, her boot went spinning away, and she stretched out her leg far to one side. Fanning out her foot, she used her elongated, prehensile toes to scrabble among the weeds. When she swung her leg back around, she was grasping my wand, and it pointed directly at me.

"And what, pray tell," said the gloating scarecrow, "do you mean to do with that? It's a talisman, you ninny. Only the one who enchanted it with his own hand can make proper use of it. Go ahead. Smite me if you can."

Sholeena's wide eyes shimmered as she lowered her brow in fearsome concentration. The whitening of her skin had fled, replaced now by an angry red. And as she pointed the wand, my magesight revealed its cascading energies. They poured forth in a torrent, lashing across the field in which I lay. The scarecrow's vines which entangled me withered under this scathing assault. And I promptly sat up amid their remains, free from my captivity.

"How?" howled the scarecrow, still reeling from the blast.

I gave him no time to recover. I peeled off the mask he had placed o'er my features, reclaiming them as my own. It was time for a face-off with my errant, former homunculus. I tried to resume full consciousness, but the horrid buzzing of Rhea's tendrils still had their hooks in me, and I was overcome. Painfully, I was ground back down as the scarecrow watched on in triumph.

But it was not I alone who had benefited from the Paluda's unexpected defoliating burst. My true homunculus, Rockytop, had shaken off his shackles as well.

"You can do it, Rocky!" I called out in encouragement.

And my homunculus didn't disappoint. He erupted forcibly. Shedding stones to the left and right, he stood up in a vaguely man-like manner, finally free of the hill he'd once been. And he sang a droning melody that was more of a rumbling din. His long-sustained rumble shook our foemen to their very cores. He stretched up and outward, then down through the spire he delved, there to grip the ley line firmly in his rocky fist. And surging up from within me, I finally found the energy to resist!

Casting off the oppressive pall of Rhea's baleful control, I faced the wretched doppelganger who had so betrayed my trust. I grappled with him for control of my limbs, winning through (only just). Tearing the crown from off my head, I regarded it and considered its fate. I decided I must end the thing while the power to do so still rested in me. It was far too great a danger to the world to wait.

The force I summoned to crush the dire artifact was immense, but she resisted it with all her considerable might. And as the two titanic forces met and vied, the spire itself did tremble. With a great snapping sound and a scream of anguish, the circlet finally succumbed. I'd barely glimpsed its shattered pieces before they crumbled into dust.

I felt the exhaustion kicking in as though I'd just run a marathon. But I was soon to discover my tribulations hadn't ended yet. Roy and Sholeena had worked themselves free and were hustling over my way, when still more grim tidings arrived.

"Brother," rumbled Rocky, "there's trouble down here below."

From his quavering tone, I could tell the news was dire.

"Our tapping of the ley line has destabilized the stone. Our reckless draw has damaged the foundations of the spire! I'm holding it together, but I can't hold out for long. The ley line's shifting and I'm beginning to tire."

I couldn't hear it yet, but I felt it through my boots, a creaking grinding trembling at my feet.

My companions approached me cautiously. I assured them it was really me, and quickly filled them in about our impending fate. According to my earth sense, there wasn't time to climb back down, and I could think of no way to survive the spire's imminent collapse.

Sholeena suggested we crawl into bob. Lloyd's void had once saved her from Master Gunther's fire spell. Alas, the opening was much too small. Moreover, I doubted the bag itself could survive such a fall. Better to be crushed outright than to suffocate slowly in an airless void.

I hugged my comrades close as the world began to tilt, slowly at first but with ever gathering speed.

Then a miracle occurred.

From between two of the dolmens, a flickering light came wavering into view. And in it, the face of an angel sharpened to form a figure we all knew. It was Gretta. Not her younger self who'd spoken along our journey's path. She was old, this Gretta. But unlike the ancient invalid we'd last seen at Conclave, from this one's eyes shone the light of reason as she frowned at us with concern. She beckoned us thither, calling out our names.

"Sholeena, Lucas, Roy. Come home. We're waiting for you. Come home."

Someone had activated the menhir at the conclave. Could one actually step through it? We really had nothing to lose at this point. Without question, we should all try to do it.

I was rhyming again.

Oberon. I had to go get him. The king of the fey must still be alive. I couldn't just leave him to his sorry fate. He'd been duped by this Rhea just as had I. I should rush over and help drag him out through the gate.

But just as I turned to race downhill while the wind went whistling past. I was saddened to see his body spill o'er the lip of the precipice.

Sholeena was tugging at my sleeve. The ground sloped upward more sharply. My body felt far too light. Among the final impressions my tired eyes received, I saw from the heavens a flash of greenish light. It streaked downward, speeding swiftly from my sight.

And then I was through, but disoriented. For the ground lay as flat as a table. I now stood on the Conclave side looking out upon Lake Placid. At the menhir stood Sybell Dunham, her hand resting flat on its surface.

"They're through!" shouted Gretta frantically.

"Close it quickly. Sybell." She urged.

The scene framed in the standing stones started to collapse. Before it closed entirely, it belched out a foul odor, and a rain of pebbles sprayed across our backs.

"That was close," said Sybell.

I thrilled to be alive as I lay panting on the ground. But I felt something within me was amiss. Peering deep within, I beheld a startling sight. My inner hill was there, but no green field abutted it.

"What happened to my meadow? Rocky, are you there?"

But an echoing stillness was the only reply.

Epilogue

"A Little Neglect May Breed Great Mischief."

~ Benjamin Franklin ~

How many times could a person almost die and not get the feeling someone was watching over them?

The wind howled against the parlor window, causing it to shudder. Our recent sojourn in the south had left me ill-prepared for the icy grip of winter here at Conclave. In the steaming jungles and stuffy marshland, I'd almost forgotten we were well into the advent of... well... Advent.

Mistress Talia had been kind enough to let us reclaim our old rooms at Julia's former estate up on the hill. Our master, now the doting grandmother of a darling baby girl, would be returning in the spring. So it was decided that we three should resume our training under Conclave's new Elven representative until then. After we'd shared our tale with the masters, they decided to grant us a well-deserved rest. The king of the spire, and indeed, the spire itself, should trouble us no more.

"Did you hear the latest from the pixies?" asked Sho, warming her feet before the fire.

"Not unless you mean that Holly's lost her baby leaves."

"Not that, silly. Queen Tinatia has taken Orenob back as a consort. He isn't king again yet. She says he has to earn that privilege among the seelie --"

"Hold on, I interrupted. He fell off the spire. I saw him do it. What's he made of to have survived *that*?"

Sholeena smiled knowingly, as only a gossip with a tasty bit of trivia could. She made us wait several more seconds before sharing it.

"The queen was *watching* that day we climbed the spire, flying high above unseen to see how it would turn out. When Orenob fell, she was stricken. She was still in love with the wretch despite his former philandering. At the last possible second, she flew down and saved him!"

That explained the green light, I thought.

"It makes sense," put in Royland. "I had wondered about that line in the verdant prophesy that said 'A kingdom will be reconciled.'"

"According to the pixie," added Sho, "she even removed all the warty boils from off his face. She left one, though, as a reminder."

I took it from Sholeena's happy expression that she approved.

It was then that Zelda arrived bearing a tray with three steaming mugs of wassail. It could be nothing else. From the holiday mixture wafted the distinct sharp scent of apples and spices. The woman was known to be a bit heavy-handed when mulling it with spirits. And from her rosy cheeks and unsteady gait, it appeared she'd done more than her share of sampling.

"Drink up," she urged us. "Mattingly wassail can warm the cockles of one's heart even on the bitterest day of December."

"My thanks, Griselda," said Roy. "What's the occasion?"

"'Tis the season, is all," she replied. "Though I must confess you're a few weeks early."

"Oh? How so?"

"Usually, it's a few days into the new year before three magi arrive from the east," she tittered.

Sholeena tried a cautious sip, then pulled a face. Smiling, she licked her lips and went in for another. We all watched with amusement as our well-lubricated housekeeper, tray in hand, made her unhurried way back toward the kitchen. I shifted in my seat to a more comfortable position and let the warmth of the hearth seep into my skin. Sholeena wiggled her long, slender toes. It reminded me of a question that had been nagging at me.

"So, Sho, how did you manage to activate my wand, anyway?"

"Easily," she replied. "When you made it, we were all joined by communal magic. Because of that, I expect Royland could use it as well. Even that crazy magic-muffling stone didn't slow it down much."

She looked over at me and grinned that wide Paluda grin.

"You should have seen the look on your smug face when it went off."

"Hey, now. You *know* that wasn't me. I was glad when you did it. It freed me. From the *vines*, at least. But on that note, how'd you get your leg loose to begin with? Your knife?"

"Nope. It was all Royland's doing."

I turned a questioning gaze on my cousin.

"Like Sholeena," he said, "I was made muzzy-headed by the power of that stone. But I've been that way many times before. It used to be my natural state. I had learned early on in life to overcome it somewhat by extreme concentration on but a single task."

"So did you manage to sneak in a 'force axe' spell?"

He shook his head in negation and took another sip from his mug.

"Nothing so energetic. Due to my affinity for insects, I was able to summon some ants to chew through Sholeena's bonds."

"Ants?"

"Yes. They were of the leaf-cutting variety I'd studied earlier. There are ants everywhere - save perhaps in the village of Nayen," he amended.

It amazed me that so small a thing could have so large an impact. It put me in mind of that old poem where for want of a nail a kingdom was lost. By extension of such logic, it was a mere ant that had toppled the spire.

"It was hard," grumbled Sholeena. "*You* try playing dead with Royland's *bugs* marching up and down your leg!"

"I was really worried about you, Sholeena," I said placatingly. "Those vines were cutting off you airway for a good three minutes, and you really looked like you were dead or dying."

"I was only faking," she assured me. "Like the merfolk found out at Indigo Bay, a Paluda can hold her breath for a *looooong* time."

I smiled at this.

"Well," said I, "what amazes me most was the manner in which we were rescued."

Turning to Roy I asked: "What are the odds they would open a portal from Conclave at the precise moment of our need?"

"Pretty good, actually," he replied, "given that one of them was a clairvoyant."

"According to Sybell, however," he continued, "it was Gretta's awakening that triggered the whole thing. She came out of her cell and wandered up into the tower of meditation, pacing about and wringing her hands in obvious agitation. When Mistress Dunham tried to guide her back to her chambers, she was struck by the vision that guided her hand at the menhir."

Royland drained his mug and set it on the table before him. He stood and stretched.

"Speaking of my grandmother, I must be off. I promised her sister I'd help get her moved to her estate this afternoon."

Roy wrapped his cherished scarf about his neck and headed toward the entry hall in search of his boots. After he'd gone out to brave the cold, it was just Sho and I. We sipped at our wassail as the fire shed its cheery glow. It was now cool enough not to burn our tongues. (The wassail, that is. Not the fire.)

"Filbert says you're a geomancer now. Is that right?"

I gulped.

Rockytop had eventually emerged from my inner hill, but he seemed shaken by his recent experience. It had to do with the ley line. The witch had never explained it very well. I wasn't sure I quite understood it myself. Touching the thing connected one to a primal force of nature, slowed time to a glacial pace and expanded one's awareness to include the whole of the earth. It gave one a glimpse of Gaia's plan, too large to be encompassed by a single mind. After the long exposure that Rocky had suffered, it had taken him a while to reassemble his individual identity.

As to my inner garden, that was gone. I suppose the destruction of the artifact had swept it away, along with poor back-stabbing old Reginald. I guess it was never really mine to begin with. Still, I would miss my vines.

"Tell Filbert he's a very smart fish, and that Rockytop says hello."

After Sholeena, too, had made her excuses and departed, I sat alone in the parlor for a time, staring into my empty mug. Despite Roy's explanation, I still thought a higher power had been watching out for us. It was more comforting to think of it that way.

Calming my scattered thoughts, I sought within. There was my inner hill, solid and peaceful. Adjoined to it, I noticed a small green spot that pricked at my awareness.

I moved in closer.

I had the impression of a blotch of green. It was small but fraught with possibility and potential...

Author's Afterword

Dear Reader,

I hope you've enjoyed this fourth installment of the "Osten Chronicles." Our heroes have certainly come a long way from their humble beginnings. I feel that I, too, have evolved somewhat as an author and storyteller. Since retiring from a career in information technology, I've taken up many interesting hobbies and pastimes. Among them have been woodwork, arts and crafts, gardening, (writing, of course), singing and even (briefly) line-dancing, for which I found I have very little aptitude.

I spend some time each week at the Delhi Senior Center, here on Cincinnati's west side. During the writing of "Bedlam in the Bog," I was even elected to the center's board of trustees. Initially, I became a member in order to join the Delhi Senior Singers, a group that entertains at local retirement homes. They say you can't teach an old dog new tricks, but I find myself in total disagreement with this maxim. The leisure time afforded me as a retiree has instead empowered me to unleash talents long suppressed by my former work-a-day existence.

Hence, one of the primary themes of "Bedlam" is facing new challenges and new situations. The characters and my readers experience many new locales, cultures, languages and ideas. Lucas is confronted with an entirely different understanding of his own identity and his magic. Another theme is kindness, with an emphasis on how the smallest act can send ripples into the future, touching many lives.

I also came to realize just how difficult it is to do quality work in a rigid format. Every now and again, I'd hit a section where the fairies had to rhyme. I hope you found this playfulness as funny as I did. It was slow work to keep the dialog well-metered and rhyming while still making sense and varying it enough to avoid tedium. It gave me a whole new appreciation for writers like Shakespeare, who had to pen entire plays in iambic pentameter.

Anyway, when dedicating a novel, I look for the things that inspired me to write it as I did. This one was difficult. There were so many possibilities. You'll note that I settled on Sister Shirley

Le Blanc. Sister Shirley runs a drum circle that met once each month in the pre-Covid era and hopefully soon will again. I attended it regularly as one of those leisure-time activities I was mentioning earlier. She is a pleasant and outgoing person, very skilled in the art of rhythm, with whom I immediately struck up a friendship.

How does this relate to inspiration for my novel? It's a bit roundabout, but here it is. I mentioned to Sister Shirley how much fun I was having in the Delhi Senior Singers. Many of the oldies we perform are quite the toe-tappers. She promptly lent me a drum (a dandy little snare drum in a rolling case) and encouraged me to try something new. Despite never having played a lick prior to my late fifties, I gave it a try. The singers loved it, and it's brought quite a bit of joy to many people ever since, myself included.

By now, you may know that I compose, arrange, and record a new song for each novel I write. I write about them in my stories, and the songs themselves relate to the novels. For "Bedlam," the song I wrote is called "Threnody of Twilight." It's the song the Paluda's sing at sunset to invoke the moon's blessing. You can find it on my website on the page relating to the fourth novel (www.thormans.org). Fear not; it's in English. And a special shout out to the Delhi Senior Singers and some of the sisters of Mt. St. Joseph for helping me record it.

Like Lucas at the novel's end, I feel as though I've just run a marathon. I think the "Osten Chronicles" could almost stand complete as a four-book series. But, as I've previously indicated, it was envisioned as a five-volume set (and I think I still have one more in me.) Look for the stunning series conclusion in a year or so. Its working title is "A Royal Ruckus." Why so long? Well, I've always disliked series which start out great, then decline in quality and imagination as they wear on. I promised myself that each novel in "The Osten Chronicles" would sparkle and take the reader to unexpected horizons. How am I doing so far? Please let me know by placing a review out on Amazon or Goodreads!

Until Next Time, Then,
Daniel Thorman

Appendix I

(Dramatis Personae)

To help you keep track of the many characters populating this novel, I've provided the following reference. This is a short summary of characters directly mentioned or encountered. Reference with care and only at need. A few of these passages may contain spoilers. Otherwise, enjoy them.

Main Characters

Lucas Harper - Having finally been selected as a journeyman mage, Lucas looks forward to learning new things as he masters his magical gift. But fate is to deal him a different hand from the one he had envisioned. Lucas is struggling to master two disciplines: geomancy, and the relatively unknown gift of verdumancy. Add to that, he now has a special relationship with the woodland fey.

Sholeena Blorlafargalish - Sholeena hails from a tribe of people called the Paludaria, marsh dwellers of Indigo Bay. Her race is semi-aquatic, having webbed feet. Her skin can change color to reflect her mood or reflexively camouflage her when frightened. Her homunculus, Filbert, is a little fish that swims in the back of her thoughts and gives her wise advice. Though sometimes timid she would dare much for those she calls her friends.

Royland Wagge - Although technically not a narrator in this novel, Royland is present throughout its pages and is quite instrumental in pursuing its quest. He considers Lucas his cousin. Sometimes grumpy and always quirky, Roy has many fine qualities and is trying to improve his social skills.

Hans and Gretta Brubaker - Also not narrators *per se*, this pair of master wizards and their antics from several decades earlier are recounted in a series of hidden records. These lead the way to adventure and intrigue. They are Royland's grandparents on his father's side.

Some People of Conclave

Lorraine - (Doña Lorraine Cordova of Alamendra) - Lorraine is a photomancer, specializing in tricks of light. Formerly one of Lucas' house mates, she is now the head of House Blue Jay. Lorraine is from Freemark Duchy, a southeastern region of Osten.

Griselda Mattingly and Jason Mills - Two servants at Mistress Julia's estate. Zelda cooks, cleans, and manages the household. She came into Julia's service as a young girl and is now growing quite elderly. Jason is a young fellow more recently come into the Mistress' service. He fetches and carries and is a 'right good Jack of all trades.'

Franklin Stein - Lucas' former head of house. Franklin is now a journeyman to Master Brayden Sheppard, head of the conclave's seneschals. As such, he is on a quest to rid the kingdom of the monster he himself unleashed. Franklin is a necromancer whose innocent experiment ran afoul of the villainous Truman Huber.

Arnold Clark - Journeyman Clark is a therianthrope serving in the seneschals. He is the lone survivor of an attack on Master Prowd's funeral barge. He swam back to Conclave to bear witness to the event. His totem animal is a leopard (and he can most definitely change his spots).

Lloyd "The Void" Bridges - Lucas' former roommate from House Blue Jay. Still an aspirant journeyman, his gift enables him to make objects vanish and reappear elsewhere. He is learning several new uses for his talents and hopes to be selected soon to become a full journeyman.

Sybell Dunham - A master of the conclave blessed with oracular visions. Sybell came into her powers later in life than most. She was consulted by the Brubakers as they prepared for their fateful mission.

Some People of Lorédon

Puquabeth Chosha Julia (pronounced jo-LEE-ah) - The sole Elven master to reside in Conclave. Her name means: 'daughter of the twilight sun'. Among humans, she goes simply by Mistress Julia. She is a wind mage and is several centuries old.

Hazhi Dia Quobias - This poet is Mistress Julia's lifemate. His name means: 'Laughs in the face of danger.' It was given to him for his devil-may-care attitude. He is a bit stocky for an elf and enjoys fine dining and a good joke.

Qenga Taliha Shunje Qua (Clarity of Thought and Spirit) - She is one of the three Elven master wizards to reside in Lorédon. She arrives in her carriage at Gentle Repose along with her apprentice and her husband, Tamil. Among humans, she goes by Mistress Talia.

Rory Nicholson - Though not an elf, Rory owns a hostelry in the border town of Ngema Sorihap. He is considered a gracious host and a superb storyteller.

Baqua Lipo Sithia (Freshness of the Morning Rain) - Mistress Sithia is the daughter of Mistress Julia and Hazhi. She is a master wizard in her own right. She and her husband, Reh, are awaiting a blessed event and live in the village of Araceae Fontes (Palm Springs).

Pachtel bo'Degh (Talon of the swooping owl) - A young tweenage ruffian from Lucas' Elven language class. His classmates call him 'Swoop.' Swoop is somewhat of a bigot and doesn't care much for humans.

Her grace, the Duchess Brighton - Her human name and title derive from the fact that her people affectionately refer to her as 'The Bright One.' She has been a leader among the elves for centuries and is revered for her wisdom and grace.

Hazhiwab Ghosha Bitig (Laughter of the rushing river) - This fox-shifting therianthrope goes by the nickname, 'Splash.' She is a journeyman to Master Shon, and helps him to keep the southern reaches clear of the abominations drifting up from the marsh.

Some Men Encountered in Eagle's Keep Duchy

Thaddeus Von Holstein and ***Brian Pendleton*** - A pair of border guards manning a lonely outpost at Eagle's Keep's western-most reaches.

Sir Charles Stapleton of Fairglen - A dauntless knight who claims to be on a simple hunting expedition. He is known to be one of the king's best men and is a terror on the tourney circuit.

Kendrick - Squire to Sir Charles with a secret past. He is kind and chivalrous, and Lucas admires his intellectual nature.

Friar Wallace - This heavyset friar is Sir Charles' spiritual adviser. He is a skilled battlefield medic and chirurgeon. Royland claims he is a 'man of secrets.' And Royland is rarely wrong about such things.

Lars - A man-at-arms serving Sir Charles. Later, he reveals his full name as Lars Templeton of Ayrshire.

Marco and ***Barnaby*** - A pair of guardsmen who escort the journeymen to Stronghold's upper levels.

Inquisitor Mattius - Described as a man with a 'salt and pepper beard and a broad-brimmed gray hat.' He is in charge of the TSA, or Theological Surveillance Authority. This group of clergymen was formed to safeguard Eagle's Keep from infiltrators and heretics. Armed with an ocular sent from Conclave, they scrutinize all citizens and travelers for the telltale glint of fey magic.

Brother Parvus - A tonsured friar garbed in brown sporting an iron cross about his neck. Gifted with a wild talent to spot fey energies, he assists the TSA in rooting out malefactors. For most of each day, he works with his fellow scribes, illuminating holy texts in the monastic library of Stronghold.

Brother Hewitt - Another mendicant of Stronghold. Brother Hewitt is the custodian of the monastic library up on tier four. He is also the treasurer for their order. He is their representative to the duke's men and enjoys a good bout of haggling.

Master Pete - Technically a wizard of Conclave, Peter Redmond Doyle has long been assigned to dwell at Eagle's Keep, the nerve center of the war effort in the south. This is due to a unique talent he and his twin brother, Redmond, enjoy. Master Redmond can convey Master Pete's words and gestures instantly over any distance. Thus, Master Pete keeps the conclave well-informed of the war's progress with his daily reports. Peter is also a photomancer, like Lorraine.

Men of Redoubt

Tim Hodges - Commands squad six. Corporal Hodges and his men are charged with keeping clear the trail leading to Redoubt from the E.K.

Richard Chapman - An expert tracker assigned to squad six.

Harold Hunt - Newly promoted captain in charge of the forces of Redoubt. Lucas and Royland first met Harold on their way to Conclave from Westarbor. He was then a roustabout working for Master Ross, the caravan boss. He departed the caravan to answer the king's call for reinforcements along the southern battle front, resuming his former rank of lieutenant.

Dave Clark - Captain Hunt's staff clerk. He is described as 'a thickset fellow with a bushy brown beard so dark as to be almost black.' Sholeena calls him Corporal Dave.

Harland Reznic and Dominik Cooke - Two master wizards of the conclave presently assigned at the war front. They are nearing the end of their one-year assignments and looking forward to leaving this god-forsaken swamp behind. Harland can move objects better than most, and Dominik has an affinity for earth and stone.

Others

Blandor - A Paluda who helps guide the journeymen to the southern border of his hunting grounds.

Filbert - A small fish swimming in Sholeena's inner pond. He is her homunculus.

Reginald - A stick-like figure who emerged from a cocoon in Lucas' inner garden. Lucas is having a great deal of trouble rearing him to be a proper homunculus.

<u>Fairy Folk</u> - Contains some spoilers! (Read the book first)

Terwilliger - A brownie and professional bootblack. He is of the Seelie court and resides at Conclave.

Fengári - Previously described as a 'bespectacled owl creature perched on a hickory branch', Fengári receives only a brief mention.

Hazel - A hamadryad living in the Perilous Glade of Conclave. She was transplanted there as a sapling. Now that the glade has been given to the fey as an embassy, she is its 'mistress.'

Holly - Hazel's daughter also growing in the Perilous Glade. She was planted there by Lucas once these lands were officially given over to the faire folks' management. Still in her first year of growth, she is already considered a juvenile.

Bogalump, the Grudge - Described as a 'frog creature smoking a long pipe,' he is actually more of a toad and not amphibious at all. He is the ambassador of the fey in Conclave.

Orenob - This be not his true name, but tis near enough to conjure by. Actually, the name of this 'unseelie king' is an anagram for 'Oberon,' of "A Mid-summer Night's Dream" fame. Lucas refers to him as a warty-faced demon. Orenob possesses the 'Heart of the Swamp,' the objective of the journeymen's quest.

Queen Tinatia - As ruler of all the 'seelie' fey, Tinatia the Fair calls and attends the Seelie Court, an occasional gathering of the fey. She is a tall fairy with dragonfly wings garbed all in green. (That is not her picture on the cover, but rather a closeup of one of her pixie subjects). In a manner similar to Orenob, the queen's name is an anagram for 'Titania,' the fairy queen of Shakespeare's fey fantasy.

Dark Dryads - A group of hamadryads who dwell within hawthorn trees in the Glade of Endless Summer.

"We are Mother Flurina, Cilia, Viola; and Yana's the youngest one there. And in seeking our blessing, I, whom you're addressing, am known as Katrina, the fair."

Appendix II
(Spells)

Fun Fact: The 'old tongue' I use for the spell verbalizations is simply Latin. You can usually plug a spell name into a Google translation to find its literal meaning. Lucas and his cohorts have learned quite a few since their apprenticeships. Below is a fairly comprehensive listing of Spells used in my novels to date:

ambulare interitus (Withering Stride)

aqua exstinguit (Water Quenches)

aquam claram (Clear Water)

*arescet et mori (Wither and Die)

*ave cantus et flores (Birdsong and Flowers)

calidus ignis ardentis (Blazing Hot Fire)

capturam petram (Catch Rock)

cogitationes liberare (Liberate Thoughts)

digitus flamma (Flame Finger)

exorcizo spiritus (Exorcize Spirit)

frigus metallum in perpetuum
        (Permanently Cool Metal)

geas silentii (Geas of Silence)

gloriabitur securis (Force Axe)

iactare spheara (Spinning Toss)

*ignis loquela (Fire Speech)

impedimente (Shield/Protect)

inexsuperabilis permanens lignea
        (Permanently Impregnable Wood)

internum calorem (Inner Warmth)

levare et colligentes (Lift and Pull)

levare et conicere (Lift and Throw)

lumina in (Lights On)

lumina quell (Kill the lights)
manent vigilate (Remain Alert)
miscere cogitata (Combine Thoughts)
motis cessabit (Calm of the Grave)
*omnino siccis plantis
        (Completely Dry Plants)
personalis zephyris spirantibus
        (Personal Zephyr)
podagra flammae (Gout of Fire)
Praefundo harenae (Dampen Sand)
praemium (Explode)
pulver in ventis (Dust in the Wind)
quaerite mihi amans (Seek my Love)
*quaerite nuntius flammae
        (Seek the Messenger of the Flame)
quomodo probatur in conflatorio mortis
        (Crucible of Death)
radet ovium (Sheer Sheep)
*repellere insectorum (Drive Away Insects)
scripturam vim extermina (Erase Writing)
spacium girabit (Rotate)
sphera de incineratio
        (Sphere of Incineration)
sternetur tinea munda (Maggot Cleanse)
suspendium tenaci (Choking Grip)
tenera pluviam (Tender Rain)
terram aratro (Earth Furrow)
ut reflectum speculum (Glass that Reflects)
viburnum pugna (Snowball Fight)
visio tenebris (Darksight)
*visus aquilae (Eagle's Sight)

Appendix III

(Elven)

For this novel, I thought long and hard about the Elven culture. I tried to go easy on the reader and not stray too far from English. But still, a surprising number of Elven words and phrases crept into some of the dialog. I hope you found this amusing and not too distracting from the story. As previously explained, I use a softened version of Klingon to arrive at most Elven words. Below is a fairly comprehensive listing of the 'Elven' phrases presented in this novel and their meanings. They are listed in the order in which they appear. Omitted from this list are the Elven names which are explained elsewhere.

"Jaweehay chosha julia" (House of the Twilight Sun)

"Jisusha jaweehay quash quin quem!"

(I greet the house. A message I bring!)

"Sowee batla shey jhey" (You honor us also)

"Quordusha tivia vam soja pop sodazh" (May our family enjoy this meal to honor our foremothers)

"biddle-tessen puqua" (round-eared children)

"Jiquosa jithosia tua" (please forgive the lateness of our arrival)

"Boma-sud Hoodah" (the singing green mountain)

"valihimay" (profession; specialty)

"broeka" (pantaloons that billow out below the knee)

"Quavo, sotto joh. Quaquova yinniway!" (Be not distressed, my lady. I will protect you with my life!)

"Iway jagha poH" (Blood enemy times)

"watheeshan" (The speech of the people)

"Ngema Sorihap" (Forestwood Village)

"*puhi Lorédon nagemmahia*"   (The beautiful, forested land of
    Lorédon)

"*nuvapua watheesh*" (The first people; the elves)

"*valladevhiwi*" (Clever leadership)

"*Ghuji quich*" (Baby Talk)

"*Rakkanach*" (Fiddle head fern)

"Sarghajib" (Horse mane; an Elven hair style akin to a mohawk)

"*Ghuji Tlhagh*" (Baby Fat)

"*Nom Quetbitig*"   ('Fast-flowing River'; The river into which
    Brooke the water nymph flows, her mainstem)

"*Wova zeja bosch tazbeth*" (Our bright and shining queen)

"*Puachoqua*" (A naturalist who sees to the health of the land;
    Sylviculturalist)

"*Venghom Ki-bodey*" (Blackbird Village)

"Ghojawi" (Students; Journeymen)

"*Waminbodocha*" (one-eyed bird thing; the Elven name for the
    Cyclochiropteans)

"*Tammanegha* of the *watheesh*" (Silent warriors of the [Elven]
    people)

𝔄𝔭𝔭𝔢𝔫𝔡𝔦𝔵 IV

(Paludas)

My third novel introduced Sholeena. She is from a tribal folk known as the Paludaria, a race of my own invention. The Paludas are a swamp-dwelling race of humans well-adapted to swimming and fishing. They have a second set of transparent eyelids that protect their eyes while under water and allow them to see better in such environs. Their toes are longer than those of most humans and are webbed. This gives them a shuffling gait on land but greatly aids them in aquatic endeavors. And as we discovered near the story's end, a Paluda can hold her breath for quite a long time.

Among other fun aspects of Paluda anatomy are the chromatorphores in their skin. These erupt to produce a protective camouflage when a Paluda is frightened (or embarrassed). Paluda's have superior communication skills because the color of their skin also reacts to their emotions. According to Sholeena, it's like breathing. These changes occur automatically in response to different feelings, but a Paluda can also make such changes on purpose. Below is a chart of some of the colors and the emotions that elicit them:

Tan:	Ordinary flesh tone, Boredom, Sleepiness
Red:	Anger, Resentment, Passion
Orange:	Amusement, Joy or Mirth
Yellow:	Doubt, Uncertainty
Green:	Nervousness, Anxiety
Blue:	Sadness, Solemnity
Purple:	Astonishment, Wonder, Awe
(Camouflage):	Fright, Embarrassment
Black:	Hatred; Intense Focus or Anticipation
White:	Nausea, Illness. Paluda dead also 'whiten'

In the Paluda language, there are many words for various shades and emotional composites such as Furious-Red, Dignified-Blue, Proper-Blue or Weeping-Blue (to name but a few).

For this novel, I had to delve somewhat into other Paluda customs and traditions. I hope you found them interesting. The song described in the story is called "Twilight Threnody" you can find the English version recorded on my website. I enlisted the aid of the Delhi Senior Singers and some of the Sisters of Charity at Mt. St. Joseph to record it. For the Paluda language, I borrowed heavily from modern-day Filipino. I liked its rhythm and flow. Below is a fairly comprehensive listing of the 'Paluda' words used in this novel. They are in the order they appear in the story.

Hindi sila marunong lumangoy tulad namin

(They don't know how to swim like we do)

Mababaw ang kanilang hininga at maikli at mahina ang kanilang mga daliri sa paa!

(Their breath is shallow and their toes are short and weak!)

Pagkatapos ay sasakay sila sa balsa... parang mga sanggol!

(Then they will ride on the raft ... like babies!)

Pagtitipon (an assembly of tribal elders; a folkmoot)

Pinuno (Leader, Chieftain)

"Kahit na hindi ka namin kilala, mukha kang isa sa aming mga tao. Sino ka?"

(Though we do not know you, You look like one of our people. Who are you?)

Ang pangalan ko ay Sholeena Blorlafargalish

(My name is Sholeena Blorlafargalish)

At ako nga ay taga Paludaria (And I am from the Paludaria)

Kailangan mong kumanta para patunayan ito sa amin.

(You must sing to prove this to us.)

Napakahusay (Very well)

Tatawagin ko ang pagpapala ng buwan kapag bumaba ang araw mula sa langit

(I will call down the moon's blessing when the sun drops from the sky)

Magsimula (Begin)

Nayon (village)

ang Garetta (the Gretta)

Magandang gabi mga kaibigan (good night, friends)

Salamat (thanks)

Ilog ng Luha (river of tears)

Galamay Palaka (Tentacled Frog)